I0652701

The Devil's Breath
- Abel Kane Book 2 -

by
John Wilson

Cover and Interior Design by Vinnie Corbo

Published by Volossal Publishing
www.volossal.com

Copyright © 2025 John D. Wilson
ISBN 978-1-963359-26-8

For Margaret and my family

CHAPTER

ONE

Abel pulled the door open and stepped in. The bar seemed darker than the moonlit midnight outside. A bouncer sat on a stool nodding, his arms crossed and resting on his bulging gut, his belly lapping halfway down his thighs. One eye twitched as Abel Kane passed him and made his way to the bar.

The dive was bigger inside than he'd expected. From the parking lot, it looked like just a storefront, but it had taken over the adjacent buildings from the inside like a cancer. It wasn't empty, either. People were clustered here and there in the dimmest parts of the space as if the few lights that were there were radioactive. An occasional loud clack emanated from the end of the building where a lone pool table with a lone player was playing with himself and probably losing.

One man was sitting at the bar. His beefy forearms were resting on the leather edge, and his grapefruit-sized fists were clenched on either side of his glass, protecting it. *From whom?* Abel wondered. His knuckles looked like walnuts. Each was tattooed with a letter. Instead of '*LOVE*' on one, both hands spelled out '*HATE*.' Regardless, Abel violated the unwritten rules and sat right next to him. The hater turned to look at Abel, eyeing the midsized young man with dirty blond hair and greasy jeans. He drew in his arms closer around his beer and turned away slightly.

Abel glanced at the bartender and caught his eye. "A Coors Light, please." The man next to him snorted. The bartender poured the beer and handed it to him. Abel twisted around on the stool and leaned his back against the bar and surveyed the place. It wasn't like his home bar, The Flying Machine, which had loud music, girls dressed to the nines, and guys strutting around like roosters. The people here were like pieces of crumpled old paper that had gotten blown around in the wind and ended up trapped in a corner of a building with other stranded pieces of trash.

Abel spun around on his stool and leaned his forearms on the bar, aping the man next to him. "This place is a shithole," he commented. No response from the Goliath next to him. The man turned further away. "You live around here?" asked Abel.

"Fuck off!" the man said without looking at Abel. Abel took the hint.

He slowly but steadily drank beer after beer, keeping pace with the unfriendly man next to him. He staved off the boredom by counting the wasted people leaving in ones and twos as the time inexorably ticked toward last call. There was a break in the exodus as a woman entered. She pushed herself past two drunks supporting each other and made her way to the bar, coming closer and closer till she was standing between Abel and the hulking man, who ignored her, hunching further over his drink.

She appraised them both and turned to Abel. "How 'bout you take me out to your car, honey?"

Abel rudely looked her up and down. She was rail thin, Casper-the-Ghost white, and had a weeping sore on the edge of her lip. The girl smiled at him. Her teeth were black—rotting. *Meth,* thought Abel. "I don't think so," he answered. Her face went empty, and he felt a pang of remorse, regretting his tone. "It's late," he added lamely.

The woman addressed her second choice. "What about you, hon? You wanna party?"

"Fuck off!" mumbled the man without looking at her.

Jeez, this guy's got a two-word vocabulary, Abel thought.

The girl's face transformed into rage. "You two faggots deserve each other!" She slapped the man's arm, sloshing his beer, and said, "You probably like the bottom." In a blink, he spun on his stool, his arm raised to strike. Even quicker, Abel leaned over and grabbed his wrist.

"Don't waste your energy. It's not worth it," he said. Then he nodded his head toward the barback. The bartender was standing there with a short billy club in his hand. "Get lost," Abel told the meth addict.

She scuttled backward into the shadows. Abel released the man's wrist. "White trash," the man said.

Ironic, given his 'HATE' knuckle tattoos, Abel thought. He upped the guy's vocabulary list to four.

"You see her before?" asked Abel.

"Yeah, she comes in every night, tryin' to get cash to score."

Hmmm, the guy can actually talk. Abel kept it going. "You come here every night?"

"Most nights."

Abel continued the small talk, keeping it light, making the guy stay engaged. "You get that ink in the joint? My uncle was up in Angola. He came back with lots of tats like that."

"Are you in the Life?" asked Hater Knuckles.

And just like that, they were best buds. The man told him about his experiences in the state penitentiary, and Abel related stories about his days in a robbery crew. The man mentioned his name was Francis, but Abel couldn't wrap his head around that and fully intended to only think of him as Knuckles. When the dick-measuring was over, they reloaded and moved to the pool table in the back.

Sitting next to the man at the bar, he had seemed bigger than your average man, but when Abel stood next to him in front of the pool cue rack, he truly realized what a behemoth Knuckles was. Abel was a rangy five-ten, but the man beside him went six-eight at least. And if Abel weighed 180, this guy went 325 plus. All meat. Looked like he coulda been a lineman in the pros or, better yet, a professional wrestler. He looked like he was made from a child's block set—a supersized version. His torso was a triangle balanced on its tip on a block that was his legs.

They played eight ball for a while, the huge guy murdering the rack whenever it was his turn to break. "Man, you look like you play pro football," said Abel.

"Yeah, played for the Saints, for a while anyway," said Knuckles. "I got hurt. When I gave up on football, I started helping a friend. You know, helped him collect on some bad loans."

"You still doing that?"

"Naw, that went sideways. I got in a little trouble. A guy was late, he couldn't take a punch, and his brother was on the NOPD."

"Man, that sucks. You shouldn't get money off the street if you aren't going to be able to pay it back or handle the vig," said Abel.

"I know—right?" said Francis. "Anyway, I can't seem to keep out of trouble since getting out."

The bartender yelled last call, so they played a final rack in companionable silence until that was interrupted by the bartender yelling closing time. They walked out of the joint, a funny-looking pair—a giant next to a shorter man who walked with a slight limp that caused him to ticktock back and forth as he tried to keep up.

The parking lot had a solitary bulb casting a dim glow, hardly enough to discern the make of the few vehicles left. It left huge pools of black shadow between the cars. They stopped in front of a sedan, a foreign job, and Abel wondered how Knuckles could fit behind the wheel.

"Are you coming by this place again?" asked Francis.

"I doubt it," said Abel as a shadow broke away from the dark space between two cars and rammed into Francis's back. He grunted but didn't go down.

"Aw shit," muttered Abel as he went in for an armlock. He got an arm bar and tried to twist Knuckles to the ground, but Francis was able to pound him in the face several times with his free hand, each time making a wet, meaty sound.

Tank, a wiry Black man and Abel's partner, was on the ground trying to tie up the man's legs with his arms, but every time he almost got his hands clasped, Francis would let go a mighty kick and knock Tank back. Abel kept applying pressure to the arm bar and tried to force the man to his knees, but he wasn't tall enough to get any leverage.

The next thing Abel knew, he was knocked on his ass by a lightning bolt. Francis was on his knees, and Tank was standing over him with the taser. Abel crabbed backward, and Tank put his boot in Francis's back and pushed him to the ground.

Tank put a knee on the man's spine and reached behind for his cuffs. He got one locked around Francis's wrist and was pulling it toward the other when Francis erupted off the ground, throwing Tank to the side. Francis whipped the loose steel cuff around and caught Abel right above the ear, then started running. Blood gushed from Abel's scalp.

Tank was up and after him. Francis was probably fast for a lineman, but he was no match for Tank. He was on the escaping man in a couple of seconds and tased him again with his backup taser. Not taking any chances this time, he sent two jolts down the line. Francis went down and laid on the ground, twitching.

Abel caught up and the two of them manhandled the loose cuff onto the other wrist. Tank zip-tied his ankles for good measure.

"Let's get him in the truck before he starts getting frisky," Abel said, gasping.

They half dragged and half carried the hulking man to the back of Tank's F-150. They managed to stand him up and tip his top half over the tailgate. Abel quickly ran a chain attached to a cargo tie-down through the handcuffs, folded it back, and snapped a lock through the links.

Teaming up on the legs, they wrestled the rest of Francis's body up and into the back of the truck. Tank grabbed another chain and put several loops around the man's legs. He snugged the lock tight against Francis's ankle so he couldn't shake the chain loose.

Tank and Abel leaned against the side of the truck catching their breath. "Jesus, Abel, what the hell were you doing in there? That took all night. I thought I was going to have to come in there and drag him out myself."

"Hey, I was busy making friends with him. You know you can't rush that." Tank snorted. "Besides, there was no way you were dragging that bastard out. Or me. Or the both of us."

"Let's go," said Tank, "before you bleed out. And don't forget to put on your jacket."

Chapter One

TWO

The Orleans Parish jail loomed in front of them. Its crisp outlines and expanse of windows were probably designed to mimic a hospital, but it couldn't hide that it was a jail. The walls topped with razor ribbon made certain of that. Tank pulled up to the guard and showed him the paperwork provided by the bondsman. The dumpy-looking deputy waved them through.

Tank pulled in front of the intake door and jumped out. Abel eased out, moving slowly. They were both wearing their windbreakers with the words *Bail Recovery Agent* emblazoned in yellow across the back. They pressed on a button, and a loud buzz could be heard through the door. They waited a few minutes and hit the buzzer again. The door opened abruptly, and a man poked his head out. He had a dab of what looked like mustard stuck in his beard.

"Watcha got?"

"We got a skip. Here's his packet." Tank handed over the same papers that he had shown to the guard at the gate.

"We're all full up. We can't take him," said the doorman.

"Wait, what?" asked Abel, instantly wondering what they were going to do with the giant chained in the back of Tank's truck. "Let me speak to your supervisor. Is the warden here?"

"It's the middle of the night, man. Nobody is here."

"Look, deputy, we got a violent felon in the back of the truck. We can't hold him all night. He's chained up. That's inhuman. He's not a dog. You make us do that, then we're coming back tomorrow, and we'll go straight to the warden and explain to him that that is what you had us do."

The intake deputy cursed under his breath, then opened the door and said curtly, "Bring him in."

"We're going to need help," added Abel. The guard dropped an F-bomb and turned around and went back in.

It took Tank, Abel, and two guards to wrangle Francis out of the back of the truck and drag him into the jail. This time it was one of the guards that took the brunt of it. The prisoner headbutted the guard right on the point of his shoulder and gave him a stinger, but all it did was amp up the efforts of the guards. They roughly kicked him in the back of his knees, then dragged him in and put him in a holding cell.

Tank wearily returned to his truck, and Abel waited around for the paperwork for the bondsman. Of course, the guards slow-rolled him, making him wait an additional quarter hour. Then, at last he had the documents in his hand, and he and Tank headed home.

The next morning, Abel picked up Tank, and they headed back into New Orleans on the I-10 Twin Span bridge. The guys lived in Lacombe, Louisiana, a tiny village on the north shore of Lake Pontchartrain. They had known each other since they were in elementary school and Thomas Cheval had jumped into a fight Abel was having with the school bully. He had bulldozed the kid and got forever nicknamed "Tank" for his efforts.

Both of them lived in homes situated back from the road, among the trees, with backyards abutting Bayou Lacombe, which meant they had a forty-minute drive back into the city to hand over the paperwork to the bondsman for the felon they had brought in that night.

Abel was looking out over the bridge at the light glinting off the water, in a daze, still tired and sore from the night before, when Tank interrupted his fugue. "Man, I sure need this payday. Things are getting tight again."

"Hey, brother, I still have some cash. What do you need?" said Abel. Tank and Abel had grown up together, they had both lost their fathers, and Tank had probably even saved Abel's life once or twice, and Abel had returned the favor. "What's mine is yours. You know that."

"Naw, it's not like that. It's not like I open my wallet and cartoon moths fly out. We're working about eighty hours per week it seems, and we aren't making shit."

"I'm feelin' it, too, but our cut on this one is going to be bigger. Keep us going for a while," said Abel.

They finished the trip, Tank's spoken worries weighing on Abel's mind. Abel parked in front of the bail outfit. "C'mon, let's get our money and go back home. See if your brother wants to go fishing on the bayou."

"Yeah, we need a break. Sorry I'm whining. I'm just tired."

The bail bond office was one of many businesses near the jail feeding off the misfortune of others. It was a small, seedy place with two desks, the kind of desks that were government surplus after World War II. They hadn't even bothered to upgrade after the Korean War or any of the ensuing conflicts. An old battle axe, Doris, usually sat at the front desk, gatekeeping for Frank Veruto, the owner of Family Bail Bonds. Abel always wondered if the word *Family* referred to Frank and his son, Little Frankie, or if Frank wanted the various felons to consider him family so they would hesitate to jump bail and screw him on the bond.

Abel never bothered to get that cleared up because he liked to minimize his time with Frank, who was an asshole of the highest order. Any conversation with Frank involved backhanded compliments, subtle condescension, passive aggression, or downright insults. But because Frank considered himself a people person, you also had to endure his ass-kissing every now and then which was worse than his contempt.

His son, Little Frankie, didn't do put-downs. That would have required some thought. Frank Jr. was an idiot, an old-fashioned idiot, when the word meant something. After working ten years for Senior, Little Frankie could just about handle filling out one of the bail forms. Abel was certain that the only reason the secretary was around was to babysit Little Frankie and make sure he didn't drool on himself. She was certainly fond of him. Maybe Frankie was her love child from Big Frank.

Abel and Tank stood there in front of the secretary waiting for her to acknowledge them. Abel was tempted to just walk around her desk and talk to Frank directly, but he was studiously ignoring them as well, his face about eight inches from the computer monitor. The only thing that stopped Abel was the certain knowledge that violating protocol would cost him in the long run.

Tank cleared his throat. A beat later the old hag looked up and acted surprised, like they had materialized out of thin air. "We brought in our skip last night. You know, Francis Marchand. The big guy. He's in holding over at the jail."

Abel handed her the paperwork. She shuffled through the documents and stamped the cover page with an old-school rubber stamp, then whirled around on her stool and slapped the papers onto Frank's desk. "Frank!" she honked.

He picked them up and went through them, acting like they were the Magna Carta. Then, he stamped them with his rubber stamp and went back to peering at the monitor. Abel looked at Tank. Tank rolled his eyes.

"Hey, Frank, how about giving us our cut?" asked Abel.

Frank turned his face away from the computer and stared at them, his eyes magnified by his glasses. He resembled a toad—short and wide with bulging eyes. "You numbskulls know I don't have that kinda float. I gotta wait till it settles out."

Tank and Abel knew that was complete bullshit. Frank's business was booming. Crime was a growth industry. "C'mon, man, that was a tough skip. Most of your other guys wouldn't have taken that job," said Abel.

"Sorry, boys, no can do." Frank turned back to his computer and refused to look at them.

"There are ten other shops that we could work with," said Abel.

"You pissants took all week on this one job. The word's going to get around that you boys can't cut it. Calm down. I'll have your money next week."

Abel was burning inside, and a fantasy spun through his head of vaulting the front desk and grabbing Frank by the collar and dragging him to the safe bolted to the floor in the corner, but Tank grabbed his upper arm and pulled him out of the office.

Abel raced out of the lot, his car spewing gravel. He was quiet for minute. "You know, going straight isn't all it's cracked up to be. How does anybody put up with this shit?" Abel had run a robbery crew for his Uncle Deacon and the Dixie Mafia since he was twenty-one, but they had disbanded the crew a couple of years earlier.

His Uncle Deacon had been the local boss for a long time but had been murdered. That and the realization that robbery had no future given the modern, digital world drove his crew to try to get out of the Life. The sheer inability to have a normal life with normal people was another reason. His sister, Callie, nagging at him to do something legit with his life had forced his decision, too. Yeah, there were a lot of reasons they'd quit.

But the straight life sucked. *At least so far,* Abel thought to himself. He turned to his friend. "What are we doing, Tank?"

"Do you mean right now or in general?" asked Tank.

"Right now, we're going fishing. No, I mean in our lives."

"Abel, you're doing what you promised Callie. You got out of the Life."

"Yeah, but this is ninety-nine percent boring crap and one percent action. Remember what it felt like to rip into Garcia's wall and find the four hundred grand?"

"What about that job when you got shot? You can't just remember the good parts. You know, we had to put up with Deacon's bullshit, too. He wasn't that much different than Frank. The way things were going, someone else was going to get killed: Harm, Rabbit, or my brother. Losing both Deke and René was tough. Hell, you and I both almost bought it."

"I know. But I miss it," said Abel.

"Me, too," Tank said.

"I was talking to your brother the other day. André is frustrated, too. He likes the computer work, but he said it doesn't have the same level of risk and excitement of all that mayhem we were into."

Tank jumped on that. "Hilarious! My bro was the one that was always harping on the danger." He adjusted himself in the seat and added, "Harm seems OK with strong-arming deadbeats."

"Harm's still in the Life. What with the loan sharking, he's rubbing shoulders with the Italian mob and the gangs. He didn't change things," said Abel.

"I had a beer with him at The Machine the other day. He misses doing shit with us. It was all about the crew to him. He didn't care what we were doing. You know, he would never come out and say it, but I felt like he was bummed," said Tank with a touch of sadness in his voice.

"We kinda left him in the lurch. I feel bad about that," said Abel. "Rabbit, on the other hand, is doing great."

"Rabbit had an out. He was always going to end up taking over his daddy's shop. Heck, he was doing that half the time when we were robbing shit. The thing that I didn't see coming was him marrying his second cousin."

"Yeah, we always thought he was going to end up getting hitched to his first cousin!" They both laughed.

There was a lull, then Tank said, "Who woulda thought that he was going to be the first one of us to get married? Or have a baby, for that matter!"

"Yeah, I know. I saw Crystal the other day. She's really showing. Rabbit was in seventh heaven, talking about being a father and all the stuff he was gonna teach the kid." Abel didn't know why exactly, but it bothered him somehow. It wasn't like he wasn't happy for Rabbit and Crystal; it was more like it made him feel like he was in one of those dreams where you'd forgotten something important and woke up all panicky.

"Speaking of Crystal, is it wrong to say she reminds me of Rabbit's mom?" asked Tank.

"Aw man, now I'm not going to be able to unsee that! And anyway, Kisha kinda reminds me of your mama."

"Fuck you, dude!"

Abel laughed and then asked, "What's going on with you and Kisha, anyway?"

"We're still hanging out. I'm not sure she trusts me even yet. Getting out of the robbery biz helped, but she's heard some stuff. She wants me to come to church more often—thinks that will drive the devil out of me, I guess." Tank was silent, lost in his head a bit, then said in a quiet mumble, "She's trying to save me."

"Dude, you don't need to be saved. You're already the best person I know," said Abel earnestly, then he changed the subject. They were straying too close to the sentimental.

"But this bounty hunting shit? I'm starting to feel like we might have to rethink that. Having to beg to get paid? Screw that! Working these kinds of hours and making 50K a year? We coulda done that with one gig. Hit a warehouse or a truck, we woulda been set."

"Practically every runner we go after beats the crap out of us. Your face is totally effed up, and the cut on your head probably needs stitches. It's not worth it," said Tank. "But are you saying put our crew back together and start up thieving again?"

"No, my sister would kill me if we did that," Abel said quickly. "Just thinking is all."

THREE

Abel was sitting in the kitchen drinking his morning coffee and listening to the mockingbird that was singing just outside his open back door. He wondered how the bird was able to sing a different pattern of notes every time it sang. He'd always thought about his own nature and felt it was in some way fixed, but the bird was able to change itself from moment to moment. Every time he walked out into the yard, it dive-bombed his head, trying to run him off his own land. He wished it would change *that* behavior.

The Gulf breeze blew through the open door bringing with it the scent of the bayou that was just down at the end of the yard—a wild, rich smell, redolent of loam, decaying leaves, and fish.

"Hey, where y'at?" said Callie, his sister, as she blew into the kitchen, interrupting his thoughts.

"A'write," replied Abel in response to the greeting that only made sense to Cajuns, particularly ones from New Orleans.

Callie got her coffee and sat down across from Abel. She was an athletic blonde and looked like she would be more at home in California than Lacombe, Lousiana. She took after their mother or at least the idealized version of their mother that Abel remembered from before the car crash that killed off both his parents when he was a little kid. A nurse at the large trauma hospital down in the city, Callie thrived on the stress in the emergency room and worked the late shift, so their paths only crossed when she had a day off.

"What the heck happened to your head?" she asked, always concerned about him, like the mother he didn't have.

"We snagged that jumper the other night," he said, then sipped his coffee.

She stood and leaned over the table, brushing his hair away from the lump over his ear. "That needed stitches. It's too late now. You're gonna have a scar."

"It'll be under my hair."

"Is Tank OK?"

"Yeah, he's fine. The guy was a beast. I knew he was big from the info in his packet, but in real life he was like Tank and me put together."

"So it basically went smoothly?" she asked.

Abel knew she wanted him out of the criminal life and working a normal job. He was also aware that Callie was skeptical that bounty hunting was an improvement. Still, he didn't edit his answer. "Yeah, except for getting the shit beat out of me, the jail refusing to take him, and Frank not paying us our cut yet . . ."

This time she was supportive. "Hey, it'll get better. You'll figure this out," she said, "and anyway, getting knocked around is better than going to prison, which was what was gonna happen to you in the Life. I can always patch you up."

Before Abel crossed over the lake, he made a pit stop at the Starbucks in Slidell. His sister tended to like half-caf brew, so their house coffee was usually thin, and he needed to top off before he faced Big Frank this early in the day.

He ordered and then went to stand by the pickup spot. Of course, they were serving the drive-through with their usual high priority and leaving the actual customers inside the store to take a beating on the wait. He fidgeted impatiently, watching all the other second-class citizens until he noticed a girl watching him. She met his eye for a second, then looked away. Abel continued to watch her. She had white-blonde hair cut short—very short, like a boy's. But oddly, the effect was to make her appear extremely feminine. Coupled with her figure, she was a knockout.

The barista called his name, and as he was reaching for his drink, he saw the woman look at him again. Abel was a decent-looking guy, but he didn't have the kind of appearance that made random girls stare at him very often. He felt a jolt of endorphins or oxytocin or whatever feel-good chemical the body squirted out when something good happened. It was the first time since his previous girlfriend, Olivia, had broken up with him that he'd been obviously noticed. Getting checked out was a nice boost before he had to deal with his tool of a boss.

On the way to Family Bail Bonds, Abel pondered whether getting beat on and not making any money was in fact better than having a robbery crew. Sure, he was hanging with Tank every day, his best friend, but the crew wasn't really together anymore, and he missed that. He grew up with those guys, and now he only saw them now and then.

When he had decided to go straight after all the shit that had happened with the MS-13 gang, he didn't think it was going to mean that they all went their separate ways. He understood that people grew up and went on with their lives and left their friends behind sometimes, he just didn't imagine it was going to happen with his crew. They were his family. The worst part was that he knew he did it to himself. It was his choices that led to this.

He pulled into the bond office, cutting short his internal monologue and jumped out of his F-150. That fucker Frank better pay him. He was sick of his bullshit and kicked at a chunk of rock in the gravel parking lot, wondering why the cheap bastard wouldn't cough up the cash to actually pave it. He sure as hell had enough money. But the whole place was a dump. Part of Big Frank's whole deal about not making enough to pay a fair cut on time, he guessed.

Little Frankie was sitting at the secretary's desk, pretending to look busy on the computer. *Probably playing tic-tac-toe and losing,* Abel thought uncharitably. "Your daddy around?" Abel asked.

"In the back," Frankie said and wiped the back of his hand under his nose, leaving a glistening trail all the way to his wrist.

Jeez. He was like a nine-year-old boy in a grown man's body—like that movie *BIG*, only minus the movie kid's heart and soul.

Abel walked to the back of the office and yelled, "Frank, you back there?"

Frank came out of the doorway that led to a dingy kitchen and an even grosser bathroom. Abel hoped Big Frank had washed his hands but didn't reach out to shake just in case. "What do you want?" Veruto wheezed out, as if he had just run a mile.

Abel could smell the edges of the foul cloud that still clung to Frank and took a step back. Like Frank didn't know what he wanted. "We want our cut for Marchand," Abel said, trying to take shallow breaths.

"Alright, alright," Big Frank muttered and went back to his desk and carefully situated his bulk onto the chair designed for a 1940s man instead of a 21st century guy with metabolic syndrome. He opened the file drawer and fished around and pulled out a packet of raggedy bills held together with a rubber band. Frank reached out with the wad.

Abel was impressed. The guy had actually planned ahead and set aside their payout. He grabbed at the stack, but Veruto held fast. "I got an opportunity for you," he said.

Uh-oh, Abel thought, detecting Frank's ass-kissing tone. Abel managed a "Give—" before Veruto rode over his words.

"A smart guy like you should be thinking about investments. You know, put some money aside and let it work for you. It's called passive investing. Soon, you'll have a wife and some kids, and you're gonna need more money than bounty hunting wages. How about you leave this with me, and I put it back into the business . . ."

"Hell no," Abel said vehemently, knowing how that would turn out, and yanked harder on the short stack of bills, wresting them from Big Frank.

"Well, just a thought," Frank said, like the guy who asks every woman he meets at a bar to have sex with him on the off chance one will say yes.

Abel turned to leave, but Frank said, "Hey, not so fast. I gotta job for you. Another one of those skips that nobody can find—a Black guy. Tank should be able to get a line on him quick."

"Yeah, every Black guy knows every other Black guy in the parish," Abel said sarcastically. "He'll use Negroogle . . . Should take us a minute."

"You and Tank come back Friday, and I'll brief you."

"A'write," Abel agreed, thinking, *What an asshole.* Then, he escaped Family Bail Bonds, definitely not letting the door hit him on the butt.

With a rooster tail of gravel spewing from his rear tires, Abel blasted out of the lot and headed for the Ninth Ward. When Isabelle, Tank and André's mama, had heard he was going down to the city, she had asked him to run an errand for her. She was a root doctor, a practitioner of hoodoo, and had requested he pick up some supplies. He willingly agreed. He knew she couldn't get it herself anymore.

A root doctor or conjuror was a person in the community that helped people with various issues in their life, like trouble with a lover, illness, or a threat from some person or situation. But Isabelle was getting on, and her last few years had been hard on her. The cataracts in her eyes had stopped her driving, and lately she had been getting lost. Most of her conversations were turning to the ebb and flow of good and evil. It was as if the regular world was moving away and the spirit world was coming closer, and it worried Abel. He and Tank had talked about it with André, but they didn't know what to do. When questioned about her well-being, she either answered in cryptic biblical phrases or got her hackles up and abruptly terminated the conversation.

They eventually stopped asking and mostly just tried to facilitate her periodic requests, which usually involved tracking down her hoodoo supplies. Hoodoo wasn't voodoo. It was an African-American folk medicine, passed down through the generations, a mixture of magical healing, charms, and practical knowledge.

This trip to the Ninth Ward was one of those scavenger hunts. Abel and the brothers knew of the likely places around New Orleans to find the powders and tinctures. They would take a list prepared by Belle in her spidery handwriting and deliver it to the proprietor of one of these shops who was usually an older Black woman, not unlike Isabelle. She'd eye the list, then give the errand boy the items or suggest a different shop that might have something she didn't. Sometimes the woman would scoff and look at them side eyed and say, "Why, you can get powdered rosemary at the grocery store—whatchu bothering me for?"

This time, Isabelle had directly instructed Abel to go to a shop in the Ninth Ward—a *particular* shop. When Abel asked why, she cast her milky eyes on him for a long moment but didn't answer. He wondered what she was up to.

Abel made his way to the address on a street off Galvez. The area was poor, but interspersed among the tired houses was the occasional tidy home, refurbs from some hurricane. The streets themselves looked like they were from a war zone, blown up and cratered, likely the last place in the city that road crews were sent. Abel expected to find a store or something official looking. Instead, it was a house, a tiny but neat house painted haint blue. Instead of just the porch ceiling, the whole house was blue. It floated in a sea of white houses.

He parked and slid out of the truck, patting his front pocket to make sure he had Belle's list, and went up to the porch. He rang the bell next to the plaque that said *Haitian Vodou Apothecary – Miss Lovelie Mondesir* and moved back so he wasn't crowding the door. He waited. Nothing. He rang again and put his ear to the door and heard a faint tinkle. He was reaching to knock when the door opened. For a moment, he thought the door had opened by itself but then realized the proprietor was bent over at the waist, her mostly bald head with a few wispy white threads of hair aimed at his belly. Her head was cocked like a little sparrow, with one rheumy eye gazing up at him.

"What's a White boy want with me?" she asked in a quavering voice. Abel felt a little frisson and wondered where it came from.

"My friend sent me here. She needs some supplies. She can't drive anymore. Isabelle Cheval." Abel realized he was babbling and stopped.

"She still up in Lacombe?" the old lady asked and took a step back into the house, beckoning Abel to come in. Abel followed, wrinkling his nose. "Sorry about the smell. It's the snakes. I don't smell 'em anymore," said the old woman.

They passed a dark room lit with red lights. Glass tanks lined the walls, and Abel could see shapes moving within.

"Frogs in there, too, but they don't stink," she muttered back at him, her back still parallel to the floor and her head peering over her twisted shoulder. She continued on into a back room at a pace that had Abel checking each step so as not to overrun her.

The reptile stench was overpowered in this room by so many other strong odors that Abel was momentarily stunned. Chemical smells he couldn't identify were overlaid by the woodsy, herbal scent of sage and the perfume of lavender. His nose stung from the piss tang of ammonia. The crone had turned and was looking up at him expectantly.

"Oh, I guess you need this," Abel said and handed her Isabelle's list.

She peered at it myopically, moving it first close, then farther and finally sidled over to the small window between two shelves, holding the list up to the feeble light making its way through the grimy window. "Yes. Uh-huh. Hmmm." she muttered to herself. She stared at Abel.

"Did Isabelle send me to the wrong place?" asked Abel.

"No, chile. Sit in that chair over there. This'll take me a while."

Abel sat and watched the woman putter about the room getting little envelopes of powders and glass vials of liquids. She took the lid off an apothecary jar and, using tongs, pulled out a large, dried spider with curled-up legs and dropped it into a ziplock bag. Finally, she stood in front of a cabinet in the corner. Pulling a key from around her neck, she unlocked the cabinet and rooted around and took out two small blue jars. She set them aside and relocked the cabinet.

She put each jar in its own ziplock bag, then carefully packed the two jars into a repurposed red plaid Walker's shortbread tin. She took her time cushioning the jars with crumpled paper, then put the tin in a larger paper grocery sack. The remainder of the supplies were placed on top, and she handed the bag to Abel.

"You take care with this. Don't drop it. Don't open that tin. Don't get it on your skin. Leave it for Isabelle. She'll know how to handle it . . . She better," the old woman said warningly. She looked at Abel expectantly.

"Oh," Abel said, "how much?"

"Five hundred." Abel's face fell. "I take Visa," she said.

After he paid, the ancient lady led him to the front door, forcing Abel to walk at her same slow pace. She opened the door for him, but as he stepped through, she caught his arm and he stopped and looked down. She painfully twisted her head so she could look up at him with both eyes. "Isabelle ain't root doctorin'. That wasn't a hoodoo list. I deal in voodoo." She quietly closed the door in his face.

He took the sack to the truck and carefully put it on the floor on the passenger side, then headed back to Belle's house. He did the trip on autopilot, barely noticing the change from land to water to land as he crossed the Twin Span bridge over Lake Pontchartrain. The light glinting off the water did nothing to distract him from his thoughts about Isabelle and her turn toward the darker religion.

The jog to Fish Hatchery Road came up, and he took the right, getting to Isabelle, Tank, and André's home on Bayou Lacombe moments later. Their house had been his second home since he was a kid. He and his sister, Callie, had lived with his Uncle Deacon, Aunt Henriette, and cousin, René, but had never really felt included. It was Tank's mama, Isabelle, who gave them the acceptance that made their childhood feel somewhat normal, that made them feel loved.

Abel went in the back door and found Isabelle in the kitchen working over the stove. "Where y'at, cher?" she asked and dropped the spoon in her hand and walked over and gave him a hug. She was a dignified lady, thin, with a regal face that had once been plump and beautiful. Now her rich black hair was mostly gray; a few strands here and there were almost white. Abel could feel the bones in her back.

"A'write," he answered, handing her the bag of supplies. "The lady at the shop said this was voodoo stuff," he blurted.

Belle scoffed. "She doesn't know nothin'! She's getting on—probably ninety-nine by now. Maybe even one hundred. Can't believe she's still moving around. Go find the boys. They's waiting on you," she said, and she hustled him out of the kitchen.

On his way out, Abel called over his shoulder, "She said to be careful with the stuff in the tin." Abel heard a snort in response.

Tank and André were down by the bayou sitting in the broken-down chairs by the firepit and staring at the ashes. There was no fire. It was ninety-three degrees out, it being July and all. Abel's shirt was sticking to his back.

"Hey, boys," Abel said in greeting.

André gave Abel a big grin. He was a giant, mostly gentle, unless he was riled. Tank was wiry and tough, but his little brother was like a big grizzly bear. If you looked at him, you might have the idea that he was slow, but you'd be wrong. He was whip smart and had ended up becoming a white hat computer hacker after the robbery crew had disbanded. Really, he was the only one of them who had landed on his feet in the straight world.

"Did ya get our money?" Tank asked Abel.

"Yeah, but that asshole tried to get me to invest it back in the business."

"Why am I not surprised?" said Tank, laughing.

Abel handed Tank his half of the money. He looked at it with a bemused expression on his face, obviously comparing it to the stacks of cash they used to bring home from a job.

"Yeah, I know. Feels like chump change. But Frank's got another job for us. He wants us to come down there Friday and get the skip's packet. It's a Black guy, so Big Frank thinks you can beat the jungle drums and find him quick."

"Veruto probably figures I know him from church or hoops, or maybe he and I used to go eat fried chicken," said Tank sarcastically.

"Speaking of food," broke in André, "I'm going down to the Quarter on Friday, and since you're gonna be there, too, do you guys want to get some barbecue for lunch? I got a line on a new place. Brisket like Houston. Burnt ends like Kansas City. Ribs like Memphis! Oooh, my mouth is watering."

"Hey, maybe we can get Harm and Rabbit to meet us there. Hell, Harm will probably be down there by the port anyway, strong-arming stiffs," added Tank.

André stood up. "Sounds good. I haven't seen Harm for a bit. Let's go on up. Mama's workin' on some stew from that pig I shot over the weekend."

FOUR

Friday morning Abel drove over to Tank's and picked him up. They had to get the info on their next job, and Big Frank was expecting them. Not that Abel really cared about Veruto's schedule—the man obviously didn't care about wasting Abel's time. It was just that Abel and Tank were both organized. Their previous life of crime had instilled in them the criticality of timing. Most robberies were all about the window of opportunity. Miss the window and you walked away with nothing. Ignore the clock and go to prison or get dead.

They hit the road, but then Abel noticed he was low on gas and didn't want to have to waste time in the city trying to find a station. He pulled up to a pump at a mini-mart on his way out of Slidell. Tank jumped out and went into the store to grab a soda for the road, calling out, "You want anything?"

"Naw," yelled Abel over his shoulder as he worked the pump. The morning sun was hitting the black and white screen, washing out the display. Abel pushed his sunglasses up on his head, then shaded the unreadable screen with his hand.

"Do ya need some help, old man?" said a person on the other side of the pump.

Abel looked around the pump, irritated, ready to make a smartass comment. It was the girl from the Starbucks. The one with the short blonde hair. He morphed his scowl into a dopey grin. "Hehe, funny," he said lamely. He tried to come up with something clever but ended up just saying, "Small world," exactly like an old man.

"Looks like you're stalking me." She laughed. "Should I be worried?"

"Wait a second," Abel replied. "You pulled in after I did! Maybe you're following me." He silently congratulated himself for not totally failing at a comeback.

The girl laughed.

Abel continued digging the hole deeper, asking the girl, "Do you live around here?"

She took pity and quit playing with him. "No, I live down near the Quarter. I share a place with some of my friends. I'm just up here on business."

"What do you do?" asked Abel, trying to keep the conversation going and knowing he was on the clock with her pump ticking in the background.

Just then, Tank rounded the front of Abel's truck and walked right up to the girl. "Hi, I'm Tank!" He held out his hand for a shake and asked, "What's your name?"

"Maria."

"Nice to meet ya. Maria, this is Abel. Abel this is Maria." Tank gave Maria a big grin, then caught Abel's eye and winked. He walked back around the front of the truck with a smirk plastered on his face.

"Yeah, nice to meet you, Maria," said Abel. "We're headed down to the city, so I better get going."

"You do that, Abel. I don't want you to be late!" Maria said.

Abel climbed up into the truck, mentally kicking himself. What was with that girl?

Tank didn't help matters by saying, "Jesus, dude, we gotta work on your game . . ."

Abel drove out of the lot and looked back at Maria. She was standing by the pump. Their eyes locked for a brief moment, and then she was out of sight. Abel shook it off and said, "OK, let's go get the packet on this runner. We need the money."

This time, Family Bail Bonds had all hands on deck. Little Frankie stared at them. The old battle-axe secretary had a big manila envelope in her hands. Veruto had spun around in his chair and was facing them, manspreading, his protruding belly neatly bisected by a belt with a big rodeo buckle. Big Frank gazed at his son expectantly.

Abel took in the tableau. Nobody said anything for a beat too long, then Frank kicked the back of Frankie's chair.

"Here's the jumper's information," blurted Little Frankie. The secretary ceremonially handed the manila envelope to Little Frankie. He stood up and walked around his battered desk to Abel. "Here's his packet," he said and presented the envelope with two hands like it was the communion chalice filled with wine.

Abel heard a low snicker from Tank and avoided looking at him, knowing they both would burst out laughing. Well, well, well, looked like Big Frank was tapping Frankie for the majors. Surprisingly, he felt a touch of pity for Veruto. The man was getting near retirement, and all he had to pin his hopes and dreams on was this disappointing kid.

"What's the story on this guy, Frankie?" asked Tank.

"His name is Faber. Uh and he's a dealer."

"What're the numbers?" Tank nudged.

Little Frankie looked over at his daddy. Frank ignored him. Frankie thought a bit and then said, "One-fifty."

Tank started to say something, but Abel interrupted. "Why so high? He's just a dealer."

Frankie's mouth worked, but nothing came out. Big Frank sighed. "He shot at the police during the arrest."

"And he's still alive?" said Tank to no one in particular.

"This guy's dangerous. We want twelve percent," said Abel.

"You guys only get eight," said Little Frankie.

Veruto overruled his son. "I'll go ten, but that's it. It'll be easy. Tank probably knows the skip."

"Yeah? How's that? There's 'bout half a million people in New Orleans," Tank said.

"Shit, you people all go to the same clubs. Y'all talk. He's about your age. You know what part of town to check out," Veruto said.

"*You people*?" Tank said.

"Now don't get all huffy," said Frank. "I didn't mean nothin' by it . . ."

Abel and Tank locked eyes, and Tank raised his eyebrows, a hint of a smile on his face. "We'll find him."

Abel added, "Yeah, no problem." He grabbed the skip packet from junior, then said, "Let's go," to Tank.

The door closed behind them and Tank said, "I'm hungry. Time for barbecue. I hope my brother got us a table."

André stepped out of the front door of the bank. He was hungry, too, and thinking about the barbecue. He had been deep in his head, analyzing the bank's security policies and definitely needed a break. Sometimes he'd get stuck on a detail, but just a little walking around would dislodge something in his brain, and then everything would become crystal and would lay out in front of him in a beautiful landscape of logic. He figured that by the time he came back from lunch, he'd be able to put in place a comprehensive plan to protect the institution from ransomware attacks.

The barbecue joint was a new place close to the bank, and there was a rush of patrons vying for seats at noon. He'd arranged with his brother and the guys to hit the place at eleven thirty to avoid the rush. He hoped Harm and Rabbit were going to show because it felt like he hadn't seen them for weeks.

Rabbit, especially, had been hard to track down since he had gotten married almost two years ago. His new wife, Crystal, jealously guarded her time with him and gave him trouble if he hung out with them too much, which was unfortunate, because he was kind of the straw that stirred the drink. Always talking. Always joking. Always giving somebody shit. Man, he missed him!

Harm was different. André felt that if they didn't keep him in the fold, he would go off the deep end somehow. In a fight or thieving a warehouse, Harm was there—the tip of the spear. But now, when they had stopped robbing places and he was off on his own collecting bad street debts, André thought that he was probably spiraling around the drain and getting depressed. After he hit up deadbeats for money all day, he just went home to his mama every night.

Then he laughed to himself, because he went home to his mama every night, too. Course, it was different! Tank was there, and it was more like it was their house, and they were taking care of Isabelle, who was getting more and more frail.

He picked up the pace. The restaurant's kitchen exhaust was hanging in the street, and he could smell the delicious oaky smoke mixed with the roasted meat perfume. His mouth started watering as he came up on another Black dude leaning against a storefront. The man was familiar. André had seen him before.

He bumped fists with the guy and stopped for a moment to chat. Turned out the guy was hitting up people for change. André reached into his pocket for a few bucks and handed it to the man. The man didn't look exactly homeless and still managed to exude an air of cool; although, something in his eyes didn't look quite right. They had an unfocused intensity.

The man fished around in his pocket and handed André a small white card, slightly worse for wear. Writing on the card read: *"I looked, and there before me was a pale horse! Its rider was named Death, and Hades was following close behind him. They were given power over a fourth of the earth to kill by sword, famine and plague, and by the wild beasts of the earth."*

Hmmm, kind of grim, André mused, recognizing the words from Revelation.

"Come to my church," the wild-eyed man said. "The address is on the card."

André flipped it over. An address ran across the top and below it was another quote from Revelation: *"When I saw him, I fell at his feet as though dead. Then he placed his right hand on me and said: "Do not be afraid. I am the First and the Last. I am the Living One; I was dead, and now look, I am alive for ever and ever! And I hold the keys of death and Hades."*

André slipped the card into his pocket and disengaged himself from the guy by saying, "Uh, yeah, I'll check it out." He continued down the street, still hearing the man talking to him, or maybe just to himself, the tone becoming more and more urgent. André ignored it, and when he hit the middle of the block, he cut across the street, nimbly dancing away from an oncoming car. He waited in the center of the street till the next lane cleared, then jogged to the sidewalk in front of the restaurant.

As he walked toward the entrance, he was suddenly grabbed on the shoulder, and a voice said, "Stop, motherfucker!" André whirled around, raising his arm defensively. It didn't protect him from being struck on the side of his head. Dazed, his ear ringing, he stepped back and looked at a swarthy man in jeans and a polo coming at him again.

"I said stop! Get down on your knees!"

"Uh, what—" André managed to get out, but suddenly someone rammed him from behind, knocking him down.

Jolts of pain exploded in both his knees. His mind went nuclear, and he erupted off the ground into the man in front of him, knocking him down on his back. André swung his arm up and down like a sledgehammer, crushing the man's nose, then up and down again.

Abruptly, he was jerked backward. The man behind him had a hold on André's neck and was brutally choking him. He clawed at the man's forearm. A roar was trapped inside of him as he kicked backward, landing on top of the man. He twisted his huge body, getting half turned around, enough to get an arm in play, and he scrabbled his hand over the man's face. Finding the man's eye socket, André jammed his thumb in, making a motion like digging out a peach pit. The man screamed, and his armlock loosened. André rolled off the man and stood, backing against the plate glass window of the restaurant.

The swarthy man was on his feet, too, facing André. Blood leaked over his mouth and dripped off his chin. "We're police, asshole. You're fucked now!"

Two cop cars screamed down the road and stopped in front of the barbecue joint, four cops boiling out of the vehicles. They rushed André, swinging nightsticks, and proceeded to club him to the ground. He didn't resist. He just covered his head with his arms and rolled into a ball.

"I didn't do anything! Stop!" he yelled.

One cop put all his weight on André's head. Another was on top of his legs. The remaining cop wrestled his arms back and cuffed him. All four then manhandled him to the patrol car and leaned him over the hood, banging his face onto the metal.

A cluster of patrons from the restaurant were standing on the sidewalk watching. "Hey, what did he do?" yelled one.

"Asshole cops!" screamed another. "Fucking savages!"

The original man with the busted-up nose ran toward the crowd. The people shrank back. "Get back inside, or we'll arrest you for interfering!"

"Yeah, fuck you! New Orlean's finest," one brave soul muttered, but the group of people edged away. A few people still had their phones up, recording the action. The people milled around, agitated.

The plainclothes cop left the crowd and went back to André, who was still plastered on the police car's hood. "I'm Detective Guidry. You're under arrest, motherfucker." His words came out nasally as he squeezed his nose to slow the bleeding.

"What am I under arrest for?" André asked.

"Jaywalking."

André snorted. "Ya mean, walking while Black."

Guidry continued, "Resisting arrest. Assaulting a police officer. We watched you do a deal with that guy up the street. Money changed hands. We saw you take something from him."

The detective started fishing through André's pockets. "Ah, lookee here." He held up a little white packet. "Looks like some smack," he crowed.

"Bullshit!" André yelled. "You fucking planted that. That guy I talked to was just a street preacher. I gave him a handout."

"Save it for the judge," said one of the uniforms, and he roughly jerked André off the hood and walked him to the back seat of the patrol car. The other cop opened the door, and then they both pushed him into the back, making sure to bang his face on the roof edge and splitting his eyebrow in the process.

André sat there, trying to calm himself. He assessed his injuries. Blood was streaming down the side of his face from his eyebrow, he could taste blood in his mouth, and when he swallowed it felt like his throat was bruised. *Probably from that choke hold,* he thought. Both his knees throbbed, and when he probed his teeth with his tongue, one of them was loose. Fuck! That pissed him off. He'd had good teeth. His arms were battered all the way up to his shoulders.

The cops got into the front seat, put the vehicle in gear, and drove down the street. *They're taking me to jail,* André thought. *All those robberies? And I get busted for jaywalking? Fuck me!*

Tank and Abel rolled down the street, scanning for LA Smoke. Suddenly Tank said, "Hey, look, there's Harm and Rabbit." Abel dove the truck into a convenient spot. Tank jumped out and yelled, "Hey, Rabbit!"

The two guys stopped walking, and Rabbit turned around and yelled back, "Tank!" Harm stopped, too, and Tank jogged up to them. He and Rabbit exchanged a bro hug, and then he and Harm bumped fists.

Abel caught up and hugged them both. "Man, it's good to see you guys!"

"Yeah, it's awesome to see you guys, too. Lately all I do is talk to my bride. I love her and everything, but I miss the crew. Marriage is great! But still wish I was robbing. But she'd kill me if I did that," said Rabbit, machine-gunning them with his mouth like usual.

"Dude, marriage hasn't changed you a bit," teased Abel. "Let's get to the restaurant. André is probably waiting for us. Hope he got us a table 'cuz I'm starved."

"We can catch up on what's going on over a couple of slabs of ribs," said Harm. "Oh, and Rabbit, I hear the salads are good, too."

"Fuck you, Harm! I'm getting brisket," said Rabbit. They all laughed at the old inside joke. One time, way back, Rabbit got a salad instead of a burger, and the crew never let him forget it. That's where he got the nickname "Rabbit"—which was perfect anyway because he talked fast and jumped around from topic to topic.

Rabbit worked at his daddy's auto shop now, and he looked the part: a mechanic, thin and antsy, with a cigarette usually clamped between his lips or jammed between two grease-encrusted knuckles, as he was talking and waving around his hands. Back in the day, he'd been the crew's car man, scouting the path to and from the gig and driving the getaway. Stealing vehicles for the job was his thing. Then he made sure the cars ran and ran fast.

He led the crew through the entrance to LA Smoke, but the guys were blocked from moving into the dining room by a cluster of people talking agitatedly among themselves. Tank brought up the rear, coming through the door and pushing Harm and Abel up closer to the group of people. Abel overheard one of the people say, "Can you believe that? Fucking cops. Beat the shit out of that guy for nothin'!"

Harm had already scanned the joint. "André's not here."

"I'll call him," said Tank. The guys milled around while Tank called. "He's not picking up."

The group of upset people had filtered toward the door and were leaving. Abel peeled off from his crew and caught up with the departing patrons outside. "Excuse me, what guy got beat up by the police?"

One of the men stopped and said, "This big Black guy got arrested by six cops out in front of the restaurant. Happened a few minutes ago."

Another one of the group added, "They beat the shit out of him with their clubs—they about killed him. 'Cept he was so big, he stood 'em off for a while."

Abel was getting a bad feeling. "Way taller than me with an Afro?"

"I recorded some of it," the first guy said. "Wanna see?"

"Definitely," Abel answered.

The man fiddled with his phone and then held it in front of Abel's face. He watched, getting a sick feeling in his stomach. "Dude, can you send me that video?"

"Sure."

Abel introduced himself, then gave him his number and waited while the video was being sent. He checked his phone and made certain he'd received it right. "Thanks, man. If we need a witness, could we call you later?"

"No problem," the man said. "We all saw it." He waved his arm at his whole group of friends. "Saw almost the whole thing. Total bullshit. Be glad to."

Abel plugged the man's name and details into his phone, then went back into LA Smoke to break the news to Tank that his brother had just been arrested.

CHAPTER

FIVE

ndré's shoulders hurt. The cops had cranked the cuffs on tight behind his back, and his shoulders didn't flex like that. He had too much bulk across his back. The cuffs had already rubbed his wrists raw, and it seemed like the policemen had taken a perverse pleasure in rounding every corner at high speed, throwing him back and forth on the bench seat. They didn't miss a bump, either. With all that turbulence and flopping around, the cuffs had been constantly yanked back and forth, and André imagined he could feel blood streaming down his hands.

On top of the physical battering, the carnival-ride motion of the vehicle was making him carsick. The strong smell of vomit, and maybe even shit, coming off the floor was pushing him toward puking, too. He hadn't thrown up in a car since he was a little kid, and there was no way he was going to do that in front of the two cops. He was covered in flop sweat from trying to resist vomiting, and he was repeating a mantra to himself: *please get to the jail, please get to the jail.*

Just when he felt he couldn't hold it back any longer, the cop car hit one last bump and sailed into the jail lot. André leaned forward and put his head between his knees, breathing quick gasps of air in a last-ditch effort to hold off vomiting.

Through a sheer act of will he didn't puke, and when the door opened, he was still panting liked a dog. Even though the cop banged his head on the doorframe wrestling him out of the back, he didn't care. He was just glad to be breathing fresh air. They frog-marched him through the intake side of the New Orleans jail and parked him in front of the deputy.

He was glad they had taken him here instead of the parish jail—the one where the sheriff's department had abandoned the facility during Hurricane Katrina, leaving the prisoners and a few guards to tough it out. The toilets had overflowed, the food had practically run out, and the hurricane had run over it like a bulldozer. That one was on the list of top ten worst jails in America. They had rebuilt the parish jail, but André doubted the staff and operations had improved.

"Book this piece of shit," said the cop. "Possession, resisting arrest, assaulting an officer—Guidry's nose looks like an alcoholic's liver."

Shit, now they were gonna make his life miserable for the next few days.

The deputy at the desk guided André through the process, getting everything from his pockets, fingerprinting, and then the mug shot. In every jail photo André had ever seen, the suspect was scowling. He'd always figured that they were just tough guys putting on a show. But standing there after being beat to shit when he was arrested, almost puking in the squad car, and having no idea what the future might portend, he realized that all those people were just miserable and frightened.

Finally, the cops pushed him down onto a chair that was bolted to the floor and released one of the cuffs, then relocked it around the arm of the industrial-strength seat.

"Have fun," said one of the cops with a sneer, then they both left the room.

André sat there for a few minutes, wondering what was next. He found out shortly. Two jail guards came into the room. One was tall with a blond crew cut and resembled a linebacker, while the other seemed almost effeminate and had a receding chin and a face covered with an active case of acne. They uncuffed him from the chair, then pushed him into the hallway and back into another room. He didn't even think of resisting. One of them was carrying an ASP, a collapsible baton, and André's arms were already bruised.

"Strip!" commanded the baton-wielding guard. André started removing his clothes. "Faster, asshole!" As the clothes came off, the other guard was searching them and putting all of André's possessions, including his clothes, into a big heavy-duty ziplock bag.

Once he was naked, they ordered him to spread his legs, spread his butt cheeks with his hands, and jump up and down. André gave them a look that said, "You gotta be kidding me," and the guard that was putting him through his paces said, "Gotta make sure you don't got nothin' in your prison pocket."

André was tempted to say, "Just pictures of your mother," but figured he'd been hit enough already. They directed him to an alcove that had a shower. He stepped in and fiddled with the controls, trying to make it warm, but it wasn't happening.

"Speed it up, dipshit. There's only one temp; this isn't a spa. You gotta minute, then the water goes off. Enjoy it. It's the last time you get wet until after your arraignment on Monday."

Fuck! He was gonna be in here all weekend. They'd neglected to tell him that during booking. He assumed he was just in for an overnighter, getting bailed in the morning by his brother. Dejected, André finished and stepped out, looking around for a towel. There wasn't one.

"Sorry, laundry service hasn't delivered any warm towels," said the alpha guard. He nudged his minion and said, "Haha, look at that big fucker's dick. It looks like an acorn!" They both laughed.

André's face remained impassive, but he felt a burning humiliation inside. He ran an imaginary film loop inside his head where he had the guard alone on the outside, and he was smashing his face like how he had beat on Guidry.

The zit-faced guard handed André a faded orange jumpsuit. As he was putting it on, he hoped it had been washed since the last inmate had worn it. He was handed a pair of limp canvas shoes, and of course, they didn't fit his size-fourteen feet. He just crammed his toes in and stepped down the backs.

The two guards moved him further down the hallway. André shuffled along, walking like he was in his mama's slippers, trying to keep them on his feet. Next was a health screening where they gave him a cursory exam, took a DNA sample by swabbing his cheek, and then drew blood. He guessed it was to check for STDs or look for drugs in his system because they weren't explaining anything. At the end, the doctor, no, the medical orderly—no way this fucker was a doctor—gave him a questionnaire to fill out, checking for health issues like a bad back or seizures and shit like that. Like these assholes cared.

And in the end, they threw him into a holding cell filled with some other inmates. The cell was about the size of his mama's living room and was filled with ten other sad-looking dudes, mostly keeping to themselves. Two Hispanics were talking loudly in Spanish to each other. Some were sitting on the floor as far apart from each other as they could manage. The few uncomfortable bunk beds were occupied already. A steel toilet sat in the corner in plain view of everybody. The stench in the cell hit André. His urge to vomit resurfaced.

The linebacker guard said, "Keep to yourself, and maybe you won't be raped," and with that cheery admonition, the two guards slammed the door behind him.

Tank's cell vibrated. He snatched it out of his pocket and saw an unfamiliar number. He swiped and put it on speaker.

"Thomas, I'm on the jail phone. They finally let me make my one call. The jail phone—ya get me?" asked André.

André never called him by his given name. The wheels turned in Tank's head. It was common knowledge that the justice system monitored the phone calls but was glad that André had the presence of mind to remind him. It told him that André wasn't totally freaked by being in county. He was still André, the thinking machine. "Are you OK? I heard you got a beatdown."

"I'm bruised up, but nothing's broken. Listen, I don't know how long I've got—there's a line waiting to use this phone."

"Got it," said Tank.

"They're holding me over the weekend. I'm being arraigned Monday morning."

"OK, we'll have an attorney there for you. What did they arrest you for?

"Jaywalking, but then it turned into resisting, assault on an officer, and the undercover detective planted some drugs, too. Smack, I think. Motherfucker!"

"OK, don't worry, brother, we'll get you out of there. Can you handle it till Monday?"

André said, "Yeah, no problem," but there was a hitch in his voice.

"Hang in there, man."

"OK."

André was choked up. Tank could hear it in his voice. It came through the shitty prison phone, and it came through all the jail background noise. Tank's words caught in his throat. "Don't worry, little brother, I got this. We'll get you out. No matter how high they set the bond. I love you, André. Keep your head down."

Tank heard a faint "I love you, brother" on the phone, and then the connection died.

They were all in Isabelle's kitchen, a normally cozy room with green cabinets and a white board ceiling, but it felt wrong. They'd all been there many times eating dinner on happier occasions, but tonight it was tense, and there wasn't any food on the table. Isabelle sat at the head of the kitchen table with her son, Tank, next to her. Callie and Abel were there. Two more chairs were taken up by Harm and Rabbit, but André's seat was empty.

It felt like one of their old planning sessions before a robbery except that Isabelle and Callie were sitting in. It didn't have the excitement of figuring out a job and anticipating the rewards; instead, it was grim and everyone was worried. André arrested for jaywalking? That was kind of the norm for a Black man in today's world, but the other charges of assaulting an office and resisting arrest, plus the bogus drug charge, escalated things. It could go south in a hurry for any number of reasons.

Tank had just finished recounting the call with André, and Isabelle had teared up and said, "I'm going to see my baby tomorrow."

"I wish we all could go," said Tank. "But we're not going to be able to see him until after he's arraigned."

"What are we going to do?" Isabelle asked plaintively. "I can't have my André go to prison."

"Tank and I are going to Big Frank's in the morning and make sure we have him lined up to front the bond. Depending how much it is, we are going to have to either use one or more of the vehicles for collateral or one of our houses," said Abel. "That is unless we can persuade Frank to do the bond without collateral."

"Riiiiight," said Tank skeptically. "I'll bring a copy of the house deed and title to my truck."

"We need to get him a lawyer, too," said Callie.

"I was thinking we could get Uncle Deacon's lawyer, you know—Hebert," Abel said.

"What? That guy let Deacon go to prison," said Rabbit.

"No, he's good," insisted Harm. "No one could have got Deke off. Shit, Deacon literally was holding those stolen diamonds in his hands when he got popped."

"They were in a box on his desk," said Rabbit.

"You know what I mean," Harm said, grumpily.

"What do you think, Mama?" asked Tank. "Hebert's got a solid rep, and he knows us and we know him."

"Can we afford him?"

"Yeah, we all have money set aside for an emergency. We'll pool it, right?" asked Abel.

"We got this," said Rabbit.

"We don't want to stir anything up until we see how it lands on Monday. Maybe it'll all go away," said Abel.

Callie put her arm around Isabelle's frail shoulders and said, "Let's hope so."

CHAPTER

SIX

Tank and Abel stood outside the courtroom on Monday with Hebert, the attorney, talking quietly. Blaise Hebert, a slim, aristocratic-looking man, dressed in a charcoal suit, cut tight, was briefing them. "This is serious. We are looking at resisting arrest, assault *and* battery on a police officer while he was in the process of performing his duties, and the possession. At least one of those is going to elevate to a felony."

"He was just jaywalking!" said Tank.

"This is bullshit," added Abel. "André doesn't touch drugs, so this is a setup. It's some racist shit."

"Be that as it may," said Hebert, "the DA may turn the tables on us and charge him with this new law 'Blue Lives Matter.' It makes the injury and resisting charge a hate crime against the cop. Another felony."

"Are you fucking kidding me?" said Abel. "He was just crossing the street to get lunch!"

"Look, we'll cross that bridge later. Today, we just need to get him out on bail so we can start putting together his defense. Let's hope this judge is rational and doesn't do something insane with the bail." Hebert shook Abel's hand

and then put his hand on Tank's shoulder as he passed him on the way back to the courtroom.

Tank went over to his mother who was standing next to Harm and an uncharacteristically silent Rabbit. Harm was shifting back and forth on his feet uncomfortably.

"We should move inside. Hebert told me it's about time," Tank told them. They shuffled as a group through the dark mahogany doors and found seats.

Then, they waited. Several groups of inmates passed through the system. A litany of charges were read, and the various defendants' pleas became a drone of noise as they waited for André to appear. Every now and then a lucky prisoner was deemed innocent, or at least there wasn't probable cause to be held, raising hope in Tank's heart that there would be a good outcome.

Then, it was time. André shuffled in, along with a line of four other prisoners in orange jumpsuits. "Oh, my heavens!" said Isabelle, when André's beat-up face came in to view.

The deputy sat the prisoners in the front row before the judge. One at a time, they stood and faced the judge. At last, André got up on his feet and stared at the judge whose eyes were cast down, reading the paperwork through his half-moon glasses.

The judge made short work of it. He read the list of charges. When he came to the assault on the detective, he grimaced. Tank knew what that meant. The judge looked up at André and asked him if he understood the charges.

"I do," said André.

"How do you plead?" asked the judge.

"Not guilty," said André vehemently.

"Hold over for trial." The judge nodded at the representative from the district attorney's office.

"Your Honor, we request that you set bail at fifty thousand dollars. These are significant charges."

Hebert stood and said, "Your Honor, please. This whole situation stems from a jaywalking incident! The defendant is a hardworking man with ties to the community. He's responsible and will attend trial. He is not a flight risk as he fully intends to prove his innocence." Hebert gestured at Tank and Isabelle. "His mother and brother are here in this courtroom, and they will be guaranteeing the bond. They are just simple people of limited means. Please take that into consideration."

But Tank already knew how it was going to go. He'd seen the expression on the judge's face. "Bail stands at fifty thousand," said the judge without looking at André, Hebert, or Isabelle.

The court deputies ushered the prisoners out of the courtroom. André hung his head as he walked toward the exit. Just before he reached the door, he looked back at Tank. They locked eyes. As he went out of the courtroom, a uniformed policeman sidled up to him and said, "You're gonna serve time, and you'll never make it back out. And in the meantime, Guidry is gonna fuck you up. Won't matter if you make bail. One of us will find you—then, you're done." André stared straight ahead and didn't acknowledge that he'd heard.

"What now?" asked Isabelle. They all were clustered around Hebert outside the courtroom.

"We get him bailed out right now," said the attorney.

Abel was already on the phone, giving Big Frank the bail number. He hung up and turned to the group. "OK, it's all set. Tank and I will go over to the jail and wait for him to be processed out. We'll get him home."

Isabelle breathed a sigh of relief, then said, "What can we do now?"

"Get him to the emergency room and get him attended to. Make sure they take pictures of his body. Get all those bruises and cuts documented. They didn't take him to the hospital before they incarcerated him, so I'm going to be building a case around how they mishandled this from the beginning."

"What else should we do?" asked Tank.

"Nail down those witnesses that took the video. Find the street preacher. Get some people to vouch for him from the church. Get me some contacts from his work. We want to show that he is an upstanding citizen who has been unfairly targeted." Hebert checked his watch. "I've got another case in a few minutes, but call my secretary. See if she can find space on my calendar tomorrow morning. Bring André and we'll start planning for his trial."

The group broke up. Abel and Tank were headed over to the jail, while Harm and Rabbit left with Isabelle. As she walked off, Tank called out, "I'll have him home after lunch."

CHAPTER

SEVEN

"So are we seeing the lawyer this morning?" asked Abel. He and Tank were standing just inside the Chevals' front door.

"Naw, Hebert was booked up all day with more court proceedings, so we're meeting tomorrow. We took André to the ER yesterday afternoon and got him all checked out, and they took pictures and shit. They got all his injuries documented. When we got home, he didn't even want to eat. He went straight to bed. He's still sleeping."

"Is he OK?"

"Seems kinda traumatized," answered Tank, concern on his face.

"He'll be OK after he gets some rest. The parish jail is chaos. I doubt if he got any sleep at all the whole weekend."

"Should we start looking for those witnesses, or do we need to start looking for the skip?" asked Tank.

"Let's wait until we talk to Hebert before we track down the wits. We probably should get started on the jumper and keep Big Frank happy. I read through the packet last night, and it turns out the guy is named Fabre, not Faber. Little

Frankie is such a dipshit. The guy's full name is Didier Fabre—he goes by Didi."

"We gonna start with friends and family as usual?"

"Yeah, he lives over by the farm country around St. Martinville, toward Breaux Bridge. His parents are still alive. They gotta place just outside Catahoula. We can go there and nose around. Check it out and surprise his parents."

"That's a bit of a drive. Wanna hit the Starbucks in Covington on the way?"

They discussed their strategy with Fabre's parents on the drive over. They never knew the right approach because the parents could flop either way: against the criminal justice system or against their wayward child. Usually, the parents tended to show antipathy toward the bounty hunters, including Tank and Abel, along with the criminal justice system which had unfairly targeted their precious child and given him a raw deal. Sometimes they bumped into a parent who felt that a bail recovery agent was the lesser of two evils. If the police picked up the skip, much worse things could happen than just being taken back to jail to face trial. Every now and then, there was a set of parents that had given up on their kid and considered them to be a lost cause.

This latter group might not hesitate to give up information on their child, but a lot of times the leads were old and stale. They were usually estranged from the jumper and had nothing to do with them, hence the poor intelligence.

When they hit the Covington city limits, Tank and Abel cut short their planning and started looking for the Starbucks. Abel saw it on the corner and made the turn, then pulled to the curb. A chorus of "Welcome to Starbucks" hit them as they entered, annoying Abel. When did that become a thing? He would have preferred to slide in the door unnoticed instead of becoming the momentary center of attention.

They made their order and then moved back away from the group of people milling around the coffee bar. There was another chorus of "Welcome to Starbucks" from the baristas, and everyone turned toward the door. An extremely attractive girl stepped in and surveyed the coffee shop. She had dark hair, almost black, cut in a way that appeared shaggy with spikes here and there. With her distinctive hair and large brown eyes, she almost looked like an anime character.

The girl started walking straight toward Abel. Suddenly, he realized that it was Maria, the same girl that he kept bumping into—only now her hair was black, not blonde. And somehow, she had managed to make it look longer and fuller. "What the fuck?" he murmured to Tank. Seeing a person once, that was just random. Twice in a week? A coincidence. But three times and in different towns? Something was going on.

"She's following us," Tank said.

Maria walked up to Abel and lightly punched his shoulder. "We have to stop meeting like this," she said. Abel laughed uneasily. She grabbed his upper arm and gently steered him away from Tank.

"Yeah, it feels like you're stalking me," he blurted out, then instantly regretted it. She was gorgeous, and he was in a dry spell. He wasn't sure that he even cared that she might be stalking him. In a way, it felt like a compliment. It was hot.

"I can see how it might feel like that. I'm sorry. It was just that when I saw you at the gas station before, it didn't go the way I wanted it to. Then I thought, well, I'll never see you again, and that made me kind of sad. So when you guys turned right in front of me while I was over in Lacombe doing errands, I thought here's my chance, and I followed you. I figured you were going to some place local, but you kept driving and driving, and by then I was committed."

"I guess I'm glad you did," said Abel.

"You guess?" said Maria. "How many times do I have to show up before you get the message and ask me out?"

"Um—"

"Why don't you take me out to dinner tonight?"

"I don't know . . . I'm sorry, there's some stuff going on in my life." Abel nodded toward Tank. "His brother got falsely arrested, and we're trying to figure out what to do."

"You gotta eat, and we can talk about it. Maybe I can help. I'm good at that stuff," cajoled Maria.

"Alright, alright. Dinner would be nice. Give me your number, and I'll call you after we get done and set it up."

"How about we make a date for Thursday night right now, that way it's set up, and then we both can go about our day?"

"OK, can you meet me at Palmettos at eight?" asked Abel.

"You mean Palmettos on the Bayou?"

"Yep."

"OK, I'll see you there." With that she turned and left, leaving Abel slightly dumbstruck.

Abel walked back to Tank who was standing there with his mouth open. "She's following you."

"She did follow us—all the way from Lacombe. But she explained it, and it made sense. She wanted to apologize for how she acted the last time she saw us, plus she's awesome looking."

"Abel, she was fine the last time. It was you that acted weird. But following you? That's a little strange."

"Hey, she couldn't help it. It's my animal magnetism."

Tank snorted a laugh.

"We're going out Thursday night."

"What!" said Tank. "That's the first date you've set up since Olivia. You've had a two-year dry spell."

"No, I haven't. I've been on dates . . ."

"Riiiight," said Tank.

They continued on till they hit Baton Rouge, transitioning from I-12 to I-10, then over the insane bridge that crossed the Mississippi, the bridge that had seen better days and needed to be replaced. Traveling up and over and through the rickety black steel girders on the top, the traffic always seemed to pause at the apex, like a Ferris wheel that stopped at its peak. Anybody with acrophobia would freak.

They traveled further west, cruising over the Atchafalaya, going over the causeway, but this time hugging the swamp. They continued south through Henderson, passing Bayou Teche, and meandered through farm country until they found Fabre's parents' house teetering on the bank of the Catahoula Coulee.

Abel pulled the truck up onto the yard, parking next to another truck. This one was an ancient Chevy, the color of the dirt that surrounded it. The home may not have been much to look at, but that was more than made up for by a magnificent chicken coop that sat to the side, surrounded by a chicken wire fence. The coop had a ramp that crossed the front of the building and ended three feet off the ground at a door that was tied up, allowing the birds free range during the day and, when closed, protecting them from foxes at night. A stooped man stood at the edge of the coop, watching them.

Tank approached the fence and called over, "Hello! Where y'at?"

"A'ight, I guess," the man called back, tentatively walking toward them and stopping a few feet away on the other side of the wire fence.

He had close, grizzled hair and fine features on his face and was still carrying the traces of a handsome man that had been worn down by age. His hands were clasped, but he periodically rubbed them against each other like he was washing them under a faucet, and now and again he took a step back, then forward like he was fidgety.

Abel tried to catch his eye, but the man wouldn't focus on him, looking instead at his ear or maybe past him at the street. "We're here about your son. He hasn't shown up to court, and now we're trying to find him. We're bail recovery agents."

Mr. Fabre adjusted his head slightly and locked eyes with Abel. "He didn't do no wrong. My boy's a good boy."

"Well, that's what the trial is supposed to determine," said Tank. "If he didn't do anything, then he is innocent until he is proven guilty, but he didn't show up."

The man shook his head disgustedly at Tank as if to say, *You should know better than that* . . . "Didi knew he wasn't going to get a fair shake. So I guess he run off."

Abel noticed the uncomfortable look on his friend's face. He knew Tank sometimes felt like a traitor to his own people. Tank wasn't positive that the criminal justice system always let the innocent go free.

A screen door slammed, and Abel and Tank turned to the sound. A large woman in a print dress and red shoes stalked toward them. "What do you want? Are you here about my boy? My Didier is a church boy. He sings in the church. You go talk to them. The reverend will tell you he couldna done those things they sayin'."

"Which church is that, ma'am?" asked Abel. "Can you tell us where to find him? His situation is going to get worse if he stays on the run."

Tank said earnestly to Mrs. Fabre, "It's better that we find him. I'll make sure he's safe, and we'll take him straight to jail and make sure he's OK."

"It's better us than the NOPD," added Abel.

"You two boys don't know nothin'. You're just chasing the money; you don't care 'bout my boy." She glared at them. "You want to find Didi? He a church boy—spends all day Sunday there."

"Where did he work?" asked Abel.

This time the father spoke. "Didi didn't do a nine-to-five. He had his own business," he said proudly. "He was always in the woods collecting herbs and getting powders and such."

"He was healing people and supplying all the hoodoo folk around here and all the way out to Lake Charles," said his mother. "He knew every root doctor round here. You go talk to his sister; she'll tell you. Didi's good boy."

Abel politely said his goodbyes and walked back to the truck, leaving Tank behind with the Fabres. Tank stepped in closer to the folks, speaking quietly and seriously. Eventually, the mother nodded a few times and stepped away. Tank pulled out his phone and typed in something with his thumbs. He shook the old man's hand, then took the mother's hand with both of his, pulling her a little closer, speaking something to her, then turned and headed back to the truck.

Tank climbed in. "Head on over to St. Martinville. That's where his sister is, the church, too."

EIGHT

Didi's mother had mentioned that the sister, Josana, was a social worker and wouldn't be home till after four which gave them a couple of hours to kill before she was available, so they went to the church first. It was an Apostolic church on the outskirts of St. Martinville.

"These folk take their Bible seriously," said Tank, as he eyeballed a small white sign that directed them to the office in an adjacent building.

"Can you tell just by looking at the church?" asked Abel.

"No, I just know. They're Apostolic, that's what they do."

Abel took Tank's word for it. Isabelle and her sons went to church regularly. Abel had tagged along when they were kids, but it didn't really stick. He wasn't an atheist. He believed in some kind of God; he knew there was something—he could feel it. But sitting in church wasn't his thing.

Tank led the way into the empty office anteroom. The room had greenish threadbare carpeting and a messy desk off to one side, covered with stacks of folded bulletins and piles of inserts. In another corner, a wooden shepherd with a broken crook leaned against the wall. A closed door with the words *Pastor Desmond Broussard* painted in script, beckoned.

"Hello!" Tank called.

"C'mon back." The basso profundo voice rumbled through the door.

Abel and Tank skirted the church secretary's desk, pushed open the door, and entered the pastor's office. Abel stepped toward the beefy man with short snowy hair seated behind another messy desk. "I'm Abel Kane and this is my associate, Thomas Cheval," he said with his hand outstretched.

The solid man stood up and moved around the desk and wrapped up Abel's hand in both of his hands. "What can I do for you fellows?" he asked in a voice that seemed to make the room itself vibrate, each syllable uttered like the lowest notes of a church organ.

"We're bail recovery agents trying to track down Didier Fabre, and his parents told us we should talk to you," said Tank.

The preacher motioned for them to sit in the chairs in front of his desk, and he settled his large frame down in his seat. He shook his head sadly. "He hasn't shown up to Wednesday night Bible study for several weeks. When one of the deacons told me that he'd been arrested, I was shocked. That boy has never caused a lick of trouble."

"Even if he is innocent, he's getting himself in deeper by jumping bail," said Abel.

"The sooner we find him, the better it'll go for him," added Tank.

The pastor looked at each of them in turn. "I don't know what to tell you. I haven't seen him for several weeks. He's a good boy, comes to church on Sunday, goes to Bible study on Wednesday, and he's been doing that since he was little. At Christmas, he and his sister take flowers to all the shut-ins. It just doesn't make sense! He's a good man. There must be some mistake."

"Do you know where he might have gone?" asked Tank. "Do you know who his friends are?"

"Well, he's friendly with everybody at church, but I don't know who his close friends are. He's quiet, keeps to himself mostly. But I do know that he travels all over Louisiana delivering natural medicines and herbs and such to folks that are interested in that kind of thing."

"Could you point us at some of those people?" asked Abel.

"I can't really say."

"You can't or you won't?" asked Tank.

"I just don't know who they are. Those people usually don't advertise themselves."

"Those people?" said Abel.

"Hoodoo folk. I have mixed feelings about them. Their beliefs sometimes conflict with the church's doctrine, but it's part of the culture around here, and I guess it doesn't do any harm. Even heard of people getting cured of what ails them, sometimes. I put it in the category of 'God works in mysterious ways.' Anyway, Didi is a good boy. I'm certain of it. I'm praying for him. Have you talked to his sister yet?"

"We're going there next," said Abel. He stood up to leave, and Tank followed suit. "Thank you, sir."

They shook hands with him again, the pastor once again gripping their hands in both of his. Abel noticed a lingering warmth in his hand as if the pastor had imparted some of his energy as a blessing.

It wasn't four yet, but they went to Fabre's sister's house and sat in their truck in front of her neat little home. The house was one of a group of four on a stubby street, but it stood out with bright white paint and crisp green trim. It reminded Abel of a cottage on a lake. Well, a cottage on a lake in one of those pictures that were sold at the mall. They waited quietly for a few minutes, then Tank broke the silence.

"Why do you s'pose that girl is following you around?" He waited for Abel to answer, but he just sat there, his forehead furrowed. "It can't be because she thinks you're hot." Abel still didn't respond. Tank laughed. "C'mon, man, lighten up. You're due. You haven't had anyone serious since Olivia. Maybe this is the one."

"Maybe," said Abel, thinking about Olivia. She *was* the one, and he'd screwed it up. Although, he couldn't figure out what he should have done. He had been honest about being in the Life and honest about some things he had done, and he had told her more than she could take. She'd broken up with him, and he still hadn't really gotten over it. She had dangled the possibility of them getting back together some time in the future if he got his act together, so he couldn't let it go and get over it because of that thin hope.

Abel was saved from more recriminations by a BMW pulling into the driveway. They got out and stood by the truck on the street waiting for Josana to get out of the BMW, Abel thinking that she would feel hesitant to get out if two strange men walked up to her car, even if it was in broad daylight.

Ms. Fabre opened the vehicle door and stood with the door open, ready to jump back in it looked like. Abel thought she looked like a younger version of her mother, wearing a bright dress with large orange and red flowers.

"We're bail recovery agents," called Tank, and he did a circle, showing off the big yellow words emblazoned on the back of his thin jacket.

"Do you have ID?" she asked.

Abel slowly started walking up the drive with his hand outstretched and his credentials flipped open. When he got within arm's reach, she snatched his ID and examined it carefully. "What do you want?"

"Your brother skipped bail, and we're trying to find him. Keep him out of more trouble," answered Tank.

"I doubt if you care about my brother's well-being," she scoffed.

"Miss, even if we don't know your brother, it's in our best interest to get him back in good shape and ready to stand trial. If he's running around free with a warrant and the cops pick him up? Anything could happen," said Abel.

"You'd be helping your brother if you tell us where he is," said Tank.

"My brother is being railroaded. Drugs? He spends his life helping people. He's got a great business. There are very few people in Louisiana that even do what he does in the hoodoo and voodoo world, and he has more business than he can handle. Drug dealing would be the last thing Didi would do, so I know the charges are bullshit." She shook her head angrily. "It makes me so mad! You should know what I'm talking about." She glared at Tank. "Working for the man," she said, sneering at him like he was a traitor.

"If I didn't feel like I was helping the skip in the long run, I wouldn't do it," said Tank. It sounded like he wasn't that sure himself.

"Ms. Fabre, we really are trying to help your brother. Do you have any idea where he might have gone? Can you tell us who his friends are?" said Abel.

"I don't trust the criminal justice system anywhere, let alone New Orleans, so I wouldn't tell you even if I knew. And if I know my brother, and I do, and if he doesn't want to be found? You won't find him. Didier is smart. Got a lot of friends. He might find you if he decides he wants to talk, but you'll never find him."

"Can you tell him to call us? I'll give you my number," Abel said.

"Like I said, I don't know where he is. But if you give me your number and he does contact me, I'll give it to him."

Abel gave her a business card with his number on it, silently laughing to himself. It felt absurd, jumping from being a robber and trying to be invisible to now being a guy that handed out little white business cards. He politely ended the interview, and they went back to the truck.

On the way home they discussed what they had found. On one hand it was a dead end, but on the other, it generated some questions about the jumper. There wasn't an ounce of information that indicated that Didier Fabre was a criminal. That wasn't their problem though. Their job was to find him and get paid. Still, it was a bit of a mystery.

CHAPTER

NINE

T he next afternoon found André, Tank, and his mama sitting across from their attorney. Hebert was in a dark gray suit with a vague chalk stripe that by its very faintness managed to accentuate the crisp white shirt and scarlet tie with indecipherable golden symbols. Isabelle appeared reassured.

Tank saw past the clothes. He saw Deacon's old lawyer, the guy that mostly kept Abel's uncle safe for all those years except for that one time. There wasn't much that Blaise Hebert could do with the case ol' Deacon handed him, what with the stolen diamonds wrapped up in a box with a bow sitting on his own desk when the detectives landed on him.

André broke the momentary silence. "What are you gonna do?"

Hebert leaned forward and clasped his hands together and said, "We're all going to do our jobs. I'm going to do the things I'm able to do, and y'all are going to do some things that you can do." Blaise looked at Tank when he said that.

Tank opened up the folder in front of him and handed the attorney some photographs. "We took these of the worst of André's injuries." Hebert grabbed them and examined each in turn.

"These are great! But I can't use them. Did you go to the emergency room?" Blaise looked up at André and got a nod. "Did you ask them to document your injuries?" Another look and an answering nod. "Good. I'll subpoena them for your records."

"Next, we're going to need some statements from witnesses. You mentioned some people at the restaurant saw this whole event. You've got to get me their names."

"I think we have them," said Tank.

"Oh, and that street preacher. We gotta track him down, too," added Hebert.

Tank turned to André. "Do you think you can remember his face and find him?"

"Well, if he's still around, I can find him. He gave me a card, and I remember him telling me the address of his church was on the card. Lucky those guys in booking didn't lose my stuff. Still have the card *and* the money that was in my wallet," he added, with a touch of amazement in his tone.

"OK, good," said Hebert. "Can you go over again how this whole thing started? How did the cops engage with you?"

"Engage with me?" André said incredulously. "They just jumped me. It was that detective, Guidry. He was in plain clothes, and he didn't identify himself or anything. He attacked me out of the blue. I just reacted."

"You sure he didn't say something first?" asked Hebert.

"Nope."

"And you weren't acting out in any way, like bumping into people?"

"No. I was thinking about food. I was hungry. There was nobody in front of the restaurant."

Chapter Nine

"Do you know him from before, somehow? Have you ever had contact with him?"

"Nope."

"Hmmm," said Hebert, making notes on his yellow legal pad, "it sure sounds like it was personal to him, like he was targeting you." Blaise looked up from his writing. "I think we're done for today. On your way out, give Emmie the address of your employer so I can start working on some character statements. Oh, yes, and the contact information for your preacher."

André's family stood up and started shuffling out. Blaise Hebert stood and cleared his throat, and they paused and turned. "Don't worry. We have a lot to work with here. I'm going to get the body cams from the uniforms. We'll pick those apart."

In the truck going home, André and Tank strategized while Isabelle sat with her head bowed. Tank said, "Let's get everyone over to the house tonight and figure out who's doing what."

"They all have jobs now. What can they do?" asked André.

Tank looked over at his little brother. "Don't worry, they're all on board. Even Harm, and I feel like we're gonna need him. Last thing he said to me was he was there for 'whatever.'" The brothers were quiet while they mulled that over. They could hear a murmur from the back seat. Every now and then a familiar hoodoo imprecation could be heard. André caught Tank's eye and raised an eyebrow.

CHAPTER

TEN

Harm should have felt his ears burning, but he was down near the port, oblivious and looking for one of his customers. Yeah, he was all about *customer service*. This particular customer, Pete, was late, and the vig was getting big. It was time to escalate the pressure, but first Harm had to find him. He worked at the port but wasn't going to be found there. Gone were the days when you could find a guy at his place of business. Well, maybe you could track a guy down at a body shop or something like that but not the Port of New Orleans, too much security.

He made the borrower turn on tracking on his iPhone when he had handed him the cash, but that connection wasn't working now, of course. Harm knew where he lived, but beating on a guy in front of his wife and kids was a last resort kind of thing. For the moment, he was checking the guy's usual after-work haunts. He wondered why these mopes always went to the same places after work. It made them so easy to find. He guessed it went hand in hand with the kind of thinking that allowed a man to borrow money on the street with its ridiculous interest rates and the chance of maybe getting a leg broken if you got behind.

This dude hit a couple of different bars near the port. They were dives. There weren't very many working man's bars left because the port area had turned into a high rent district over the years. But there had to be places for the riffraff; they were thirsty, too. The kind of places where everything was sticky and smelled sour and had bathrooms that were one step above a third world hole in the ground still existed, and Harm knew 'em all.

He parked by his first choice and went in. Harm was a medium-sized man who looked like a hillbilly with large hands and forearms that were corded with muscles and tendons, the blood vessels prominent. A shockwave of menace preceded him wherever he went without any conscious effort on his part. Out of the corner of his eye he noticed the bartender reach under the counter—maybe to reassure himself that his shotgun was still sitting on its shelf.

Harm ignored the barkeep and stepped deeper into the space, took off his sunglasses, and scanned the joint. Pete saw Harm before Harm saw him, and Pete jumped up, banging into chairs and tables enroute to the back door. Harm went from full stop to full speed as he ran along the bar, catching up with the welsher just as he banged on the emergency bar on the back door. They both went through and ended up rolling on the ground, Harm's grip on the man's collar keeping him down.

Before Harm could do anything, Pete swung wildly and managed to catch him square on his nose. Harm saw red. He climbed on top of Pete and started hammering him in the face. Pete was only able to put up one arm in defense because Harm had Pete's other arm tangled up with his left leg. After a few good hits, Pete started getting better at blocking Harm's punches. Then, Pete started bucking, trying to get Harm off his chest. Harm changed tactics, stiffened his hand, and stabbed Pete's throat. Gagging sounds came out of Pete's mouth.

Harm climbed off of Pete and stood over him. Blood was dripping from Harm's nose and running into his mouth. He spit the blood onto Pete's face, then kicked him in the ribs. Pete's gagging sounds turned into a grunt, and he tucked into a fetal position.

Harm bent over and yanked the chain connected to the man's wallet and pulled it out of his pants. He riffled through it, collecting thirty-eight dollars. "Shit!" Harm said angrily. "You owe three grand with the vig."

Pete, who was still on the ground, rolled up in a ball and protected his head, saying, "I'll have it on Friday. I promise."

"You better or I'm going to your house, and I'll hurt you in front of your family. They probably don't even know you're drinking and gambling away the food money, ya fucking deadbeat."

Harm turned and walked away, the fight giving him a sense of déjà vu. But it wasn't that vague, unplaceable familiarity kind of thing. He knew exactly what it reminded him of. The fight that got him drummed out of the Rangers. The start of his slide from having a purpose to this bullshit—beating up guys to collect on their bad debts.

He didn't feel much for most people except for his mama, Callie and Abel, and the other guys in the crew, but he had a glimmer of something like compassion for these poor sons of bitches. Maybe it was because he was kinda at rock bottom, too.

The fight with his captain was just like this fight—a ground and pound. He had ended up on top of the guy, just like today. Only he didn't stop hitting the motherfucker. Two of his Ranger buddies had pulled him off eventually.

It didn't matter that the captain had been picking on him, doing one unfair thing after another. The guy had hated on him from the moment he'd laid eyes on him. It was pretty much straight to the brig and an other-than-honorable discharge for Harm after the fight.

Harm sighed and tried to push the bad memories out of his mind with about as much success as usual. One more stop, one more deadbeat, and he could go home. He got in his truck and examined his nose in the rearview mirror. Not too bad except for the blood mustache and clots around his nostrils. He spit on his sleeve and tried to clean up, then drove the seven blocks to the next sad bar, parked, and went in.

The acrid smell bit into his raw nasal tissues, and he grimaced as he looked around. This time, the delinquent saw him at the same time Harm laid eyes on him. Harm could see the man mouth the word *fuck*, but he didn't run away. He rubbed his face and then just hung his head, waiting for Harm.

Harm walked over and pulled out the chair and sat, looking at the guy. At least he knew this particular loser. They had history. They had gone to high school together back in Slidell. It was a blast from the past when the guy had hit up Harm for five large. They had talked over old times, and Harm had even remembered the guy's name before he introduced himself.

The asking-for-money conversation was always happy and optimistic. The mope always convinced himself that it was just a blip, him being short that week. But this pay-up discussion was going to be grim, and Harm could tell Justin knew it. It was written on his face.

Harm expected Justin to have an attitude. Instead, he had an air of defeat that conflicted with the fierce tattoos on his neck, the usual white supremacist bullshit: swastikas, eighty-eights, daggers, and even a bulldog that was framed by the vee of his unbuttoned shirt collar.

Justin said, "I don't have it," and he looked at Harm with something like hope. Maybe he felt Harm was a kindred spirit because Harm looked exactly like the kind of guy that might be in the Aryan Brotherhood as well. But he wasn't. Harm didn't have positions, and he wasn't a joiner. He didn't harbor feelings of hate. Well, unless someone did something to one of his few friends. He basically didn't feel anything for anybody outside his circle.

"You told me you'd have the 5K plus the five hundred by today. How much do you have?"

"Nothin'."

"I just kicked the shit out of another welsher a half hour ago. You still have your job?"

"Yeah."

"How 'bout I take your car, and we'll be even?"

"C'mon, man, then I won't be able to get to work," whined Justin.

"What did ya spend all your money on?" Harm asked, wondering why he bothered. He didn't give a fuck.

"Medicine for my mother. Insulin. She has the diabetes. That shit costs fifteen hundred a month." The guy had lucked out mentioning his mother. He had said the one thing that Harm could relate to.

Harm didn't have the energy to push or maybe the fragment of sympathy he felt made the difference. "Ya gotta week. But it's gonna be another five for the vig. You better bring the whole six *G*s. If you don't have it, I will fuck you up, and then you won't be able to take care of your mama and buy her medicine and shit."

"Thank you. Thank you, thank you. I won't forget. I promise I'll have it. I owe you. I mean it."

"Yeah, we'll see," said Harm, pushing the chair away from the table. He left without looking back.

Harm's mama always waited to eat dinner till he showed up, and he hated to make her wait. He headed home, crossing the High Rise bridge, the Twin Span, then on through Slidell. Suddenly, he was on his street and couldn't even remember driving home. Just as he turned into the broken-up driveway and drove onto the yard, he got the call from Tank.

ELEVEN

H arm came in the back door of Isabelle's house and into the kitchen. The first thing he did was ask for Callie.

"Dude," jeered Rabbit, "it's your lucky night. She's in the dining room." Harmon's monster crush on Callie was no secret, but she was having none of it. To her, it would have been like dating a brother. He was sentenced to the friend zone. It didn't stop him from dreaming, though.

Abel came in from the dining room and said, "We're all in here, c'mon." He noticed Harm's red and swollen nose and added, "Jeez, what happened to your beak?"

Harm ignored him and went in and sat at the dining room table. The guys always left the seat next to Callie open so Harm could sit next to her. They knew it was never going anywhere, but they enjoyed putting Callie on the spot, and the awkwardness was delicious.

They were all there. Isabelle was at the head of the table, hands clasped in front of her, along with Callie, Harm, Rabbit, Abel, Tank, and finally, André on the other side of his mother.

The second Harm was comfortable, Rabbit jumped on him. "So what happened to your nose? Looking for love in all the wrong places? Didja put it in someone else's business? Some deadbeat pay off his loan with his fist? Car accident? Or did Pinocchio loan you his nose?"

Harm looked at him with irritation, his usual expression when interrogated by his best friend. "Naw, some guy caught me with a wild swing. I ended up throat punching him. Calmed him down in a hurry. What sucked was that all he had was thirty-eight bucks."

"You need a new job," said Abel but then clamped his mouth shut, likely remembering that it was he that shut down their robbery gig. Harm eyed him with an unreadable expression on his face.

Tank changed the subject. "Abel's got a new girlfriend," he said just like he was still in elementary school.

"Why am I the last to know?" asked Callie, glaring at Abel.

"Yeah, she's been stalking Abel for a while. We've bumped into her three times. It's definitely not a coincidence."

"Is she hot?" asked André.

"Smokin'," said his brother.

"Then she must want something 'cuz there's no way some random hotty is going to be hitting on Abel and stalking him," teased André. They all laughed.

Abel's feelings were slightly hurt after the shot from André, but he pushed it down, glad that André was able to make a joke rather than moping about his own situation.

Callie said, "I can't believe Abel even managed a conversation, given how hot this girl is supposed to be."

"Oh, believe me, I jumped in and smoothed things over. I had to tell the girl Abel's name. He was too tongue-tied," said Tank, adding insult to injury.

Suddenly, Isabelle chimed in, "The beautiful belladonna flower is deadly poisonous." Which pretty much killed the mood. André caught Tank's eye, and he grimaced. Isabelle had lately been saying the occasional nonsense, and her sons were concerned she was showing the first signs of dementia. Or it could be her hoodoo was getting stronger, and she was seeing things at some deeper level that they didn't understand; although, the consensus was she was probably losing it.

Still irked over the razzing, Abel wrestled everybody back to the topic at hand. "How are you doing, André?"

They all turned to him and Rabbit said, "Yeah, man, this is super unfair. You didn't do nothing."

"I couldn't sleep last night. I just lay there going over and over in my head what happened. One minute I was walking across the street, thinking about lunch with you guys, and the next thing, that Guidry cop was hitting me. It feels like it's just because I'm Black. You know, it's always there, the Black-White thing. I can usually ignore it, but this was different. It was like I could feel the guy's hate," he said with a hitch. "I wanted to hurt him. I wanted to shove that hate back into him."

It killed Abel to hear that tone in André's voice. He was always the gentle giant trying to make peace. That was what made him the maddest, that some bastard could somehow change who André was.

"Alright, we've got work to do," Abel said. "Hebert needs statements from those witnesses. I'm going to track them down. They told me they saw the whole thing. One guy said it was just another case of WWB. You know, walking while Black."

Tank said, "Abel, you and I can talk to Big Frank and see what he has to say about Guidry. Frank's been in business forever. Maybe he knows this guy."

"Yeah, while you're doing that, I can talk to some people down in the city and see if I can dig up anything on that asshole, too. A guy doesn't just do that shit randomly. I bet he has a past," said Harm.

"That's good, Harm. Thanks," said André.

"André, what about that man that they said sold you drugs?" asked Abel.

"I'll go with you, bro," said Tank. "We'll stop in and talk to Frank and then go find that street church."

"I think that's all we can do for the time being," said Abel. "And Tank, we can't forget the skip. We still have to find him. We need the money."

"Who you chasing after now?" asked Belle, speaking for only the second time that evening. Normally she would be talking away, but maybe she was upset and distracted by André's problems.

"Didier Fabre," Abel said.

"Didi?" asked Isabelle, astounded.

"What? You know him, Mama?"

"Sure do. He's a fine young man. If I can't find something here and there, he can get me some of the rarer plants. In fact, he supplies most of the hoodoo apothecaries round here." She sighed. "What are they sayin' he done?"

Tank told her. "The police say he was dealing and that he fired a gun in their direction."

"Well, I don't believe it. He wouldn't touch the drugs. He's a good church boy. Fire a gun? He'd carry a cockroach outta the house instead of steppin' on it," she scoffed.

"We've talked to his parents, sister, and pastor, and they all say the same thing. I've heard he's a good boy so many times, I'm beginning to believe it," said Abel. "But we gotta find him. That's our job now."

"Yeah, we just find 'em and then let the courts figure it out," Tank added.

Isabelle said to her son, with a touch of sadness in her voice, "Like a Black man can count on the courts in Orleans Parish."

"Anyways, we're going to go see Lovelie Mondesir down in the Ninth. If this Didi is supplying her voodoo place, then she may have a line on him," said Tank.

CHAPTER

TWELVE

The next morning found Abel and Tank parked in front of Lovelie Mondesir's Vodou shop in the Ninth Ward. They had talked over their strategy on the trip down from Lacombe and hoped that Tank being Isabelle's son might put them on Lovelie's good side and allow them to get some solid information on Didi from the voodoo apothecary.

As they walked up to the porch, Abel thought he noticed a curtain move in the window abutting the entrance, and when he rang the doorbell, the door was pulled open abruptly before the last tones of the bell died out.

It was the same as the last time he had stood on her porch. Lovelie stared up at him from her hunched posture, her head even with her chest, the shoulders curled in at the top like bird's wings.

"Whatchu want?"

"I was down here a few days ago getting supplies for Isabelle Cheval—"

Lovelie interrupted. "All sales are final! No guarantees! No returns!"

Tank and Abel exchanged grins. "Isabelle didn't have a problem with the supplies I picked up before. We just want to ask you some questions," Abel said.

"What questions?" Lovelie asked suspiciously. "I remember you, but who's this fine young man?" she inquired, eyeing Tank.

"I'm Thomas Cheval. Isabelle's son."

Old Miss Mondesir's face relaxed a bit. "You do take after your mama. Did she send you down here to talk?"

"No, we're looking for Didi Fabre. He's in trouble, and we're trying to help him," Tank answered.

"Trouble? What kind of trouble? He's a good boy."

Abel stifled a sigh and said, "Yeah, but even good boys sometimes get in trouble with the law in Orleans Parish. He jumped bail, and if we don't bring him in, he's gonna be in deeper trouble."

Lovelie looked at Tank. "Are you a bounty hunter, too?"

"I'm a bail recovery agent, Miss Lovelie. We just need to find him so he can get this mess cleaned up. We've already talked to his family and the preacher. They couldn't or wouldn't help us."

"Do you have any idea where he might be?" Abel asked. She tilted her head up and looked him in the eye with much less warmth than how she'd been eyeing Tank.

Tank gave Abel the side eye, and Abel shut up. "Miss Lovelie, my mama said Didi supplies a lot of voodoo apothecaries. Do you know where he's at? Everybody's saying that Didi's a good boy and that he wouldn't do anything wrong. So there must be some mistake, and we gotta get him back before a judge and get this cleared up. Else, he's gonna be on the run, and he won't be able to work the voodoo trade. It's the best thing for him; otherwise, he's just going to be in worse trouble. If some deputy comes across him before we do, who knows what'll happen."

Lovelie responded to Tank. "He might be in the swamps northwest of Lake Maurepas. He's got a shack up off the Blood River. Don't know exactly where it is.

Didi was going up there and living in his shack off and on, searching around for some of the rarer plants deep in the swamp. If you want to find the shack, you'll have to find his girlfriend first. She lives over in Killian."

"What's her name?"

"Margaret," answered Lovelie. "He brought her here once. She a skinny White girl. Palest girl I've seen. Curly red hair and freckles. Lotta freckles."

"Do you know her last name?" Abel asked.

"They never told me, though I doubt I'd remember. Killian is small, and the girl is distinctive. She'll be easy to find. And if you find Didi? Don't tell him I told you. He's the best gatherer in Louisiana; I don't want to lose him." She raised her bony hand and gently touched Tank's arm. She caught his eye. "Give your mama my best." Then, she stepped back into her foyer and slowly closed the door in their faces.

Killian wasn't a town. It was a tiny word in the middle of a large green splotch on the map. All the green was wooded swampy ground to the west of Lakes Maurepas and Pontchartrain. South of Killian was the Amite River and north was a leg of the Tickfaw. It joined up with the Blood River, and together they flowed their black water into Lake Maurepas.

There was nothing to Killian but a police department, a Dollar Place, and two Baptist churches barely a mile apart. Abel and Tank figured the Dollar Place was their best bet.

They went in the door and encountered the dreary sameness that was all Dollar Places. It was a store that sold everything that you'd need to get along for a while, including food, if all you ate was soda, Pringles, and Cheese Doodles. The items in the store were all around a dollar but so cheaply made that when they inevitably broke, you didn't care. You just went back and bought another.

Abel and Tank meandered over to the cashier who was a White girl. With freckles. And red hair. Abel elbowed Tank. It wasn't that big of a coincidence. If you were a girl who wanted to work in that pitifully small town, you didn't have a lot of choices.

"Hi, are you Margaret?" Abel asked.

"Yeah. Who's asking?"

"I'm Abel Kane, and this is Thomas Cheval. We're looking for Didi and heard that he has a place up here. Have you seen him?"

"Are you the police?"

"No, we're bail recovery agents. We're trying to keep Didi out of more trouble," said Abel.

"Ha! You mean bounty hunters."

"We're more like clerks. Just trying to keep the system moving and make sure people get their chance in front of a judge," answered Tank. "Do you know where he is?"

"I don't know where he is now, but I saw him a few days ago. He passed through here on his way to his shack in the woods. I told him he was stupid for running. Everyone knows he didn't do anything. He shoulda just stayed put. The judge would have seen that it was all bullshit."

"Can you call him on his cell?" Tank asked.

"Cell reception is shit here," she said.

"Where's his shack?" asked Abel.

"There is no way you're gonna find it without directions. You can drive all the way around, go up to Springfield, then down 1037, then cut over on some back roads, but you're still going to have to hike through the woods to his place. Or you can go up to the Blood River Landing and see if someone will rent you a boat and go down the river a piece and tie right off on his dock. But you'll need a map."

"Can you show us on the map?" Tank asked.

"No, it's not on a regular map. I'll have to draw it, and it's going to cost you."

Abel sighed. "How much?"

"I'd ask for a cut of the bounty, but I know I'd never see it. So you got to pay me up front. How about a hundred?"

Abel turned to Tank. "You got any cash?"

Margaret snorted. "We ain't hicks up here. You can Venmo me."

Abel took out his phone, got her number, and handled the transaction.

The girl pulled out a strip of cash register tape and picked up a pen off the counter. She proceeded to draw a map on the paper starting from the put-in at the Blood River Landing. Tank took it when she was finished. It was somewhat distorted given the confines of the strip of paper, but it didn't look too complicated.

Abel peered over Tank's shoulder. "Are there any landmarks when we get off the Blood and go left on that little branch that goes to his shack?"

"It's simple. Take the Blood for about a mile, and when you see the first left—take it. Then the next right. You'll see his shack. It's back a ways, but he has a little dock to tie off his pirogue."

They thanked her and went back to the truck and drove up to the landing. As dead as Killian was, Blood River was the opposite, filled with river rats, boats, docks, and a happy bustle of excited people itching to get into the swamps and lakes. It was no trouble renting a pirogue with a small motor at the marina.

The boat and the motor were designed to handle the shallow water of the marshes and waterways in the area, so it was perfect. It came equipped with some paddles and a pole in case they had to tip up the motor to get over a snag.

Abel and Tank got in the rented boat and started up the river with Tank commenting a little late that they could have come back the next day with their own boat and saved the fee. They were a bit demoralized after coughing up a hundred for Didi's girlfriend and the fifty for the boat and all the driving around. They could see their payout dwindling as the expenses spun up like the numbers on the gas pump, with more to come probably.

Their life had sure changed from always being cash rich from their robbery gigs and being able to buy the best of things without worrying about it. Paying attention to expenses and all the nickel-fritzing, as Tank called it, was beginning to be a pain in the ass. Living the straight life was a lot harder than it looked

Abel put those thoughts out of his head and gazed at the banks of the river. "Man, these woods are thick. If Didi is at the shack and he decides to run, we'll never find him."

"Yeah, maybe we go in real quiet, and I'll get out of the boat and crawl up the bank and stage myself between his place and the woods. That way if he runs, I'll have a fighting chance before he gets in deep and we lose him."

Abel said, "A'write," then cranked the arm on the motor to guide them toward the left fork he could see ahead. Changing direction caused enough disturbance in the water that it kicked up a mullet which flew through the air and landed with a slap that they could hear above the purr of their trolling motor.

They veered left at the junction, and then they both stared at the bank, looking for the little inlet that Margaret had mentioned. The elephant's ears crowded the banks and hung over the black water, making Abel worried that they'd miss the opening to Didi's shack, but shortly a break in the vegetation appeared, and Abel slowed the boat and turned in. Up ahead, they could see a few posts in the water with some flimsy planks nailed to them.

"That must be Didi's dock," Tank whispered. "Slide over to the bank here."

Abel complied, then leaned over the side of the boat and grabbed a handful of plants to stabilize the pirogue. Tank slipped over the side, barely making a splash, and stood in the waist-deep water. He grabbed some stalks and tried to pull himself up onto the shore, but his feet slipped out from under him and dumped him flat on the bank where he unceremoniously slid back into the river. He tried again, worming his way up the bank on his belly, and made it far enough to grab a sapling which allowed him to stand up. He looked down at his pants and shirt, which were covered with black mud and grinned. "Glad I wasn't wearing my favorite shirt," he whispered.

Tank turned and creeped back into the woods toward Didi's place, while Abel goosed the motor enough to allow him to glide up to the dock. He tied off, then gingerly climbed up onto the rickety dock, thinking that Didier Fabre might be a "good boy," but he sure wasn't a builder of any talent.

Abel walked up toward the shack, which was a sorry affair of weathered boards. Some logs gave it structure with tar paper here and there holding it all together. There was one window and a crooked six-inch galvanized pipe chimney.

He went up to the door that was open about an inch and knocked. He waited. Nothing. "Didi! Are you in there?" he yelled. He waited some more. "Didi, I'm coming in. I just want to talk." Still no response. He slowly pushed the door open, standing to the side.

He peered around the jamb at the gloomy interior, the light from the window illuminating the inside enough for him to see that the one room shack was empty. "Tank! C'mon out. He's not here."

Abel heard some crashing in the underbrush, and then Tank was by his side. They went in one after another, the place so small they had to stand close to each other. There was a little table, a beat-up ice chest, and a cot with a rumpled sleeping bag on it. In one corner, connected to the galvanized chimney was a little cast-iron stove with a skillet sitting on it. The frying pan had a skim of white grease.

"Man, I wonder how he got that stove here?" Abel marveled. "It must weigh a buck fifty."

"Yeah, but other than that, this place looks like a homeless guy's squat," said Tank.

"I'm sure he just sleeps here now and then. He's probably out in the woods most of the time anyway. But damn it! He's gone."

They poked around the place, but there was nothing really to look at. The cooler still had some ice in it, but it was almost melted. There was a bunch of plants bundled together with rubber bands and a half-empty carton of eggs, the cardboard limp from the water in the bottom of the ice chest.

"Looks like we just missed him," Tank theorized.

"Do you think Margaret saying that the cell phone reception sucks was bullshit? And maybe she called him the second we left the Dollar Place?"

Tank shrugged and said, "Maybe. But she sure didn't hesitate to rat him out for a quick hundie. We should sit on her for a while—see if Didi shows up. Anyways, let's go. I need to get my clothes changed. If that's not mud in my underwear, I mighta had an accident."

Abel laughed and left the shack. He stopped and looked around, seeing the black water down by the makeshift dock and feeling the surrounding woods. The bayou was his playground, but this place was gloomy, despite the high sun—almost sinister. A movement off to the left caught his eye. A man deep in the trees was staring at them.

CHAPTER

THIRTEEN

Abel dashed into the woods, the branches slapping him in the face. Tank crashed through the brush behind him. Fifty feet in, the forest went dark as if a cloud had passed in front of the sun. The man remained ahead of them, tantalizingly out of reach. He stopped and turned, looking back at them—a Black man but with an odd, whitish face. Abel and Tank slowed to a stop, and for a few frozen moments they stared at the man. He abruptly dropped and disappeared. They chased to the spot where he had been standing, but he was gone.

They cast about the woods but didn't find him. It was as if the man had turned invisible. "You did see that man, right?" asked Abel.

"Yep. The guy was like a ghost."

Abel suddenly got a chill on the back of his neck, and he whirled around. Nothing. He still felt like he was being watched, and his skin crawled. "Let's get the fuck outta here."

"I'm with you," said Tank, his voice a little funny.

Callie was in the kitchen opening cabinets when Abel walked in. "How was work?" he asked.

"The ER was busy last night. Two GSWs, an eight-year-old child with a neck wound and her older brother who was shot twice in the chest. Both his lungs collapsed. He was circling the drain when the EMTs brought him in, and we managed to save him, but his little sister was collateral damage and she died. I wonder whether that was just God's punishment making him suffer the rest of his life with guilt because he'd let his sister get killed over some gang business. Fucking gangs! It's depressing."

"Man, that's sad."

"Where've you been?"

"Out on the Blood with Tank, chasin' down a lead on Fabre. Just missed him."

"It seems like this one is taking you guys a while. I'm surprised Veruto hasn't cut you loose."

"I don't get it. You bugged me for five years to give up the Life, and now you're busting my chops about the straight job I've got."

"I've been thinking. This job doesn't suit you. You could do so much with your life. I told you I would support us both while you went to college. You're smart. For some reason, people look up to you. Running around chasing after skips is such a waste."

"I got my GED, just like I promised. I went straight. Are you ever gonna be satisfied?"

Callie sighed. "I'm sorry. It's just that I can see that you're not exactly happy. Bounty hunting is for people that have no other options. It's beneath you. I love you! I want you to have a good life. And you know what? You're dragging Tank down with you."

"That's kinda brutal!" Abel said, but in his heart, he knew it was mostly true. The bounty hunting was bullshit. For one thing it just felt wrong. Like they were going after their own people, poor bastards just trying to get by in a world that didn't have a place for them.

Harm was Harm. He was never going to fit back into the regular world after Afghanistan, and Rabbit always had his dad's auto shop to fall back on. Plus, he was married with a kid on the way. It had snuck up on them, but he was a regular guy now, all the way over the line. André had landed on his feet. He had skills. If he got through this situation, he was gonna be OK, but he and Tank were just treading water, neither here nor there.

"What's for dinner?" he asked, to shut up the little voice looping in his brain.

"Nothing!" answered Callie, frustrated. "You promised to get stuff yesterday."

Callie's tone triggered the little voice in his head again, and he said, "I'll go now. Get us some steaks."

"Hey, Abel! Where y'at?"

Abel glanced away from the two thick rib eyes he was eyeing through the glass at the grocery store's meat counter. It was Olivia and her little boy, Owen. His heart gave a little hitch. It almost hurt. She looked the same as when they had first met, short black hair in a pixie and the lithe body of a dancer. He answered, "A'write."

"No, really," she repeated. "How are you? You look kinda tired."

"Yeah, maybe I am. Had a late one last night."

"A date?"

What did it matter to her? he wondered. They were never getting back together after he put her and Owen in danger. "No, I'm not really dating that much. We're trying to help André."

Olivia went on like she didn't care whether he was or wasn't dating. "Why does André need help? Are you guys back robbing people?"

"No. I figured you mighta heard André got arrested for jaywalking, and the cops beat him up and he fought back, which turned it into a big deal. Now he's got to go to court, and they're accusing him of holding drugs that they *supposedly* found on him. It's all bull, but there's some heavy charges, and he's facing real jail time. It's his word against a bunch of cops. You know how that goes."

"Oh, I'm sorry to hear that. That is so unfair—André is such a gentle giant. Please let me know what happens with that. How's bounty hunting going?"

"Great! Tank and I are retrieving a lot of jumpers." He wasn't going to get into how demoralizing it was dealing with Big Frank or his conflicted feelings about bringing in guys that were no different than he was or the fact that they weren't exactly making bank. He had told her two years ago that he was going straight, and he didn't want her to hear all his misgivings.

He turned the conversation back on her and Owen. "Owen, you're a big kid now! How old are you?"

Owen held up a hand and an extra finger from his left. A boy of few words, just like when Abel had first met him two years ago.

"Do you still like trucks?" Owen nodded. He didn't know why, but he wanted Owen to speak to him. "Do you remember when we went fishing? Maybe someday we could do that again." Owen looked at him with a serious expression, then gave him the tiniest of nods. A warm feeling flooded through him. He wished he could take Owen out on the bayou. It was messed up—Olivia didn't want to be with him, but he wanted to be there for her kid—have some kind of connection. He didn't want Owen to grow up without a father like he did.

Olivia interrupted his thoughts. "So how do you like regular life? Do you miss all the action?"

He wasn't going to tell her how boring it was or how much harder it was to make a living or that he missed being part of a crew that felt like family. He wasn't going to mention how it felt to watch that family, the people he grew up with, separate and grow farther and farther apart.

"It feels good to not have to look over my shoulder for the cops every day," he said instead. And even that wasn't exactly true. He missed the excitement. All that risk and danger made the other parts of his life come alive like a pixelated TV screen suddenly snapping into focus.

They were standing off to the side of the meat counter with people milling around them, but Olivia seemed oblivious. "What's it like being a bounty hunter? Doesn't it feel like you are on the opposite side now?"

"There is kinda this thrill of the chase, which is pretty cool, but we're going after a guy right now, a Black guy who everybody says is a good boy. It's not like he's a vicious criminal." He changed the subject. "Did you hear that Rabbit is going to be a daddy?"

"No! I forgot that he was even married. Can you text me his phone number? I'd like to give him my best wishes."

He immediately pulled out his phone and sent her Rabbit's number, then said, "What's going on in your world? I haven't seen you at The Machine for a long time. Are you still waitressing?"

"Nope, I'm working at a law office as the receptionist. They're super nice there. They're helping pay for me to get a degree in paralegal studies. If I get that, I won't have to depend on my mom helping us out."

"That's awesome. Sounds like you've got your act together." He nodded at Owen. "What's going on with this little guy?"

"He just finished kindergarten, and he's excited about first grade coming up. Right buddy?" She looked at Owen expectantly. Owen cracked a real smile that lit up his face.

"Any news from your previous situation?" He didn't want to ask outright about Owen's father in front of him.

"Still out of the picture."

"That's good, right?" He looked at Olivia's cart which had a big container of ice cream sitting on top. "Man, I've talked and talked, and your ice cream is probably all melted."

She looked down and smiled. "Yeah, I'm gonna have to swap it with a frozen one on my way out." She walked around the cart, gave him a quick hug, then wrestled it toward the freezer section. She looked over her shoulder. "It was nice talking to you."

Abel watched them leave, Owen walking next to the cart, his hand latched onto the side. Before they turned out of sight, Owen looked back at him, dragging his feet till his mother pulled him around the corner of the aisle. The expression on his face caused Abel to stand there for a minute trying to decipher what it meant, then he pushed his own cart out of the way and walked briskly to the toy aisle.

Quickly, he scanned the shelves, turning his head left and right as he speed-walked down the aisle. There they were! The Hot Wheels section. He snatched two with the brightest colors and headed to the cashier. Olivia and Owen were heading out the door just as he parked himself in the express line. There wasn't anybody ahead of him except a little old lady who was paying her bill with a check. Damn it! Time stopped moving. C'mon, c'mon . . . She painstakingly tore the check, and the cashier, as impatient as he was, grabbed it and stuffed it in the cash drawer.

Sensing Abel's urgency, the cashier ran the two cars through the scanner. Abel handed her a five and grabbed the cars, saying, "Keep the change" over his shoulder as he jogged out of the store. Olivia was closing the rear door of the car as Abel sprinted down the lot with his funny left-right wobble, shouting, "Liv!"

Surprised, she looked up. She stepped to the back of her car, waiting for him. He stopped in front of her, out of breath. "Jeez, I guess I'm out of shape."

"What's wrong?"

"Uh, nothing. I have something for Owen. Can I give him these little cars?"

"Sure," she said, a bemused look on her face.

Abel went around and opened the door. Owen looked up at him with that same expression he'd had on his face back in the store. Abel held the cars out to him. "Do you still like these cars?" Owen reached out and grabbed Abel's hand instead of the cars. Abel's eyes started to sting, and he blinked them fast.

"Are you coming to our house?" Owen asked, breaking his silence. Abel dropped the two cars in Owens lap and put his other hand on top of Owen's tiny hand, covering it.

"Maybe someday." He stepped back, gently shutting Owen's door, then opened the driver's door for Olivia. She got in and started the car, then reached over and tugged the door closed. Abel watched her put the car in gear, and just as he thought she was going to back out, she rolled down the window.

Looking him straight in the eyes, she asked, "Do you ever think about us?" Then, she looked over her other shoulder to check whether it was clear and neatly pulled out. Once again, Abel stood and watched them leave.

Sitting down at dinner later with Callie, he told her about bumping into Olivia and Owen. "What do you think she meant—*do I ever think about them*? Why did she ask that? She didn't even give me time to answer."

"Well, for sure she's thinking about you and her, and some part of her wants you to know that. But she's got mixed feelings and is like fighting with herself about you."

"What do I do? Should I call her up? I mean, if she's fighting with herself, I don't want to crowd her, right?"

"Yeah, don't call her. That's a bad idea. You told her you're out of the Life. She saw you in the flesh. She saw how you feel about Owen, and if she has any clue, she could tell how you feel about her. It's plastered all over your dopey face. Let that sink in for a little while. And then, maybe you do something."

CHAPTER

FOURTEEN

Abel was in a rocker on the Palmetto's porch, absently scanning the people walking up to the restaurant. He'd arrived right on time and had been rocking back and forth for fifteen minutes, waiting for Maria and mulling over his conversation with Olivia.

Breaking out of his reverie, he reached into his pocket to fish out his phone and find out if Maria was blowing him off when he saw her hurrying up the pavement with a harried expression. He stood, and she rushed up the steps saying, "I'm so sorry I'm late. There was an accident on the Twin Span."

"No problem. I was killing time thinking about all the things I have going on." He stepped in and gave her a hug and stepped back, taking her in. She was breathtaking. Her floral sundress was held up by tiny spaghetti straps, showing off her perfect café au lait skin. High heeled slides placed her almost at his height, and he noticed the slightest edge of a tattoo peeking above the edge of the dress just where the strap attached, sending his mind off on a tangent.

"C'mon." He took her hand and pulled her gently into the restaurant.

Palmettos was white tablecloth Gulf Coast dining, and the waitstaff was impeccable. The maître d' sat them in the dining room in a little out-of-the-way corner, where the dark mahogany woodwork contrasted with the stark whiteness of the tables. Abel shook his hand, transferring a twenty, and the man gave him a nod before discretely backing away. Instantly, a server approached and took their drink order.

"I love this place," said Abel. "Have you ever been here before?"

"No, but I'm starved. I hope the food is as good as the service. I can tell when a place is well run. I'm involved with management myself."

"Really? What do you do?"

"I'm the manager of a community outreach organization. We try to keep young men out of trouble, help the elderly, education, that kind of thing."

"That sounds difficult but worthwhile. It must make you feel good at the end of the day."

"Yeah, but you take your eye off things for a minute, and it all goes upside down," Maria said, gesturing with her hand. "Anyway, enough about me. Every time I see you, you're going somewhere or in a hurry. What's all the drama?"

"No drama, it's just my job. I'm a bail recovery agent." Abel noticed a quizzical look on Maria's face. "Like *Dog the Bounty Hunter* on TV," he added.

Maria's expression resolved. "Oh, you hunt down bad guys who don't show up for court?"

"That's right!"

"What's that like?" she asked. "Is it dangerous?"

"Naw, it's mostly just talking with people till you find the skip. I mean, the person who jumped bail."

"Then where did you get those bruises on your face?"

"Well, sometimes it gets a little rough. I'm surprised you wanted to go out. I kinda look like a thug."

Maria laughed. "Yes, you look tough—that excites me." She reached across the table and lightly slapped him on the arm, laughing. "I'm kidding. I thought maybe you fall down."

Abel smiled as drinks were placed on the table. When the waiter had finished taking the order, he picked up his bourbon, and the lone ice cubed clinked against the glass as he leaned back in his chair and inadvertently sighed.

Maria looked at him with concern. "You say your job is easy, but you seem sad. Why do you sigh?"

Abel thought of all the things that were going on. André's arrest, Isabelle's mental state, tracking down the skip, and the difficulties of making a living in the real world. He couldn't really go into that history and tell her he used to be a pro robber and complain that going straight wasn't all it was cracked up to be. It was hard. And not really fun. And all the guys were walking around kind of bummed, missing the Life.

He picked the safest topic. "I'm worried about my friend, André, who got arrested the other day. He's Tank's younger brother. You already met Tank. André was literally walking across the street, minding his own business, and the police attacked him and busted him for jaywalking. They beat him up but then blamed it all on him and said he had drugs on him. Blah blah blah . . . Same stuff you see on YouTube."

"Have you known Tank and André a long time?"

"Practically all my life—we're like brothers."

"Where did this attack happen?"

"Outside the Quarter, in front of a new barbecue place."

"That kind of stuff happens in my neighborhood all the time. Many of the young men I work with are immigrants, and they are targeted by the police. We have a strategy to deal with it. The officers involved get tracked, and we look for patterns, and then we report them. What we've found though, is that it's the same cops doing it. A handful. The rest of the NOPD seem like they are trying to do their job, or maybe that's just what I want to believe."

"Well, these guys were not trying to do the right stuff. It was bull—I mean, they sure looked like they were randomly picking on a Black guy for no reason."

"Do you know the name of the cops that were involved?"

"The main guy was a Detective Guidry."

"I don't remember his name, but I can go back and check our records and see if there is anything relating to him."

"That would be great. If we could find that it's a pattern with this guy that would sure help André. I don't want to make tonight a bummer, so let's talk about something else. Tell me more about your life."

"Haha, my life is boring. I want to hear more about you. Have you always been a bounty hunter?"

And then just like every other date, Abel had to start the bullshit about his past. It was the main reason why he had wanted to get out of the Life. There was no way he could have an intimate relationship with anybody outside the criminal world. If he came clean about his past, then it was the end of things. That was what had happened with Olivia. And even though he was trying to change his life, he didn't have enough history on the right side of the law to compensate for all the criminal acts he'd been involved in.

He went down the same path as always, guaranteeing that this relationship would be built on lies and ultimately doomed. Abel sighed again. "No, that's a new job Tank and I are trying. We used to help out my uncle in his warehouse and junk shop. It sounds small time, but we would get big truck lots of stuff, closeouts, and excess inventory from businesses. Sometimes we were dealing in heirloom jewelry, too. But he passed away, so now we're doing the bail recovery thing."

"You and Tank working in a warehouse? To me you look like the kind of guys that are going places. Was that a better living than this bounty hunter job?"

"Well, yeah, we moved a lot of goods. It required a lot of planning and logistics. My uncle was in the business a long time and had a ton of connections, so we received a huge amount of inventory." The not quite lies rolled off his tongue, and he hated himself.

Maria must have had some sense that he was shining her on because she continued to probe his past, picking around the edges of what he said. Abel continued to dance around his past, telling fairy tales until he said, "Wow, I should have brought my résumé!" He instantly regretted his tone, figuring that would be the end of any future with her.

Maria gave him another arm slap and a chuckle. "Abel, if I am going out with you again, I need to know who you are. But, I'm sorry. I am too big nosed."

Their food arrived, saving Abel from more awkward lies, and he directed the conversation back to Maria's life, while the part of his mind that never shut off wondered if this relationship could really turn into something.

FIFTEEN

"Dinner!" called Harm's mother, a short, mousy woman with black hair shot with gray.

Harm walked the seven steps to the kitchen from his bedroom and sat down at the table that looked like it was from the fifties with its chrome legs and green Formica top. The table had been laid with two place settings and was covered with various plates and bowls of food. It was enough food to feed six people.

"Here, Harmon, let me dish it up." Harm's mama half stood and leaned over the table and filled his plate with roast chicken, stuffing, mashed potatoes, green beans, and two slices of what appeared to be Wonder Bread. "We'll eat the Jell-O mold for dessert," she added. Harm eyed it, smack in the center of the table, green and quivering in the place of honor. Tiny marshmallows were suspended in the goo and nestled between strands of what looked like sauerkraut. The gelatin clashed with the color of the tabletop, making him feel slightly queasy.

"So how was your day?"

Harm thought about answering truthfully and telling her about chasing deadbeats all around the docks and threatening them but just sighed. "Typical day. I originated some loans for some folks and handled some payments."

Ever since his daddy had run off fifteen years previously, he'd become the man of the family. The handyman. The breadwinner. The companion of his mother, and her sole connection to the outside world. He wasn't mad at his mama, but he resented his father for leaving him in the role.

He had thought he had escaped it all when he joined the army straight out of high school. Being a soldier had been the best time of his life up to that point, and he had thrived. If there was anybody that was meant to be a soldier, it was him. It was a perfect fit. He was motivated, strong, relentless, and didn't lose any sleep over any philosophical questions about the sanctity of life. Predator and prey? The circle of life? He understood it intuitively. He'd hunted all his life and knew it was simply eat or be eaten.

It didn't hurt that to some degree he was sociopathic or psychopathic or maybe just autistic. He had some issues with understanding people and feeling other peoples' feelings and knew that about himself, which was why the army was the perfect spot for him. No one would notice.

But then it all came crashing down. It was Harm's fault that he had been drummed out of the service, but that didn't stop him from feeling bad about it. He didn't mind being a good soldier and taking orders as long as the guy giving orders was in it with him. The chain of command didn't give him any problems except for the captain, who somehow got off on ordering people around and managed never being in the shit when the bullets were flying. Eventually, they got in a fight, and then he was out.

And here he was back at the kitchen table with his mama. She continued to fuss. Her whole reason for living, her very definition of self, was to take care of him. He knew she loved him, but it was a weight, like he lived on a planet with twice the normal gravity.

"Do you want more potatoes?" she asked and then plopped them on his plate without waiting for his answer. Harm withdrew into his own head again, planning.

He had collections to do the next day down in the city, and then he had to drop off the cash to his boss, Anthony Maroni, a loan shark with loose connections to the remnants of the Italian Mafia. New Orleans was overrun by Black gangs, Mexican cartels, white supremacists, motorcycle gangs, and who knew what else. It was chaotic and fluid, but there were still threads of the Mafia even after the Feds had busted Carlos Marcello for RICO back in the eighties.

Strong-arming for Maroni was where he'd landed after Abel and the crew broke up, but he generally tried to keep a distance between the Italians and his friends and family, figuring there was no advantage to having Anthony Maroni familiar with those kinds of details about his life.

Still, Maroni was hooked up, and Harm thought about breaking his own rule for André's sake and asking him about Detective Guidry. The mob had lines into the NOPD, so it might be worthwhile, but it was problematic in that André was Black and Harm looked like a redneck Aryan Brotherhood member. He didn't want to discourage that misperception as it gave him an aura of menace even beyond his own force field.

"Harmon! Hello, are you there?" His mother jolted him back to the dinner table. She was leaning over him again, this time spooning a collapsing green blob of Jell-O next to his uneaten mashed potatoes and gravy.

Harm forced himself to engage with his mother, and they finished the meal discussing Isabelle. Harm mentioned some of the odd things Belle had said, and they talked about the possibility of dementia while they were cleaning up. When they finished, they moved to the couch and spent the rest of the evening watching TV in companionable silence, Mrs. Jolly's favorite pastime.

"What do you got for me?" asked Maroni. He was sitting across from Harm at Café du Monde and had a dusting of powdered sugar all over the front of his starched sky-blue shirt from the multiple beignets he had stuffed into his mouth one after another. Even though his navy blazer was split open across his wide belly, he had still managed a snowstorm of sugar on it as well.

The boss insisted on meeting at the popular tourist location every time Harm had a drop-off. The beignets were dependable there, but Harm preferred New Orleans Coffee & Beignets on St. Charles, where they were just as good or better, especially the chocolate ones, and you didn't have to fight the crowds.

Harm wiped his hands with a napkin and reached into his pants pocket and drew out a thick wad of bills, organized from singles to hundies, folded into a packet, then handed it to Maroni. "Almost ten grand."

"Who and how much?" Maroni asked as he reached into his blazer and pulled out a little black book with a pen clipped to it.

"Rendall, four thousand; Mendoza, five hundred." Harm continued through the list and finished it with, "And four-fifty from St. Clair from the other day."

Maroni hunched over the little journal and made cryptic notations next to several entries. "St. Clair's behind. He's not even keeping up with the vig. Put some pressure on him." The boss stood up and handed Harm five hundreds along with a piece of paper torn from the back of the journal with names and amounts on it.

Harm eyed the list, stood as well, and said, "I'll get these by the end of the week." He looked at his boss. "Hey, don't you have a line into the NOPD?"

Tony Maroni sat back down. "What's up?" His caterpillar eyebrows bunched together, creating two vertical slashes between them.

"No big deal, just a friend of mine got jumped by a detective named Guidry in the police department. They threw a mess of charges at him, but it's complete bullshit, and I wondered whether this cop has some kind of problem. If he has a history, maybe my buddy's lawyer can use it in his trial."

"Are you talking about a real friend, or do you mean you're in trouble with the police?"

Harm laughed. "No, not me. A real guy. Used to be in a crew together. No big deal. I was just thinking maybe I could help him. We go way back."

Maroni visibly relaxed and sat back. "Jeez, I thought you were in trouble!" He knew shit flowed upstream when the cops were involved.

"Anyway, do you know of any guys that might have some info on this asshole detective?" asked Harm.

"Yeah, I got a guy in the department. But he won't talk to you unless I talk to him first. Here's what I'll do. I'll give 'im a call. If he's willing, he'll call you. It's not going to be cheap. He'll hit you for five hundred minimum. What was the detective's name again?"

"Guidry. And thanks, Tony. I owe you one."

As Maroni wrestled his bulk back up out of the chair, he said, "Yeah, don't forget it." Harm, still sitting, watched him leave, wondering whether he'd get a call.

SIXTEEN

L ater that night, Harm was sitting on the couch with his mother again, watching some mind-numbing sitcom when the vibration of his phone pierced his fugue state. Pulling it out, he saw that the screen said *No Caller ID*. He jumped up from the couch, his mother looking on with concern.

"Just work, Ma. But I gotta take this." He answered the call as he went out the front door.

"Hello?"

"Yeah, this is a friend of a friend. I've got something for ya, but it's gonna cost you a grand."

"That's steep, man!"

"Yeah, well, you're messing with some people that are dangerous, and I'm going way out on a limb just calling you. And I'm only doing it 'cuz I owe your friend a favor. Get me?"

"Yeah, I get it."

"Do you have the cash? I don't take no Venmo shit!"

"The money's no problem. When do you want to meet?"

"I want this off my back, so tonight. I hear you're up in Lacombe. How about we meet at midnight at the back of the parking lot of The Flying Machine? And be there exactly at midnight or I'm gone. You know the place?"

Harm said, "Yep," and the connection dropped as soon as he spit out the end of the word.

Immediately, Harm dialed Rabbit. "Yo! Come get me at eleven. I need your help."

"What's up?"

"I'll tell you when you get here." Harm dropped the call and went back into the house.

His mother was just where he'd left her, staring at the TV. "Everything OK?" she asked, absently.

"Yeah, but I gotta go out a little later. Rabbit and I are going to The Machine."

Harm went out to the garage and navigated past the lawn mower and gas cans to get to his little workshop in the back where he did his gun maintenance and loaded ammo. Next to the workbench was a large floor mounted Barska gun safe.

Placing his index finger on the reader, he unlocked the safe and scanned the interior. It was a big rifle safe and had twelve positions for long guns. Most of the positions were taken up with hunting rifles, but there was a short shotgun and two AR15s that had been tweaked with bump stocks. The top shelf held his two registered Glocks, but the next shelf down had several anonymous throwaway handguns. Harm removed two and set them on the workbench, a Ruger 9 mm and a Smith & Wesson .38 Bodyguard.

They were stubby pistols designed for concealed carry and used mainly for personal protection. The guns were put in the safe clean, but he had time to kill until Rabbit showed up, so he got out the cleaning supplies, donned blue nitrile gloves, and broke down each gun in turn. He brushed them with CLP fluid, then put them back together and made sure the action was smooth. Carefully, he wiped the gun with a cloth, then he loaded the weapons, rubbing each bullet with the soft rag.

He didn't expect to need the guns with Maroni's dirty cop, but you never knew what was going to go down, and he preferred to have guns that he could toss immediately without worrying about 'em, especially with a cop, where the scrutiny was going to be next level if something happened.

A quiet rumble sounded outside the garage, then abruptly stopped. Rabbit had arrived. Harm walked out to the drive wondering what vehicle Rabbit was driving. The sound hadn't been from one of Rabbit's usual rides. But Rabbit changed cars like other people changed their underwear and seemed to have a never-ending supply of cars running through his daddy's auto repair shop. This one was a Mustang. It had a dented grill, but Harm knew the engine would be mint. Rabbit didn't run with anything that didn't work or lacked a monster top end.

"Dude, what's going on?" Rabbit asked.

"I'm meeting a guy at The Machine. He's a cop that's in Maroni's pocket and has some info on that asshole detective that fucked up André. C'mon in here. I've got you a burner."

They went into the garage and stood in front of the bench. Harm handed Rabbit the Ruger. "These are clean, so don't handle the bullets. I wiped them. Oh, and be careful, your gun has a hair trigger. It has hardly any pull."

"Got it," said Rabbit as he took the gun and stuck it in his waistband underneath the back of his shirt.

Harm went over to the gun safe and took a pouch from the top shelf and rooted around in it, finally coming out of it with a packet of bills that he stuffed into the front pocket of his jeans. Shutting the gun safe, he turned to his buddy. "Let's go. The guy's expecting me at midnight."

Rabbit drove, of course. He'd been their crew's wheelman forever, and even though Abel and the guys had disbanded their robbery team, it didn't make sense not to take advantage of his skills.

The Flying Machine was in Slidell, the next town over. Lacombe didn't even have a gas station, but Slidell, though small, was a real town with real amenities and was the first city encountered when you exited the Twin Span bridge that crossed Lake Pontchartrain if you were trying to get out of New Orleans to the north.

The Machine was their home away from home, and Rabbit navigated to it unconsciously. They talked strategy on the brief ride, and as they pulled up near the entrance to the bar's parking lot Rabbit slowed to a stop and let Harm out. He immediately skulked into the shadows at the edge of the lot. Rabbit continued on into the lot and found a pull-through spot aimed right at the lot's exit.

Meanwhile, Harm had snuck up to the back of the lot, looking for the cop. From behind a sedan, he could see a vehicle underneath some trees with the vague shape of a man sitting behind the wheel. Suddenly, the man's face was lit with a bluish light. Harm's phone buzzed in his pocket. He snatched it out of his pocket and brought it to his ear. "Yeah?"

"You here?"

"I'm looking at you."

"Alright, walk over here with your hands up and keep them that way."

Harm put the phone back in his pocket, looking around as he did so. Slowly, he stood up and walked toward the cop. As he moved into the open area in front of the man's car, he stared at the cop, watching for movement, willing his eyes to see more than they were capable of in the midnight light. His back itched, like he could feel someone aiming a rifle at his spine. Finally, he reached the cop.

"Give me the money," the man said.

Up close, the cop was nondescript, but Harm could smell the sour tang of body odor wafting up through the window, and every time the cop spoke, a small storm front of halitosis assaulted Harm's nose. He wrinkled his nose and breathed shallowly through his mouth to avoid the rancid fumes.

Harm could see a gun in his hand, and he took a step back and said, "I'm reaching for the money."

"Slow!" the cop commanded.

Harm dangled the packet of bills in the frame of the window. It was snatched out of his hand.

Harm kept his distance, safely out of smell's way. "What do you got on this asshole Guidry?"

"You want to stay away from the guy. He's bad news."

"I already know that. What kinda bad news?"

"I'm putting myself in danger, man. It's not just Guidry. There are others, and I don't know who they all are. They could be watching us right now."

"Bullshit. This is a completely random hookup. What are you talking about?"

"Ya know the Feds put a consent decree on the NOPD after Katrina?"

"What the fuck are you talking about?" Harm asked.

"The NOPD was a complete mess before the hurricane. Went back years. Corruption. Police brutality. Randomly shooting Blacks. It all came to a head after Katrina when the Feds stepped in. The brass and the government worked out a deal, and the NOPD was supposed to clean up the shit, and they were given a few years to clean house. The Feds have been eyeballin' them since."

"What does this have to do with Guidry?"

"Do you think the Feds can just waltz in and like magic all the bad shit disappears? No. The payoffs still happen. The racism, the beatings, the faked evidence—it's still going on. It's just hidden better, and the brass turn a blind eye. Hell, some are a part of it. I've even heard that they've killed cops that have tried to out them. Make it look like a drug bust gone bad or some such shit."

"What does this have to do with these fuckers just randomly jumping my friend?"

"I don't know, man. I think they do it for fun or some white supremacist shit. I've heard that this Guidry has some axe to grind, and he gets off on putting n—Blacks in jail on bullshit charges. It's like a game. Most of Robbery/Homicide is in on it. The White ones, anyway. Is your friend an African–American?"

"This is all just talk. I need something hard."

"I don't have anything hard. I don't know you. I'm not going to hand you my ass. I just do my job, take my piece. This is a favor for Maroni. This was a one and only, 'cuz those dudes'll put me in the swamp."

"I can't do anything with this." Harm whipped out his pistol, shoved it in the man's ear, and pushed his head against the headrest while simultaneously jamming the cop's gun against the side of the window opening with his left hand. "Give. Me. Back. My. Money."

The cop said, "Wait. Wait!" Harm backed off the pressure a bit, and the dirty cop pushed the gun out of his ear. "Look, you didn't hear this from me. And if you say you did, I'll come after you myself."

"Yeah, yeah."

"Guidry has turned the department into his own personal business. He has an income stream completely outside his salary which he calls his second pension. It's set up for all his buddies, so they all have his back. They talk about it all the time and act like they deserve it because they're always in danger and the community is better off because of how they 'manage' the crime."

"More bullshit! How am I going to move on that?"

"Guidry and his buddies hang out at a social club. They run the pension out of there—it's how they launder the money. It's in the Seventh. Just for cops. Cops like him."

"It gotta name?"

"The Blue Wall."

Harm silently backed into the trees and watched the cop rub his ear, then peel out of the lot. He speed dialed Rabbit and heard the vibrating buzz of another phone behind his back. He whipped around his gun and aimed at the sound.

"Dude! It's me. Put your gun down before you pop me."

"Fuck!" said Harm. "I told you to watch the front."

"If I did that, I couldn't be watching your back, now could I? I thought I was going to have to nail the guy when you went psycho there for a second. I heard the whole thing. That's fucked up, man. Anyway, as long as we're here, let's go in and get a beer and figure out how we're going to crash The Blue Balls."

"Wall."

"Whatever."

A bel's phone on his bedside table vibrated. He rubbed his eyes and reached for the phone and noticed that it was 11:45 pm. The book he had been reading when he fell asleep was uncomfortably jammed between his armpit and the mattress.

"Hello?"

"Hola, Abel, I hope it's not too late?"

"No, I was just reading." Abel briefly wondered to himself why no one ever admitted that they were really asleep. "What's up?"

"Oh, I was just thinking about you and wanted to hear your voice. I had a great time at the Palmetto, but I wanted to apologize, too. I felt like I gave you the third degree."

"No, it's all good. I'm glad we're getting to know each other."

"Haha, good, because I want to know more about you. Have you always lived in Lacombe?"

"Well, I used to live in Houston when I was really young, but my parents were killed in a car wreck, and my uncle and aunt took us in and we grew up in their family."

"That is so sad. Do you think of them often?"

"Not very much anymore. Lacombe is my home. All my family and friends are here."

"Do you have other close friends besides Tank and André?"

"Yes, Rabbit and Harm. I've known them since we were kids. We were a group, you know? Did everything together: hunting, fishing, and hanging out. But when my cousin died—René—things fell apart. We're still recovering."

"Oh wow, you have had some tough times. How did René die?"

"He got mixed up with some wrong people and was killed. It's still kind of a mystery."

"I'm so sorry. It's hard to move on when there isn't any closure."

"Even though he was my cousin and sometimes we didn't get along, we grew up together in the same house. We were like brothers, and I miss him. He was so full of life. You should have seen him . . ."

"What about Harm and Rabbit? Do they live in Lacombe?"

"Yes. The five of us live within a mile of each other."

"That's good to have your best friends so close, and it's nice to hear more about your life. Thank you for sharing. Now I have something for you."

"You found something about Detective Guidry?" asked Abel, excitedly.

"Yes, I checked around. This Guidry is trouble. He hassles everybody but saves his worst for Blacks. If he hits a drug house, or sees a real drug deal go down, he takes the money and leaves the dealer in place so he can hit him again later. If a person is innocent and Guidry doesn't find anything, he'll plant evidence and make up lies to keep his arrest numbers up. The other detectives that are in with him back him up."

"That's what he did to André."

"Yes."

"Wow, you must be really plugged in with the gangs."

"Oh no! I work with the boys in the neighborhood to keep them OUT of the gangs. In this case, I had helped the sister of this man get placed in a work release program. She stayed out of trouble, went on to community college, and is now married with two children. Her brother owed me a favor. I called him. Like I said, neighborhood outreach."

"That's good info—thanks."

"Now that we got the questions out of the way, maybe it's time for me to let you go back to sleep. I'm in bed, too," Maria said in a completely different tone. "Don't you want to know what I'm wearing?"

EIGHTEEN

Abel pushed through the door of Family Bail Bonds followed by Tank and André. The little bell attached to the doorframe tinkled. The place was oddly empty; even Little Frankie wasn't sitting there wasting space. A low, guttural grunting could vaguely be heard coming from the back room.

Abel looked at Tank. "I think someone's hurt." The noise stopped abruptly.

"I'll be right out," someone yelled from the back in an odd voice. André started grinning and gave his brother the eye.

Tank caught on, too, and chuckled.

"What's the joke?" asked Abel.

"You'll see," answered Tank between suppressed snorts.

Doris, the secretary, came out of the back, fluffing her big hair out and running her hands down her dress, tugging here and there. "Frank will be out in a minute; we were just organizing some record boxes."

Maybe there was some truth that Little Frankie was the product of Doris and Big Frank. Maybe it was common knowledge they were a family unit, and that was the reason it was called Family Bail Bonds. He was probably the one out of the loop. *Had he ever asked Big Frank about his life?* Abel asked himself.

"What do you need, boys?" boomed Veruto, coming out from the back and pulling his pants up tight under the overhang of his belly.

"We just have a quick question, and we'll get out of your hair. It's unrelated to Didi Fabre. Do you know anything about a Detective Guidry?" asked Abel.

"Sure. Everybody knows Guidry—the original big swinging dick. What do you want to know?"

"What's the story on him? We heard he's dirty."

"Yeah, that's the word, although nobody has pinned anything on him. Lots of complaints by the public and some other uniforms, but the NOPD brass has his back. He keeps the arrest numbers up, mostly Black folk. He's got a thing for 'em. Why did you say this has nothing to do with Fabre? Guidry was the arresting officer. Didn't you read the jacket on Fabre that we gave you?"

"What?" said Tank. "How did the arrest go down?"

"Fabre resisted and Guidry's guys beat him up, and they found a significant amount of dope on him, and of course, Fabre did have that gun, too."

"Were there any wits?" inquired Abel.

"Nope. Fabre made bail because his pastor spoke up for him. Then, he took off and screwed me on the bond, and you guys got the case."

Abel, Tank, and André exchanged looks.

"How are you guys coming with Fabre? Got any leads?"

"Yeah, we've tracked him down to the Blood River area. We're close," said Abel.

"Well, hurry up, times running out," groused Frank.

"OK, we'll get after it. Thanks," Abel said over his shoulder as the boys headed out to Tank's truck.

In the parking lot, they batted around the implications of Guidry being the arresting officer for Didi. "What if Didi's arrest is just as much bullshit as mine?" André asked.

"Yeah, all the more reason to find him fast. We gotta talk to him. Maybe we can help the both of you," said his brother. "Meanwhile, let's track down the witnesses to André's arrest and see if we can't get them in to make a statement."

Abel scrolled through his phone and then dialed the phone number of the man from the restaurant. The witness picked up, and Abel went through explaining who he was and what he wanted, and the man—Joseph St. Claire—agreed to meet them for lunch at the same barbecue place where the original arrest went down.

"Good," said André. "I never got to eat that day. That was almost the worst part of the arrest." He gave a sad chuckle.

Tank peeled out of Veruto's lot. "Where to?"

"Let's kill some time in the Quarter, then head over for lunch. Might be the last time I see the place for a while," said André, and he gave another depressed laugh.

Abel leaned over the seat and squeezed André's shoulder. "Don't worry, man. We're gonna fix this. I promise."

Tank drove around the French Quarter for a while, and then they headed over to the restaurant. They found a parking spot across the street from the joint. The live oak smoke filtered across the street, beckoning, and Tank stepped out into the road, following his nose. André came around the front of the truck, grabbed his brother's shoulder, and dragged him back to the curb. "C'mon, man, let's go up to the crosswalk."

Tank followed him, saying under his breath, "God damn it."

The three of them walked back down to the barbecue place on the other side of the street. St. Claire was waiting for them in front of the place. He was a solid, heavily bearded dude, also in his late twenties or early thirties. He had a single tat on his left arm of a yin and yang symbol and a full sleeve of cartoon characters on his right arm, with Bugs Bunny taking center stage on the forearm. They introduced themselves all around, and André said, "Thanks, man. I remember you guys talking shit to the cops while they were beating on me. Thanks for trying to do something. You could have just ignored it."

"It was bullshit. Had to do something. I wish we coulda stopped the beating, but the cops were pushing us back."

"Let's go in and eat something, guys. Joe, we got your lunch. Eat all you want."

"You guys can call me Joey."

By the end of the meal Joey had agreed to follow them to André's attorney's office and give a statement and pass the video on to Hebert.

Once that was taken care of, the boys headed back to the neighborhood around the barbecue joint. André pulled the card the street preacher had given him out of his wallet and punched the address into the map on his phone. Eventually, they pulled up in front of the street church.

Oddly, the place reminded Abel of the sex trafficking location they had busted up a few years earlier. It was a storefront with soaped words on the grimy windows: *God's Bounty.* And in smaller letters: *Free food inside – Open 24x7.* There was a line of bedraggled men coming out the door and winding a little way down the sidewalk.

André led the way through the door, gently moving the waiting men aside. They stared at him mutely. Their body odor was strong—no place to wash on the street. Abel accidently bumped into a young woman carrying a black trash bag, who was missing all her upper front teeth, making her look old beyond her years.

"Don't touch my stuff, man!" said the woman in barely understandable words.

"Sorry," muttered Abel.

They went past the people in line and into the building proper which was much smaller than it looked from the outside. There were some chairs scattered in the open space with a lectern in front. On the right was a plastic table with a big soup pot, napkins, disposable bowls, and a torn open box of spoons, some spilling onto the table like a pile of pick-up sticks.

Behind the pot was a man with a ladle in his hand. "That's him," said André, nodding in his direction. André walked up to the man. "Do you remember me?"

The street preacher looked at him over the pot of soup. "Yes," and he paused, then said in a different voice, "Do not fear what you are about to suffer. Behold, the devil is about to throw some of you into prison that you may be tested, and for ten days you will have tribulation. Be faithful unto death, and I will give you the crown of life."

"You're right," André said. "I'm in trouble. Can you help me?"

"I can help anybody who wants to hear the word of God."

"Can you come with me and talk to someone and tell them what happened between you and me the other day when we met in the street?"

"No, I can't leave here. Who'll feed my people?" he said and waved expansively at the line of people with the ladle.

"We can do it while you go with my brother," said Tank.

"I feed these people with the words of the Lord. They're not here for the soup." He looked Tank in the eye. "Can you do that?" Tank was silent.

Abel asked, "If we bring someone here, will you talk to that person and tell them the truth?"

"I always speak the word of God. It's the only truth."

"Will you tell the attorney what happened?"

"Of course, for it's the truth."

"OK, we will be back in a while," said André.

"Come before dinner, or I'll be busy."

The guys turned to leave, and the preacher touched André on the shoulder with the ladle. "Those whom I love, I reprove and discipline, so be zealous and repent."

They left the storefront ministry and headed back to Tank's truck. "Do you think that guy knows what we've done?" asked André.

NINETEEN

Tank and André finally got home after running around New Orleans all day. They dropped off Abel and continued down Fish Hatchery Road, then pulled into their own driveway less than a quarter of a mile away. Just like Abel's house, their home backed onto Bayou Lacombe, and when Tank jumped down from the truck the unmistakable smell of the bayou hit him. Others might have found it off, but to him it was integral to his being.

They walked up to the porch through the spreading branches of the live oaks that were constantly growing toward something that they could never quite reach. André ducked under a low branch that Tank was always meaning to cut but never got around to it. Their mother was sitting on a rocker under the shade of the porch's haint blue ceiling enjoying the soft Gulf breeze that was gently blowing.

"Hi, Mama," said André and he passed her by and continued into the house, a downcast expression on his face. Isabelle looked after him with concern.

Tank stopped and sat on the porch swing facing her. He pushed off with one foot and the swing moved back and forth with a faint squeak. Neither spoke for a minute, Tank watching his mother for a sign of her mental state. Was she his lucid mama that bore him, raised him, cared for him, and fed him, or was she this new person that forgot something he had told her an hour earlier and often seemed to be talking nonsense?

"Were you able to talk to the people who witnessed the attack on André?" she asked, pointedly refusing to call it an arrest.

"Yes, we got 'em to go in and make a statement to Hebert, and then we saw the street preacher, too," he answered, relieved that it was his mama in front of him still. "Hebert is sending down his investigator to get what he has to say on record."

"Hmmm, I hope it helps." She had a look on her face similar to the expression André had been carrying all week.

"Get this though. Frank Veruto told us that Didi was arrested by Guidry, too."

"Really?"

"Yeah, and it went down the same as with André. Supposedly, they roughed him up. I'm starting to think that Fabre was telling the truth when he said they planted the gun and drugs."

"Are you boys going to stop chasing after him?"

"Mama, you know we can't do that, even if we wanted to. It's our job now."

"Do you have any line on Didi at all?"

"Yeah, we're going back up to the Blood River Landing tomorrow and are gonna sit on his girlfriend. I think she was shining us on a bit, sayin' there wasn't anything between 'em."

"When are you going up?"

"After lunch. André's going with us. Maybe keep his mind off his troubles."

"You should let Didi know what happened to André. Y'all should be working together."

Tank got up from the swing. "I'm hungry. I'm going to get a bite."

"There's pimento cheese in the fridge. That is unless André has eaten it all by now." Tank headed for the door and Isabelle called out, "Think about what I said. Maybe you should help your brothers . . ."

He went inside wondering just exactly what she meant. Or was it just more confusion?

Abel, André, and Tank had been parked down the road from the Dollar Place in Killian since lunch. They knew Margaret, Didi's supposed girlfriend, was inside working the cash register because André had gone in first thing to check. He had aimlessly walked around and bought some snacks, and when he was checking out, he hit on her.

He broke the ice talking about how dead the place was and wondered whether she got bored. She volunteered that her shift ended at 4 pm and that she couldn't wait to get out and go home. André offered to stick around and take her out to dinner, but she shut him down saying, "I got a boyfriend already, and I don't play around. We're serious."

The guys passed the time eating the snacks, watching the door of the Dollar Place, and ribbing each other until a few minutes before four when a silver-gray Chevy Malibu limped up, driving on a balloon tire from some previous flat. A woman got out and went into the store.

"Heads up," said Abel. "Looks like shift change."

"Yeah, here is where we find out how serious Margaret is about Didi," said Tank.

"Or vice versa," added André.

Margaret came out of the Dollar and drove off in a vehicle just as decrepit as the other clerk's Malibu. Tank waited a beat until she had turned onto the road and headed toward Killian and then eased after her. They tracked her at a distance as she passed through the center of the town, and when she reached the outskirts, they saw her make a left.

Abel said, "Get up on her!" and Tank scooted up closer and turned into the neighborhood moments later. She was already a few blocks ahead pulling into a driveway. Tank automatically slowed down, then made a right like they had other places to be. The guys waited a few minutes, then circled the block, coming up to Margaret's house from the other direction. "This is a good spot," said André, and Tank parked on the side of the street in front of a house that they assumed to be abandoned given that the roof had partially caved in.

"Another Katrina casualty," observed Abel. He paused, then said, "This is perfect. We can see anybody coming or going. Now we just wait."

"She's either going to take off and find Didi, or Didi's going to show," said Tank.

"Or she's gonna eat dinner, watch the tube, then hit the sack," André said. He settled back in the seat and reached into the Dollar Place sack on his lap. "Lucky, I thought ahead and got rations," he said as he tore open a new bag of Doritos. Abel snorted and rolled down the window.

Nothing happened for a while as the guys watched the little white house that seemed still, almost empty, even though they'd seen Margaret enter more than an hour earlier and knew she hadn't left. Her car was in the driveway, and there was another old truck that was missing its tailgate parked diagonally across the tiny front yard that was mostly devoid of grass. The home had one window on each half of the front that was bisected by the door. One of the windows had blinds that were broken and hanging at an angle, giving the place the appearance of a face with one eye winking.

Tank groaned. "My butt's tired. I'm tired. Let's call it."

"No, man, let's hang a bit more. I got a feeling," said Abel.

They waited another ten minutes, then André crumpled up the Doritos bag and threw it on the floor.

"Dude!" said his brother. "There's a trash bag hanging right in front of you . . ."

André ignored him and said, "Yeah, she's done for the—" as the front door opened and a large White guy with ginger hair came barreling out and down the little stoop and across the yard, heading straight toward them.

"Uh-oh," murmured Abel as they watched the V-shaped guy running toward them who was growing in size the closer he got.

Tank moved to get out, but André reached over and touched his arm. "Wait."

The behemoth, who was like a polar bear to André's grizzly bear, slowed down when he got close to their truck and slapped the hood with a meaty hand. "What do you want, assholes?"

Tank cranked down the window a few inches. "Do you want to talk? Are you gonna be calm?"

Margaret, who had slipped out the door and followed in the giant's wake said, "These're the guys looking for Didi."

André didn't wait for an answer and got out and headed around the front of the truck with Abel one step behind. As André came around, the ginger took a step back as he got a good look and realized that he wasn't the biggest guy in the room. Tank took the opportunity to jump out as well.

They all faced each other in a rough circle and Margaret said, "Like I don't know you followed me over here from the Dollar? You've been sitting out here for over an hour. You can't do that!"

"Ma'am, we are just doing our jobs. Didi skipped out on his bail, and we have to bring him back," said Abel.

The girl snorted. "Ma'am?" She gave a derisive chuckle, then said, "I told you before, I haven't seen him, and I don't know where he is now."

The big man was eyeing André and jockeying for position. André noticed and said, "Relax, hoss, maybe we can help Didi. He should talk to us."

"Yeah, we've got some new information about his arrest. That detective? Guidry? He's got a thing. Has it in for Black guys. He did the same thing to my brother." Tank nodded at André. "He's out on bail right now."

"Didi should call us. We can share information. It could help all of us," chimed in Abel.

"This is some bounty hunter bullshit," scoffed Margaret.

"Nope," said Tank. "My brother didn't do anything, and Guidry and his guys beat him and arrested him. He's lucky he's even on the street now 'cuz he whooped up on that dirty cop bastard."

"Helping André comes way before pulling in Didi." Abel reached in his pocket and got a business card and held it out to Margaret. "Please have Didi call us. We can help each other."

Margaret eyed Abel's outstretched hand. "I ain't saying I know where Didi is, but if we talk, I'll tell him to call you." She grudgingly took the card and put in in her pocket.

"Please tell him to call. I'm in big trouble, too. We got to help each other," said André.

The red-haired giant glared at them. "Now get back in the truck and git the fuck outta here," he growled.

The guys got in, and as they drove off, Tank said, "I was kinda looking forward to seeing you two go at it, André!" They all laughed.

"It woulda been epic," added Abel.

"Yeah, the last thing I need is another arrest for assault and battery for pounding down a White guy. Anyway, that guy didn't look too smart. I woulda handled him with my razor-sharp wit. He's the kinda guy that has to shave his ginger back hair."

Tank laughed. "What does that have to do with anything? And anyways, are we giving up on Didi's bounty?"

"Yeah, fuck that chump change. Maybe he can help with André's case. I hope he calls."

CHAPTER

TWENTY

They were in their favorite bar in Slidell, The Flying Machine, like the old days—back before René had been killed. It was a big operation with several bars and a large outdoor dance floor and stage. The Machine was just about the only social scene in Lacombe and Slidell unless you were willing to make the trek over Lake Ponchartrain on the Twin Span. During the week most of the people didn't make the effort. Thursday night there was a big turnout, about as good as Friday.

Abel, Tank, André, Harm, and even Rabbit were on the patio just off the dance floor, sitting at a table that had some distance from the stage so they could talk. Not like when they were younger, where they would sit in front of the speakers and melt their eardrums. The waitress had dropped off a bucket of Abitas and then moved on without stopping to chat. That would have never happened if René had still been with them.

"Man, I miss him," said Abel. "Do you realize this is the first time we've all been back here together since he died?"

"Was killed you mean," said Harm.

Tank said, "Yeah, fucking MS-13. Those assholes got what they deserved. The hogs ate every last bit of them. André and I were hunting back at the wallow, and the place looks like nothing happened there. No trace."

"Gone!" chimed in André. "Pig shit, washed away by the rain."

"Abel, did you ever hear anything more about that MS chica that René was mixed up with?" asked Rabbit, who was out of the loop now that he was married.

"Nope. I asked around and even went down to the El Luz Loco, but nobody would talk to me."

"What didja expect, gringo?" commented André.

Harm added, "Anyways, I'm all over the place, even the Ninth Ward. Haven't heard anything about the MS. Either killing off their leadership wiped them out, or they've gone deep."

"Well, when I went to The Loco, it was still filled with Latinos. I saw guys with MS tats, a few anyway," said Abel.

"That doesn't mean the Maras are still in business. You can't take off your ink," said Rabbit, then he rattled off: "Maybe they all went south of the border for a little vacation. Maybe they went straight like us, washing dishes in the Quarter or going to community college or—"

"Yeah, yeah," interrupted Abel, trying to shut off the spigot. "André, where are we at with Hebert and your court dates?"

"Hebert is making progress. He's got statements from all the witnesses. The preacher says that it wasn't a drug deal. And he's no fly-by-night dude. He's been there serving soup for more than a year, and everybody down there knows him. Plus, the card that he gave me was in my pocket, and it's on my intake inventory.

"The other guys that saw the arrest gave a statement saying that the police started pounding on me for no reason and never identified themselves, at least until the uniforms showed up. They said that Guidry was talking racist shit, but I don't remember that at all. Anyway, they are willing to take the stand.

"He's got my hospital records, and he ordered the body cam footage, although I don't think the detectives had cameras, just the beat cops."

"When's the trial?" asked Harm.

"Hebert's strategy is to find enough evidence that Guidry is profiling and has racist motivation. He's already filed some motions, so that's gonna slow shit down. Give us time to put together that story."

"It's lucky you don't have a record. He can build a pretty good case that you have a good character," said his brother.

Rabbit chuckled. "Yeah, given all the shit we've done, that's a miracle. Jeez, we almost got caught when that check shop gig went south."

Harm elbowed him. "That wasn't even close! If I remember, I was calling time, and we were outta there before the four-minute clock ran out. And if you weren't driving like a soccer mom, we probably woulda had an extra minute to spare . . ."

"Wait a second! You're not gonna find a better driver than me. I've been in the car with you driving, a-hole. You drive like your mama or a little old Asian lady with a hat. Lucky to have me!" erupted Rabbit.

"Enough!" said Abel, but he was laughing. "We have to figure out how to get something legit on Guidry. A game changer. Any ideas?"

Tank said, "Why don't I dangle myself in front of Guidry while you guys record it on your phones. He attacks me and plants stuff on me. Boom—we're done."

"Well, maybe . . . But when Isabelle has both of her sons in jail, she'll either kill me or curse me. Not havin' that," replied Abel.

"I could go through the court records and find all the cases involving Black guys, get the arrest reports, find out if it was Guidry that made the arrest and then compare it to all the arrests of everyone else and see if there's a pattern," said André.

"You could do that?" marveled Rabbit.

"I guess it would take a lot of time," answered André.

"Why don't we just creep The Blue Wall?" asked Harm. "That's supposed to be their after-work hangout. Maybe we can find some shit on him and his buddies."

"Yeah, that's a good idea. Maybe we could bug the place, too. André do you still have all that surveillance gear from that job where we were trying to make sure that warehouse was empty?" asked Abel.

"Yeah, but man, that stuff is not that good. It's UHF. It's more like a walkie-talkie," said André."

Rabbit said, "But it worked. We could hear like everything that was going on."

"Yeah, it kinda worked. I got three transmitters, and they run for a few days on batteries."

"They're small, right? We just go in after everyone leaves and hide them around the place," said Tank.

"Yeah? No," replied André. "They broadcast on open channels. There could be fifty dipshits using each channel. Plus, somebody has to be nearby with the receiver. Then, we got to set up some way to record it."

"But we could do this. Right, André? Worth a shot at least," said Harm.

"I suppose we could dump the output from the earphone jack to an A to D converter and then to some software on my laptop. There's some freeware out there that records multitracks for music. Easy to use that."

"Alright! Done," said Abel.

"Wait," interrupted André. "All you guys are forgetting the hard part. We have to sit nearby with all this gear. We have to be in a car with all the receiver shit set up. Someone's gonna see us."

"André, André. Simple. I'll drive one of my cars down there, and you can have all this shit set up in the back seat. Easy peasy. And if I see someone coming toward us, I'll take off. Give me a chance to do some real driving for once. Hey, I'm happy being married, but sometimes it gets boring, ya feel me?" spewed Rabbit.

"Wait! There's no way we're putting André on the scene," Abel said.

Harm said, "This stuff can't be that complicated. André can train me and Abel. We'll take shifts." He thought for a minute, then added, "And for that matter, we don't want Tank sitting in a car near those racist motherfuckers."

"Maybe so, but I'm going in with you guys. I'm gonna drop an upper decker in their crapper."

They all laughed, then Abel said, "Let's do this tomorrow night. Harm and I'll come over in the morning, and you can show us what we need to know. OK?"

"Sure," said André. "Plus, we got to talk about their alarm system and what you guys are going to have to do if they have one."

"Cool," announced Rabbit as he stood up. "Now I gots to get home to my bride. She doesn't like me staying out late. This is our TV night, and I already missed *This is Us.*

Harm snorted and shook his head. "Dude, you are so whipped."

Abel stood as well and said he was going to hit the road, and Tank groaned. "C'mon, this is the first time we've been out in a while."

"Sorry, man, it's just that being here makes me think of René. It's hard. I'm just gonna call it. Maybe we need to find a new place. But look, drink some beers for me, and I'll see you guys tomorrow."

Abel left the guys sitting around the table looking a little bit dejected, and that bummed him out even more, but it was just too soon. He left the patio and walked through the main building with his head down. As he walked past the front bar, someone said, "Why so sad?"

Startled, Abel looked up, into the eyes of Maria. What the fuck? How was she always showing up? How did she know he was at The Machine? "What are you doing here?" he asked abruptly and immediately regretted his tone.

Maria stepped aside and gestured to a girl standing off to the side. "I'm here with my cousin, Carlita." The girl looked at Abel impassively. "Carlita, saluda a mi amigo."

"Hola, Abel," the girl uttered grudgingly with a strong accent.

"Forgive her," said Maria. "She's just up for a visit. A distant cousin and she doesn't speak much English."

Carlita continued to stare at Abel, unnerving him. She was as tall as him and whip thin. Her face had a mannish cast, and one of her heavy eyebrows was split down the middle. The eye under the bisected brow had a little mark beneath the corner. Abel realized that the blemish was actually a tattoo. A teardrop.

"But why are you here?" asked Abel, still struggling to catch up.

Maria laughed musically. "Can't a girl check out her boyfriend's favorite place? I was showing Carlita the sights, and I thought I would take her up here because she is from the country. She was getting tired of the city."

Maria turned to Carlita and spoke rapidly in Spanish, then fished in her purse, pulled out her keys, and handed them to the girl.

A faint smile graced Carlita's lips as she said, "Sí, sí." She bowed slightly at Abel and backed into the crowd.

"There." Maria punched Abel in the arm. "Now I can talk to you!"

"Wait, what? You blew off your cousin?"

"No, no. She was getting tired and wanted to go."

"But you were showing her around . . . How will you get home?"

"Abel, you have the Uber! Anyway, she knows that I like you. She didn't want to be—how do you say it— a blocker?"

Abel didn't bother to correct her. He adjusted his mind and said, "Can I get you a drink?"

"Oh, Señor Abel, it is my turn to buy. Do you like whiskey? Haha, you thought I was going to say tequila." Without giving him a chance to answer, she whirled around and headed to the bar.

It kind of felt to Abel that he was suddenly dealing with a female version of Rabbit or maybe a tornado. He watched her slip through the crowd, the people parting like magic. The bartender served her immediately. That never happened to Abel; of course, he wasn't an eleven like her. But come to think of it, even the female bartenders who were sevens never served him that quick.

She navigated the crowd as if she was coated with oil and handed him a whiskey. A large whiskey. Maria grabbed his sleeve and dragged him over to an out-of-the-way corner. She chattered while they were drinking their whiskeys, telling Abel about growing up with her cousin, Carlita. Abel tried to insert a question here and there but could hardly get a word in.

Maria switched gears. "So you didn't tell me. Why do you look depressed?"

"I think I told you about my cousin, René. You know, he died a while ago. He loved it here. René ruled the place. Everybody knew him here. I haven't been back since."

"Oh, I'm so sorry. How did he die?"

"He was killed in some kind of attack. We don't really know what happened. But yeah, I guess being here just brought it all back to me. Made me kinda sad."

"That's terrible. I'm sorry I am holding you here when it is making you feel bad. Don't you live around here? Let's go to your house."

Surprised, Abel started to say, "Uh—"

Maria took his sleeve and started to guide him to the door. "C'mon. You can make me a cup of coffee, and then I'll call an Uber."

They drove back through Slidell and into Lacombe, then Abel turned on Fish Hatchery Road. Maria had chattered the whole trip home, making him wonder whether she'd had too much coffee or something stronger. It was a little bit out of character based on his previous experiences with her. He gently put his hand on her hand as he turned into his long driveway, then navigated through the trees until he reached his house. Several lights shown through the windows, casting a warm glow onto the lawn.

It looked like someone was home, but Abel knew the house was empty because his sister worked the second shift at the hospital and wouldn't be back till the morning. He went around his truck and opened the door and reached for Maria. Taking his hand, she stepped onto the running board, then carefully onto the uneven gravel drive. Her high heels sunk in, and she reached down and pulled one off, then the other, steadying herself by holding tighter to Abel's hand.

They walked up the front steps, and Abel let go of her hand so that he could unlock the door. As it opened, Maria grabbed Abel's upper arm, squeezing his bicep, and pushed him urgently through the door. She kept pushing until he was up against the living room wall, Abel compliant, letting her lead. She took his shoulders and he slid his hands around her waist, pulling her in. They leaned close in unison and kissed. Gently at first. Tentative touches. Then, more fiercely.

Maria broke away and stepped back, reaching her arms around her back. Abel touched the corner of his mouth with his tongue, tasting the iron tang of blood. She moved her arms down decisively, and her dress fell away. The incandescent light lit her in warm tones like candlelight. Stunned, Abel was transfixed. Maria stepped in, brushing her mouth against his cheek, and whispered in his ear, "Where's your bedroom?"

The morning light burned through the window heating his face as he slowly came awake, the memories of the night strobing through his mind in flashes. He languidly rolled over and reached for Maria but found only a warm spot. Abel jumped out of bed and pulled on his boxers and hustled into the bathroom.

When he was finished, he went into the kitchen and found Callie sitting there drinking coffee.

Seeing the look on his face, Callie said, "Wow! Nice to see you, too." Abel rearranged his face and laughed. She added, "You missed the famous Maria by ten minutes."

"How did she leave? She didn't have a car."

"Some girl came and picked her up."

"Hmmm, what did you guys talk about?"

"She was in a hurry, like she wanted to be gone before you woke up, so I thought she was embarrassed about doing the walk of shame thing, but she did say that she really liked you."

"Is that all?"

"She said to tell you she'd call you later. I didn't even know you guys had a date last night."

"We didn't. We bumped into each other at The Machine last night. She was there with her cousin."

"Abel, believe me when I say this because I love you like a brother. But . . . you're good looking. And you're smart and funny and you've got game. It's just that she's like way out of your league."

Abel, kind of hurt, said, "I'm not that bad."

"It's not that. It's that she could get any guy she wants. Any guy! You know how René had that thing, that smell or whatever, that made every girl he bumped into want to be with him? She's got the female version of that."

"She's not like René."

"That short hair? And that cut? On any other woman that would look like shit."

"Now you're just being catty."

"No. On her it works. It looks exotic."

He sighed. "What are you saying? 'Cuz I know you're getting ready to tell me."

"I'm just saying I don't want you to get hurt. And why haven't you talked with Olivia? I think you guys should get back together."

"You know what happened. It's not my choice."

"I just wish you could fix things."

"OK, OK. Message received."

"Abel . . ."

"I'm going back to bed."

TWENTY-ONE

After dinner, the guys cruised around The Blue Wall in one of Rabbit's muscle cars disguised as a beater. The vehicle was rusty and dented on the outside, but the guts were top of the line. Rabbit had taken an old Crown Vic Interceptor from the early 2000s that had been driven hard and upgraded just about everything. It had started life as a patrol car, so it was a solid high-speed chase vehicle, then he'd bored out the cylinders and added a four barrel with scoops built into the grill, netting him more horsepower and torque. Now it was a beast.

They didn't figure they'd need Rabbit's wheelman skills that night, but you never knew. If creeping The Blue Wall turned into a situation of poking a hornet's nest, they were prepared. Rabbit could outdrive any cop and had proved it multiple times during some of their robberies back in the old days when they were still knocking off places.

They cruised the alley behind the bar and checked out the back door as they drove slowly past. "A dead bolt and a lock on the knob," reported Abel.

"We can rake both, and no one will hear us back here at three am," said Tank. "Did anyone see the phone SNI?"

Harm said, "You think these guys are going to have a lame ass alarm hanging off the phone line? If they have a system it's going to be a direct line or Wi-Fi."

"I betcha these cocky bastards don't even have a system. They're the police. Who's gonna rob 'em?" said Rabbit.

"We're just gonna have to be careful tonight. Look close before we go in," said Abel. "We can work around what they have."

"Fuck that! Rabbit, park this bitch. I'm going into the Wall to check it out," said Harm.

"Wait a second, we don't want to tip our hand to Guidry," said Abel.

"Look, y'all know I can fit in. I still look like a soldier. And they don't know me from Adam."

"Yeah, Harm looks like a jarhead, still high and tight. Or a white supremacist hillbilly for that matter. Hell, they'll be buying him drinks," said Rabbit.

He drove around the block and found a spot down the street with a good line on the front door. They watched for a while as the occasional obvious cop in street clothes entered the bar.

"Harm looks just like those dudes," commented Rabbit.

"I'm going in," he said.

Harm let the door shut behind him, and he stood there a moment letting his eyes adjust. He turned around and scanned the doorframe quickly, then turned back to face the inside and walked through the tables, past a pool table, and up to the big slab of distressed mahogany. The bartender eyed him with an uncertain look on his face which Harm ignored.

"Can I get a Purple Haze?"

The bartender slid down the bar and drew the beer, then scuttled back to Harm, placing the beer on a napkin. He didn't say anything but looked at Harm expectantly.

Harm dropped a ten on the mahogany and said, "Thanks." The man looked like he was going to say something. Harm turned and leaned his back on the bar. He could feel the bartender's eyes like an ant was crawling on his neck. He drank some of his beer and surveyed the place.

It looked like a neighborhood bar with a dartboard, tables here and there, and clusters of men and the occasional woman with half her head shaved close. The odd man was still in uniform. An out-of-place whiteboard hung on one of the walls, unreadable in the dim light.

Harm checked out each table one by one. His eyes flicked past one table, then snapped back. There was Guidry holding court like he was king of the castle, leaning back in his chair with his arms spread wide and propped on the backs of each chair next to him. One of the chairs had a man in it, but even that didn't stop Guidry from spreading out, taking up the space that was his due. Three other occupied chairs surrounded the table in an uneven pattern, each holding a minion. The men gazed at their boss, hanging on his every syllable.

Moving his focus off the detective, Harm examined the corners of the space, searching for cameras and motion detectors. Nothing. He dropped his gaze to the whiteboard and casually took his phone out of his pocket like he had a call, moved his thumb over the screen, and then started moving toward the board, acting like the person on the other end was reporting something vital. When he was near enough, he made sure that the phone captured the writing on the whiteboard, then ended the video recording that he had started while he was standing at the bar.

Glancing back at Guidry, he caught the tail end of a gesture, and one of the minions got up and headed his way. Shit. So much for flying under the radar. The man came up to him, getting one step too close. He was tall, well over six foot, and thin with the rounded over look of someone who was perpetually ducking through doorways. The features of his face were well formed, almost feminine, but his posture took away from that handsomeness and made Harm feel like screaming, "Stand up straight, soldier!"

"I haven't seen you here before," he said. "I'm Randy."

Yeah, I bet, Harm thought. *You're practically in my pants.* "My name is John. John Smith. Yeah, yeah, don't say it. My parents couldna given me a worse name. Wish they'd named me Xavier." *Crap, I sound like Rabbit.*

"Nice to meet you, John. What district do you serve?"

"District?"

"Yeah, you're a cop, right?"

"Uh, no," mumbled Harm.

"You know this is a cop bar, right? Actually, it's a private club. Everyone in here works for NOPD. And pretty much no sheriff's department deputies, either."

Harm said, "Well, I'd heard that this was a police hangout. That's why I'm here. I'm thinking of trying to get in the department."

"We get a lot of wannabes in here all the time. We usually shuffle them out the door. But you look like ex-military. Didja serve?"

"Yeah. A Ranger—in the 'stan."

"Wow! I heard that sucked." Randy turned and motioned to Guidry. The detective stood up. "Let me introduce you to the man."

Guidry approached and held out his hand to Harm. "Shane Guidry." He enveloped Harm's hand and squeezed. Harm clenched back, matching Guidry's pressure. They looked each other in the eye for a couple of beats, then Guidry backed off his grip and let go, stepping back.

Randy introduced them. "Detective, this is John. He's thinking of trying to get on the force. He's ex-mil. A Ranger."

"When did you get out?" Guidry probed.

Harm made a gamble. "A couple years back. To be honest, I got discharged. I punched my captain. A Black guy."

"Did he deserve it?" asked the detective.

Chapter Twenty-One

"Yep," Harm said adamantly.

"Well, son, we could use guys like you on the team."

"Guys like me?" Harm asked.

"Stand-up men that can be counted on. Like us." Guidry gestured expansively at the room.

Harm looked at the room that was populated by White guys and a few White women. "Yeah, I think I would fit right in. Is it hard to get hired?"

Randy said excitedly, "Do decent on the test and we can put in a word for you. That goes a long way."

"If you got any other questions, you can come talk to me," offered Guidry as he headed back to his seat.

"He's a great guy," said Randy.

"Say Randy, what's this whiteboard all about?"

"Aw, it's just kinda a game. We keep track of arrests that we all make. We all put in money, and at the end of every quarter the guy with the most arrests gets to keep the pot."

"I get the column with all your names on it, but what are all the letters and numbers mean?"

"Like the A's and B's and C's are race. And the numbers are for the number of charges that get filed. There's some formula that calculates how many points the guy gets."

"Hmmm, sounds like fun," said Harm. "Looks like Guidry is kicking ass."

"Yeah, but he's a really fair guy. If he wins, he splits the pot with the next guy."

Harm stood there, bullshitting with Randy as long as he could take it, until finally he'd had enough and made his apologies. He looked around one last time, making sure he had the details committed to memory, then clapped Guidry's boy on the shoulder and made his way out of the club.

Walking down the street casually, he looked over his shoulder, then slipped into Rabbit's Interceptor. Rabbit hit him in the face with his mouth shotgun. "Dude! What happened? We thought we were gonna have to storm the place. Is it alarmed? How many people were in there? Was that dick Guidry there?"

Abel reached over the seat and grabbed Rabbit's shoulder. "Hey, man, get us out of here so we can relax and listen to what happened."

Rabbit shut his mouth and started the muscle car, feathering the gas to dampen its normal growl. The vehicle rolled off from the curb, and Rabbit found the nearest side street to get it out of sight. Taking random turns, he eventually found a doctor's office that was closed for the day and pulled into the small lot.

Harm gave a quick dump of what happened. The boys were extremely interested in his take on Guidry. They were surprised that the detective seemed to be somewhat charismatic.

"I guess that makes sense. If he was an asshole to everybody, he wouldn't have lasted long in the department. Especially given his supposed behavior," said Abel.

Fiddling with his phone, Harm brought up the photo of the whiteboard and showed it around. "Maybe André can figure out what this all means."

Abel said, "And let me get this straight, you didn't see any alarms or magnetic switches on the door?"

"Nope. No glass breakers, no obvious cameras, and no panel."

"Cool. We can go in the front. I think we're all set. Let's go get sumpin' to eat. We can get a steak, then go to Café Du Mond and hang out till it's time to hit the place," said Abel.

Three am. They cruised past The Blue Wall. The street was quiet. The bar was quiet. And dark. Inside and out. Rabbit circled the block, then entered the alley behind the club. They inched past The Blue Wall's back door.

"Stop!" hissed Abel. "I see the SNI. It's seven or eight feet off the ground. Put the car close to the side of the building."

"Harm didn't see an alarm up front. Why are you messing with that?" asked Rabbit.

"No sense in taking chances," said Tank.

Rabbit jockeyed the vehicle closer to the building, putting the hood directly under the phone company's box. Abel got out and awkwardly clambered onto the hood of the Interceptor. He silently cursed his leg. It had never been the same after he broke it in the car crash when he was a kid. He carefully stood up. He took the phone box tool out of his pocket and unlocked the SNI. He lit the box with his phone. Simple. Only the blue and white pair was connected. One phone line. He carefully bent the blue and white wire back and forth till it snapped at the terminal. Good. Now it looked like it had just broken on its own. He closed the box and relocked it, then climbed down off the hood. "Go!"

Rabbit glided down the alley while Abel held the door closed. As soon as the Interceptor exited the alley at the far end, Abel half opened the door and pulled it shut. Rabbit circled the block again.

Tank asked, "Think we should wait a bit and see if they're monitoring the phone line for a break?"

Harm answered, "Naw. These dipshits are so cocky they wouldn't imagine someone hitting their place. There weren't any alarms, and the front door is wood with a residential dead bolt. Cake. We'll be in and out."

"Just circle and post up where we were earlier," said Abel.

Two minutes later they were down the street from The Blue Wall. They conferenced their phones and each put in one Bluetooth earbud. Then the guys rolled out of the muscle car like ninjas, leaving the three doors slightly ajar. Rabbit stayed behind the wheel. Outside man.

Keeping to the shadows, Tank skulked up to the door of the club. Harm was positioned directly across the street, and Abel was in the doorway of the building next to the bar.

Abel heard the lock rake buzz and then the snap of the dead bolt. The door rattled and Abel heard a whispered "Fuck!" The lock rake rattled again as Tank unlocked the doorknob lock.

"We're in!" came over the phone conference.

Abel saw Harm cross the street. He waited a beat, and then he hustled down the sidewalk and entered the bar, seeing Harm already stationed by the door, gun out and looking past Abel. Abel kept going through the bar and on into the back room. Tank was still in the front, pulling the audio gear out of his backpack, getting ready to plant two of the bugs.

Abel found the office and went in, closing the door behind him and started shining his phone flashlight around systematically. There was a file cabinet in the corner and a computer on a wooden desk that looked like it came from IKEA. That was it. This'll be quick, thought Abel, instantly regretting it, knowing karma was a bitch.

He scanned the desk and took a quick photo of the desk calendar that had shit written on every square. He moved on to the computer and rebooted it, repeatedly hitting F12 until it opened up the BIOS screen. Abel changed the boot setting to work off the USB port, then inserted a flash drive and rebooted the machine one more time. He let André's code go to work and turned his attention back to the desk.

The middle drawer contained the usual bullshit but also a Post-it note with *pw=whitepower.* "These guys really are stupid turds," he said out loud, then he laughed because he hadn't really needed André's heavy-duty hacking setup to get into the machine. The computer hard drive was whining in the background doing a low-level copy. André had figured out some way to goose the machine and make it go as fast as possible.

Abel slid out the side drawers one at a time. The top one had a manila folder with a handful of papers. He snapped a photo of each. Abel heard Harm through the earbud. "Hey, are you almost done, Abel? We've been here ten minutes. We need to roll soon."

"Tank, are you ready to put the third bug back here?" asked Abel.

"I'm coming, I'm coming," Tank responded.

Abel was rifling through folders in the filing cabinet as Tank entered. "Move over," Tank grunted, as he worked his way past Abel around to the back of the desk. He pulled out the chair and stepped on the seat so he could stand on the desk. He reached up and moved a ceiling tile up out of its frame.

"Shit!" Tank cursed, wiping his face.

"What?"

"Rat crap . . ."

Abel continued flipping through the folders. It was all business papers, time cards, and receipts.

He moved down to the next drawer. It glided out. Just whiskey bottles. He lifted one out and checked the label. "Shit! This is a bottle of Pappy!"

"Too bad you gotta leave it," said Tank. He jumped down off the desk and adjusted the calendar and the chair. "Is this done?" Tank asked, pointing at the computer.

"Does it say it's done?" asked Abel.

Tank jiggled the mouse and the screen lit up. Written across the screen in big letters were the words *I'm done, motherfuckers!* He shook his head; André could afford a sense of humor because he was sitting home safe. He snatched the flash drive out of the port and pocketed it. "Let's go!"

Abel took one last look around the office and started to leave. He stopped and went back to the computer and pressed the power button, shutting down the machine. Wouldn't do to leave André's work plastered across the screen.

When he stepped back into the bar area, he heard Rabbit's urgent voice in his ear, "Po-po! They're heading toward the club."

Abel yell-whispered, "Tank! Behind the bar!"

Harm said in a calm voice, "I see 'em. Stay down till I give the all clear or you hear me shooting." He kneeled down next to the door, hidden from the street.

Behind the bar, Abel was crouched tight next to Tank. Abel felt him move, and in the vague light, he watched him take his gun out of his rear waistband. Blind, hidden behind the bar, he felt his own tension escalating and could feel the butt of his gun digging into his belly. He reached down and the Glock was in his hand.

Mumbling voices were heard from the street. Abel stopped breathing. A loud rattle, as the cops tried the door. Then dead silence. Abel took a breath. Bang, bang. Something hammered on the door. Another loud noise. It sounded like the cop was jerking the door in the casement. Abel's heart was screaming.

"Fuck!" said Tank in a strangled whisper. "They're coming in."

TWENTY-TWO

The guys were dead quiet and the police went silent. Abel held his breath. Then he heard the scrabbling sound of the cop trying to fit a key in the lock. "Get ready!" Abel grunted, his throat squeezing the words. Tank raised his weapon.

The thumping roar of the Interceptor blew up the night. Four hundred horsepower dumped into first gear, the tires screaming, then dropping an octave as they grabbed asphalt.

Three gunshots ran together like one, and then they heard a faint "Fuck you, PIGS!" followed by the Interceptor's thunder, followed by the lesser sound of another engine.

Harm was up and running toward them. "They're chasing Rabbit! Go, go!"

Tank jumped to his feet, yanking Abel up by the collar. They banged into each other when they came up on the back door. Harm ran his hands over the door till he caught the dead bolt and flipped it. They burst into the alley.

"Wait!" Abel commanded, just short of a shout. "Give me the rake!"

"No time!" said Tank.

Harm grabbed Tank from behind, fixing him in place and reached into Tank's backpack. He handed Abel the lock rake.

Abel buzzed the dead bolt but couldn't get it to turn. "Fuck me!" He yanked it out and reinserted it. He held his breath for a few seconds, then let it out slowly. Holding the lock gun loosely, he buzzed it again, giving it just a little bit of torque—babying it. The bolt slipped home.

They backed away from the door and started moving down the alley away from the bar, automatically separating, keeping hidden in the darkest shadows.

After their escape the previous night, Abel, Harm, and Tank were parked down the street from The Blue Wall with their surveillance gear set up in the back seat of another of Rabbit's never-ending supply of anonymous beaters. Harm had taken over Rabbit's wheelman role as his pregnant wife wouldn't give him a kitchen pass two nights in a row.

Tank was riding shotgun keeping his head on a swivel, checking the neighborhood, and eyeing the police hangout. Abel was bent over the gear that rested on the bench seat in the back of the car. The vehicle was parked about a block away from the bar. It had to be fairly close because the listening devices they had planted could only transmit somewhere between one hundred and two hundred meters, and if there were buildings in the way as was the case with The Blue Wall, that distance got shortened.

It was five o'clock. Prime time for the cops to stop on the way home to grab a beer and decompress. Abel figured they'd hang around till the conversation lagged inside the bar, and if it never did, the crew would stay till lights out.

They had planted three bugs and the off-the-shelf receiver they had gotten from André had a receiving channel for each. From the receiver a cable snaked to a laptop that was running a digital audio workstation called

Cubase LE that allowed the sound to be recorded as individual tracks. Later on, André would be able to work with the audio and enhance it as necessary.

While Abel was fiddling with the gear, Tank asked Harm, "So how did Rabbit get away from the cops last night? Did he have to dump the car?"

"Nope. They never caught up, but after about a mile he parked in a Quick Stop and then walked away. He lurked around the neighborhood until he figured the heat was off, then went back and picked up the Interceptor."

"Was he bitching like usual?"

Harm laughed. "No! He was glad to get out of the house. Told me he hadn't had that much fun since the old days. Plus, he said that he might as well be out running around because Crystal isn't sleeping so that means he isn't getting any sleep either. She's got heartburn."

"Man . . . who woulda thought that it was gonna be Rabbit settling down?" Tank said with a touch of amazement tinged with sadness.

"Yeah, I thought for sure it was going to be Abel, all pussy whipped by Olivia."

"I heard that!" groused Abel.

Tank and Harm laughed.

"Can you hear anything?"

"A lot of mumbling, a lot of fuck-yous, and a lot of laughing. Basically, about the same as listening to you guys."

"Now, now," said Tank

"But you guys need to be quiet. I'm having trouble hearing. And I'm probably missing half the shit that's going on because I'm jumping between the three conversations. André is going to have to listen to each channel all the way through. Take him all day."

Harm looked back at Abel. "Are we wasting our time?"

"Let's give it a bit."

They sat in the car quietly for most of an hour, Harm quietly looking forward, Tank gazing back at The Blue

Wall. Every now and then, Tank whispered that another cop had entered the place.

Tank broke the silence. "Anybody notice that stank? Smells like somebody shit themselves."

Abel held up his hand. "Someone's yelling something." He adjusted the earbud in his right ear and leaned into the computer like that was going to help. "I think the guy said, 'It's time to put your stats up on the board.'"

"What else?" asked Tank. "Do you hear anything else?"

"Shush!" hissed Abel. "You sound like Rabbit!

"Someone is saying . . . Wait. Something . . . then the N-word."

"What, the po-po using the N-word?" Tank snorted.

"There's a lot of noise. I can't hear any more. I think it's people getting up and moving around."

"Hey, someone's coming toward us," interrupted Harm. He started the car and said, "Get down, Abel," out of the corner of his mouth. He pulled forward and passed the man. "Not a uniform. But he walks like a cop. Probably one of Guidry's guys. White. Buzz cut. Big fat gut. Walking down the street like his cojones are one size too grande."

"Yeah, he walks like a rooster," agreed Tank. "His head and butt have to counterbalance that belly. How about we drive around the block and park on the other side a few blocks before the bar?"

Harm drove around the block taking it slow, then eased into a spot about a block and a half shy of The Blue Wall.

"You gotta move closer. There's a lot of static," said Abel.

Harm inched closer.

"That's good!"

They sat like that till a few minutes past midnight, keeping low in the car, not having to worry much because there was very little traffic going in or out of The Blue Wall.

Then Harm broke the silence. "Can that rig take care of itself? I think we should leave the car here and come back tomorrow morning."

"Yeah, too many cops are going to be walking around when they start to close up," added Tank. "If we leave the gear, maybe we'll catch some final wrap-up conversations that'll tell us something."

"OK, let's do that. Tank and I'll come back tomorrow and get the car and the recordings and give them to André." Abel rooted around in the footwell and came up with a ratty blanket that looked like it had been used to cover a corpse. *Well, that explains the smell,* he thought, then dragged it over the receiver and laptop.

They waited till the street was empty, then quietly exited the vehicle and walked back the way they had come. When they had turned the corner, Tank said he was going to call André to pick them up.

"No, dude! We'll Uber!"

"Shit! That's gonna cost us fifty bucks!" said Tank.

"Jesus," said Harm disgustedly. "I got it. I know you guys can't afford it. What with your five-figure straight job."

"Don't I know it," Abel said morosely.

CHAPTER

———

TWENTY-THREE

ndré answered the ringing doorbell and found Olivia standing on the porch holding a basket. Surprised, he said, "Hi, Olivia! It's been a while." He stepped out and bent down and gave her an awkward hug.

They parted and Olivia offered the basket. "I made you some cookies. Not sure what you like, but I figured you can't go wrong with chocolate chip."

"You got that right!" said André. He took the basket and peeked under the napkin on top.

"Sorry to just drop in on you like this, but Abel told me about your situation, and I wanted to check in and see how you were doing. See if I could do anything to help."

"That's nice of you," André said. He stepped back and beckoned her into the house. "C'mon, let's sit in the kitchen a bit. There's fresh coffee—perfect with these cookies."

They settled around the table with their coffee, and Olivia said, "I don't know how you're set up attorney-wise, but I talked to my boss about your problem. He's big on social justice issues and offered to help if you needed it. He said he'd give you the friends and family discount. That's like thirty percent off the regular fee schedule."

"Wow, that's nice of him and you for thinking about me. But I think I'm good at least for now. We're using Hebert. He was Deacon's old lawyer and so far, so good."

"Well, if things change keep it in mind. Anyway, how are you doing? It must be hard. It's so unfair."

André had been acting stoic around the guys, but somehow Olivia's sympathy affected him. He choked up a bit and said, "Thanks." It came out a little squeaky. He cleared his throat and said, "Let me tell you what happened . . ."

Abel answered his phone. "Hi Tank. What's up?"

"Abel!" He heard some low muttering.

"Dude, I can't hear you. Why are you whispering?"

"Abel! Olivia's here," Tank whispered louder.

"What? Why?" Abel asked.

"She's talking to André. Here's your chance to see her again. You gotta come over here!"

"I'm not sure she wants to see me."

"She didn't just come here to see André. She's checking in on us. She's gotta be thinking about you again. C'mon, man!"

"OK," said Abel.

He hung up and headed to his truck, driving the short distance to the Chevals' house. Pulling into the driveway, he saw that Olivia was getting into her car to leave already. He jumped out and hurried up to her as she slammed the door shut. She looked up at him through the window.

She sat there for a few beats, then rolled down the window. "Hi, Abel. I guess someone told you I was here?"

Abel thought about making something up but then told her Tank had called.

"Yeah, I figured. I saw Tank lurking out in the hall."

"He's just looking out for me, I think." Abel cleared his

throat. "It felt like we didn't finish our conversation when I saw you at the store."

"What else was there to say?"

"Uh, I guess I was wondering if you were feeling any different?"

Olivia looked up at Abel. She didn't say anything, her face working through unreadable emotions. She finally broke the silence. "I don't have time to talk about it now. I have to pick up Owen. Can you move your truck?"

"Uh, sure." Abel went back to his vehicle and backed out. Olivia came out of the driveway and then headed off. He said out loud, "Nice to see you, too. Let's set up a time to talk," then sighed.

TWENTY-FOUR

The cliché black Lincoln pulled up to the curb on Magazine. The back door popped open, and Tony Maroni leaned his head out. "Get in." Harm climbed in as his boss slid over.

"Drive," commanded Maroni to the soldier behind the wheel.

Harm almost said, *Jeez, Tony, you've been watching the Godfather too many times* but bit his lip; you never knew what mood the guy was gonna be in. One minute he was all sweet and asking about your mama, the next minute he might be threatening to crush your balls. Plus, when you got a call out of the blue from Tony, you were more than likely on his shit list. It was probably a good time to be kissin' ass rather than bustin' ass.

Maroni interrupted Harm's train of thought. "Did my source inside the department help you out the other day with your problem?"

"Uh, yeah." That was about all Harm could muster up on the fly given that the cop had basically given him jack-shit, but he didn't want to bad mouth Tony's guy.

"I asked him for a favor, so if he didn't help you out, then I need to know."

"He gave me some background info on Guidry."

"So what you're saying is, he didn't give you shit." Tony leaned back into the corner and gave him the eye as he adjusted his crotch.

"No, he didn't give me anything that I could directly use."

Tony gave a disappointed grunt. "I'll lean on him again, but I need you to do something for me."

Aw, there it is, Harm thought, the mystery of the back seat meeting becoming clear. "Whatddya need? Some deadbeat stiffing you?"

"No, this isn't work related. It's sensitive. Can't use one of my other leg breakers; this needs finesse."

That felt like a compliment. Maybe he was moving up in the org. Harm's interest was piqued. "How can I help?" he asked.

"It's a family matter. My daughter is mixed up with the wrong guy."

Harm gave an internal groan. What the fuck? "Isn't she in college?"

"Yeah, she'll be a senior in the fall, then she's going to law school unless this asshole derails her."

"Don't these things just come and go, and it'll take care of itself? Why don't you talk to the guy?"

Maroni snorted. "My wife's a romantic. She doesn't see what's going on. If I try to do something and they find out, they'll kill me. I've gotta keep my distance, you know, have plausible deniability, but I've checked this guy out. He's one of those muscle heads—at the gym all the time. Ten years older and drives a forklift at some warehouse. They're on different trajectories. The day she gets outta school, she'll be making more than him, and things'll go south, what with all that 'roid rage. I don't want my baby to get hurt."

Chapter Twenty-Four

"Do you want me to fuck this guy up?"

"What!? No! I just want you to scare him off. Finesse for Christ's sake! If I wanted to hurt the guy, I coulda used one of my own meatheads."

Harm couldn't help letting out a sigh. Fucking gray areas, he knew he was out of his element. "A'write, where am I gonna find this hump? Ya gotta picture and a name?"

Harm handled the muscle head. In the end, the guy had started crying, leaving Harm feeling like he'd kicked a puppy. Maroni had wanted finesse? Finesse my ass! How was that going to work?

In return, the next night Harm got a call from Maroni's cop. They set up the meet just like last time. "You asking for another thousand?"

"Nope, this one's on the house."

Maroni must have reminded the guy who he really worked for, Harm thought as he went out to his garage to prepare for the encounter. He didn't call Rabbit, figuring he could handle the guy himself, but he did take his drop gun, a taser, and a block of cash just in case.

This time Harm got there way early and right on time. The guy entered the lot, Harm's eyes tracking him all the way to the back. He didn't detect any further activity—no additional vehicles coming in, no people in the distance lurking about. But you never knew. He didn't really know what the relationship between Tony and this dude was. The guy could just decide to cut threads if Maroni pushed him too hard, and Harm would be the first snip, so he stood in the trees waiting and watching.

Nothing. Then more nothing. Harm texted the cop. "Stay in the car, put your hands on the steering wheel, don't move. I'm coming over."

Like a ghost, Harm popped up outside the cop's window, startling him. The man jerked, and Harm tapped the window with his pistol. Harm leaned in to watch the guy's hand as he carefully lowered the window, making sure the cop didn't have a gun stashed somehow.

The window hit bottom, and the cop said, "Get that gun out of my face!" Harm pointed it off to the side.

"What do you got?"

"Can I smoke?"

"Sure." Harm figured that had to be better than the man's apparently chronic breath issues. Harm stepped back as the guy lit up. "A'write. Ya got anything I can use?"

"Yeah, maybe something. Listen! This can't come back to me or I'm dead, got it?" Harm nodded. "No, I mean it! I'm sure that Guidry has dumped guys just on a suspicion that they're gonna rat."

"For what?" asked Harm. "You haven't told me anything that would warrant that kinda response. I get that they may be taking payoffs for turning a blind eye, but probably there are a lot of cops doing that."

"No, this is way beyond that. They're active criminals."

"Cops have been corrupt since the beginning of time," Harm commented, still not impressed.

Irritated, the cop continued, "I'm not talking chump change, asshole. I'm tryin' to tell you . . . Big money. Drug money. Millions. Money they'll kill to protect."

Harm started to get interested. "Maybe that helps, but I need something hard. Some place to hook in and unravel this motherfucker."

"Have you ever heard of the Bandidos?"

"You mean the motorcycle gang outta Texas?"

"Yeah, not as big as Hell's Angels but one of the top four and just as bad. They're the gang that was involved with that shooting in the parking lot of the Twin Peaks in Waco. It was in all the news. They're based in this little town south of Houston called San Leon and have the meth trade sewn up over there. And I don't mean that little burg, I mean all of Texas."

Small world, Harm thought. That was where Abel was from—where his parents had died. "So what does Guidry have to do with them?"

"Do you know what a *support club* is?" The cop didn't wait for an answer. "It's like a subcontractor. They're tied to the big gang, but they don't advertise it. They do a lot of the drug smuggling and other violent crimes for the big club. In New Orleans, it's the Bastards. They work for the Bandidos, and they're next-level bad. I'm saying cartel bad. Cut off heads bad."

"What are you saying? Guidry is tied to these fuckers?"

"Exactly what I'm saying."

"Spell it out," said Harm.

"Guidry's crew protects the Bastards, and he gets paid outta The Bastard's meth trade."

"A'write, now we're getting somewhere. What does this have to do with the whole Black thing and all the bullshit arrests."

"For Guidry, it's like killing two birds with one stone. He's a hard-core white supremacist, which goes along with the whole motorcycle culture. They are all racist motherfuckers. He believes that Black guys belong in prison. That's part of his 'community service.' But really, I think it's more about numbers. He lays off the Bastards, so he's got to puff up his numbers somewhere else. It's just a smoke screen. And I don't know anything more than that."

Harm doubted that but said anyway, "Yeah, that's good stuff. Thanks."

"OK, can I go now? Or are you gonna go back and whine to Maroni and get me in deeper shit? I don't want to hear from you anymore. I'm probably a dead man already."

"Yeah. Get the fuck outta here." Harm stepped back and the cop tore off.

TWENTY-FIVE

The door opened and André jerked up, then sank back down when he realized it was his mother. He adjusted the pillow under his cinder block head.

Isabelle said, "Child, you've been thrashing around all night. Have you gotten any sleep?"

"I don't think so."

"I know you have a world of worry right now, baby, but is it something else? Is there something that I don't already know?" She sat down on the edge of the bed and tugged the covers up to his chin, patting them in place. A glimmer of the old Isabelle could be heard in her voice. "I can't help if I don't know."

"Mama, I'm scared." He started to cry, and the bed shook slightly in time with his shuddering sobs. Isabelle climbed onto the bed next to her son with her cheek on the pillow next to his head and an arm draped over his mountain of a chest.

"It'll be OK," she whispered over and over, as she rode out his spasms.

Eventually his body quieted, and the bed was as still as a windless lake. "What if they send me to jail?" he whispered. "Deacon came back a different person. I don't want that to happen to me."

"Baby, Abel's uncle was a different person when he went in. Prison barely changed his black heart. You ain't nothing like Deacon. It's not going to happen. We won't let *it* happen. Hebert is good. Your brother will do everything he can to prevent it. Abel, too—Harm and Rabbit. They are all out beating the bushes trying to come up with something against this Guidry monster."

"I gotta be real, Mama. It could happen. I feel like I'm in a dream and I'm trying to scream and nothing's coming out of my mouth. It's not fair."

"Honey, it's never been fair for a Black man in this country. It's your turn to walk up the mountain. You gotta be strong. Didn't Jesus carry his own cross in Jerusalem?"

"I'm not Jesus. Maybe I deserve this. Maybe this is God's way of punishing me."

"Baby, God may be testing you, but he isn't punishing you. He knows what's in your heart, and so do I. I won't let anything happen to you." André felt his mother's body stiffen and a steely note enter her voice. "I have resources."

In the same tone, she added, "It's time you start fighting for yourself. You go find that Didi. Maybe you can help each other."

Exasperated, André said, "Tank and Abel have been trying to find that guy for a while."

"Oh, I'm sure if you go lookin', you'll find him. Tomorrow morning, you get up and start doing for yourself. God never meant for you to give up. He expects you to fight for what is right.

"Now you get some sleep."

André opened his eyes, his brain already spinning from his night of disturbed dreams. Planting his feet on the floor, he stood. His plans for the day were somehow fully formed as if Isabelle had planted a seed and it grew while he slept. He'd stop at Hebert's, get an update, and grab a copy of his arrest report. He showered, picked out his matted hair till it was in its full glory, then hit the road. The bank computer security job had to go on the back burner; today he was going to attend to his own security.

Hebert was his usual self, nattily attired in a navy windowpane plaid suit. Today he was even wearing a five-button vest. He warmly reached out and shook André's hand and at the same time clapped him on the shoulder. "How you holding up?"

"OK, I guess. To be honest, I bounce back and forth between optimistic and scared to death."

"I can imagine, and I'm not saying you shouldn't be worried. This is serious business, but we've got a lot to work with. You've got a big group of people in your camp."

"Would it help my case if there was another guy arrested by Guidry in a similar way?"

"You bet. We could use that to show that he's got a pattern and that he's working another agenda. It would definitely weaken the case against you. Who's the guy? You got a line on him? Has he been convicted already?"

"Whoa! I've got to track him down. It was such BS that he jumped bail."

"Isn't that Abel and Tank's job?"

"Yeah, but I've got some ideas. Can you give me a copy of my arrest report?"

"Sure. I've got a call with another client, but I'll have my assistant run it out. Wait here."

A few minutes later, a buttoned-up girl just as put together as Hebert brought him a manila envelope. André lifted the flap and pulled out the paperwork, scanned it quickly, and stuffed it back in. "Thanks," he said as he left.

Next stop was Blood River. The Dollar Place again. André entered the empty store, asking himself how the place even stayed in business. There was hardly anybody around; the area was mostly swamp. To him, stores like that were like parasites that fed off the disadvantaged, people who didn't have money or access to anything better, and the stores eked by with the same fraught existence as the people they served. He really didn't know why the place bugged him so much. Maybe, it served a needed purpose. Maybe the locals wouldn't have any place else. Shit, he sounded like some depressed asshole, he thought disgustedly.

Margaret looked up from her phone as she heard him approach. "Jesus, not you guys again."

"No! It's just me. I'm not a bounty hunter. I'm just a computer guy. I told you before, I got arrested just like your boyfriend." André wrestled with the manila envelope and handed her the arrest report. "Read it! I bet it's exactly what happened to Didi."

She set her phone down, and he watched her lips move as she read the report. Every now and then she snorted or scoffed. Finally, she looked up at him.

"I talked to my lawyer. He said Didi and I could help each other. Please get him to call me."

"What's your number?"

A few hours later, André's phone rang. "This André?" a deep voice asked.

"Yes,"

"This is Didier Fabre. I hear we need to talk."

"Thanks for calling me. I think we can help each other. Can we meet up?"

"OK, show up at the Dollar Place tonight at ten. A friend of mine will bring you to me."

"Can I bring my brother and his friend?"

"The bounty hunter dudes?"

"They aren't doing the bail recovery thing. At least not with you. I swear."

"If they do any bounty hunter shit, I'll drop back into the woods, and nobody'll ever find me."

Chapter Twenty-Five

"They won't. I promise. See you then."

Abel, Tank, and André stood in the Dollar Place parking lot at ten. It was empty, and no cars passed on the road. The night air was still humid, and the chatter of the cicadas from the surrounding woods assaulted their ears. A waxing moon was up, casting a vague light on the canopies of the nearest trees gently moving in the Gulf breeze. When you stared at the trees, the moving branches and leaves seemed to form faces that would appear and disappear. If you were alone, and in a certain frame of mind, you might be spooked.

Abel smelled the funk of the Blood River on the wind. He breathed deep. "Smell that? Man, I love that." He breathed in again, then said, "Where are these guys?"

"Think they stood us up?" asked Tank in a whisper.

"Nope! I know he's coming," answered André. "And you can talk normal for Christ's sake. We want them to know we're here."

The guys stood around for a few more minutes, then they heard someone call, "Over here!" A Black guy materialized at the edge of the trees.

"Ya didn't bring anyone else didja?"

"We're by ourselves."

The man waved them over. "C'mon. I'll take you to him."

André jogged over, and Tank and Abel followed. The man disappeared into an opening in the woods. "Stay close," he called over his shoulder. "It's dark." Mr. Obvious.

But they couldn't stay close; the man moved fast like he knew the place. Inevitably, they got strung out. Soon Abel was by himself. The light from the moon filtered through the trees, providing just enough illumination to keep him from banging into low-hanging tree limbs, then the call of the cicadas stopped, and all he could hear were the sticks and dead leaves crackling under his feet. Unnerved, he began to imagine that he was passing people in the woods. At least he hoped he was imagining it. They were dark shadows apart from the trees with ghostly white faces. He started to lose it a little bit and picked up his pace, moving faster and faster, not quite panicked, his head turning back and forth toward each black shadow at the edge of his vision.

TWENTY-SIX

A large man materialized from the trees, and Abel dodged left, then accelerated and burst through the trees into a clearing. The man popped out of the woods behind him and stopped, guarding the faint opening. He had some kind of skin condition on his face—here and there were patches without pigment, freakishly white against the black—and he was pointing a handgun vaguely in Abel's direction.

André and Tank were standing in front of Abel, quizzical looks on their faces and even a slight hint of a smile on Tank's face.

"Man, you look like you've seen a ghost!" said Tank.

"Yeah, he's as white as a sheet . . ." added André.

"He's always as white as a sheet," continued Tank.

"Jeez, shut up!" said Abel.

"I see you noticed my friends," said the lanky Black man with the mini-Afro, who was positioned behind André. "Just some guys making sure that you boys weren't pulling some bounty hunter bullshit." More men filtered out of the trees. Each had white faces— paint or dust or something—but the effect was spooky.

"What's with the ghosts?" asked Abel.

"We kinda like the effect Kevon's fucked-up skin has on people, so from time to time we go ghost mode, too. If you're in the voodoo business it helps to look the part. Plus, every now and then we come across some tweakers and growers out here in the woods, and it makes 'em keep their distance usually. They don't know what they're dealing with."

"Yeah, I get it," Abel said.

"Look, Didi, we're done with the bounty hunter stuff. Don't worry about that anymore," said Tank. "We're tired of chasing after you. We need to work together. Both you and my brother are in trouble, and that takes precedence over any pissant bail recovery payout. And anyway, you've been one step ahead of us since we started looking. Effing frustrating."

"About that . . ." said Didi with a chuckle. "C'mon." Didi led them to the back of the clearing where there was a stump with a sawed off top and a fat tree lying along the length of the clearing. The lower part of the tree was naked of branches, and Abel and the brothers sat down in a row on the trunk like they were on the couch in the living room watching TV. They eyed Didi, who had already taken the stump.

The guys looked at Didi expectantly. Oozing palpable charisma, Didi said with a smile on his handsome face, "Yeah, sorry. It was easy to keep away from you guys. I've been getting information about you all along."

"Wait, what?" exclaimed Abel.

"Yeah, Lovelie called me and Maggie right from the get-go. When you guys were at my shack on the Blood, I was watching you from the woods the whole time. Maggie called me right after you talked to her at the Dollar Place."

"I knew she was shining us," said Tank.

"They weren't the only ones. My mama called me, my sister called me, the minister called me. Hell, even Isabelle called me a few times."

Chapter Twenty-Six

"What!?" Tank, Abel, and André practically shouted in unison.

Didi was laughing now. "A traitor in your own camp. She was pumping you guys and calling me and giving me a heads up."

"Why would she do that?" murmured Tank.

"'Cuz we're friends. I've been getting her plants for years. She knows I'm innocent." Tank and André were both shaking their heads, baffled—their own mother.

Didi changed course and asked them why they thought they could help him and what they wanted from him. André, comfortable with a person that had likely experienced the exact same trauma, dumped a torrent of words describing what he'd been through. Didi inserted *yeps*, *I-hear-yous*, and *exactly-the-sames* like rocks in André's river of recounting.

Finally, André slowed down until he completely stopped talking, leaving the clearing still, except for the sighs of the treetops in the Gulf breeze. "Let me tell you my story," said Didi.

"I'd been up on the edge of the Blood, where I'd found a good source of ribbon grass—you know, basket grass. I was digging it up and harvesting the roots. The folk call it 'Devil's Shoestring,' 'cuz it 'trips up evil.' Lovelie is always looking for it because everybody uses it for protection."

"Protection from what?" asked Abel. He'd been interested in Isabelle's hoodoo since he was a kid, even though he didn't really believe it was real.

"Protection from curses, breaking bad luck, binding an enemy, ya know, that kinda thing.

"Anyway, I had it, and I drove back to the Ninth and stopped at Lovelie's place. Can you believe that woman? She's gotta be a hundred and she still goin'."

"Maybe she's been taking some of her own *medicine*," said Tank seriously. Abel knew he wasn't a skeptic. Tank had seen too many things over the years.

Didi continued, "I hung around and talked with her. She tried to give me some cookies she baked, but they were kinda greenish—who knows what was in 'em. I finally ended up taking them. They're probably still in my car. Last thing she said was she was needin' some rose of Jericho, although that's not sumpin' I find out in the swamp. I got a guy who imports it from Asia.

"I left there, and since I was down in the city, I thought I'd go on over by the courthouse and stop at this little butcher shop off of Tulane that I like and pick up some andouille."

"Not the nicest of areas," said André.

"Yeah, but the meat at this place is amazing. Definitely worth it. I'm just sitting in my car down the street from the shop, putting notes into my phone about the other things old Mondesir wanted, and someone raps on my window. I look up and it's a cop."

"Shit!" said Abel.

Didi slapped at a mosquito biting his neck and then continued, "I had both hands on the wheel, but the dude motioned to roll down the window, so I rolled it down about three inches. He's in full uniform, but there are three other guys in plain clothes behind him. I knew they were cops, too, because of the way they were standing, ya know?"

It wasn't really a question, but André echoed, "I know," like an amen at church.

"I asked them why they were on me like that, and the uniform said they'd had a tip that a guy fitting my description was dealing smack in the area. Selling 'H' to people being released from the jail who were jonesing and needed to score. Told me I looked 'suspicious.'

"The cop wanted me to roll the window all the way down, and I tried to say it was fine the way it was, but the three men behind him took a step forward. That scared me, so I reached to the door to press the button, and suddenly the guy went apeshit and screamed, 'HANDS ON THE

WHEEL.' His voice cracked like he was thirteen and I woulda busted his chops, but I was startin' to freak, too."

"Jesus," said Tank.

"Well then, the cop dropped back with his buddies, and all of 'em had their guns drawn and pointing at me. I kept yelling, 'You got the wrong guy,' 'I haven't done anything,' and 'I don't have a gun.' They made me get outta the car, and they tried to push me to my knees, and I resisted just a little bit. I didn't want to bang my knees on the concrete. That was a mistake 'cuz then they started to go to town on me. The four of them were hitting and kicking me, and if I put my arms around my head to cover up, they kicked me in the guts. And when I rolled up, they booted me in the kidneys. That really hurt. I thought they ruptured something inside of me.

"One of the guys yelled, 'He's got a gun!' But that was bullshit. I don't even own a gun," Didi said with an aggrieved tone.

"It's lucky they didn't kill you right then and there," Abel said.

"It was in my mind, believe me. I just stopped moving and put my arms out to the sides. I musta looked just like a rag doll because they stopped beating on me. One of the cops kneeled on the back of my neck, grinding my face into the road, and another locked up my wrists in cuffs. Two of 'em yanked me up onto my feet. I had some blood in my eyes, but I could see enough to see a gun lying there on the ground. They were sayin' it was mine. It wasn't.

"Suddenly, one of the plainclothes guys says, 'Lookee here.' I see him standing by my car door, and he has a plastic grocery sack. He reaches in and his hand comes out with some packets, and I hear: 'Looks like we got some Cinnamon.' I didn't say anything. I knew I was being railroaded."

"I'm sure the body cam on the uniform is going to show that the whole thing is bogus," said André.

"Nope. I'm pretty sure he was always facing away when the shit was going down. He wasn't the one kicking me. It was the other three. Probably only the stuff that they kept saying is on the tape. You know, like 'He's got a gun,'" Didi said, gloomily.

"And anyway, that body cam recording will probably disappear before the trial, knowing these dudes," Abel commented.

"Wasn't there anybody standing around, watching this shit go down?" asked Tank.

"Naw, the area was empty. I found out later the guy had closed down the butcher shop. A wild goose chase right from the start. I guess the area had gotten too rough for him."

"And was Guidry one of the cops that was pounding you?" asked Abel.

"Yeah, and he was the one that told me I was being arrested for dealing, resisting arrest, concealed carry without a permit, and get this, firing the gun. The whole thing was completely made up. But there were four of them to one of me. Who are they gonna believe?"

"That's almost exactly the way it went down with me," said André. "You have to talk to Hebert, my lawyer."

"Why? I don't think I'm gonna get a fair trial, regardless. This Guidry has got too much weight, got a lot of friends. Two Black dudes ain't gonna shake that up."

"Yeah, we're working on that," Tank said. "Turns out this guy is into a ton of criminal stuff on the side. We just found out that he's shielding the Bastards motorcycle club's drug trade."

"That sounds like a lot of noise. You got any proof?"

"Not yet, but we will. We're workin' on penetrating Guidry's inner circle," Tank said.

"That's not enough for me to come in, especially when one of Guidry's detectives whispered to me that if I didn't shut up about how the arrest went down, I'd be getting worse than Angola," said Didi. "I'm stayin' lost, but how about you give me Hebert's number? I'll call him, tell him my story, and I'll listen to what he has to say."

"That sounds OK, and meanwhile, we'll be doing our thing, trying to get something hard on Guidry," said André.

"I can help you if you need it. Me and my ghosts can be hard if we need to. You got my number." With that, Didi stood up and he and his friends stepped back into the trees, leaving the guys to reverse their path through the woods to the Dollar Place.

CHAPTER

TWENTY-SEVEN

Harm's mother had gone to bed, and he was sitting on the couch watching TV with the volume turned down low and the captions turned on. His hearing had never been the same since he'd got out of the Rangers. He'd probably fired hundreds of thousands of rounds, including all his training and the multiple tours, and now he had trouble understanding words if there was any kind of background noise at all. TV was the worst. Even if it was quiet, sometimes it sounded like all the people were speaking with mush in their mouths. Despite all that, he heard a knock on the front door. First, it was a small sound which his brain barely registered, then a sharp rap.

He got up quickly to stop the door knocker from waking up his mama. He looked out the window. Isabelle? He couldn't remember the last time she'd come to his house.

Pulling the door open, he asked, "Is everything OK?"

"No, not really. Is your mama awake?"

"She's asleep." Harm stepped out onto the porch and closed the door behind him.

"Good, I wanted to talk to you." Harm looked at Belle expectantly. "I need you to get me in front of Guidry."

"Why me?"

"Because you won't try to stop me," Isabelle said with certainty.

"Do Tank and André know you're talking to me?"

"They're out with Abel tonight. I don't want you telling them about this, either."

"Uh, OK." Harm didn't really understand why he was instantly agreeing with Isabelle. He could never quite admit to himself that she sort of frightened him in some deep weird way. "When do you need to see him?"

"As soon as you can arrange it. At the police station."

"But why?"

"I need to talk to him. I'm going to ask him to let go of André."

"Isabelle, this guy's a hard case. He's not going to back off."

"I'm André's mother. I think Guidry will listen to me."

Harm didn't believe that for a second. "OK, let me make some calls and as soon as I find out when and where, I'll come over."

Harm knocked gently on Isabelle's back door moments after the sun had risen. It had taken him the whole weekend, but Maroni finally leaned on his dirty cop connection. The cop had called him, all pissed off, but Harm had managed to calm him down and squeeze him for Guidry's whereabouts. He was getting deeper and deeper into Maroni's debt and wondered what else he was gonna have to do to clear the obligation. Harm pushed that worry back and knocked again.

Isabelle opened the door and beckoned him in. "The boys are still asleep. Do you want some coffee?" She poured him a cup after he nodded, and they sat at the table.

"When can I see him?"

"He's in his office at the department tomorrow morning after nine. It's some bureaucratic thing. Every week, no matter what he has going on, he spends the morning doing paperwork or some such bull—uh, stuff."

"That's perfect. Thank you, cher. Can you come get me tomorrow morning, early? Like this same time?"

"Sure, but I don't think I should let Guidry see me."

"Don't worry. It'll just be me going in to see him. You just have to get me there."

Harm sat in his truck and watched Isabelle knock on Lovelie Mondesir's door. She was dressed in a long sleeveless dress that hung loose on her bony frame, and Harm was sure that it was her church outfit. A big flowery purse hung off her shoulder. Belle had insisted that they stop here first, saying it might take a minute. Harm wasn't sure whether she meant it was going to be a short or a long stop, but he settled in, turning up the AC, and closed his eyes after watching the creepy old lady usher Isabelle in.

Startling him, Belle opened the door. Harm eyed the clock. He'd nodded off for almost an hour. He straightened up and popped his neck. "Didja get what you needed?"

"Yes, Lovelie was very helpful. Please take me to Guidry."

Harm heard the impatience and didn't say anything else. He pulled away from the curb and headed out of the Ninth toward the NOPD Investigation and Support Bureau.

As they were driving, Isabelle was busy. First, she snapped on a pair of blue nitrile gloves like he'd seen in the doctor's office, then she reached into a brown paper sack by her feet that she'd brought from home and retrieved a little blue jar, the kind he'd seen in his bathroom forever. She unscrewed the lid and set it on the console between them. Harm noticed it was filled with the same goop his mother used every night.

Next, she pulled a gallon-sized ziplock bag out of the sack. Folding the ziplock's lip over on itself, she bloused the bag, and set it on the floor between her feet. When they stopped at a light, she carefully pulled a vial from her purse, unscrewed the tiny lid, and poured some of the contents into the little blue salve jar. She carefully screwed the lid back on and dropped the vial into the ziplock at her feet. Reaching into her purse, she came out with a tongue depressor, and stirred the contents of the salve jar. She dropped the stick into the ziplock. Finally, Isabelle screwed the blue jar's lid on. Taking a handkerchief out of the purse, she wiped the jar, wrapped it up in the cloth, and placed it back into her big purse.

She leaned back in her seat and let out a long breath as Harm slowly accelerated. She was holding her gloved hands in the air like a surgeon, and she carefully removed them and dropped then into the ziplock bag. She snapped on a new pair and bent over and closed the ziplock tightly.

Then she delved back into the bottomless purse and pulled out some long formal gloves and carefully threaded them over her already gloved fingers. When she was done, the white gloves reached to her elbows, making Belle look like she was going to a cocktail party from the fifties.

Harm glided up to the curb in front of the NOPD Bureau and stopped. "Just go in there and ask for Guidry at the desk." He watched Isabelle walk up to the door.

Inside, she asked the deputy if she could see Guidry about André Cheval. The cop grabbed the phone and made a call, then told her to take a seat in the lobby. Somebody would come get her.

While she was sitting there, she put her big purse in her lap and rooted around inside with both hands. Eventually, she finished and set the bag in the chair next to her with her right hand. Her left arm she rested on the chair arm, her hand held stiffly away from the fabric. Soon, the door to the back emitted a loud clicking noise, and a uniformed deputy came out.

He made his way to Isabelle, his eyebrows registering some surprise at her getup. "Follow me." They went back to the detective's office, and he motioned her in. "This is the lady," he announced.

Guidry stood up from behind his desk and motioned to a guest chair, then he parked his ass on the desk in front of her, looking down. "What can I do for you, ma'am?"

Isabelle tilted her head back and looked at him. "My boy, André? You arrested him the other week. He's a good boy. He wouldn't do any of those things you said he did."

"I hear that all the time," he said. "Usually, mothers are the last to know."

"He's got a good job. He goes to church. He doesn't mess with drugs."

"I'm sorry, ma'am, but he assaulted an officer. That takes it out of my hands. I would like to help you, but he's in the judicial system now. His lawyer can explain all that to the judge."

Isabelle looked up at Guidry's implacable face. "Please help my son. Can't you talk to the judge?" She stood up and grabbed Guidry's hands with her own. "Please, I beg you."

Guidry tried to take his hands away, but Isabelle held on for a beat. He looked over to the deputy still standing by the door. "We're through here." He turned back to her. "Sorry," he said, dismissively.

The deputy escorted Isabelle all the way to the street door at the front of the Bureau and politely opened the door for her. She walked out and stood by the curb. In a minute, Harm drove up and stopped. He got out and ran around and opened her door. She avoided touching anything as he helped her up.

He got back in and pulled away from the curb, headed home. "What's that gonna do to him?"

"Make him stupid. Then make him sick—very sick." Belle had a slight smile.

TWENTY-EIGHT

A day later, André was in Abel's living room moving furniture around. He'd taken a painting down from the white plastered wall next to the front door and had jockeyed some chairs around so that they faced the wall along with the couch that was already situated in the right direction. The net effect was of a little movie theater that was showing the screen of his laptop via a projector resting on the coffee table.

Abel dragged in a cooler filled with beer on ice and said, "Wow! Big screen Panavision. Should I make some popcorn?"

Before André had a chance to give a wiseass response, the front door banged open. It was Rabbit, of course, making his usual entrance. Eyeing the display on the wall, he said, "Are you giving us a security presentation? 'Cuz if you are, you're about a month too late. The horse is outta the barn—"

"Yeah, yeah," said André, amputating Rabbit's flow of consciousness. "Beer in the cooler, Abel's making popcorn." Abel snorted.

Harm and Tank rolled in together. "Who called this meeting?" Tank asked, knowing full well his brother was going to give them the lowdown on the surveillance data from the bugs and the analysis of the computer and paperwork they'd found. Abel shook his head, marveling at the fact that they had never changed from their thirteen-year-old shtick, him included. It was comforting.

"Where's the beer?" Harm asked. Abel pointed to the side of the couch. Harm sat down next to the cooler.

"I get the sweet recliner," said Rabbit, plopping down on it.

Abel and Tank sat on the couch with Harm, and André pulled up a kitchen chair next to the coffee table and put the computer on his lap. There were the sound of keystrokes, and a picture of the bayou was cast onto the wall.

"You've been working at the bank too long, André," said Rabbit.

André ignored him and moved on to the next slide. "We got a good haul of information from the place. Obviously, these guys believe they are bulletproof and don't have a clue about information security—ironic, really. But good for us."

For the next half hour, he gave a corporate-like analysis of what they had pulled out of The Blue Wall, telling them that the data roughly fell into three buckets: the bogus arrests, the money flowing in and out, and their involvement with the Stand Tall Boys.

He took them through the whiteboard with all the names on it that had been set up at the bar. André had been able to look through the parish court records that were freely available online and do inmate searches through the Sheriff's portal. He couldn't completely prove that all the arrests were like André's and Didi's, but he had found enough information here and there to see that many of the people were Black or Hispanic and that there was a picnic basket full of charges for each. Almost every time, there was a resisting arrest charge and felonies.

The money was covered next. André had found a spreadsheet documenting the financial situation. He pressed a key, and a sheet showing a list of transactions was displayed on the wall. "I uncovered this stuff, and some of it's in code," he said.

Harm said, "This goes right along with what I learned the other day. Guidry and his guys are working with the Bastards motorcycle club. Those must be protection payoffs from them. According to the dirty NOPD cop I talked with the other day, the detective and his men are giving the club inside info on raids, telling them when to lay low, hitting competitive stash houses, and guarding shipments."

André jumped back in. "It sure looks like the cops are using the bar to launder the drug money. But I can't exactly prove that the money flow isn't legit. I think we would need a forensic accountant to examine the books to prove anything."

"Still good info, though," said Abel. "We're getting dialed in on these sons of bitches. We're gonna break 'em and put 'em in Angola."

"Anything else we need to know?" asked Tank.

"Yeah, I looked at the photo of the desk calendar. Two things jumped out: there were some days that had the word *shipment* on it, one in August, one in September. The one next month had asterisks and underlining that about tore through the paper. I wonder if that is a big load of drugs coming in."

"Ya think?" said Rabbit, snidely.

"You said two things. Just the shipments or something else?" asked Abel.

"Right," said André. "Toward the end of August, there was another day that was all highlighted and doodled on. It said *STB Rally.*"

"For a second, I thought you were gonna say STD Rally! Ya know, Sexually Transmitted Disease Rally, which woulda been perfect for Harm. He could get all undercover and penetrate the organization . . ." Rabbit waited for a laugh. Nothing. "C'mon, guys, you get it?" Harm rolled his eyes.

Tank sighed. "Guess you haven't seen the news. Got your mind on bein' a daddy. STB—Stand Tall Boys. They're having a big rally."

"I knew that," said Rabbit. "Just tryin' to lighten the mood."

"Anyway . . ." continued André, "I got into their email, too. When you guys hit the place and ran my hacker, it installed a keylogger."

"A what?" asked Rabbit.

"Some code that watches everything they type in and sends it to me."

"You can do that?" asked Rabbit.

"Yeah, your wife probably put one on your computer and knows exactly what porn you're watching."

"No way!"

André chuckled. "Anyway, I got their Gmail password. Most of the emails were about running the bar, but I did find some stuff from the Stand Tall Boys. One of the emails gave the details of the upcoming rally and when they wanted Guidry's guys to show up. Apparently, these things get pretty intense because Antifa shows up, and they are just as psycho as the white supremacists."

"This is getting complicated," said Harm. "What's Antifa again?"

"An antifascist group. Basically, these white supremacists have like a Nazi ideology, which is fascist."

"Not helping, Abel! What's fascist?" asked Rabbit. "This is like history class."

"And we know how much you loved history. Like how many times did you skip it in high school?" said Tank.

Chapter Twenty-Eight

"I had history class?" said Rabbit, and everybody laughed.

"Fascism is where there is a dictator who puts down the masses and keeps in control with violence. So just like the Nazis with Hitler. Big on nationalism and racism. Like they were 'pure blooded Aryans' and therefore good, and anybody else like the Jews and Blacks were bad," said Abel.

"How do you know all this shit?" asked Rabbit, seriously. "You skipped as many history classes as I did."

"True," said Abel, and everybody laughed again. "What do we got? What do we do here?"

"I've been thinking," André said. "With the whole whiteboard contest thing we can show they are going after a certain class of people. Maybe they can get away with that in ones and twos, but with all the names, and the fact that they are incenting each other in a contest, it's pretty much a slam dunk that that is profiling, violation of civil rights, not following due process or whatever. It's wrong and we just hand all the data to Hebert, and he can wrap it up and put a bow on it."

"Yeah, that's good," said Abel, "but that's stuff that people and lawyers and judges can argue about forever. We need to nail them with something hard."

"I gotta toehold with Guidry's butthole buddy, Randy," said Harm. "I'll work that and worm my way in. Try to get details on both the rally and the motorcycle club."

"Yeah, get something concrete so we can set something up and catch 'em in the act," added Abel.

"I'll help Harm," said Rabbit. "I'll have his back and his front!"

Harm blocked Rabbit as he reached over to pop Harm in his nut-sack, on automatic, his expression not even changing.

"What can Abel and I do?" Tank asked his brother, completely ignoring Rabbit and Harm's interaction.

"There's still tons of stuff I haven't combed through. Maybe there's more stuff about the STBs."

"Haha, STDs" said Rabbit.

CHAPTER

TWENTY-NINE

Abel and Tank pulled into Family Bail Bonds and sat there for a moment, gearing up for the next few minutes. They had decided it was time to face the music with Veruto and inform him that they had not been able to find Didi. They rightly figured that telling Big Frank that they had a crisis of conscience, didn't believe in the justice system, and were hoping that working with Didi would help André was not going to fly.

"Alright, let's go," Abel said with a sigh.

They jumped down from Abel's truck and trudged to the door, knowing they were headed for a shitstorm. Tank stepped in first but stopped abruptly, and Abel bumped into his back. "What the eff?" murmured Tank under his breath.

Abel stood next to Tank, surveying the office. The desks had been pushed back against the walls, opening up the space, and Frank, Doris, and Frankie were doing calisthenics. Big and little Franks were performing jumping jacks, and Doris was doing pirouettes like a ballerina, occasionally stopping and raising her leg with pointed toe in some dancing motion that the guys vaguely recognized. She was dressed in stretchy yoga pants, and when she spun around there was a sight that Abel and Tank could not unsee. Both the Franks were dressed in yellowed T-shirts and cargo shorts with brilliant white crew socks pulled up to midcalf. A span of pasty flesh bridged the terrain between the socks and shorts, and Little Frankie's shirt was too tight, broadcasting an unfortunate case of man boobs. The exercisers slowed to a stop one by one and ended up standing in the middle of the room, staring at them like deer caught in the headlights.

"What can I do for you boys?" asked Frank, acting like nothing out of the ordinary was happening.

Abel couldn't let it go. "You guys on a health kick?"

"Doris's idea," said Frank, passing the blame. "She thinks we're getting out of shape. They are," he said, nodding at his mate and son. "I'm still wearing the same pant size as I was in high school."

True, thought Abel, although that was because his pants were pulled up underneath his prodigious gut and held in place by a belt cinched so tight there were gathers in the waist. His years of sitting behind the government surplus desk had wasted away his legs and butt, transferring the mass to his belly.

Doris gazed at Frank fondly. "Frank is still a dreamboat. Looks exactly like when we first met." Tank subtly elbowed Abel. "I'm just worried about his heart. His daddy died of a cardiac arrest as a young man."

Frank rode over Doris. "As long as you boys are here, help me move this furniture back. You, too, Frankie."

The men quickly dragged the desks and chairs back into place, and Veruto waved to the seats. "Have a sit. So, what's going on? Didja finally track down Fabre? I'll be honest, I expected more from you," he said, trying to shift the balance of power back away from the awkwardness of being caught in the act of family exercise.

"Well, it turned out to be harder than you thought and we figured. We did all the usual stuff: talked to his parents, his sister, his minister, his girlfriend, and his customers. We couldn't track him down. All his people were convinced that he's innocent, so no one was inclined to help," said Abel. He felt a little guilty shining Frank on but not too guilty; Veruto was never dealing with them in good faith, either.

Tank jumped in before the inevitable onslaught from Frank. "We even tracked down his shack in the swamp offa the Blood. Couldn't find him."

The guys stopped their lame explanations and girded themselves for the inevitable salty response from their boss. Instead, he surprised them and went a slightly different direction—disappointment. "Well, boys, it's a write-off. I'm not sure you're cut out for this game."

"Wait a second, Frank, this is like the first time we couldn't bring a guy in," said Abel, getting defensive and forgetting for a second that they purposely didn't bring in Didi.

"I don't know, boys. The mark of a true bounty hunter is the ability to step up your game when you need to, leave no stone unturned, you know—when the going gets tough the tough get going."

"I don't think he's even in the state anymore," said Tank.

"Guess you guys are gonna lose your payout, and I'm going to be taking a big hit. I was counting on you guys, was gonna give you extra, pay you a bonus."

Right, thought Abel, knowing Frank well enough to let that particular speck of bullshit slide straight out the other side of his brain.

"This is going to piss off Guidry; mess up his conviction rate."

"Wait, Frank, don't you think it's bogus that Guidry and his crew are making all these bad arrests?" asked Abel.

"Not my problem," said Veruto. "That's the court's job. I bring 'em back in, let the justice system take its course." Tank rolled his eyes.

"Didn't you guys say Tank's brother is also caught up with the detective? He's not a guy you wanna get on his bad side," continued Big Frank.

"Guidry doesn't even know we are on the case," said Tank.

"Yeah, but he knows I fronted the bond or he could find out easy enough. And let me tell you, that guy's a piece of work. I don't want to make him mad. He's a full-service asshole. You should hear what he did to Little Frankie the other day. Made him cry. Tell them, son."

Suddenly put on the spot, Little Frankie stared at them with his bovine eyes. "Dad!" he exclaimed, outraged.

"Now Frankie, tell 'em what happened."

Silence. Frankie continued peering at them, then sighed, the air bleeding out as if he had a slow leak, his shoulders dropping and rounding. He grudgingly began. "I had some papers to drop over at the court, so I drove over there the other day. I got a sweet spot in the employee lot of the parish prison. A friend of mine—"

"Not important!" said Big Frank. Abel was stuck on the fact that Frankie had a friend with enough pull to get him a spot that close to the court.

Frankie continued, "It was pretty crowded, but I saw a pull-through and slid in even though it was super tight. All good till I opened my door and accidently spanked this car next to me. I mean, it was no big deal. The car was an old wreck, already dinged up pretty bad. I got out like nothing happened; you know, squeezed out the door but didn't hit the car again. It was just that once."

"Uh-huh," said Tank.

"Anyway, I didn't notice anybody in the car, so I just started walking down the lot toward the courthouse."

"Yeah?" said Abel, hearing the tension rise in Frankie's voice.

"All of a sudden, somebody grabs my shoulder and says something like 'Hey, you SOB' and whirls me around, and I'm standing there looking at Detective Guidry and some other guy. Guidry says, 'You hit my car and dented the door.' I said the door was already scratched, but he wasn't having it."

"What a prick!" said Frankie's daddy.

"The detective told me I had to pay him one hundred dollars, and he wanted it right then. I pulled out my wallet, but all I had was a twenty. I showed them the money, but then the other guy hit me in the chest with both his hands, knocking me back.

"Guidry told me I was going to jail for damaging city property. I kept telling them I was sorry and would pay for getting their car fixed. The guy pushed me again and knocked all my court papers from under my arm, and they started to blow around the lot. The papers blew away under cars and shit, and Guidry said, 'You're going to jail boy,' and I kinda started crying about then."

"Aw," said Abel, and Doris let out a sniffle.

"I was standing there in front of them crying, and Guidry said something about squealing like a pig, then he twisted my titty. Hard, not like a joke. Hard like he was trying to hurt me." A tear rolled down from the corner of Little Frankie's eye.

He snorted, then continued, "They both started laughing, and Guidry said, 'Jeez, boy, can't you take a joke?' then they walked off like nothing happened."

Frankie lifted his yellowed T-shirt up over his nipple. An ugly purple bruise discolored his man boob.

"Ouch! That's gotta hurt," said Tank.

"He thinks he's King Shit. A real bully," added Abel.

"See what I'm saying, boys? Guy's a psycho."

"When he hears Fabre is not around for his trial, he's gonna be pissed."

Abel said, "We can keep looking but haven't seen any signs of him so not gonna promise anything."

"Well, boys, no payday I guess."

"You got anyone else needs tracking down?" asked Tank.

"Nope, got a handle on things right now," answered Veruto.

Abel grabbed Tank and hustled him out the door, and as they hit the parking lot Abel said, "Well, that went better than expected." Tank laughed.

THIRTY

Harm didn't like having to-dos hanging over his head, so he had jumped on the task of getting with Guidry's guy, Randy. He had gone back to The Blue Wall immediately after André's presentation and vultured the place at a distance, figuring that it would be easy to pick out Randy when he left given that he looked like Ichabod Crane.

He'd gotten lucky and caught sight of Randy leaving the building just shortly before 11 pm and had followed him home. At least he guessed it was Randy. Could there be two tall scarecrows in Guidry's crew? Randy's place was a shotgun-style house in an area that was being gentrified. It was probably worth some decent bank even though the home looked like it was in the beginning stages of a rehab. Harm wondered whether Randy had inherited the place or whether it was more evidence that he was dirty. There was no way Randy could afford the area on a cop's salary. Maybe Randy still lived with his parents.

Harm had put a pin on his map and sent the address and license plate to André, knowing full well that he'd have the guy's particulars by morning. It would be nice to know his last name at least, then they could start taking the guy apart.

After that, it had been simply a matter of waking up early, tracking the man to the police bureau on South Broad, then tracking him after work. Well, it had not been that simple, since it involved a parking garage, catching him when he was leaving, identifying his vehicle, and following him over a couple of days.

He finally managed to *bump* into Randy at a Quick Stop as he was getting a tin of Copenhagen chewing tobacco. Harm waited till Randy was backing away from the counter and said, "Hey, man, aren't you the guy I met at The Blue Wall?"

Randy looked at him blankly for a second, then got a wide stupid smile. "Yeah, the other day. I remember you!"

Harm whipped out his hand. "John Smith."

Randy grabbed his hand deep, imitating how Guidry had taken Harm's hand back at the bar. "Randy Williams. Nice to really meet you."

Harm said, "Kind of a coincidence, right? I'm coming in here to get a can of Cope, and there you are. Buying the same dip. I like the wintergreen though. Anyway, I'm glad I bumped into you; I did want to talk a bit about the force. How about I buy you a beer, and maybe I could get some advice from you."

"Sure," said Randy. "I got time."

"A'write. Let me get my chew, then I know a place where we can knock some back."

Harm knew about every bar in New Orleans, so he led Randy to the closest dive, one where the people minded their own business as they slid into alcoholism. They parked on the street, and Harm waited by the door till Randy caught up. They entered the bar through a door that was propped open with a trash can.

"Hmmm, nice place," said Randy. "Looks like we gotta get you a better job. You know, upscale your life a bit."

Harm laughed. "Hey, man, the place was close, and the beer is cold . . . and cheap!" He wasn't going to say that no one knew him here.

"Yeah, that works," said Guidry's man.

They parked at a booth in the dingy place, the place dim even though there were hanging lights over every table. The bulbs were dusty and fly specked and casting a bare glow that amplified the orange tone of the unfinished pine tabletop. "What's your poison?" asked Harm before he went up to the bar to buy the round.

Harm, or John, as he was known as for the moment, placed the glasses on the table and sat. "So what would be my first steps if I wanted to get on the force?"

Randy took Harm through the process of applying, training, and probation, and Harm managed asking legitimate questions in all the appropriate spots. He occasionally dropped tidbits from his time in the military that made him appear to have relevant experience. It wasn't pure fabrication; there really was a lot of overlap.

Harm summed it up. "Just like the Rangers. Periods of utter boredom punctuated by shit-your-pants excitement."

That elicited a laugh from Williams who then said, "Exactly!"

They were quiet for a minute. Harm was thinking about the times when the excitement was probably better described as terror; although, he wasn't willing, or maybe able, to be that honest.

"All you gotta do is go to any of the district police stations and pick up an application. But here's the key. On the form where it asks for references, put down Detective Shane Guidry and my name, too. When you get the forms, call me, and I'll help you finish them off. Then, you'll be a lock."

"Thanks. That's awesome." Harm whipped out his phone and got the man's number and put it into his contacts.

"You're welcome. We'd love to have a guy like you on the force. A military guy. A hard guy. We've got too many namby-pamby millennials now. I guess it's a sign of the times. Ya know, I almost joined up when I got outta high school. It was between the Marines or the department, and I chose the police. But I always wondered what being a jarhead woulda been like."

"I was an Army Ranger, not a Marine, but man! I've got some stories."

"Let's hear one. What did you really do to get discharged? You don't seem like the kinda guy that fucks up."

Harm thought a minute, getting his story straight. He decided to just tell it like it happened but with the one change—swapping out the White captain with the fictional Black officer. "Maybe I don't seem like a fuck up, but I sure as hell screwed the pooch and blew up my military career. I was gonna be a twenty-year man."

"What happened?" asked Randy.

"I was doing well, you know, leading patrols. Putting my ass on the line, keeping the new guys outta trouble, and generally being a go-to guy. I wasn't just kissing ass; I loved that shit. Just like with my buddies when I was growing up. I was running around the bayou, having fun, and stirring up mayhem.

"All good, right? Then this new captain rotates in. A Black guy with something to prove. He seemed OK at first. Polite and friendly. Maybe too friendly. But he was an up-and-comer, so he starts volunteering us for all sorts of stuff. Things we had no business doing. Stupid, dangerous shit. Trying to be the biggest dick on the block and make a name for himself to his superiors."

"Sounds like bullshit, man," said Williams.

"Ya know, Randy? I get it. We all want to be somebody. He wanted to be a general. The problem was, he was throwing us into it, and he didn't have our backs. After a while, we started noticing that he'd get us in the line of fire, and then he would disappear. Or if something went wrong, it wasn't that he'd made a bad plan, it was that we screwed it up."

"That isn't that much different than the force, to be honest," said Randy. "Some guys are just politicians, and you can't count on them. Guidry isn't like that, which is why I respect him. He's right there in the shit with us. Anyway, sorry. Keep going."

"So there we were in some pointless firefight and we're running out of ammo, I drop back to the tactical, and as I walk around it, I see the captain hunkered down behind the wheel, sitting on his heels with his hands over his ears. He mighta even been crying."

"Shit," said Randy. "Frickin' coward."

"Anyway, we lock eyes. But I decide to pretend like it never happened. I ignore him and grab some ammo and run back to the guys. We continue shooting but then decide to back out. We disengage and get the hell outta Dodge. The Cap's regained his composure, and I don't say anything to the men."

"Are they all like that?"

"Who?"

"The N-words," said Randy, sarcastically.

"Pretty much," said Harm, ticked off that he had to say that shit since cowards and assholes were distributed fairly evenly across all the men regardless of race, creed, or color.

"But how did you go from there to getting kicked out?"

Harm continued, "I thought that the captain woulda dropped it. I never said anything to anybody about it. But I couldn't look him in the eye. He'd be giving me some bullshit order, and I couldn't stop myself and I'd look away. For some reason, I couldn't forget it and neither could he. It became a thing. The guy couldn't let it go. He started really fucking with me. Shit details. Night watches. Missions that were gonna get me killed."

"Fucker!" Randy said.

"I was like, this bastard isn't going to break me. I was gonna ride it out, but it was like a rubber band that you pull on till it snaps. And it wasn't just me. He started acting like everybody was out to get him. Then, one day he starts ragging on one of my guys for something that he himself did, and I snapped. I jumped him and beat the crap outta him till I got pulled off. And then I was done and out. Lucky, I didn't get court-martialed and put in the brig."

"Man, that sucks."

Harm leaned back in the chair, depressed after the telling. It was exactly how it had gone down. Well, except for the fact that the captain was really a third-generation White soldier from West Virginia, a legacy graduate of West Point, and a disgrace to his granddaddy. Even to this day, he wished he'd handled it differently, though. He wished he was still a Ranger. It had made him feel like he was somebody.

"Was it all like that?" asked Randy.

"No. Like anything, there were some good things and bad things. The best thing was to get a mission, plan it out, and then execute it. Of course, things would go castors up, and then you had to adapt. If you achieved the objective and nobody got hurt or killed, you felt awesome. Man, you felt invincible. Alive. The colors were brighter, the air smelled better, and it felt like the guys on your team were your family."

"Even the Black dudes?"

Jesus, this guy is an asshole. "All the guys in my unit were White," made up Harm. "I was able to cherry-pick my team," he continued, laying it on. "That way I didn't have to watch my back." It about made him puke, but he figured there was no such thing as too much for this motherfucker.

"Tell me about one of those missions," begged Randy, like a little kid asking for another bedtime story.

Harm obliged. "OK, one time we got directed to hit this village in Kandahar. There were some insurgents hiding there, using it as a base. It was kinda like the center of operations, and we were supposed to raid it, get whatever intel was lying around, blow up ammo and weapons, and kill any obvious enemy. Oh, and not hurt any innocents in the village.

"See that's what these ragheads would do, embed in a village of regular people—women and children and old folks. You couldn't tell who was who. But this time, we had some solid intel that they were in a particular building. We were supposed to do a surgical entry. Get into that building and then dine and dash. If you know what I mean."

"Yeah, yeah, I know," enthused Randy.

"So we get all ready, then creep in at zero dark thirty." Harm laughed to himself, talking bullshit that he'd never heard anywhere but TV. "But get this, they had the place surrounded by *fel murgh*. That's Dari for 'elephant chicken.' Like a turkey, and they make a fucking racket. The birds heard us or sensed us and started going insane. People were rolling out of the huts like fire ants. I guess it's the Afghani national burglar alarm. We pulled back to base, laughing our asses off."

"You guys bag the mission?"

"No. Like I said, we adapted. The first time we only had one sniper on overwatch. The next time, we went in with four and sneaked in like Indians from downwind. We got in close, and the snipers took out the birds. We waited till we saw the exploding feather balls and went in. Scarfed the intel, blew the building, and while we were exiting stage left, the guys on overwatch were popping the towel-heads shooting at us."

"What intel did you get?"

"The usual shit: papers and laptops."

"Anything good?"

"Jeez, I don't know. We just hand if off to the spooks."

"That was cool, though," Randy said, suddenly animated but slurring a little and talking loudly. "You should definitely join the NOPD. The training would be a no-brainer for a guy like you. And who knows, we could probably fast-track you and get you working in some capacity in Guidry's organization. Maybe even sooner rather than later."

"What do you mean? I don't think no matter how good I might be that I'd be a detective anytime soon."

"Well, Guidry's got a lot of stuff going on. Some undercover stuff, some community stuff, things outside the force. We do some security for various organizations, that kind of thing. I bet he'd bring you in on that. Are you interested?"

Hmmm, thought Harm, *here we go.* "Sure! In the police or not, I could use a side gig."

Randy said, "I'll talk to Guidry. Maybe we can use some extra help on some stuff we got coming up. I'll let you know. Anyway, I'd better roll. Thanks for the beer, man." He laughed. "And the stories!"

"I have to go, too. I'll walk out with you."

They stood up together and headed out the door that was still propped open with the trash can. Harm was a few steps behind Randy as they went out, and he watched Williams bull through the door just as a solid-looking Black dude was coming in. It was like a game of chicken, and neither Randy nor the Black guy made room for the other.

Randy purposefully bumped the man with his shoulder, and the guy stumbled into the trash can and almost fell. Drunk Randy was acting like a tough guy and showing off. It was with a certain pleasure that Harm watched the Black guy get his balance and push Randy violently against the wall of the building.

Then, it was on. They stood toe-to-toe going at it, but it was obvious to Harm that the Black guy knew what he was doing. He was pounding Randy with combinations, occasionally doubling the body shots. Williams was getting his ass handed to him.

Aw shit, thought Harm. He was going to have to do something.

THIRTY-ONE

The two fighters had circled around so that the Black guy's back was toward Harm, and Harm could see Williams's face over his shoulder. It already had red blotches where some of the Black dude's punches had landed. Randy was wobbling on his feet and if he got popped one more time, he was going down and then Harm would have to drag his Ichabod Crane-ish body out of there. Randy looked past the Black guy and caught Harm's eyes. Harm could see the fear.

Harm stepped in, driving with his hip, and landed a blind side punch about eight inches above the guy's belt on the right side of his back and squarely over his kidney. The man grunted and fell to his knees. Noises like the bleating of a sheep came out of his mouth. Harm sincerely hoped he had pulled the punch enough that he hadn't ruptured the poor dude's kidney.

Having been punched in the kidney before himself, Harm sympathized with the man on his knees and knew the guy would be out of commission for at least a minute, and if he had actually torn the organ, the guy would need an ambulance. He did feel bad. He wasn't a total psycho. It was just that André's needs were the mission, and the line he had in his head put this victim, a guy he didn't know, on the side of collateral damage.

Harm stopped dealing with his momentary guilty conscience and moved past the downed man and grabbed Randy by the collar. "Let's go!"

"What? Where?" asked Williams, dazed and confused.

"Outta here," said Harm, dragging him along. "Shut up."

Harm hustled Randy into his truck and drove out onto the street, throwing a rooster tail of gravel that sounded like metal rain as it landed on the few vehicles in the parking lot.

"I know you wanted to give that guy the boot, but we had to leave. It wouldna looked good to have one of NOPD's finest, drunk and standing over a vic when the troops showed up. And that guy was only gonna be on his knees for a minute. And if he got up, he woulda started up on you again. And just being real, dude? He was eating your lunch for breakfast!"

"Yeah, I guess I bit off more than I could chew, but I ain't gonna let no coon own the road. But then, no worries, my buddy Big John steps in and puts the guy down with one punch. Man, you paralyzed him."

Harm grunted, noncommittal, like it was no big deal, and except for the minor angst of nailing somebody who didn't deserve it, it wasn't.

Randy continued on, "You know, sometimes you meet someone and they talk the big talk. You never know till it goes nuclear whether it's all bullshit, but you're the real deal, dude."

"Big talk?" asked Harm. "I haven't told you the half of it. What do you think spec ops do? Just the training is more shit than you've ever seen in your whole life."

"Have you ever killed anyone?"

"Of course. We weren't over there playing touch football."

"No, I don't mean sniping someone from one thousand meters. Up close and personal, with your hands."

"Yeah, a few times." *More than a few times,* Harm thought, but he wasn't going to tell this puke his life story. "When you got to take a guy out quiet, it's always close work. Messy."

"Holy shit," said Williams with a trace of envy, going all fanboy. He wasn't going to let it go. "What's that like?"

Harm decided to give him a taste. "OK, say you got to get in a building and there are two guards outside and there is only one of you. The guards are on opposite sides of the building. They can't see each other but they can hear, and it's dead quiet outside. You have to put the guys out of commission silently. Make a mistake killing the first one, one tiny noise, the other guard will raise the alarm and be coming in on full auto. You're dead, and there aren't any second chances like all you pussies think 'cuz you've learned about fighting from a video game.

"So you sneak up on one guard. Haha, that's bullshit right there. If he's any way alert, he's gonna hear you creeping in. You get close. Not all the way in. You've made sure you don't have a smell. No soaps with any kinda man perfume. You come from downwind because you can't erase your smell completely. You cover your pits and your balls with a compound that stops you sweating because when you're amped up for a kill your body starts to smell like a wild animal.

"Then, you wait. He's gotta be distracted. Some sound from in front of him, he looks at his phone, he lights up a cig, anything. Because humans can tell if someone is coming from behind—it's a fucking caveman thing."

Randy wasn't interrupting and was listening, rapt. Harm went on. "The second he's not paying attention, you slide in. A rag in one hand, a blade in the other. Reach around and cover his mouth with the rag, while you cut his throat all the way to his spine. The instant the knife cuts the windpipe, you drop the rag over the wound. You think cutting someone's throat is quiet? Fuck! The air in his lungs blows out of the gash you just made. It makes a sound very few people have ever heard. So the other guard would be saying, 'What the fuck?' and would be coming in guns blazing. You gotta muffle it.

"Then, you got to go do it all over again with the other guard. But this time you don't have all that extra time to do it careful. The bowels of the guy you just killed are gonna let go, and you better hope it's not loud enough for the other guard to hear. Regardless, in a minute there's gonna be the smell of shit on the breeze, and you've run outta time."

"Fuck . . . that's intense," said Randy in a voice that almost sounded like he was turned on. "But the fucking towel-heads deserved it right?"

Harm didn't mention it wasn't Afghanistan. He wasn't going to tell Randy that it was right there in Louisiana, when they had had the run in with the MS-13 gang a while back. That had been as intense as anything in the 'stan.

Randy changed gears. "You're legit, man. I bet I can get you hooked up in a pretty decent gig with Guidry and the guys. You interested? What are you doing for money right now? Where do you work?"

Ahhh, here is where it starts to get tricky, thought Harm. "I work security for some people. But you know I can't really say much more. You know, Fifth Amendment. I don't want to incriminate myself, you bein' the po-po and all." Harm gave a short laugh and punched Randy in the shoulder, like it was a joke.

Randy laughed like he was in on it, then asked, "Think the coast is clear back at the bar?"

Harm and Randy did a drive-by of the bar, but there was some action in the parking lot. Four Black men were standing around the guy that Randy tangled with who was making large gestures with his hands, obviously still upset. "Hmmm, could you drop me at my place? I'll get one of my friends to help me get my car later," said Williams.

Harm nodded and waited till Randy gave him directions to his place, not giving any indication that he already knew the location from his previous stalking.

Harm caught up with Abel later that night to give him the lowdown. They were on the back porch, enjoying cold beers and the soft Gulf breeze, although Harm was nursing a slight feeling of disappointment. He'd hoped that Callie might have the night off, and he would see her. At some level, he knew it was never gonna happen, but that didn't stop the longing he'd had for her ever since they were kids. Early on she had looked up to him because he was several years older, but by the time Callie was a teenager, Harm was firmly cemented in the family zone.

He sighed and started briefing Abel. "Didn't take long. I'm in with Williams. He even took me to his house and showed me around." Harm detailed what happened right down to the kidney punch and mentioned that Randy had posters of Snoopy and Charlie Brown over his bed. They both had a good laugh but agreed it was pretty weird, especially that he let Harm see his bedroom decorated that way.

"Do you think that's some kind of code?" asked Abel. "Does it mean he's gay or something? And he was signaling that he's interested in you?"

"Oh, he's interested in me. But I didn't get the gay vibe. He imagines he's a warrior, and I'm like the guy that he imagines himself to be. And I don't mean that in a big-headed way. It just means he thinks he's a tough guy and maybe coulda, woulda, shoulda been a soldier."

"Is he dangerous?"

"Well, let me put it this way. If he was by himself, he's not doing anything, but if he was there with his buddies, he'd be all brave and might do anything.

"I mean look, I'm convinced he started that fight with the guy at the bar because I was there. On one hand he wanted to show me he was a tough guy, but he knew I'd step in if things went south. And when he got clocked a few times, he sure started looking to me for help.

"He's definitely the kinda guy that would follow someone else's lead. So if he's out with Guidry and that crew, and they start mixing it up? He's gonna jump in, too."

"He said he was gonna tie you into some Guidry thing?"

"Yeah, he promised he was going to hook me up, and I hinted that I was not necessarily on the up and up. We'll see."

"No way are they going to pull you into the drug stuff, but I can see them recruiting for the white supremacy side of things. I don't see that we have a whole lot of time to wait on this dipshit. Let's get an application to the NOPD, fill it out with fake info, then ask Randy to check it out."

"OK, it'll give me a chance to work him some more. Keep the pressure on."

"Just be careful. Williams may be a pussy, but from what you've told me, Guidry will cut off your head if he smells something funny. There's no way that the Bastards would be dealing with a lightweight," said Abel.

THIRTY-TWO

Harm pulled his truck into Mr. Walker's auto repair shop at lunch time the next day looking for his buddy. When Abel shut down the robbery crew, Rabbit went back to working with his daddy full time. He'd already been working a lot for his dad even when they were thieving, but he transitioned to fixing vehicles six days a week after they busted up the crew.

It was no secret this was OK with Rabbit's wife. Crystal wanted her husband out of the Life completely. Her plans did not include a baby with a crook for a daddy.

No one saw Rabbit getting married, especially Harm. He'd been blindsided. Harm had figured that he and Rabbit would be hanging out till they were old men. He had his feelings about Callie, and knew at some level they would come to naught, but somehow, he never imagined Rabbit having any real feelings for anyone or wanting to settle down. He was too jittery and wild. Rabbit had been a player like René, although not in the same league.

Now he had a wife and a baby on the way and was working at a repair shop that was mostly on the up and up, and Harm was down in the city consorting with mob types and not even Dixie Mob guys but real Italian mafia dudes that he barely trusted. It was a far cry from working with his best friend who had had his back since elementary school and vice versa.

God damn it, he missed the old Rabbit, Harm thought in a rare moment of self-awareness, then chastised himself. Rabbit wasn't gone. Rabbit was right here. Harm wasn't alone. He had his mama and Abel and the rest of the guys. Anyways, he figured, Abel wasn't going to keep up this charade of going straight. It wasn't working out for him. The crew was going to get back together, and they'd be pulling the big jobs again and life would get back to normal. Rabbit would start driving for them again, and he and Rabbit would be working side by side.

Harm jumped out of the truck and headed into the shop, looking for his friend. The office door had a little bell that tinkled when it was opened and an electric doorbell that rang deep in the bowels of the shop. A smell that was a concoction of gasoline, the stench of burned oil, the tang of man sweat, and cigarettes hit his nose. Everyone thought that the office had been painted an off shade of orange, but it had been bright white in the fifties, then it was coated with seventy years of smoke.

Mr. Walker was sitting behind a desk, peering at a computer screen through a pair of cheaters, his few remaining strands of hair standing straight up, glued that way probably by the same black oil that was smudged on his forehead. He looked up. "Where y'at, Harmon?"

"A'write," said Harm to the man that was his idea of a model father, given that his own daddy had been pretty much a failure in that department. "Still working in finance down in the city." Mr. Walker laughed, knowing what Harm really did.

"Rabbit around?"

"He's down in the grease pit over'n bay four."

Harm went through the door into the shop where he was instantly assaulted by the chatter of a pneumatic wrench on top of country radio blasting out of the speakers in each bay. He passed through the bays, greeting each mechanic, old dudes that had been there as long as Rabbit's dad. The last guy was shining a shop light on the underside of a gas tank, scrutinizing a gas leak while holding a lit cigarette in his left hand. Harm just shook his head.

When he got to bay four he saw a cherry Mustang parked over the hole in the floor. Putting one hand on the door for support, he bent over and yelled, "Dude, you down there?"

"HARM!" came the shout from the pit. "C'mon down, man!"

"No way, I'm wearing clean clothes. Git up outta there. Let's go talk out back."

"A'write, I'll meet you out there in a minute."

Harm walked out the open bay and went around to the back, an open field that doubled as a parking lot, which was populated with wrecks that went all the way back to the garage's very beginning. In the middle of the lot, surrounded by vehicles, was a tiny amphitheater of busted up car bench seats, some of which looked comfortable, while others had wicked looking springs poking through. Harm chose one without an anal probe and sat in the center of car seat Stonehenge. Rabbit appeared moments later, wiping his hands with a towel. A faint scent of orange GOJO wafted over.

"What's up?" asked Rabbit.

"Haven't heard from you for a few days, just checkin' on ya. I mean, you don't call and you don't write," he said, only half teasing. "I have to track you down here in a grease pit where you're working like a regular dude."

"Yeah, the world's changing. What with the kid coming, Crystal is sayin' I should be thinking about how to make things more secure. That I oughta take over the shop. She knows my pop is ready to retire."

"Man, if you do that it's gonna conflict with any jobs we get," said Harm.

"Jobs?"

"When we start the crew back up and Abel hooks us back into the Dixie Mob. You running this place is gonna cut into how much time you can scout jobs and wheel."

Rabbit got a funny look on his face, like he suddenly realized his friend had gone mental. "Number one: Abel's not startin' up robbing again. Number two: André, Tank, Abel, me, and you have straight jobs now."

Harm said, "I'm not working a straight gig."

Rabbit continued like he hadn't heard, "I don't see Abel giving up on the Olivia thing, and that means he's gotta be outta the Life. And no way will Crystal put up with me going back to thieving and being gone all night and all the other bullshit."

Rabbit stared at him. A few beats went by, then Harm said, "We'll see. I don't think Abel and Tank like what they're doing," but it sounded weak.

Rabbit said, "If Abel and the guys decide to go back to that, I'd have to rethink things." He wiped his face with the towel. "Harmon, I want to ask you to be the godfather of our baby."

There was dead silence. Finally, Harm said, "Godfather? But why?"

"Dude, you can be so stupid sometimes! You're my best friend! Plus, I can't think of anybody better at protecting his family and friends."

"Rabbit, I don't know anything about raising a kid."

"You don't have to raise a kid; a godfather doesn't do that. You're just around, like an awesome uncle, and God forbid something happens to both me and Crystal, then you step in and help make sure everything is gonna be OK for them. The kid would go to my sister or parents, not you."

"I just kinda watch over the kid?"

"Yeah, but if for some reason there was a threat or danger? I know you would be like a Goddamn Angel of Doom."

"Yeah, you're right. I don't know about the uncle or the father stuff, but I would rain down holy terror on anybody that threatens you or Crystal or anyone in our crew or their families. You'd do the same."

"Hell yeah."

Rabbit waited a beat, then said, "So you'll do it?"

"Yes. I'd be honored."

"Great! I'm going to announce it at the gender reveal party."

"What the eff is a gender reveal party?"

Rabbit got all rabbity. "It's when you have a party similar to a baby shower, only men can come, not just women, like with the baby shower, and part of the celebration is telling everybody whether the baby is gonna be a boy or a girl. The cool thing is that the guy gets to figure out an awesome way to show what it's going to be. Maybe shoot off blue fireworks for a boy or let a flock of doves loose that are all dyed pink. I've been thinking on it for weeks."

"What are you going to do?"

"Can't tell. Crystal would kill me. But it's gonna be epic."

THIRTY-THREE

Randy Williams was sitting across from Detective Guidry in The Blue Wall office. They'd had to move back there because the main area was getting raucous. It was 7:00 pm and the troops had had a couple of hours to get a load on, so they needed a bit of privacy to talk over their *extracurricular* activities.

Guidry had gone quiet while looking at the computer screen, and Randy knew not to interrupt his chain of thought. He leaned back in his chair, thinking about his house and what he was going to do next. He had his eye on a sweet vintage mantle that he'd seen at an antique store in the Seventh to put over his fireplace. Just as he was mentally demolishing the old mantle, Guidry turned away from the screen and cleared his throat. Pulling himself out of his *Architectural Digest* fantasies, Randy sat up straight and looked to his boss.

Guidry said, "I'm thinking about the rally. We're supposed to help them keep things under control to a degree, but they expect some protesters, and they actually want some chaos. The press is going to be there, so the Stand Tall guys want it to look like they're the ones getting picked on. They want protection if things get too out of hand."

"But if the press is going to be there, we can't be seen there, right?" asked Williams.

"Right, we need to keep our faces covered. Also, I'm thinking we pull in a few of the Bastards to help with security. They can get *their* faces plastered all over the news."

"I've got an idea along those lines. Why don't we pull in John Smith? Then we kill two birds with one stone," said Randy. "We check him out, and he helps front for us."

"Who's John Smith?"

"You know that cop wannabe that was in here the other night? I bumped into him the other day, and it turns out he's solid. One of our kinda guys."

"He's not a cop."

"Yeah, but I was thinking we need a few guys that are like civilians for stuff just like this. When we need to hide that we're police. Just like your idea with the Bastards. Plus, he wants to be a cop, and I'm going to help him with his application."

"Why are you so hot for this guy?" asked Guidry.

"He's a stand-up guy. I got more detail about how he got drummed out of the service. Altercation with a Black officer. Man, that would be hard to take, wouldn't it?"

"It could be bullshit. You know how incompetent people make excuses when they fuck up."

Randy was too clueless to recognize Guidry's jab. "No, this guy is for real. We were leaving this shitty bar in a dark area, and I got in a little tussle with a Black dude as we were leaving the place. The fucker wouldn't give me space. We were going toe-to-toe, and Smith just stepped in and hit the guy. One punch in the guy's back, and he dropped straight to the floor. He didn't get up. Probably ruptured the guy's spleen."

"Kidney," corrected Guidry, who was no stranger to punching people when they weren't looking. "Spleen's in the front."

Chapter Thirty-Three

"Right, whatever. The point is, we can use this guy. Let him get on camera at the rally. It's perfect. I already told him that maybe I could get him some work, and believe me, he'll fit right in. If he shaved his head, you'd think he was a skinhead, not just some bald Southern boy.

"He told me some stuff about the military and what he did. Special forces. He's a killer."

"Sounds like you're in love with this dude," said Guidry.

"No. I mean he's killed people before. He told me stuff, detailed shit. Stuff people couldn't make up. I believe him."

"You sound like some teenage girl with a crush." Guidry laughed.

Frustrated, Randy went on, "Man, listen to me! I'm standing there getting beat on by the Black bastard, and I looked over his shoulder, and I saw Smith's face. It was all stone and dead eyes. He didn't even hesitate, walked straight up, and dropped this muscly motherfucker to his knees. The guy couldn't get up. He was making these noises like his insides were broken."

"What's he do for a living?" asked the detective. "Why's he looking for a new job?"

"He was pretty vague. Said he worked security for some people. He hinted that he was mixed up with some people on the wrong side of the law; although, he made it sound kinda like a joke. But that's good. We don't need some goody-two-shoes."

"Alright, alright. We can bring him on to help with the rally, but he's your responsibility."

"Great!" enthused Randy. "I'll let him know."

"OK, now let's talk about the next shipment for the Bastards."

CHAPTER
———
THIRTY-FOUR

Abel waited outside the Bywater Bakery in the upper Ninth off of Dauphine. Sitting at a gray metal table with the red barn building looming over him, he looked around the neighborhood, on the watch for Maria. She'd called him the previous night and set up the "not a date" meeting, promising some information that would help with the André situation. Olivia briefly popped into his mind. He tried to push her back out. Maybe it was time he got over her.

He looked around. The bakery was in a mostly gentrified neighborhood of shotgun houses and bungalows that were loaded with character and painted teal, orange, yellow, and every other color. The damage from Katrina was mostly erased after fourteen years, and the whole area of Bywater, in fact, was better off than other parts of the upper Ninth Ward, like the blighted zone around Press Park.

Abel felt a hand on his shoulder, and he jumped. "Abel, I startled you! I'm sorry," Maria said with a devilish smile on her face, obviously not sorry in the least.

She was dressed in a black pantsuit like she was going to the office, an office that a movie star had to go to. The outfit didn't really resemble the thing you see in your head when you hear "pantsuit," but Abel didn't know what else to call it. It had a blazer with notched lapels, and she was wearing that over a low-cut silk blouse with the faintest of pink tones. The pants tapered to high heels the same color as the blouse. Her look was finished off by large black sunglasses and large dangling gold earrings.

Abel scrambled to his feet and gave her a hug. "I saved us a table," he said obviously. "Why don't you sit, and I'll go in and grab us something. What would you like?"

"A black coffee and something sweet. You pick."

Abel went into the bakery, a charming place that smelled of cinnamon and coffee, and ordered Breakfast Gumbo, which was a fusion of chicken andouille filé gumbo and scrambled eggs over grits. For Maria, he got a slice of praline King Cake. He ferried two coffees out to the table and went back for the food.

When Abel set down his plate with its pile of food, Maria laughed, then said affectionately, "Mijo, you must still be growing!" Abel laughed along with her.

They ate for a few moments in communal silence, then Maria said, "I have a little trip planned. I tracked down a former gang member who had some dealings with Guidry, and he agreed to talk to you."

"I thought that when you were in a gang, you were in for life," said Abel.

"Apparently, it depends on the gang and the gang leaders. This boy's mother was very ill, and he needed to care for her. They say blood in and blood out, so I doubt he is actually out of the gang for real. But maybe they don't expect him to show up anymore. Like he is retired?"

"Why would this guy help me?"

"Because I asked him to. I helped him find medical care for his mother. And he isn't going to talk about the gang. He's talking about Guidry. When we finish here, we're going to the other side of the canal to his house. I'll drive us there, then bring you back here."

"Sounds good," said Abel as he continued to plow through his monster breakfast.

Maria had finished and was leaning back in her chair, sipping her coffee and surveying the neighborhood. "Someday, I would like to live in a place like this," she said wistfully.

"It's nice, isn't it?" said Abel, although he preferred to be surrounded by a little more nature.

She stood up. "Are you ready to go? This guy is waiting on us."

Abel pushed back from the table and sighed. "This place is great. I hear their sandwiches are pretty good, too."

"I thought you were going to spend all morning eating. I was worried my guy might run off." She said it with a smile but wasn't really teasing, then she gave him a light punch on the shoulder and managed to sell a more convincing I'm-kidding kind of laugh. "C'mon, my car is right down here."

They walked down Independence a couple of blocks until Maria stopped at a brilliant black Lexus so neatly tucked between two cars that it must have required a chauffeur's parallel parking skills. Maria popped the locks, and Abel slid into the death seat.

He sniffed and said, "Wow still has that new car smell." He was too polite to ask how she afforded a new car on a nonprofit's salary.

Maria pegged the steering wheel and squeaked out of the tight spot, then it was a dizzying series of lefts and rights until they were in an area where the houses were sparse, and here and there were fields of green weeds. Abel figured that Katrina had destroyed the homes, and they had finally been demolished and carted off, and nature had done what nature does—cover over the scars.

She pulled up in front of a duplex that had been painted a custard color but had splotches of black mold.

The house on the left had a cratered roof and busted out windows and a front door with a faint X on it, while the right-hand home was still intact. It had what appeared to be a dry roof and even some sad curtains hanging in the windows.

Maria shut off the engine and glanced at Abel. "Let's talk to this kid. I hope he didn't have a change of heart and take off." She popped the door and stood in the street waiting for Abel to join her, and together they walked up the short drive to the house.

There wasn't a porch, just a cracked slab in front of the door, and Maria stepped up and pounded on the door with the side of her fist. "Juan! We're here!" She waited, then pounded again. "Juan!"

The door opened a foot, and Juan leaned his head out. "Shh," he said with his finger on his lips. "Mi mama está durmiendo."

Maria tipped her head toward Abel. "Inglés!" She motioned to Juan to come out as she stepped back off the stoop.

In the light of day, Juan's ink jumped off his pale skin. His pimply face had no tats, but his skinny white arms poking out of an even whiter T-shirt were covered in sleeves. Among the green skulls with long hair, tombstones, guns, skeletons with cigars, and women's faces was a large 'MS' prominent on his right bicep. A '13' adorned the left.

Abel's mind jumped, and he felt a moment of disorientation as the image sent him back in time to his crew's conflict with the Mara Salvatrucha gang, and he wondered whether this guy had been one of the men that had killed his cousin René or his Uncle Deacon. Rage stabbed his brain, and he clenched his fists. Juan took a step back in alarm. Maria grabbed Abel's arm and gently squeezed.

He got control of himself and let out a shaky breath. "I'm sorry, I thought you were somebody else." Abel realized that the guy's face didn't have any MS-13 tattoos or teardrops or any of the other flags of a banger who had performed numerous murders. The Maras didn't allow just anybody to ink the letters on their face or neck. Maybe this guy hadn't even been involved with the MS back then.

"This is Juan," Maria said, still holding Abel's arm. "He knows some stuff about Detective Guidry.

"Juan, this is my friend. Please tell him what you told me."

"Maria said you wanted to know about that cop, Guidry." Abel nodded. Juan continued, "I seen him a few times back when I was in a gang. Some of my clique was sellin' meth, so I knew what was going on. I didn't do no sellin' myself, but sometimes I had to help out. Like when some money or drugs was moving. I had to be there. Like security."

"How did you see Guidry?"

"Do you know how the drug thing works?" asked Juan.

Abel did. He'd had to mule drugs when he was a teenager to help his family make ends meet while his Uncle Deacon had done a nickel up at Angola. No one pays up front at the street end. Maybe on high the drugs were paid for up front, but in the dealer hierarchy, one level would get the raw pure product without fronting cash, those people would cut it and package it, and then it would work its way down through a network of people until it was on the street corner. The money made a similar trip back up the network. Each level took their allocated profit.

If it wasn't done that way nothing would move because the lower down the totem pole you went, the less likely anybody would be able to get cash together. This system worked because the dealers knew that if they screwed the people above them, they'd be hurt or killed and maybe their family, too.

"The drugs came from the Bastards. I heard they worked for the Bandidos. Our clique got it from them. It would get cut and bagged, then our boys would sell it all over the Ninth."

"I thought the Thirty-Niners and the G-Strip gangs had the Ninth," said Abel.

"Naw, we got some turf, too. Someone worked all that shit out. The morenos have the smack. The Bastards have crystal, and MS-13 sells for them. There was trouble before, and the motorcycle guys were muy horríble, and maybe your amigo Guidry smoothed things over so everybody happy."

"You said you saw Guidry," said Abel.

"Sí, when I used to be in the gang, I would be there when we paid the Bastards for the crystal. The club like to have Guidry with them, so everybody knew they had the NOPD on their side."

"When was the last time you helped out?"

"A couple of years ago. But I heard that Guidry doesn't show up all the time anymore. It's some freaky tall guy and maybe some uniforms."

"Where would this go down?"

"Different place every time. It's a lot of money. People are careful."

"Don't the street dudes turn it in every day?"

"More like every hour. The money is always running, but it slows down as it goes up. The bigger the pile gets, the more security."

Abel asked, "Would you make a statement about Guidry's part and what you witnessed?"

Juan laughed derisively. "Gringo, you are loco!" He looked at Maria.

"Gracias, Juan. Vete, ahora."

Maria waited till Juan was out of earshot, then asked, "Did that help? I should have told you beforehand that this was just between you, me, and Juan. OK? He's not in the gang anymore. Anyway, let's get back to your car. I have some work to do before lunch, and I know you're busy, too."

The drive back was quiet. Abel was mulling over what he'd heard, trying to figure out how to use it and what the next steps were. Maria seemed lost in thought. Abel hoped that she wasn't regretting connecting him with Juan.

As they got near the bakery, Abel directed her to where his truck was parked, and she pulled up behind. When Abel got out, she got out, too, and accompanied him to his vehicle. Abel popped the door locks, and Maria reached out and lightly touched his arm.

"Remember, I'm trusting you to keep Juan out of anything you're doing. The Maras would kill him if something he said came back on them. They'd yellow light him if they knew he even talked to you."

"What's that?"

"He would be beaten severely, almost killed but maybe dropped off at a hospital—given a chance."

"I hope you aren't having second thoughts. Don't worry. I won't say anything that will get Juan in trouble. Hearing from another person that Guidry is up to his neck in drugs and crime is very helpful. It says we are on the right track, and eventually, we're going to get the evidence that will help with André's case, so thank you."

"You're welcome, and now that I know that these guys are involved with that detective, maybe I can ask around and find out more. Maybe I can find out when and where the next handoff is."

"That sounds dangerous! Don't do that!" said Abel.

"I know these people. I've helped many of them. I won't do something stupid."

Abel put his arms around her and hugged her while whispering in her ear, "Be safe. I care about you." Maria tilted her head up and kissed him.

She whispered back, "Maybe this is kind of a date after all, no?"

Knowing he was going to be down in the Ninth, Abel had asked Isabelle the night before if she needed anything from Lovelie Mondesir's apothecary, so after Maria had dropped him off in Bywater, he went back over the canal and navigated to her unusual house.

Just like last time, he rang the bell, the wizened face peered at him through the curtained sidelight, and then the door slowly opened. "What do you need now, boy?" Given that she was probably about a hundred, Abel figured that anybody below sixty looked like a boy to her.

"Isabelle needs a few more things," answered Abel and handed her the short list.

Lovelie stepped out into the morning light and held the list up close to one eye. She moved the list back and forth, apparently trying to find the sweet spot on her retina. "Hmmm, what is she doing?" she mumbled. She turned and slowly shuffled back inside.

Abel followed her and said to her back, "You know we found Didi. He told us you knew where he was and that you were warning him all along." She stopped and slowly turned around, looking up at him through a few wispy strands of hair, her head cocked in that odd way that made her seem like a little bird. She gave a tiny chuckle, then turned and continued past the snake room.

Lovelie put together the bag of supplies, shaking her head the whole time, then ran his VISA card, which still struck Abel funny. This little old lady, probably born during the First World War, was completely caught up with the times.

Abel constantly checked himself so he didn't run over her heels as she shuffled him back to the front door. Closing the door on him, she said, "You tell her boys to look after their mama."

While he was walking to his truck thinking about the old lady's final words a white sedan drove slowly passed. The woman driving turned her head to look at him. She continued staring woodenly as she drove past like some image on the computer screen that scrolled from right to left. Abel knew her.

THIRTY-FIVE

"Did I do OK, jefa?" asked Juan.

"Speak English!" ordered Lúcido, or Maria as she was known to Abel. "You can go now."

"Sí, boss," replied Juan as he exited the cramped office of the El Luz Loco bar.

The Loco was on the fringe of the Ninth Ward and was one of the spoils that transferred to Lúcido in the power vacuum that followed the decimation of the leadership of the New Orleans MS-13 by Abel Kane's crew a couple of years back. Mara Salvatrucha was a gang that had started in Los Angeles in the seventies and eighties. Originally, their purpose had been to protect Salvadoran immigrants, but the MS had since evolved into an international criminal organization.

It was unusual for a woman to run a clique for the Maras, but Lúcido was no ordinary woman. She was formidable.

Normally, the Mara Salvatrucha cliques had a backup leader waiting in the wings so that if the leader was killed, the second-in-command could step into the top spot and they could continue making money without skipping a beat, but Lúcido had engineered the death of leaders number one and two by manipulating the situation with Abel and his crew. Then, she personally murdered the next guy in line. No one else stuck their head up.

She had replaced the dead men by pulling in a female sicario from Honduras—another rarity—and elevated the only other MS-13 member with a brain that she trusted. They sat across from her in the little office, Carlita on the left, a wiry girl in a White man's V-neck T-shirt that contrasted with her arms which were covered in full sleeves of dark green ink, and Luis on the right, next to the doorway, a handsome man in khakis and a starched blue oxford shirt. He resembled George Clooney, a Hispanic George Clooney, and had the bookish air of a professor.

Before Lúcido had promoted him to second-in-command, he'd been the bartender of The Loco and had managed to avoid most of the physical mayhem required from a MS-13 soldier. But he was smart, almost as smart as Lúcido. She and Luis had even been lovers in the past and had eventually parted friends or as close to friends as possible, given her latent sociopathic tendencies.

The three of them had just finished ensuring that Juan would keep his mouth shut about talking with Abel Kane. They waited till Juan had gone, Luis even standing and peeking out of the office door to make sure. When he sat back down, he said, "Lúcido, I still don't get what you're doing with Kane. Why don't you just kill them all and be done with it?" He nodded at Carlita. "Send her up there. That's what she does." Carlita smirked.

"That pendejo and his men hit us for a million dollars. Probably more than a million. They killed Alverez. They killed Hector, my cuñado—the last of my family! And killed how many of our men? What, ten? Just killing Kane isn't enough. I'm going to make him suffer. I don't understand why you don't feel the same way!"

Chapter Thirty-Five

"The time to do something about it was two years ago."

"I've been working this since Hector and Alejandro were killed, but we were in no shape to do anything then. All the leadership was dead. Most of our cash gone. We had to rebuild, and I had to get the clique behind me. Doing something quick that failed would not have helped my long-term plans or my reputation."

Carlita was watching the back and forth, like a police dog, itching for the command to attack. First she looked at Lúcido expectantly, then back at Luis, her expression darkening and a corner of her lip pulling back.

Luis continued to prod, too familiar, like former lovers sometimes did, not meaning any disrespect, but Carlita didn't know the history. He said, "OK, yes, certainly we're stronger now, but I don't get what you're doing. The money is nothing to us now! With the income from the expanded crystal business we've made that back and more. How is dating him going to make up for what they did to us?"

"I'm getting close to him. I'm meeting all the people in his world. I need to find out everything he cares about and all the men in his crew—the men who murdered our men, our leaders. And when the time is right, I'm going to hurt the people closest to him. Take all his money. Take all his men's money. Kill them, then kill him."

"You are making things too complicated. Have our sicario kill them, and move on. You have a business to run. Why don't you tell Guidry that Kane is circling around, asking for information about him? Let him take care of Abel Kane and his crew. You already got him to arrest one of Kane's men, after all. I still can't figure out how you managed that."

"Guidry is a stupid whore. He'll do anything for money. A racist whore. He has a thing for the morenos. That includes us, by the way. He thinks we're barely one step above the Blacks. It's just we're making him money. I gave him more money and pointed him at Kane's gigantic friend. It was like throwing meat in front of a dog. And now all Kane and his men can think about is keeping their friend from going to prison. I'm in their life, and they are oblivious.

"But I'm not having him kill Kane and his men. Guidry already knows too much about us, and I don't want him any deeper in our business. His usefulness is about over.

"And as far as why I am going to all this trouble? It's about leverage. Know what somebody cares about, then you have ultimate power over him, and when I look into his eyes when he sees what I've done, it will be so satisfying.

"But enough of this, Luis! It is the same thing over and over with you. You're always talking about respect. You say you don't get enough respect from our men. Yes, you are organized. You are careful. You are smart. Do you think if that is all you are the soldiers will respect you? To lead, men must admire *and* fear you. Our soldiers know what happened. They didn't expect us to do something immediately, but they expect us to do something eventually. Something terrible and fearsome. They must know we will do what it takes. This is not business. This is personal. For all of us."

THIRTY-SIX

The cell phone quietly rang like an old desk phone, and Abel rolled over in bed and reached for it on the nightstand. It was Maria. "Hola, mijo," she said sweetly. "Did I wake you up again?"

"No, I was just lying here, thinking about you. I'm glad you called. What's going on with you? Are you in bed, too?"

"Are you going to ask me what I'm wearing?" she said in a teasing voice.

Abel laughed. "No . . . but what are you wearing?"

"Oh, you would like it. It's black, and you can see through it. Maybe I should come over tomorrow night and try it on for you."

"Uh," managed Abel, his mind taken over for a second.

"I could come over in the evening, and you could take me on a romantic boat ride on the bayou."

"That sounds awesome."

"I'll bring a little picnic, and you can bring a bottle of wine, OK?" Maria purred. "I'll be at your door around seven thirty. Bye-bye."

Lying there, Abel stared at the flickering patterns from the moonlight through the trees outside his window. The shapes crawled around the wall as the leaves and branches were cast about by the breeze off the bayou. He watched but didn't see them; his mind was on something else.

The sound of a car pulling into the driveway drew Abel out of his chair, and he set his book down and walked to the window next to the front door. He pulled the curtain aside and looked out to the yard, reminding himself of Lovelie Mondesir's actions every time he visited her. He laughed to himself, thinking, *I'm like a hundred-year-old lady*.

Maria walked up the stairs of the wide covered porch and knocked, saying musically, "Abel, I see you."

He opened the door, and he opened his arms wide and hugged her, then pulled her into the living room. "What have we here?" he asked.

Maria held up a basket. "I brought food!" Abel pulled open the basket with a finger and peered in. "Pork pupusas with some sour cabbage and empanadas de leche for dessert," she added.

"Mmmm, sounds good. That will be easy to eat in the boat. I have some white wine in a cooler."

Abel stepped back and appraised her. "Am I wearing the right clothes for a boat trip?" she asked. She had on a short pale green skirt that showed off her legs and a pink tank top, an eye-popping combination.

Just right for the temperature but mosquito bait. "Perfect! We're going to need bug spray when we go out though. The mosquitos get pretty fierce when the sun goes down.

"C'mon." Abel guided her through the kitchen and out the back door, through the screened in porch, and then down the yard past the firepit to the dock, where he had his pirogue tied up. The flat-bottomed boat was all set to go with two paddles that they wouldn't need, two life preservers that he hoped they wouldn't need, and a cooler of wine, which he knew they were going to need.

Maria looked at the paddles dubiously. "We have to row this boat?"

"No, only in an emergency. There's a trolling motor on the back. It does all the work; we just sit back and steer. Here let me help you get in." Abel held her hand as she stepped down and sat, the skirt riding up her legs, giving Abel's heart a jolt.

He climbed in and then leaned over and untied the line holding the pirogue tight to the dock. The boat drifted away from the dock, and Abel flipped the switch on the electric motor. A low whine filled the air as the boat glided out to the middle of the bayou.

Reaching back, he picked up the can of bug spray and said, "Let me spray you, or you're going to get eaten up." Abel leaned forward on his knees and lifted the back of her hair off her neck and gave a quick shot on her neck and shoulders, then handed her the can.

"This won't keep you from eating me up later, will it?" Once again, Abel's heart rate spiked, and his mind went down that path. He laughed. "Let's turn around and go back right now!"

"No, mijo, you promised me a romantic boat ride, and I promised you something else." She used her purring voice. "For later."

Abel laughed again and goosed the throttle on the boat. They surged forward and continued up the bayou. They moved through the water, passing through a tunnel of overarching trees, most of them water oaks draped with Spanish moss, but where the water opened to the sky, the banks were lined with elephant's ear and American holly, which were waiting a few more months to cover themselves in bright red berries.

They reached Abel's favorite spot. The trees pulled back, the banks flattened, and the bayou opened up, allowing the setting sun to illuminate the space in a special light. It was quiet and calm, and it was the one place where he felt connected to the earth and at peace. The feeling that there was some reason to life, some higher spiritual plane, was strong here. He remembered telling Olivia how he felt about the location but didn't break the silence with Maria. Instead, he watched her back as she looked around. He couldn't tell whether she felt the same as he did.

Eventually, they reached a flat open area stretching away from the water on their right. Abel stopped the pirogue and let it drift. He went into tour guide mode. "This is a pig wallow. At night, feral hogs come here and roll around in the mud to cool off and coat their skin to protect it from insect bites. The ground is practically covered with them."

"You're exaggerating!"

"Nope. Every sow produces about ten piglets per year. The population goes up fast."

"You've seen this?"

"We all hunt back here."

"You eat these pigs?" she asked, sounding uncomfortable.

"We usually get the young boars; the old ones taste pretty gamy and wild."

"Mijo, you are like the hunter from Snow White! Don't you think this is a good place to have our picnic?"

No, actually Abel didn't. This was where they had had the confrontation with the MS-13 two years ago. He had very visceral memories of the place. The Maras had attacked them in their homes, and Abel and his crew had escaped into the bayou. The gangbangers had chased them to this place, and Abel and his friends, being in their element, had ended up killing most of them. They had stripped the banger's bodies and left them for the pigs. After a few days, there weren't even bones left.

"Let's go back to that big open area. It will be light there longer. The sun is setting, and this place is already getting dark." Abel reversed course and navigated back to the cathedral-like space.

The setting was beautiful with the sun at the perfect angle to light the opening with an orange light that transitioned to blackness as you looked deeper into the trees. Abel cut the motor, then dropped the anchor, fixing them in the middle of the channel.

Maria gasped. "Look!" A doe and a fawn at the water's edge jerked their heads up and stared at the boat. Slowly they backed into the trees.

Abel smiled. It was why he liked the place. Even the animals felt that it was a safe place. He had come here with Olivia a few times and once with her son as well. They had fished at a boundary of sunlight and shade under a live oak canopy and had caught a fish. Abel could remember the expression of delight on Owen's face. It was one of those memories that stayed alive because you called it forward often.

A rustling brought him out of his reverie, and he reached out to Maria to take the pupusa she offered. He set it on his lap and opened the cooler and pulled out the chilled bottle of wine. The bottle beaded with condensation in the humid evening air.

The food was delicious and they ate in companionable silence, watching a large great white egret fishing in the shallows. The bird was not as skittish as the deer and ignored their presence until Abel let out a contented groan and said, "That was so good!"

"Thank you," Maria said, then carefully inched her way to the back of the boat and sat next to Abel. He put his arm around her, and they sat like that until the sun touched the top of the trees, and Abel turned and kissed her, holding it softly for a moment.

"I think we better get back to your home before it gets too dark," Maria whispered.

The trip back seemed to take longer, Abel not knowing whether it was because it was dark or because of his anticipation of what was to come. He steered the boat to its home by the dock and quickly tied it in place. Jumping out onto the dock, he moved over to Maria and helped her out, then started for the back porch but realized she wasn't following. Instead, she was standing at the end of the dock, first looking upstream, then downstream, as if she was trying to commit the view to memory. Finally, she turned and walked up toward Abel on the lawn. Together, they walked up and into the house.

The light was on in the kitchen, and Callie was sitting at the table with a book and a cup of coffee. "I thought you were on a date," said Abel, a little irked. He had planned on having the whole house to himself with Maria.

"Yeah, so did I," said Callie, sounding bummed. "The guy was nothing like his picture and was pounding shots and super obnoxious. I'm glad I drove separately. I blew off dinner and left."

"That's right, chica! You don't need to settle for some pendejo. Abel tells me how smart you are. Now you and I can get to know each other better."

"Abel, I like this girl!" said Callie.

They all sat at the table for a while, drinking the rest of the wine from the picnic, while the two girls felt each other out and became more familiar. Callie told Maria about Abel, embarrassing him but making Maria laugh. Maria kept the conversation rolling. She had a knack for drawing more and more stories out of Callie, getting her to paint a good picture of what it was like growing up with Abel. He in turn started in on Callie, talking out of school like siblings do, and they continued through another bottle of wine.

Finally, Callie said she was going to bed, and the two women hugged each other. "I'm so happy we had this chance to really talk. I can see why Abel likes you," said Callie. As she left the kitchen, she caught Abel's eye and winked.

Abel started to clean up the table, but Maria grabbed his arm. "Mijo, you can do that tomorrow." She grabbed his arm and led him to the bedroom.

Later, Abel got out of bed and picked the pillows up off the floor and gave one to Maria, then pulled the covers up to her chin. She giggled. "Do you think your sister heard me?"

"I think our neighbors heard you," said Abel.

"Really?"

"No, I'm kidding. We were quiet, and Callie is a deep sleeper." *Not really,* thought Abel ruefully; he knew Callie was gonna bust his chops the next day.

He went to the kitchen and got more wine and brought it back to the bedroom. He handed her the glass and then got into bed next to her. "You know, it's the weirdest thing. The other day I was doing some errands in the Ninth, and when I came out, I swear I saw your cousin drive by."

"It could be. She decided to stay here for a while, so I helped her find a place. But for you to see her? It means we are connected."

It seemed like it to Abel, the way they had kept bumping into each other and that she seemed like she really knew him. It did feel like they were connected, not the same as with Olivia, but it was strong. Maybe you never connected the same way with different people, which made perfect sense but made him feel a little sad.

"Don't you think I should meet all the rest of the people in your life?" she asked, looking him in the eyes.

"Yes, I want you to. Rabbit is having a party to celebrate their baby that is due. He and his wife, Crystal, are having a gender reveal party. Do you want to go to that with me? I can introduce you to just about everybody in my world."

"Oh, mijo, I would love that." She snuggled up to him.

THIRTY-SEVEN

On Saturday afternoon, Abel and Tank were standing in the parking lot in front of Rabbit's father's auto shop. Tank was keeping Abel company while he waited for Maria to arrive before they went in to join Rabbit and Crystal's gender reveal festivities. They were discussing how to get incriminating evidence on Guidry so they could alleviate André's escalating anxiety.

"Harm is getting inside it seems like," said Tank.

"Yeah, but I'm worried it's gonna go too slow, and André's running out of time. We either need to find a person willing to take the stand and blow up Guidry, or we have to get video or some other solid proof that shows he is so morally bankrupt and corrupt that all his actions are discredited. Otherwise, it's just going to be André on the stand putting his word against a bunch of cops, and you know how that's gonna go."

Abel's next words were interrupted as Maria came walking up the street. "Hi Abel, hi Tank. I didn't know it was going to be this big of a fiesta! I had to park like fifty cars back. I was rethinking my shoe choice."

She was wearing spiky heels, and Abel figured the second they got into the backyard, Maria would be punching holes in the lawn. She'd be in her bare feet in a second, like every other girl probably.

Maria got close and wrapped her arms around Tank, giving him a warm hug like she'd known him forever, then moved over to Abel, wrapping him up and packaging a kiss along with it. She stepped back and said, "I'm sorry I'm late."

"No problem, the party's just getting going. C'mon, we'll take you back and introduce you to everybody."

Tank added, "Yeah, they can't wait to meet you. Everybody is a lot more curious about you than whether the baby is going to be a boy or a girl!"

"Oh, great," said Maria. "Abel can't be the only person to have a girlfriend! Don't you have one?"

"Yes, Kisha. I left her back at the party while I was talking to Abel out here. She's probably getting mad that I've been gone so long."

The three of them trekked past the shop on the gravel driveway that passed the junkyard and went all the way back to Rabbit's parents' house. They had been able to hear faint music while they were in front of the shop waiting for Maria, but every step closer to the party, the zydeco got louder and more raucous. As they passed the trees at the rear of the junkyard, the Walker house came into view, a white structure with black shutters and a screened porch that wrapped around the house.

The trio skirted the house and went around back, navigating the ever-growing crowd of people. Lacombe and Slidell were small towns. Actually, almost one small town, they were so close together. So practically everybody who was a long-time resident was invited. Everybody knew everybody, and there was no sense hurting people's feelings when you had a big backyard.

A wall of barbecue smoke hit as they moved past the back of the house into a giant yard filled with pop-up tents, umbrellas, a makeshift stage with the band working furiously, and an array of black cast-iron smokers off to the side. You would think one barbecue pit would be enough if you were from New York City, but this was Louisiana, and there was boudin and andouille sausage, briskets, a whole pig, and rafts of smoked oysters coming off in waves.

Rabbit's parents were stationed at the top of the yard, welcoming the guests as they made their way into the party, and Abel headed directly to them. Anyone could see that Mr. Walker was the oak that spawned the acorn that was Rabbit. Walker was a gangly man with corded hands that no matter how much he had scrubbed, the grease still filled the cuticles and pores of his fingers. A stupid, happy grin was plastered on his face, his two front teeth stained yellow from incessant smoking.

Standing next to Rabbit's daddy was his plump mother. If his father formed Rabbit's body, his mother formed his personality. A torrent of welcome spewed from her as they neared. "Tank! We've been waiting for you! Where's Isabelle? We haven't seen her. Callie's already here. Oh, Abel, this beautiful person must be the girl we've all been hearing about. Welcome, cher!" She stepped up to Maria and enveloped her in a giant embrace.

Abel finished hugging Rabbit's daddy and turned to catch the half smile on Maria's face. They locked eyes and Maria winked at him, acknowledging she knew she was in for an afternoon of over-the-top greetings. The five of them chatted for a few more moments, then Mrs. Walker shooed them into the party with a "Go show off your girl, Abel!"

Abel and Tank knew everybody they encountered so were making slow progress through the crowd when suddenly someone put their arms around Abel from behind and lifted him off the ground.

"Rabbit! Put Abel down! You told me you were going to behave!" scolded Crystal.

As Tank hugged Rabbit, Abel turned to Crystal, amazed at how much bigger she was than the last time he'd seen her. They embraced, Abel leaning in awkwardly over her giant belly to kiss her on the cheek. They both could hear Rabbit chattering to Tank, and Crystal laughed in Abel's ear. "He's beside himself!"

They disengaged, and Rabbit switched his attention from Tank to Maria. "Whoa, Abel you weren't kidding! Maria, you're hot! Way prettier than even he said." Then he clapped Abel on the shoulder. "Way to go, dude."

Crystal rolled her eyes and said, "He's right though. I'm jealous of you! What I wouldn't give to be able to wear that little sundress. You're beautiful, and I can see why Abel is taken with you. I'm Crystal, by the way."

"I'm Maria Portillo. Don't be jealous of me! I envy you. I wish I was going to be a mother; I think about it all the time. You're radiant!"

"Oh, stop. I feel like a beast. I'm huge." Crystal pulled her slightly away from the group of guys, and the two of them continued talking.

While they were gossiping, André, Kisha, and Harm showed up. Kisha clamped onto Tank possessively.

"Man, this is a great party, Rabbit," said André. "I've already eaten two dozen oysters. Then Tank left Kisha alone, and I had to dance about ten songs with her."

"Had to dance with me?" said Kisha.

"Yeah, André. You're lucky anybody will dance with you. Your shirt looks like a sweat grenade blew up in it," said his brother.

"Haha, alright!" said Rabbit, and he yelled over to his wife, "Crystal, stop monopolizing Maria! Abel's got to introduce her to everyone else."

Crystal and Maria edged back into the group, and André put out his hand and said, "Hi, I'm André, and this is Harmon." Harm nodded politely to Maria.

Maria grasped André's upper arm with her left hand and tilted her head up to look at his face. "I've heard so much about you." She glanced at Harm. "I know all about all of you. Abel is so fortunate to have such good friends. It's all he talks about. I can't wait till he meets my friends."

Tank put his arm around Kisha and said, "Maria, this is my girlfriend, Kisha."

Maria held out her hand to shake Kisha's, but Kisha brushed it away and put her arms around Maria. Pulling apart, she said, "I couldn't wait to meet the girl who bagged Abel. He's been moping around for two years, and now look at him." She gestured at Abel. He had a grin on his face, happy that finally all his friends were meeting Maria.

Just then, the band picked up the tempo. "C'mon, let's dance," said Kisha, grabbing Tank. Abel took Maria's hand, and they all headed for the dance floor, which was a portion of lawn in front of the temporary stage.

Soon they were all sweating like André in the August heat as they danced to the heavy beat and the rattling of the frottoir. The dancing was kind of like swing but sexier, more like salsa. Maria picked it up easily. She and Kisha took it next level where Abel and Tank could barely keep up.

Finally, Abel raised his arms yelling, "I give!" and took Maria's hand and pulled her out of the crush. "Let's grab some of this food." They made their way to the tables by the smoking barbecue pits and several white pop-up tents lined up in a row that shaded tables of food.

They each picked up paper plates, and Abel doubled up his plate, knowing he was going to need the extra support. They worked their way down the length of the buffet, Maria taking little bits here and there, while Abel loaded up on brisket coated with crispy black bark, spicy boudin, and a pile of blackened shrimp. He found room on the extra-large plate to cram on potato salad and corn and bacon maque choux. Fried okra was tucked into the crevices, and then finally he put a layer of smoked oysters and raw oysters on top.

Carrying the precarious structure, he and Maria walked to the tables, Abel walking gingerly to avoid losing the second story of oysters fragilely balanced on the meat foundation. They found an empty table and Maria sat. "Do you want beer or wine?" he asked.

He came back with two bottles of beer and placed the frosty bottle of Abita in front of Maria, tears of water dripping immediately off the bottle onto the table where they formed a pool. She picked it up and drank a long swallow, thirsty from the dancing. She looked at Abel's plate and chuckled. "Mijo, your appetite still amazes me! I can't figure out why you don't weigh three hundred pounds."

They ate for a while, then Callie appeared and sat down and said, "I'm glad you're here, Maria. I'm tired of people asking me when you two were going to show up." She looked at Maria's plate, then Abel's. "I guess my brother didn't leave you any food. You probably haven't been to a full-on Cajun barbecue before with Abel. You need to make sure you get in the line ahead of him if you don't want to go hungry."

Maria laughed, then said, "Ahhh, he's just a growing boy, aren't you, mijo?" Then, she leaned over and kissed his cheek and ruffled his hair.

Abel pushed himself away from the table and said, "Maybe I should stop. I'm getting full."

"Yeah, you're the master of restraint. You already ate everything but one oyster," said Callie, laughing.

"Oh, I missed that!" He brought it to his lips and nudged it into his mouth with the little fork.

Suddenly, André plopped into a seat at the table followed by Tank and Kisha. "They're getting ready to speak. Rabbit's all excited about it," said Tank.

A server came by with a tray of fizzing champagne flutes, placing them on the table, and admonishing them that it was for the toasts. The band suddenly stopped playing. There was a squawk of feedback and then a clatter as Rabbit dragged a dining room chair onto the plywood stage and climbed up, standing above the crowd with a microphone in one hand and a glass of champagne in the other.

Abel and the rest stood so they could see above all the people. Harm and Crystal were on each side of Rabbit with both sets of parents, all holding flutes of champagne which glowed golden in the late afternoon sun.

Then Rabbit was Rabbit, thanking everybody for coming, cracking his usual jokes, getting sentimental for a minute talking about how much he loved Crystal and how excited he was about being a father, how he and Crystal wanted to be as good of parents as their own. He waved his arm expansively over the crowd and said he was glad that his kid was going to get to grow up with all his friends and family. He pointed down at Harm with the microphone, then said, "And my best friend, Harmon, has agreed to be the godfather!" The crowd cheered.

When they quieted, Rabbit continued, "Now everybody raise your glass to my wife, Crystal, who's done all the hard work so far!" A hundred or more glasses were raised, with Rabbit's the highest, glinting in the sun.

Suddenly, the wine in his glass turned blue. Then here and there in the crowd, peoples' glasses began changing from gold to blue also. People started laughing and cheering again, but then other glasses began to turn a pinkish hue. People were holding blue and pink glasses, and a confused buzz went through the group of partiers.

Rabbit gave the confusion a chance to build, stretching out the drama, then said, "HA! I know you're confused by our big reveal. Or some of you think it didn't work. NO, it worked perfectly! We have big news! We're having twins! A boy and a girl!" Then, he tossed down his drink.

The crowd swamped the stage knocking Rabbit off the chair, but the microphone was still on, broadcasting the congratulations and best wishes out across the lawn.

"Holy shit," said Tank. "I didn't see that coming!"

Abel said, "Yeah, vintage Rabbit." He headed for the stage with the rest of the crew.

Later, after the excitement had quieted some, Abel, Tank, and the others were able to get together with Rabbit, Crystal, and Harm. The group was still bubbling with excitement, laughing and high on their joy for the prospective parents, the first of their group to move on to the next stage of life.

"How did you make the champagne do that all at the same time?" asked André.

"Your mother, of course! Isabelle helped me set it up. Although, she didn't really want me to do that. She thought I should have just kept it between me and Crystal, but Crystal wanted the big gender reveal thing, so finally Belle relented and helped."

"But how did you get it to turn all at once?" asked Maria.

"Harm was watching the time and kept saying, 'Keep talking' till the right amount of time had gone by. When he told me to wrap it up, I made the toast."

"I still don't get it," said Abel.

"Voodoo magic," said André in a spooky voice.

"Did you guys notice it smelled funny when it turned color?" said Harm. "I was afraid to drink it."

Callie teased, "You better get used to funky smells now that you're gonna be changing their babies' diapers."

"Wait, what? The godfather doesn't have to change diapers. Does he, Rabbit?" Harm had an aghast look on his face. "You didn't tell me that!"

"Uh-oh," said Tank, and he abruptly elbowed Abel and tipped his head. "Look!"

Abel saw his former girlfriend, Olivia, walking across the lawn toward the group.

"Congratulations, Rabbit! Congratulations, Crystal!" she said when she reached them. She embraced Crystal and then stepped back, appraising her. "You look beautiful! And with twins. That's so exciting! I'm sorry I wasn't here for the big reveal. I heard it was amazing."

She looked around at the group, fixing her gaze on Abel and Maria. There was an awkward pause. "That's Abel's new girlfriend, Maria," blurted Rabbit, not able to handle the uncomfortable situation for even a second.

Abel said, "Hi Olivia, this is Maria; Maria this is Olivia, my former girlfriend."

"Nice to meet you, Maria."

"You look older than I was expecting," said Maria. "I thought you would be his age or younger for some reason."

"I am younger than Abel, and what business is it of yours how old I am?"

"I'm sorry, you just must be tired." She eyed Olivia's dress. "And too busy to shop."

Abel started to say, "I think—" when Olivia interrupted him.

"You know, I didn't expect Abel to bring a street pro to a baby shower. Looks like we both got a surprise!"

Maria's face darkened, and she stepped toward Olivia.

"Holy shit! There's gonna be a catfight!" Rabbit whisper-yelled to Harm.

THIRTY-EIGHT

allie watched Abel step between Maria and Olivia. Maria's face was contorted in stormy anger. But then, instantly, her rage dissipated, and Maria's face became calm like the surface of the bayou.

As Abel backed away from Maria, he gave Callie a look. Callie took Olivia's arm and said, "C'mon!" She guided Olivia away from the group and took her over to the tables by the barbecues at the far side of the yard. On the way, she grabbed two beers from under the tent. "Let's sit," she said to Olivia.

"No, I just want to go! Everybody's staring at me."

"OK, I'll walk you to your car." Callie handed the beer to Olivia. "This'll help."

They walked around the front of the house. "I'm parked in the lot in front of the garage," said Olivia.

When they got to the garage, Olivia pointed out her car, a dark metallic flake Corolla that changed colors between blue, purple, and black as they approached.

"Wow, nicer car than that old wreck you used to have."

"Yeah, I got a better job. It was used. Someday, I'll be able to afford a new car," she said as she walked around the car to the driver's door.

"Wait, don't leave yet," Callie said as she leaned against the car parked next to Olivia's.

Olivia in turn leaned against her Toyota and sipped her beer. "I just came to wish Rabbit and Crystal good luck. I know Abel and I aren't together, but that doesn't mean I have to turn my back on them and Tank and everybody, right?"

"Yeah, I know. I get it."

"I wasn't trying to start any trouble. I just saw you all there and thought it would be rude and chickenshit to not go up and say hi like a grown-up. I wouldn't have gone over there if I had known Abel was there with a new girlfriend."

"He said he saw you and Owen at the grocery store the other day. He should have mentioned he was seeing someone then. We talked about it, and I gave him shit for not telling you."

"Is he serious about that bitch?"

"She's not a bitch. At least, I've never seen that. I don't know what happened. Maybe she was jealous. You look great. And maybe she senses that Abel still has feelings for you. You're a threat."

"He still has feelings?"

"Olivia, be honest. You didn't come here just to congratulate Rabbit and Crystal. You were hoping to see Abel, weren't you?"

"I told myself it was just to see Rabbit and Crystal, but maybe underneath I was hoping to talk to him. I guess I still have feelings for him. But it looks like he's moved on."

"I know that you guys weren't together very long before, but Abel was super upset. He was always a little bit sad underneath; God knows he had his reasons. But when you guys met, he was truly one hundred percent happy. I'd never ever seen him like that. And basically, he's been walking around like a zombie since all that stuff happened.

Chapter Thirty-Eight

"He's not like that with this girl. And anyway, I know he still loves you. You need to talk with him before he gets too far down the road with this girl, if you still want to be with him."

Olivia opened the door to her car, pausing before she got in. "Yeah, I better figure out what I really want. Easy right?" She sat, then pulled the door shut.

Callie watched Olivia drive away, staring at the car until it disappeared, thinking about her big brother.

Meanwhile, back at the party, Abel had just finished discussing what had happened with Maria. He'd never seen her angry before, so he was unsettled. She hadn't been that contrite and felt her behavior had been justified, reasoning that Olivia had had two years to fix things up with Abel and she hadn't. Maria wrapped up her explanation: "And then she shows up out of the blue all 'Hi Rabbit, congratulations Crystal, oh Abel, I miss you,' and shit. I mean, she knew I was with you."

Abel could see arguing further was pointless and was saved from more fruitless discussion by the arrival of Isabelle.

"Hi cher, so this is your new friend I've heard so much about. Maria, is it? I'm Isabelle Cheval, Thomas and André's mother."

"Thomas?" said Maria.

Abel jumped in. "Tank's real name. I almost forget sometimes. I've been calling him Tank since the day I met him in third grade."

"Oh!" said Maria with a big smile, seemingly recovered from the previous drama. "I'm pleased to meet you. Thomas and André are great guys."

"Thank you. I'm so glad you're here with Abel. He's been alone too long."

Isabelle acted genuinely pleased to meet Maria, but something seemed off underneath her superficial cheer.

Abel had known Tank's mother since he was a kid; she was the closest thing he had to a mother, and he could detect a note of something other than friendliness in the set of her mouth.

They all chatted about Rabbit and Crystal's impending twins for a few more minutes, then Maria gently excused herself, explaining she had another event. Isabelle squeezed Maria's hand and moved on, then Abel walked Maria back to the street where she was parked.

At the car, Maria hugged Abel and then said, "I guess I overreacted to Olivia. She hit a nerve, and I said some mean things. I hope you're not mad at me and that your friends don't think I'm a psycho."

"How could I be mad at you? Anyway, my friends have seen everything. Don't worry. It's probably forgotten already."

The rest of Abel's crew were still standing in a loose group. They watched Abel and Maria walk off, and as soon as they rounded the corner of the house, Rabbit said, "Wow, that was like dropping a match in a can of gasoline sitting on a pile of dynamite." He threw his hands up in the air. "BOOM!"

"Yeah, lucky Abel stepped in front of Maria or Olivia's face woulda been rearranged," said Tank.

André said, "Classic Rabbit party! We'll be talking about this for a while!"

"**R**andy! This is John Smith," announced Harm through his burner.

"Hey, man!"

"Uh, I tried to do my NOPD application, and I'm stuck on the question about my discharge. I'm not sure how to answer that."

"Look, I'm busy right now, but do you want to come by my place tonight after work? We can have a few beers, and I'll help you with the application. You're doing the online app, right?"

"Yeah, online. Tonight, sounds good. Can you text me your address again?"

"Sure. I'll see you around seven?"

"A'write. I'll get out of your hair, thanks."

Later that night, Harm pulled up in front of Williams's house in one of Rabbit's loaners from his fleet of anonymous vehicles that he maintained. As usual, it was nondescript on the outside but souped up on the inside. This time Rabbit gave him a Honda Civic as a joke, knowing that having to drive a rice burner would freak him out. Harm liked to drive big vehicles with lots of metal, the better to stop a bullet. Harm took the car but hated how all the other cars on the road towered over him.

The second Harm knocked on Randy's door, it was yanked open, just like Williams had been waiting on the other side, desperate for John Smith to show. *Jesus*, thought Harm, *this guy is kinda pathetic.*

Randy stepped out and gave him a man hug like they were long lost friends. "C'mon in, dude. Let me show you what I've been working on since you were here."

It was only a few days since Harm had been there, so the guy was an eager beaver or maybe just had no social life, no family, no friends, or nothing else to do. His previous assessment of the guy being kinda lonely seemed accurate.

For a second, as Randy showed him his latest projects, Harm forgot that Williams was the enemy. He actually enjoyed seeing what Randy had done with the place in the short time. In Harm's fantasy world, he'd have a house and a wife like Rabbit, and they'd be fixing up their own place together. Far in the distance, he felt an ache. Finally, they landed in the kitchen.

They sat at the kitchen table where Randy had set up his laptop. Harm surveyed the room. The remodel was complete, and the room was stocked with high-end appliances. He thought about his mama and their old avocado-colored appliances. There was no way this guy afforded all this on a cop's salary.

"Let's get your application in," said Randy, interrupting Harm's thoughts.

"So the problem was that when I filled out the application, it asked about my military service. If I put I was dishonorably discharged, it says my application is going to be disqualified automatically. The thing is, I wasn't *dishonorably discharged*, I was *discharged without honor*."

"I don't remember that question. What do they ask exactly?"

Chapter Thirty-Nine

"If I was dishonorably discharged."

"So, the answer is no, you weren't dishonorably discharged."

"Yeah, but are they going to bag me during the interview?"

"I don't know. Let me call a guy I know tomorrow. And maybe if you pass the online questionnaire part, we can do something for you in the interview. Guidry has a lot of reach.

"Speaking of which, I talked to the man, and he thinks we should get you involved in some of the other things we are doing. Kinda like a tryout. Maybe start getting you some money on the side."

"What? I could always use a little more scratch."

"It's not police work. Not sanctioned by NOPD. It's just some security work we're doing on our own time, so it doesn't matter that you aren't on the force. Have you ever heard of the Stand Tall Boys?"

"Vaguely. Aren't they those white supremacists that are always stirring shit up?"

"They're white nationalists. Something different. They're just lookin' out for the White man who can't catch a break anymore. They go back all the way to the end of the Vietnam War when the federal government betrayed the soldiers."

Harm smelled bullshit but didn't follow up, figuring that Williams was just spewing talking points of which he had no clue.

"Basically, they're dudes that refuse to apologize for creating the modern world. Who built this country? We did, and we want to restore things so that we get what we deserve. We need to close the border, make sure that we can keep our weapons so that the government doesn't overreach, and strengthen the families. You know, the man does what he's supposed to do. Bring home a paycheck and support his wife, who's taking care of things in the home."

Harm doubted that Randy had thought up any of that himself, but he could tell that Williams believed what he was saying. At the end of his spiel, he was spraying saliva with vehemence. He figured that maybe Guidry felt that way too somewhat, but he firmly believed that that asshole was just chasing the money.

"Is the man himself going to be at this rally?" asked Harm.

"You mean Guidry? Yeah, he'll be there organizing the guys."

"I've thought about this shit a lot. When I got back from the 'stan, I was worse off than when I went in. I was trying to do the right things by my men, and they fucked me over. I'm in."

"Great!" said Williams excitedly. "Guidry is firming up the details. It's this weekend, up in Houston. We can carpool." No way was Harm going to carpool with this guy.

"You said we'd be doing security. What do you actually mean by that?" asked Harm.

"The way these things go, there's usually some screaming liberals protesting. You know, walking around with signs and shit. But they're pussies. The real problem is Antifa. Those bastards think we're trying to take over the country, and they aren't afraid to get tough."

"OK, I've heard of Antifa, but I don't know much about 'em," said Harm, although he actually had a pretty good idea what they stood for. They were a loose group of far-left militants that opposed what they believed were fascist, racist, or otherwise right-wing extremists. He just wanted to hear what these tools thought of them.

"Like I said, they think we want to do a coup or something—think we want to take over. We don't want to blow up America. We love America! We just want what we deserve and to go back to the way things were, where the White men who did all the work to build this country were treated with respect and were the head of the family.

You know, where women and Blacks and spics all know their place. Get the country back to being God fearing and righteous, like it says in the Bible."

Harm doubted that this dipshit had ever cracked open a Bible. As far as he could tell, none of these people said anything that remotely correlated with the words of Jesus. Not that he was an expert or anything. He never went to church. But he could tell BS when he heard it. This was just another bunch of people grabbing for power and cash.

"So how tough are these mofos?"

"We've had some run-ins with them, and it's gotten physical. It seems like it's escalating. It could get dicey. Are you up for it?"

"Am I allowed to bring a gun? Or two?"

"We'll all be armed."

"Yeah then, no problem. Look, I've gotta run, but give me a call as soon as you get the details from Guidry so I have time to get my shit together."

Randy walked Harm to the door and gave him another man hug on his way out. Harm couldn't leave fast enough.

FORTY

E ven though Harm had Guidry and André on his mind, it was Friday—payday. The day that he made himself available to his clients to take their payments. That meant he had to set up at his usual place, the decrepit bar where he'd got his nose banged up the last time he was there. Given all that had been going on it seemed ages ago, although his nose was still tender, and a yellow crescent could still be seen under his eye.

He'd gotten there at three thirty and parked himself at a table with his back jammed into the rear corner of the room where he had a good eye on the entrance. He nursed a cup of coffee while he waited for the first mope to show up. In general, he didn't have to go after the guys that owed Maroni. They all knew that if they missed, they'd end up owing a lot more money. Further, they'd heard of people getting their legs broken or other misfortunes for being delinquent.

The negative consequences for not paying off their loans were mostly mythical though, because if you made a practice of breaking a guy's leg or kneecaps, then how was he gonna work and ultimately pay you back? That's not to say it never happened. It was just infrequent, very infrequent. Rarely did things escalate to physical violence like Harm's last altercation with Pete, where he'd ended up in the alley behind the bar with Pete who got in a lucky strike on Harm's nose.

Harm had started out with Maroni in the leg-breaker role, being called in whenever that was needed, which was fairly often across Maroni's whole organization, but had since graduated to handling loan origination and collection.

Most of the borrowers had blown credit, and Maroni's loan sharking was their only outside source of money other than working, so they made an effort to be responsible—at least the kind of responsible that a gambler or guy that could barely make ends meet and had an emergency could manage. That meant they mostly ended up eventually paying back the loan and the vig.

For Harm, it was an exercise in trying to maximize the collections. He worked with the delinquents, sometimes cutting them slack, sometimes talking tough, sometimes beating on some dude who was egregiously stringing him along, just to send a message to all the other guys. It was a bit of a dance, with a little acting thrown in, but ultimately basic customer service. He was like the loan officer in a bank except that it was illegal, and the vig or interest was outrageous and highly profitable to Maroni. And just like Bank of America, it was Harm's job to loan money and generate more profits.

One of the things Harm found interesting about the whole process was that after a certain amount of dealing with a borrower, he sometimes became their confidant or therapist. Maybe it was just because he was sitting behind the table, or maybe it was because of the balance of power since he controlled the money. He wondered whether it was simply due to the mope having to own up to somehow screwing up his life so bad that he had to go to a shark for help, that asking for life coaching wasn't that much of a leap.

In any case, it was not a role he wanted. He was probably the last guy on earth who should be giving out advice to anybody, given that he'd been kicked out of the military, lived with his mom, and was strong-arming for the mob. That said, when some dude asked for his advice and the answer was obvious, he was gonna give it.

He was thinking about the guy from last Friday, who had described all his money woes and wanted to know which thing he should pay off first. Harm knew it was cutting into his own end, but he told the guy that it didn't make any sense to borrow money from Maroni at their outlandish rate to pay off another debt. That was a merry-go-round that was never going to stop turning. But did the guy listen? Apparently, the collector calling him to pay off a medical bill in the present seemed worse to the guy than Harm or another of Maroni's minions coming after him in the future. Maybe the unpaid medical bill was blocking some needed medical care that was urgently needed.

The more you questioned these guys, the deeper into their lives you fell, and the weight of it all started to press on you, too. As Harm was ruminating, he'd been casually watching the door, expecting to see one of his loanees trickle in. Instead, a woman stepped through the door, the bright outside light putting her in silhouette. When the door closed behind her, her face became clear. It was Maria. What the fuck?

She didn't notice him back in the corner as she made her way to the bar and leaned in to talk to the bartender. The low murmur of conversation reached him, but he couldn't make it out. The bartender stood up straight and waved his arm around the bar. Harm could hear the negative tone in his voice and watched Maria turn to look, following his expansive gesture.

She saw him sitting in the corner, and there was a sudden expression of recognition in her face. She walked towards him.

"Hi, Harm! Wow! Small world. What are you doing here?"

"I meet with my clients here on Fridays. They'll start coming in a few minutes. But why are you here?"

"One of my charges is in trouble, and he hangs out in this place. I set him up with a job, and the business owner told me he hasn't been showing up. I went to a lot of trouble to get him that job, and he's got a baby and a baby mama to support. I'm actually kind of pissed and am trying to track him down. Do you mind if I sit?"

"No, have a seat."

"Ay, I'm tired. I've been looking all over, and it's hot out there."

"Yes, that's one reason I do business here. The place is a dive, but they aren't stingy with the AC."

"So, Harm, Abel tells me you guys go way back. How did you all get together?"

"I'm a couple of years older than Tank, Abel, and Rabbit, but Rabbit and I were best friends and he was friends with Abel and Tank, so we all started hanging out. There's not much to do in Lacombe, we lived near each other, and we all liked to hunt and fish.

"Didn't Abel tell you all that?"

"Probably, but it's hard to remember it all. He's got a lot of friends. Did you work with him before he was doing this bail recovery job?"

Harm wondered why she cared. Maybe she was just trying to make small talk. "Yes. I helped his Uncle Deacon at his pawnshop, too. His uncle put us all to work."

Maria switched gears. "I didn't see you with anybody at Rabbit's party. I figured a handsome guy like you would have girls chasing after him. You are muy guapo."

The way she said the last bit kinda made Harm uncomfortable. It wasn't what she said, it was more how she said it. She had like a force field she projected—an animal, sexual vibe. He could literally feel it. It didn't feel right; she was Abel's girl. "Uh, no, not right now. I'm in transition."

From what to what, he didn't know. He hadn't had a real girlfriend in a while and didn't really feel motivated to get one at the moment. Somehow, it felt like if he did that, it would be the end of his dream about being with Callie, and he guessed he wasn't ready to do that, even though everybody told him it was never happening.

She switched subjects again. "I'm worried about André. Helping him and paying legal fees costs a lot of money. It doesn't seem like you guys are rolling in that kind of cash. Abel said it wasn't a problem, but I'm worried."

"I think we have it covered," said Harm.

"I don't think bounty hunters make very much money, at least the way Abel described it. Did you guys make a lot when you were working for his uncle?"

Harm was getting a little uncomfortable with this line of questions. In fact, all her questions were uncomfortable. Pretty much talking to anybody other than his mother and Rabbit and the rest of the guys was a little difficult for him. "Uh, we're all chipping in some, and André has a good job. But maybe you should ask Abel this stuff?"

"Yeah, you're right. And anyways, I have to get out here and track this kid down. If he doesn't get back to work, he's gonna get fired." She pushed the chair back and stood.

As she started edging away from the table, she blasted him in the eyes with a piercing look. Harm didn't know what to make of it. Was it a come-on? Was it anger? Whatever it was, it was intense, and he was glad to see her go.

He sat there for a few minutes, thinking about what had just happened. It was weird. The more he thought about it, the more unsettled he became. The tone and the questions were wrong somehow. He felt like he had to tell Abel, but how do you tell your friend that you think something is really wrong with his new girlfriend?

On his way out of New Orleans, he called Abel and told him he was stopping by later, and then he spent the rest of the drive home thinking about what he would say or whether he should say anything at all. He'd landed on saying something by about fifty-one percent to forty-nine, so he was worried how Abel would take what he had to say. Abel was a fair guy, but even good friends could get crosswise if you messed with their love life.

FORTY-ONE

It was after nine, and Harm and Abel were sitting on the back porch drinking beers with the lights out, watching the fireflies flicker down by the bank of the bayou. They'd been idly talking about what it was like working for Maroni, when Abel said, "So what's on your mind? I know you didn't come over here to talk about work."

Harm shifted in his seat uncomfortably. "I don't know how to say this."

"Spit it out, dude. You know we can talk about anything."

"I know, but I could be completely off base. You can just tell me I'm an asshole and to fuck off, OK? It's about Maria."

"C'mon, man, what?"

"I think there's something off with her." Abel stayed quiet. "I was sitting in my spot down at Doucet's, you know, that dive bar near the port, waiting for guys to show up to make their loan payments, and Maria walks in."

"What?"

"Yeah, small world, right? She talks to the bartender for a minute, then she sees me and comes over. We went through the whole it's-a-coincidence thing. But the thing is, it didn't feel like random."

"Did she tell you why she was there?"

"Yeah, she said she was lookin' for someone, and this was his hangout. I mean, it could be." He shrugged his shoulders. "But the vibe I got was, she was lookin' for me. She started pumping me for information the second she sat down on how much money we had and what I used to do for Deacon. She made it sound like she was just concerned about André and paying for his legal fees and shit."

"What did you say?"

"I said we had it covered, but she should talk to you."

"It sounds to me like she's just trying to make friends with all of you guys, trying to fit in."

"Probably, right? You know I'm not very good at reading people sometimes, so this is probably way off, but I felt like she was coming on to me. She said some things."

"Like what?"

"Uh, that I should have girls crawling all over me and that I was handsome and shit."

Abel laughed. "Dude, you are handsome! She was just trying to get on your good side. You're quiet and maybe a little intimidating, and she was trying to break the ice."

"Yeah, maybe. To tell you the truth, at the end, I couldn't tell whether she was making a move or super angry at me."

Abel laughed again. "Join the club. Ya think I can figure women out? Look what fuckin' happened when Olivia showed up at Rabbit's. Look man, don't worry about it. She can be intense. She's one of those fiery Latin women. I'm still getting used to it."

"You're right. I've blown this all out of proportion."

Now that Harm had gotten that off his chest, he relaxed. They pounded a few more beers and strategized about Guidry and the Stand Tall Boys rally that was happening the next weekend up in Houston, then Tank and André showed up.

Tank grabbed his beer and sat down. "Who called this meeting?"

André said, "I think it was Abel. He texted that he had a cooler of Abita. It's good timing because we should talk about The Blue Wall data that I've been messing with."

"Weren't you going through all that to see if there were other arrests like you and Didi?" Abel asked.

"Yeah, I went through the whiteboard stuff and some records off the hard drive and found five other situations like mine. Black guys and Mexicans having rough arrests and having dope planted on them."

"How do you know that?" asked Harm.

"Some guys were in the parish jail, so I visited them, and when they heard what happened to me, they told me their story. They all denied that they had drugs on them—well, at least hard drugs. Some people I couldn't track down, but I did talk to their families."

"That's good. What did Hebert say?" asked Abel.

"That it was going to be helpful but probably not be enough. Like when I got arrested, there were four cops including Guidry and just me. So, their word against mine. And all the other arrests were probably the same situation."

Tank said, "We need more. We have to dump so much shit on Guidry and his guys that the judge and jury can't ignore the smell."

"Yeah, the rally is this weekend. Williams and Guidry basically want me there to help with security. Williams wanted me to carpool with him, but I'm driving up to Houston and meeting him there."

"Tank and I will head up there, too. We'll lurk around and keep an eye on Harm and see if we can catch Guidry and his boys doing anything illegal or at least over-the-top white supremacist stuff," said Abel.

"If we get Tank arrested, Isabelle is gonna start doing the dark voodoo on us," said Harm.

"Man, that's not funny. I'm worried about her," said André. "She's hardly talking to us. She is up in her room doing something. I don't know what. Or talking on the phone with Lovelie, and if we show up, she gets all quiet and whispery and shit. She's hiding something."

"She's getting worse. I think she really does have Alzheimer's," added Tank.

"When I saw her, she seemed fine," said Harm.

"When was this?" asked Tank.

"A while ago. She had me take her down to talk to Guidry."

"And you are telling us, now?" said Tank, his voice rising. "What the fuck?"

"What was I supposed to do? She made me promise not to tell you guys. You remember what she did to Garcia and those other MS-13 assholes. I don't want to get on her bad side."

"My mama is never gonna do any bad shit to you, Harm. You know that, man," said André.

"I hate to break it to you guys, but I've seen some spooky stuff with her. She's had me do some things. You know I love your mama, but she shows me a different side than what you all see. It's like she thinks I'm on her team. Like me and she have to do the bad stuff, to protect all you guys. Man, I don't know. She always says don't tell y'all."

Tank asked, "Well, what did she say to Guidry?"

"She wouldn't let me come in to see him with her. It was weird though. Real hot outside and she was all dressed up, even wearing long gloves like she was at a party or something."

No one had a solid guess for what she was up to. André figured she was down there begging on his behalf.

Harm said, "You know, I hear you guys tease her and are skeptical, especially you Abel. But I've seen some stuff. Do you remember when I hit Alverez's house a couple of years ago? She had me get some of his hair from his hairbrush. When I dropped it off afterward, she was not your mama. She was something else. Scared the piss out of me, and you guys know I don't scare easy."

They talked it over some more, but by then they were all half in the bag and weren't getting anywhere, so they called it.

Abel went in and tried to go to bed. He was in a weird sleep limbo when he thought he heard a knock on the door. He ignored it. Then, the doorbell rang. He groaned and rolled out of bed, taking two tries to get his pants back on. Jesus, it was almost midnight.

FORTY-TWO

Abel peered through the sidelight. It was Olivia. He flipped the dead bolt and yanked open the door. "What? What's wrong? Are you OK?" he asked blearily.

"Uh, yeah. I'm sorry for coming this late. I thought you always went to bed late. At least, you used to."

"The guys were all over here. I had a few beers—made me sleepy."

"Are you going to ask me in or just talk to me on your porch?"

"No, sorry, c'mon in." He backed up and waved her in. "Make yourself comfortable. Can I get you a drink?"

"You got any beer in your fridge?"

Abel laughed. "Help yourself. I'm going to grab a shirt."

He came back into the front room and sat across from Olivia. She'd gotten him a glass of water and an Abita for herself. She nodded at the water. "Figured you needed that more than another beer."

"You got that right. I can't drink like that anymore."

"Dude, you're twenty-nine. You're not over the hill yet."

"Yeah, I guess. I think I just fell asleep, and then the doorbell rang. I feel out of it. What's up? Is Owen alright?"

"Yeah, he's fine. My mother is watching him. By now he's been asleep for about four hours."

"Speaking of your mother, how's she doing? Is she still working?"

"She's working part time. Things are gonna get easier in the fall. Owen will be at school most of the day. My mom's going to be working less, so she can watch Owen when he gets home from school, and that will free me up so that I can do more studying and work more hours."

"That's good. Owen sure seemed excited about school."

"Do you remember way back, when school was a fun thing to do?" Olivia asked.

"Yeah. I can remember the day I met Tank because René and I had gotten into a big fight with Henrí—some bully. I can remember it like it was yesterday. Tank jumped in and helped. He started pounding on Henrí and never stopped. That's why we called him Tank."

"And you guys are still friends today. It's a hard thing to do to stay friends with someone. It always seems like something eventually happens and blows it up. Kinda like what happened at Rabbit's party. I'm sorry for how I acted. I'm embarrassed, and it makes me cringe to think of it."

"Ahhh, don't worry about it. Every party has some drama. And to be honest, it was Maria who acted out. I don't know what came over her. I haven't seen her act like that before. She said the next time she sees you she'll make it right."

"Really?"

"Her exact words were 'You'll see. We'll be good friends.'"

"I'll believe that when I see it."

Abel laughed. "She's pretty intense."

"You like that?" Oliva asked, with a certain tone, the one Callie was always using with him.

"Uh, I just started seeing her. Don't know where it's going."

"Where do *we* stand?" She stared at him, almost belligerently. "Are we done for good?"

"Wait a second," said Abel. "You were the one that called it quits."

"What did you expect me to do? You put me and Owen in danger!"

"Time out!" Abel said angrily. "What are you doing? Why are you here? You know I'm sorry. If I could take it all back, I would."

"I don't know why I'm here!" said Olivia, instantly contrite. "I'm all mixed up." A tear rolled down Olivia's face. "I don't want to lose you."

"You just see I have a girlfriend, and now you want me because you can't have me," Abel said bitterly.

"No, that's not it. I miss you. I know I said I needed time to figure things out. And when I saw you at the grocery store, it got crystal clear to me. Why was I upset about something between your uncle and my father? We were both victims. My dad has been dead for twelve years. Deacon's dead, Hennie's dead. Your cousin René is dead. At least you have your sister and your friends. I've got my mom and Owen.

"You're not robbing anymore, and I want you in my life. I want you in Owen's life, and I saw you with him in the store. You want him in your life."

"Why did you wait till I was seeing someone else?"

"Is it too late?"

"I don't know."

"We already have something. Doesn't that count more than you just starting out with a person you hardly know? Callie told me you've been moping around for two years. Are you all of a sudden over me? I mean I get it, if that's the case. Maria is awesome looking, but I don't know, and it's not fair for me to say, but I get bad vibes from her."

"I guess I just gave up, and when this girl popped into my life, I suddenly started feeling good again. But then I saw you and Owen, and it brought back a flood of feelings. I miss the little guy."

"He misses you, too. After he saw you, he couldn't stop talking about you and going fishing and were you going to come over and stuff like that. He's growing up, and he needs a good man around. How else is he gonna know how to grow up right? I mean, know all that man stuff you're supposed to know. If he's just around me and my mom, it's gonna warp him." She laughed.

"You want us to get back together? Is that why you came over?"

"Yeah, I guess. I told myself that I just wanted to apologize for acting like a jerk at the party, but I probably was hoping deep down that we could put all the bullshit behind us and move forward together. I'm so proud of you for getting out of the Life."

"I feel like my emotions are being jerked back and forth."

"Are you mad at me? Are we done?"

"No, I feel confused. I finally felt like I was moving on with my life. And now this."

"I'm sorry. I guess I was just hoping it wasn't too late."

"I never felt something for anyone like I felt with you and Owen. You guys made me feel good inside. It felt right. But then all that stuff happened. A part of me knew it was never going to be possible, and when you said we were over it was like, of course, how could we be together? But I never gave up, and then Maria showed up, and I started to let it go.

"I think I need some time to get my head on straight so that I can say hell yes or hell no. Right now, my feelings are just swirling around. I had finally decided you were gone for good, and now you're telling me you're not. It's going to take me a minute."

"I know you're confused and probably mad at me, but is there a chance for us, do you think? Do you still have feelings for me?"

"I don't think I've ever stopped having feelings for you. But now things are all complicated."

"Yeah and I woke you up, and you're half drunk and I'm pressuring you. I'm gonna take off and let you go back to sleep. Just promise me you'll think about it, and call me no matter what side you land on. You owe me that." She gave Abel a quick hug, then let herself out. Abel stood there and watched her go.

He went back to his bedroom and started climbing back into bed. Suddenly, his phone rang. Jesus, now what? He picked it up and looked at the screen. It was Maria. It was like she had ESP. He set it back down and crawled under the covers. The phone rang a few more times and then stopped.

FORTY-THREE

arly Saturday morning, Harm was heading west on I-10 to the Stand Tall Boys rally in Houston. Every now and then, he checked his rearview. Abel and Tank were hanging tight.

He had made arrangement to hook up with Williams, so when they all got close, Abel and Tank were going to peel off, park, and then track back to him, and Guidry, then lurk around him all day. Harm wasn't going to have anything on him other than his burner and gun, but Abel and Tank had been equipped with small GoPro cameras and external directional microphones.

André had mounted the cameras and directional mics inside fanny packs and rigged them with holes so the camera and microphone could record the scene. All Abel and Tank had to do was put on the little pouches, turn on the cameras, then stand facing the action, and the rig would record whatever they were facing. The idea was to wear the bag over one shoulder like an ammo belt, and then they could adjust the position higher or lower on their torsos as needed.

Both Tank and Abel were going to be trying to capture Guidry doing something that would highlight his racism or catch him in the act of something illegal or violent—anything that would look bad for a policeman and cast doubt on his character.

They hung with Harm all the way into Houston, getting as close to the George R. Brown Convention Center as possible. Harm found a parking garage that allowed people to park on the weekend.

They all got on speaker and discussed their next steps. Harm had parked on a different floor, already starting the process of distancing themselves from each other. They decided that Harm would leave the building and dawdle on the sidewalk, while Abel and Tank geared up, then exited themselves.

Once they got street level, Harm started moving, and Abel and Tank let him get some distance before they started after him. He headed to the Discovery Green Park across from the convention center where he had agreed to link up with Williams and Guidry.

After a short walk, he found the green space across from George R. Brown and headed to the meeting place, the Monument au Fantome. As he walked up to the structure, he marveled at what some people considered art. Maybe he was the one with the problem and was just clueless, but he eyed the red, white, and blue construct that was plopped down in front of the beautiful green space. He figured he ought to make an effort to appreciate it, but he just didn't get it.

As he was standing there, ogling the art, he heard, "Smith! Hey, John!" He looked deeper into the green space and saw a group of men in a small cluster. He waved and walked around the installation and made his way to the group. They were all obviously cops of some sort—they had that look and were dressed in tactical gear—no NOPD uniforms or anything like that but wannabe military gear that fanboys could get off the internet. He noticed that they were all armed, openly carrying, and some men even had AR15s. Most had stretchy neck gaiters that they could pull up if they wanted to hide their faces, and one or two of the men had expandable batons poking out of their pockets. Back in the day, Abel's crew often carried those, too. They were useful for disabling people without killing them.

Williams grabbed Harm's shoulder and introduced him to the clustered men. Randy said each guy's name, and by the last one, Harm had already forgotten the first. "Guidry will be here in a minute, he just texted," Williams announced.

While they waited, Harm endured the inevitable small talk which was always super difficult if he was with people he didn't give a shit about. Randy went on about his trip up from New Orleans, which Harm found amusing, thinking that Williams must not get out of the city much. The I-10 corridor was a monotonous ride through construction that never ended.

Wait, that was unfair, the section over the Atchafalaya wasn't bad. He and the guys periodically fished the swamp, and parts of it were positively medieval. If you were deep in the swamp, anything could happen. He bet if you pumped out all the water, you'd find a thousand human skeletons.

Guidry finally showed and walked directly up to Randy and asked, "Are we all set?"

"Yep," answered Williams. "I coordinated with the Stand Tall security, and we have our spot to patrol."

"What exactly are we supposed to be doing?" asked Harm.

"Who are you?" asked Guidry.

"Uh, John Smith. We met at The Blue Wall."

Randy jumped in. "Remember? We talked about this the other day. He's that Ranger I told you about. One of our kinda guys. He just put in his application at NOPD."

"Oh, OK. Uh, Randy, what are we doing here?" asked Guidry with a slight hesitant note in his voice.

"Look, guys, we're just helping out the Boys. We got our sector, and we hang there while the rally is going on. Our job is to protect the rank-and-file Stand Tall people from any Antifa or Black Lives Matter people that threaten us. And I expect some action because the NRA convention and gun show over at the convention center is going to draw a lot of supporters and protestors," said Randy.

"What are the rules of engagement?" asked Harm. "I mean, do we pull our weapons? Do you think it's gonna get physical?"

"Well, first off, we aren't here in any official capacity. We're here on our own personal time, exercising our rights to congregate and freely speak as US citizens. We have the right to defend ourselves. So if some Antifa asshole starts acting up, we can defend ourselves. Just watch us and follow our lead," said Williams. "Oh, and keep your face covered."

"OK," said Harm, thinking, *If you are just here protecting your rights, why are you covering your faces?*

Harm had been watching Guidry while Randy delivered his spiel. His face had a weird emptiness. Harm had expected Guidry to be leading the show; he was the big dick, after all. Instead, he was deferring to Randy and had an air of confusion about him. The detective actually looked a little sick. His face had a yellow cast like he was jaundiced or something. Weird. He wondered whether Isabelle's voodoo had kicked in.

Randy finished up the briefing. "The events are going to start around one, after lunch. I suggest you guys go take a piss break and get something to eat, and we'll meet back here at twelve forty-five and head on over to our sector. If we get separated, or ya got questions, text me."

Harm was hoping that he could escape for a few minutes and sync up with Tank and Abel, but as the group was dispersing, Randy buttonholed him. "C'mon, man, let's grab a quick bite. Nothing worse than putting down a riot on an empty stomach." Harm gave an obligatory laugh.

They picked a taco truck parked with a group of other food trucks that were taking advantage of the congregating people and then walked back to the meeting place to sit and eat their lunch. Harm worked his weak conversational muscle. "I really liked your house, Randy. Having a kitchen with those fancy appliances must really make cooking fun."

"Yeah, man, I love to cook. I thought, I've got the money. Why don't I spend it on something I like."

"I wish I could do something like that myself, but that shit's expensive. You must be doing great work in the police department."

"No, man, the police don't pay shit, but Guidry set up something sweet. It's a good gig, and when I hit my twenty, I'll be all set, what with the NOPD pension, too."

"What do you guys do besides the police work?"

"You know, stuff like this, outside security work."

"You can make all this extra money just doing part-time security?" asked Harm, incredulously.

"It depends who you are doing security for," said Williams with a wink-wink in his voice.

"I hear you. I was doing something similar for a group like that a couple of years ago. It pays pretty well," said Harm with a similar tone. "Now, I've moved up to a more managerial role. But it's not what I want to do forever."

"We're tied into some situations that are very lucrative. Guidry has put together a whole organization outside of the public safety work, and we could sure use a guy like you with your skill set, 'cuz it can get a little intense. And if we can get you on the force, then that's even better for you. Then you'd get medical and pension on top of the side work."

"What's the deal with Guidry?" asked Harm.

"What do you mean?"

"I just noticed that he seems sick or kinda out of it today. He's deferring to you a lot."

"Well, I run most of the day-to-day stuff now. It's like he's the CEO, and I'm the executive officer."

"No, something more than that. Like he's confused."

"He's been under the weather for a couple of weeks, so maybe that's what you are seeing. Guidry is super smart and tough, so I figure he'll—"

"Hey, look." Harm noticed some of the other cops approaching. "Anyway, that sounds good. Let's talk about this more, later."

Randy corralled the cops, but Guidry hadn't appeared so he had to send out a couple of guys to track him down. Eventually, the detective meandered back, and then they had to wait a few minutes for the two men that Williams had sent out to hunt Guidry down. It was a bit of a shit show, but they finally got their act together and headed to their sector.

While Harm was cementing himself into Guidry's crew, Abel and Tank were orbiting his position at a distance. They had been out at the street between the park and the convention center where there were food trucks, porta-potties, and a small number of Houston police managing the traffic and crosswalks. Abel was struck by how few there were given what he thought was the potential for trouble due to the convention goers and rally.

The park was filling up with people, so many that they were spilling into the Avenida De Las Americas, making it easy for Tank and Abel to split up and almost disappear. They were separated by twenty or thirty yards and could keep track of each other while watching Guidry's team at the same time.

Abel eyed Harm until he must have felt the weight of Abel's gaze because he looked up, his eyes searching the crowd till he found Abel. He gave a slight nod, and Abel stepped back into the crowd, reassured that Harm was in place without any problems.

The crowd was growing, and the noise was getting louder, and if you were seeing it from some NSA satellite, it probably looked like mold growing in a petri dish, as the people coalesced into three distinct groups.

Abel took stock of the people. There were the Stand Tall Boys in their black faux military gear, armed with a hodgepodge of weapons, some with AR15s or holstered pistols and some carrying a variety of baseball bats and clubs, looking like the townspeople ready to hunt down Frankenstein, but all bristling with aggression. They seemed to have brought their fan club, a group of regular people, all White, milling about on the outskirts of the Stand Tall group and carrying signs that said things like 'Women for Trump,' 'Blue Lives Matter,' or 'Don't Tread on Me.' They acted like they were at a festival, hugging and high-fiving, and taking selfies with their arms around each other with big smiles on their faces—oblivious to the roiling tensions around them.

On the periphery were the Black Lives Matter people, Blacks and a mix of White people tending to late middle age or older, that gave the vibe that they were protesting the latest book censoring at the local library. They held up signs, too. Abel noticed one that read: 'This Flag Belongs to all Americans, Not Just Some.' These people were starting to chant slogans over and over, but they didn't project the aura of violence like the Boys or the final faction that had set up camp facing the Stand Tall Boys.

These people were dressed all in black, too, but it wasn't military garb. It was more like an informal uniform: black hoodies and work shirts and black jeans. This collection of people was evenly split between women and men, unlike the all-male misogynistic fraternity of the Boys. Their faces were covered with black scarves and gaiters, but it was obvious there were women given the size difference of the participants of this mob.

These folks were carrying signs that read: 'No KKK,' 'No Trump,' or 'No Fascist USA' and had started to yell stridently. Abel noticed one sign that said, 'Everyday antifascist, come for the anarchy, stay for the soup,' and then there was a picture of a Campbell's soup can with the stylized SS logo that appeared as two runic *S*'s next to each other. He didn't understand it exactly, but he got the message.

They faced the Stand Tall Boys, and it felt to Abel like an old medieval battle where the combatants were arrayed across from each other, poised to fight, but still in the early stage where they needed to ramp up their courage by yelling insults. Abel could feel the tension in the air building like the electric field that grew around a thunderstorm.

At first, he thought that if things went south the Antifa would easily get their asses kicked by the Boys, but then he noticed that all the flags that the Antifa people were carrying were tied to thick wooden staves—obviously disguised clubs. The Stand Tall Boys had more guns, but the Antifa seemed to be lit with a furor that was visceral. It felt like a building demolition where the siren had just gone off, warning of the imminent explosion.

The Stand Tall group had prepared themselves and come with an agenda. They'd set up a small portable stage with a sheet of plywood resting on some low supports, and their leader was standing above the fray speaking into a microphone connected to a public address system. Abel tried to listen, but it was difficult to pick out the words over the BLM chants and the bullhorn-driven words being squawked from the Antifas.

More and more people were arriving, packing themselves into the gap between the Boys and Antifa, and Abel lost sight of Harm and Guidry's guys and was getting further from Tank. He started moving around trying to get a sight line, and then his phone vibrated. Tank had texted him: "this shit is getting ready to blow, are you feeling it?"

Abel texted back: "yeah, I'm coming over to you."

He moved through the crowd, pushing his way through the clusters of men and women and walking around people that were on the ground. The tone of the Stand Tall leader's rhetoric had shifted from strident to reverent, and many of the people were down on their knees praying over clasped hands while others were looking skyward and waving one hand in the air.

Abel got to Tank's side and his buddy yelled into his ear, "Look at those assholes! They act like they're in church. That Stand Tall motherfucker is preaching hate, and they're waving their hands and shit like they're hearing the Word."

They stood and took it in for a minute and watched the kneelers get up as the religious tone of the speaker reverted to a harangue. The crowd resumed waving their American flags. As the words of the speaker got louder and more intense, the people surrounding the Boys started yelling along. Their faces were red, and their neck veins were bulging. The words were indecipherable, but the peoples' mouths were open, and the sound was like the braying of a hundred donkeys.

Abel leaned into Tank and yelled, "This is getting ready to pop. We need to get over by Harm so we can catch this shit when it goes nuclear!"

They bulled their way through the tightly packed folks who had gotten between the Stand Tall Boys and the Antifa group, pushing aside the people in red, white, and blue clothing and the women holding up signs, all standing shoulder to shoulder, yelling and thrusting their fists in the air. They broke through to the cordon of Stand Tall security surrounding the mass of the Boys and followed the line of armed men till they came upon Harm standing with Williams's and Guidry's men.

They posted up at the front of the Stand Tall audience and turned on their recording rigs. Abel also took out his phone and started to record Guidry's group who were, at the moment, facing the crowd at Abel's back. He was having trouble keeping his position because the people behind him were constantly pushing against him and knocking him one way or the other. It was like trying to stand in a heavy surf. Tank was a few steps away, fighting the same battle with the sea of people behind him vying for a front row seat.

For a while, the situation stayed stable despite the buffeting, and Abel had a chance to take a closer look at the Stand Tall Boys in front of him. They were acting like they were the stars of the show. Strutting around and laughing and pointing here and there at the crowd before them, they didn't appear to be concerned about the Antifa mob behind the regular people.

Maybe they couldn't hear what the Antifa were shouting. Maybe their own sound system was drowning out the growing ire that Abel could hear coming from behind him. But then the leader of the Stand Tall Boys started yelling, "Fuck Antifa! Fuck Antifa! Fuck Antifa!" and then the demeanor of the Boys standing inside the line of Stand Tall security abruptly changed.

They started chanting in unison with the leader. "Fuck Antifa! Fuck Antifa! Fuck Antifa!" Then the crowd picked it up and started becoming more active. Abel got knocked hard and almost lost his feet, but Tank reached out and steadied him. They got tight together like two warriors in a shield wall, bolstering their position, and aimed their cameras at Guidry's men.

The sound of the crowd turned more frantic and the "Fuck Antifa!" shouts abruptly changed to "They're coming!" or "Watch out!" or "Help!" Abel could feel the party atmosphere around him evaporate and change to fear, and he stopped being able to understand the shouts as the milling people around him started trying to escape the Antifa that were pushing them toward the Stand Tall Boys.

Abel glanced over his shoulder and could see the black-clad Antifa surging toward him and the crowd of regular people parting to let them through. It was frightening to see the pillar of people, in black from head to toe with old-school chemistry goggles over their eyes, brandishing their wooden cudgels in a solid formation and pushing aside the crowd. They looked like a horde of insects. He pushed Tank and yelled, "Move!" getting him going in the direction that would take them out of the direct collision between Antifa and the Boys that was imminent.

They escaped out from between the two opposing forces and situated themselves to capture the action around Guidry's team. Abel held his phone as high as he could to make sure he caught what was happening. It was easy for him to keep his body aimed at Guidry because Harm was wearing a gaiter that had a red and black pattern and had promised to stick to the detective's side. Guidry had pulled up his neck gaiter as well, and you could no longer tell it was him. *Shit,* thought Abel, *that's gonna be a problem,* but he kept on recording.

As the troop of Antifa approached the Boys, there was a moment when everything paused like a bus that was teetering back and forth halfway over a cliff and you didn't know whether it was going over the edge or not. Then, one of the Stand Tall men pushed his way to the front of his pack and brought up a can of bear spray and spewed it across the chasm between the two factions. The Antifa front line started screaming and pawing at their faces, and the line fell apart.

The men behind the burned Antifa surged forward and started swinging their flagstaff clubs. The sprayer was hit in the arm and dropped the can of pepper spray. Then it was on—a melee of furious people, attacking and defending. It was chaos. No real guns had been fired yet, but a group of the Boys were shooting paintball guns on automatic.

Because they were all roughly wearing the same black clothing, it was hard for Abel to tell who was who, but he kept his recording rig focused on the Guidry line as best he could, and Tank did the same. Abel was thankful that Harm was wearing the colorful gaiter and standing next to the detective, otherwise he would have lost the man in the confusion. Guidry was beset by a force of Antifa people who were trying to breach his team's section and was flailing away with a nightstick. Harm was at his side helping, blocking with a baseball bat but not taking any swings.

Just as Guidry was rearing back to hit the Antifa man in front of him, Harm reached over and yanked down the covering on Guidry's face. Abel caught Guidry's exposed face, his expression contorted in anger, as he swung the club down on the Antifa attacker. It struck a glancing blow above the ear. A spray of blood could be clearly seen, and the attacker dropped to his knees. Abel caught it all on his phone that he was holding above the fray. He hoped he'd captured it on his GoPro, too.

The man next to Guidry screamed something to the detective and pointed at Abel who was still holding his phone on high. Guidry and the man erupted off the line and ran toward Abel and Tank. Harm chased after them.

"Fuck!" yelled Tank, and he grabbed Abel and shouted, "RUN!" They took off toward the convention center. They reached the Avenida De Las Americas. The violence from the park had spilled into the street where some Houston police were trying to intervene. Tank and Abel had to use the sidewalk, and they continued running, pushing people out of the way, trying to gain some distance on Guidry. They passed a parked truck with its passenger window broken out and two men brutally fighting within. The man closest to them had blood coursing down his scalp.

Suddenly, a cluster of black-clad men appeared on the sidewalk in front of them—more of Guidry's men. Abel and Tank slowed, and then Guidry caught up to them. "Give me your phone, motherfucker!"

The phone was still in Abel's hand. "Why?"

Guidry pulled his weapon and held it at his side. "Give me the phone! Your wallet, too. And those purses you have strapped on. Everything!"

One of Guidry's men grabbed Abel's arm and wrested the phone from his hand. Tank swung, smacking Guidry's man on the side of the head. Abel grabbed the guy and tried to get the phone back. In almost one move, Guidry raised his handgun and fired.

CHAPTER

FORTY-FOUR

Harm had been standing next to Guidry, fending off the Antifa psychos, when he realized their plan wasn't going to work. They had orchestrated this big effort to catch the detective in the act, but his face was covered by the gaiter. Abel and Tank's recordings were probably useless. So Harm ripped down Guidry's face covering. The detective didn't seem to notice in the heat of the battle, but he sure as shit noticed Abel standing there waving around his phone above the fray and aiming it directly at his face.

Guidry had seemed a little confused and fucked up before the fight, but he was operating on all cylinders now, and he launched himself at Abel. *Oh shit,* thought Harm as he took off after the detective. Williams was on the move, too, and the three of them, one after the other, chased Abel and Tank through the maelstrom.

They ran past the statue where they had met earlier and were gaining on his friends, but then Abel and Tank hit the sidewalk and went left and started to get some distance. Guidry was ahead of Harm, running pretty fricking fast for an old man, and Harm thought about pulling his

Glock and slowing him down permanently, but there were too many random people around.

Abel and Tank kept running into folks, but the people, once knocked out of the way, left a clear path for Guidry, Harm, and Williams. The New Orleans cops were catching up to his friends, and Harm was furiously thinking on how to get Abel and Tank loose without giving himself up in the process. They were almost on top of his guys, and Harm wasn't getting any brilliant ideas.

Then, Abel and Tank slowed down abruptly, stopped by the remainder of Guidry's men that had taken the hypotenuse. His buddies were in between two sets of bent cops who were ready to do anything to cover their asses. Guidry pulled out his gun and demanded Abel's phone. He resisted, of course, then one of the corrupt cops grabbed at it, and Tank weighed in with a right.

Guidry raised his Glock, and Harm reacted instinctively by knocking the detective's arm up as he pulled the trigger. Guidry started turning toward Harm, saying, "What the fuck?"

Harm snatched his own pistol out of his ComfortTac belly band and jammed it into Guidry's neck. "Don't move!" Harm snarled. Guidry was left with his weapon pointed toward the sky.

Williams started reaching and Harm said, "Don't!" Randy stopped, and Abel and Tank started edging backward down the sidewalk. "Drop your pistol," Harm growled at Guidry, and when he complied, Abel and Tank took off running.

The cops were frozen, but Harm knew he just had moments before they were going to swarm him. He took off at a sprint down the sidewalk.

Harm caught up with Abel and Tank as they rounded the corner and slammed on the brakes. The three of them casually walked into the Marriot Hotel. The guys fast walked their way through the hotel and popped out of the side door and directly into the parking garage. In minutes, their trucks were back on the street and heading to Lacombe.

On Sunday morning, everybody except Rabbit was clustered around André's computer monitor watching Abel's video footage from the rally. The earlier footage caught all of Guidry's men standing around next to the weird piece of art in the park, their faces exposed, proving that they were at the rally. But when they fast-forwarded to where the rally blew up, they weren't so lucky. Most of the action was of a group of men with their faces ninety percent covered, and because the recording had been done with the GoPro hidden in Abel's fanny pack, it turned out that a lot of the footage captured of the scene was too low and was constantly being obstructed by people running around between Abel and Guidry's men. The images were chaotic.

Abel said, "In just a minute, Harm yanks down Guidry's gaiter." They stared at the screen. Suddenly, Harm reached over and pulled down Guidry's face covering. A flash of white appeared on the monitor, but then the camera was obstructed. The picture changed direction, and the focus started bouncing around. First it showed the ground, then bodies, then sky, then ground.

"That's when Guidry started chasing us," said Tank.

"Let me see whether I can isolate Guidry's face." André dialed the images back and froze the screen on the flash of white when Harm had pulled down the face covering. It was clearly a side view of a face but blurry.

"Shit! I mean, I know that's Guidry, but I knew that was Guidry standing there. Do you think other people would be able to identify him from that?" asked Abel.

Tank asked his brother, "Can't you enhance the image?"

André fussed with the mouse for a few minutes. It didn't make much difference. He leaned back in the chair and sighed. "Let's look at Tank's footage."

André played all of his brother's recording. It wasn't any better than Abel's and didn't even capture the moment when Harm exposed Guidry's face.

"Well, that was a bust," said Tank.

"I can't believe I let that guy get my phone. I'm sorry, André."

"That wasn't your fault, Abel," said Tank. "I shoulda reacted quicker and stopped that dickhead."

"Guys, nothing ever goes alright when you're in the shit. At least we can prove that Guidry and his men were at a fascist white supremacy rally in Houston," said Harm.

"That pretty much shows that they are racist mofos, at least," said André. "I have a meeting with Hebert on Tuesday. I'll take this over there and see if he thinks it will help the case."

"Yeah, it's gotta help some, right? We have a lot of stuff that makes this guy look bad," said Abel.

"Tell Hebert I'll go on the stand and tell all the stuff I saw," said Harm.

"Thanks," said André. "That rally was a shit show. You guys coulda got fucked up bad. Thanks for trying. I love you guys." He plastered a smile on his face. "I'm sure that video will help." But he didn't sound like he believed his own words.

FORTY-FIVE

André and his brother sat in Hebert's mahogany-paneled waiting room, sunk deep in a plush couch, talking low. Tank was getting worried but was trying to sound optimistic. André wasn't having it and was fairly depressed.

"I guess it was my turn, and I'll just have to take my lumps. It's not like this doesn't happen on a regular basis to every other Black dude in America. Or maybe it's just karma for all the other shit we've done. Ya know, it is what it is . . ."

"Man, I fucking hate that expression! No, we aren't just going to roll over and take it up the butt."

"Even if I get off? I can pretty much write off my security business. What company is gonna have a suspected felon handling their financial security?"

"Naw, man. When we stomp on Guidry and get you off, people are gonna be lining up for your business. You can turn this into a positive."

André sighed, not buying his brother's unrealistic take.

Hebert's classy assistant, Emmie, popped her head out from behind the door to the inner sanctum. "He's ready for you. C'mon back."

The brothers stood and followed her to the conference room, a solid room, with a solid door and a heavy conference table. Hebert was sitting at the head of the table like he was the CEO of a large corporation. In front of him were stacks of multicolored folders, papers roughly protruding from each.

"Have a seat, guys. Let me bring you up to speed."

Tank and André sat next to him, and Hebert pushed away from the table so he could look directly at them without having to turn his head constantly. "I've been going back and forth with the DA on the charges, and basically, he's being a hard-ass. The counts against you are resisting arrest, possession of narcotics, and assault of a police officer."

"What happened to the jaywalking?" asked Tank derisively.

"That is just an infraction and not even a misdemeanor. We don't have to worry about that," said Hebert."

"Are all those charges against me a felony?"

"Unfortunately, yes."

"Even the resisting arrest?" asked Tank.

"They're saying he resisted the arrest with violence so that turns the resisting into a felony."

"That's so unfair. They didn't identify themselves! They attacked me, and I was just defending myself."

"Don't worry. We'll get into all that at the trial. The good thing is that they haven't decided to charge you with the Blue Lives Matter hate crime designation, which would add another count."

"When do I go to trial?"

"It's not on the docket yet, which is not surprising. Since you got bonded out, they have one hundred and eighty days to bring you to trial."

Chapter Forty-Five

"I've got to wait for five more months with this hanging over my head?"

"Yes, it could be that long. I'm sorry. But I think we have a lot of mitigating factors, what with the witness statements and character witnesses and such. I know it's hard. You've just got to hang in there and trust me and trust the system."

André didn't have a whole lot of trust in the *system,* but he bit his lip. "Let me show you some things we've found," he said instead and opened up his laptop.

He took Hebert through the video footage of the rally and Hebert watched, rapt. "That's pretty good and is going to help. It's too bad you can't make out his face while he's hitting that other guy, though. They can make the case that while you showed Guidry was there at the rally, it's not provable that that was him hitting the Antifa guy. They could say he was there in support of the BLM guys, and then he looks like he's unbiased, and it makes his statements about you being a criminal stronger. Could bite us in the ass."

Tank groaned. "This is all bullshit! Abel can testify that he talked to a gang member who told him that Guidry handles protection for The Bastard's motorcycle club and their meth trade."

"Will the gang member testify?"

"Uh, no," said Tank.

"That will probably be treated as hearsay. We can get it in front of the jury, but it will probably get struck off, and they will be instructed to ignore it."

"What about all those cases I showed you, where they did this same shit to other brown people? Like what they did to Didi," asked André.

"Oh, Didi called me by the way and is going to retain me, and who knows, at this point that might help. Also we might get Harmon up on the stand, and he can verify that it was indeed Guidry, but then maybe the prosecutor impeaches him with his military record or just says what else is a good friend going to say.

"Look, guys, we've got a lot of stuff that points to these cops being suspect, and we might be able to convince some jury members that there are problems with the state's case, but there's nothing ironclad here. If I was the prosecutor, I could pick the evidence apart. I'd like to go into trial with a slam dunk or have enough dirt that the DA realizes he's holding a bag of shit and drops the case."

"So are you telling us we got to catch Guidry and his crew in the middle of something and document it so it will hold up in court?"

"Yep. Right now, we might have one of those death by a thousand cuts things and hope the jury sees it, but I don't think we're there yet."

André slumped, defeated. "I don't know how we're going to get that."

"A lot can happen between now and then. I've heard of cases where the arresting officer dies, and then they have to drop the case. If this guy is mixed up with the wrong people, anything could happen," said Hebert. He stood up and ushered them to the door. Squeezing André's shoulder, he said, "Hang in there, André. Don't worry, this is going to work out OK."

The brothers walked out to the parking lot. *Did I just hear what I think I heard?* Tank asked himself incredulously.

CHAPTER

FORTY-SIX

"**A**bel, it's me," said Tank. He and André were driving home from Hebert's office. "Hebert said the video footage we brought to him wasn't enough," Tank said into the phone. He listened for a bit. "Yeah, that little snippet of Guidry's blurry face will help, but it isn't a slam dunk. And I have to talk to you about some other stuff. I'll track you down tonight." He was quiet, listening to Abel, then said, "OK, catch you later."

"What did he say?" asked André.

"He was disappointed, but before he hung up he said we'll think of something. And you know? He's right. We will. We always do."

The phone rang again, interrupting the encouragement. Tank answered and went quiet, then said, "I'm glad you called. We heard from Hebert that you reached out to him. Let me bring you up to speed on our end." Tank went through the rally and aftermath with Hebert, then wrapped it up. "So if I were you, I wouldn't come in just yet, Didi. We've got to get a solid piece of evidence that completely invalidates anything official Guidry has been doing."

Tank paused to listen, then said, "Thanks for the offer. As soon as we come up with a plan, we'll let you know. And if there is something you can help with, we'll definitely tie you in."

André started talking, but Tank held up his hand. "Thanks, man, yeah and you call me if you hear anything new on your end." He hung up, then turned to his brother. "I wanna talk about what Hebert said . . ."

"Hola, Abel! Is this a booty call?"

Abel laughed, then sat up higher in the bed and adjusted the pillow behind his back. "No, I just wanted to talk."

"What's going on? How's the André situation?"

"Not so good. We thought we had enough to show that Guidry was mixed up with the whole white supremacy, neo-Nazi thing, and we showed all the evidence to the attorney. But he basically said it wasn't enough. I was worried before but thought we would figure something out. Now, I think we're running out of time, and there is a pretty big chance that André might get convicted. That'll kill Isabelle."

"That's terrible. What are you going to do?"

"I don't know! We have to catch Guidry in the act of doing something horrendous and somehow be able to get that into André's trial."

"When is the trial?"

"It hasn't been scheduled yet. It can be up to six months. We still have time, but Guidry has been able to cover up his corruption for a long time. He's smart. I don't know how we're going to get the goods on him. I'm really worried. I don't want André to go to prison. I know what jail can do to a person. My uncle went to prison. Fuck! André didn't do anything wrong. He was just defending himself."

Abel took a breath. "Let's talk about something else."

"Can we talk about us? Are you seeing anybody else besides me?"

Chapter Forty-Six

"No!" Abel responded quickly. "How about you?"

"Me neither. I think that maybe you and I should start thinking this is a real thing."

"Me, too." Abel cleared his throat. "We should take this next level. You've met my friends and family. I've only met your distant cousin."

"Do you want to meet my parents? Are you ready to take a trip to El Salvador?"

"Uh."

Maria laughed. "Maybe we should start with just my friends around here."

"Yeah, that sounds good."

"And now that we've got all that settled, don't you want to know what I'm wearing? I'll give you a hint. It's black and very tiny and very soft . . ." she purred.

CHAPTER

FORTY-SEVEN

Harm was sitting in his truck psyching himself up to drive down into the city. Maroni was expecting him to show up at Café Du Monde for a status meeting. The man had been talking about Harm creating a report describing his collections, using Excel or some shit. It killed him. Being involved with Tony was getting to be like working at a real company. The way André described his job at the bank was exactly the stuff he was dealing with. Tony must be reading business books or something. He knew Rabbit and the guys thought he was still working in the Life, but it felt to him like he'd gone straight, too.

He sighed and reached to turn the key but was interrupted by the buzzing of one of his phones. The left pocket—the burner. He pushed back in the seat, straightened his leg, and dug the phone out of his tight pocket. It was Williams. He put it to his ear. "Hello?"

"I'm surprised you answered, you fuck!"

"Wait, what? Who is this? Why are you mad?" Harm tried to put the right amount of confusion in his tone.

"Don't give me that shit, Smith, or whatever your name is. I've been checking on you and can't find a trace.

You fucked me, man! Guidry is pissed about the shit you pulled, and he blames me."

"You got it all wrong, man! I was looking out for you. Guidry was going to shoot those guys. There were cops right down the street. You idiots would be in jail right now if I hadn't stopped Guidry. If you haven't noticed that guy is fucking loony tunes."

"Yeah? Then why did you run off with those guys that were recording us?"

"I didn't run off with them. I was chasing them."

"Nice try, asshole. Guidry told me you pulled off his face covering."

"What are you talking about? When?"

"I thought we were friends. I'm a detective, asshole. You think you can hide from me and Guidry?"

Randy stopped ranting, and Harm realized he'd hung up. He grinned and wondered whether Williams had bought any of his bullshit. He hoped they did try to come after him.

The guys were sitting at The Flying Machine going through their fourth bucket of Abitas. Rabbit had gotten a kitchen pass because Crystal's mother was visiting from Shreveport, and his wife wanted some alone time with her mama, so Rabbit had taken the opportunity to get some alone time with his buds. "Man, this is awesome. I'm glad we're all here. It still hurts that René is gone though." He raised his glass, and they all held up their beers. Even Abel was able to put on a smile, albeit weakly.

"We need to do this more often. I know it's mostly my fault, being wrapped up with all this marriage and baby stuff, but I promise I'm going to fix that. I'm going to set up something with Crystal so that we can do this regular."

Harm clinked his bottle against Rabbit's, and Abel said, "Yeah. I agree. We kinda let this go, and it's my fault, too. It was hard to come here. Made me think too much about René." In his head, though, he knew Rabbit was on a one-way trip. Yeah, Rabbit missed hanging, but when the babies came, nothing was gonna be the same. Rabbit was full tilt married and a soon-to-be daddy, and he wasn't going to let the old business get in the way. He just didn't know it yet.

Harm interrupted Abel's train of thought. "Williams called. Boy was he pissed! I tried to shine him on some, but I don't think he bought it."

"What did he say?" André asked.

"That he and Guidry were going to come after me."

"You used a fake name and fake plates and a burner," said Tank. "How're they going to find you? New Orleans is a big place."

"I hope they do find me."

Tank said, "About that . . . when André and I were meeting with Hebert, the last thing he said was that if Guidry disappeared, then the prosecutor might drop the case."

"Hebert told you to kill Guidry?" Abel asked incredulously.

André said, "No, I think he was just telling us what could happen. You know, all possible outcomes. He wasn't telling us to murder Guidry."

Tank snorted. "Nah, he was definitely saying to do Guidry. I'm not saying we kill him. Just that's what our lawyer said. So maybe he's worried that things are going to go south."

Harm spoke. "The fucker deserves it; he's bad deep down."

"I'm with him," said Rabbit.

Abel laughed and squeezed Rabbit's neck. "Says the big tough baby daddy!" Everybody laughed.

He continued, "Check this out. Olivia came over and said she wanted to get back together."

"Last night?" asked Tank.

"No, that night we were all drinking on my back porch."

"Yeah, like that narrows it down," said Tank. They all laughed again.

"Dude, you're on fire! Do you think you can keep 'em both on the line?" asked Rabbit.

"Rabbit!" said Tank with a groan.

André said, "That's the way you lose both."

"Abel's been dopily in love with Olivia since the first time he laid eyes on her," continued Tank. "What are you gonna do, Abel?"

If anybody had been watching Harm's face, they would have seen it go through a series of expressions. It settled in a slight frown as he looked expectantly at Abel.

"I love Olivia, but I just don't know whether she and me can make it work after all that happened. I don't want to waste anymore of her life if it's not going to work out. And this thing with Maria is pretty intense."

"I'll bet!" said Rabbit with a smirk plastered on his face.

"C'mon, man, I'm serious. All these thoughts and what-ifs are running around my head. Maria wants me to meet her family and friends. She wants to take it next level."

Harm had a vague expression of disappointment on his face. Abel didn't notice. Harm stood up. "Guys, I hate to break up the party, but I've gotta be down in the city talking to Maroni first thing. I need to roll."

"Bro, we all came in the same truck," said Rabbit.

"I'll Uber."

Abel said, "Hey, man, are you OK?"

"Sure, I just noticed the time. Maroni wants an Excel spreadsheet status report of my *clients*. Can you believe that shit? I've been working on it all day. If it wasn't for YouTube, I wouldn't of had a clue."

"Man!" said André. "You shoulda called me. I would have showed you all you needed to know in fifteen minutes."

"I didn't want to bother you."

Chapter Forty-Seven

"Ahhh," said André, "call me next time."

"Let's all go," said Abel. "We'll drop you off first, Harm."

They closed out their tab and walked out to the lot, all of them a bit subdued, the turn of the conversation at the end somehow a buzzkill. Tank had driven so André had shotgun automatically, not because he was Tank's brother, just that there was no way he was going to fit in the back seat with two other men. Both Harm and Abel managed to bookend Rabbit in the middle, and they spent the ten-minute trip home purposely crushing him at every turn, then laughing.

Tank turned into Harm's house, and as the headlights swept along the shrubs next to the driveway and landed on the open garage, three men boiled out of the space like cockroaches running for cover when the kitchen lights were flicked on.

Tank slammed the gearshift into park, and all four doors of the truck blasted open. The crew fell out and ran after the men.

FORTY-EIGHT

The three men were already thirty yards down the road. Rabbit was hot after the men with Tank on his shoulder. Harm was pounding after them. One of the men turned and took a snap shot that went over their heads. Rabbit instantly veered off the road and dove into the ditch at the side of the road. The rest of the crew followed, André grabbing Abel by the arm and dragging him into the culvert with him. Suddenly, a vehicle screamed down the road, blowing past them. The crew scrambled back up onto the road and sprinted back to Tank's truck, Abel taking up the rear.

"You guys go! I gotta check on my mom!" yelled Harm.

"I'll stay with Harm!" shouted Rabbit. "We'll follow you in a minute. Don't lose them!"

Abel and André were barely back in the truck when Tank started reversing out the driveway. André had to grab the oh-shit handle and lean out to get his door. Tank cut the wheel and hit the gas. "Buckle up, motherfuckers!"

Tank reached the main road. "Right or left?" he yelled.

"Left—I see them," yelled his brother. Tank hit the brake, steered inside the curve, then feathered the gas and did a partial drift through the intersection, getting on Hwy 190 toward Slidell. Tank saw the lights ahead and put the hammer down, but the other car was doing the same. Brake lights flickered ahead, and Tank ate up some ground. The gap between the two vehicles opened and closed, but they couldn't catch up. Then, they hit Slidell, and things got interesting.

Slidell was not a big city and it was late, but still there were enough cars ahead of the sedan they were chasing to slow it down. The thieves or whoever they were didn't seem to care about the traffic laws as they were blasting through each intersection with impunity. Still, Tank was able to keep them within eyesight by violating a few statutes himself. Abel hoped Tank didn't T-bone anybody.

The sedan went south and took the Twin Span, heading for New Orleans. Tank followed. The guys had been quiet except for the occasional frantic "Look out!" yells as they were careening through Slidell, but the relative quiet of the highway allowed Tank to break the silence. "Now what? Do you want me to move up and pit 'em?"

André answered, "Naw, at these speeds, if we spin them, they could go over or one of us gets killed."

"Yeah, I got a better idea." The thrill of the chase and the adrenaline was wearing off, and Abel had had a chance to think. "Drop back, but keep them in sight. As soon as we pass another car, pull behind it, and put out your lights for a bit. And if it's another Ford truck, that would be even better."

Tank laughed. "What are the odds of that?"

André took the question seriously. "Pretty good. The Ford truck is the most popular vehicle in the Gulf Coast area."

"Doesn't really matter. It'll just looked like we dropped the chase. We can jump into the left lane every now and then with our lights out and goose it and keep the distance between them and us short. We want to find out where they live. So we just go low profile and try to track them home," said Abel.

"Yeah, we need to figure out what we're dealing with here. Who are these motherfuckers?" Tank said.

Abel's phone rang. It was Harm. "Is your mom, OK?" Abel put the phone on speaker and leaned in between Tank and André.

Harm's voice came out of the phone, and Abel held it up so that the brothers could hear over the road noise. "She was awake while the guys were creeping the garage. She heard a noise and looked out the window. At first, she just thought it was us getting back but then realized they were smaller than us."

"How could she tell that?" asked André.

"Pretty easy to see that someone is tinier than your giant ass," said Rabbit's voice chiming in from the background.

"I don't know," said Harm. "Secret mother shit. It doesn't matter. She then tried to call me like fifty times. The ringer on my phone was off. She was super pissed. Anyway, are you still on those guys, or did you lose them?"

"We're on them and almost over the bridge. Don't bother rolling after us. We're lurking way back and gonna try to track them home. See if we can figure out who they are. We'll come back to your place after we track them down."

Harm said, "A'write," then dropped the call.

The boys came out on the south side of the lake, all three of them tracking the taillights of the sedan. They had played the game of right lane, left lane, and lights off, lights on, for the whole trip over the water and hoped that the men were confused about which vehicle was actually following them. And truth be told, they weren't positive that they were still following the correct car, either.

When the sedan exited the High Rise bridge, Tank followed, still keeping as much distance as he could. For several minutes, they chased the car through surface streets, trying to stay close enough to see it but not give away that they were there. Then the car ahead took a left. Tank sped up and turned, but the sedan was gone. He hit the gas and came to a four-way stop. They checked the crossing street. Nobody.

"Fuck me!" said Tank. "They musta known it was us all along."

"That's not certain," André said. "They could have just fired it into any garage along here."

Abel put a pin on the location on his map app. "Let's box this area, anyway."

Tank drove in ever widening circles. They never found the guys. But then Abel said, "Doesn't this place look familiar to you guys?"

"Not to me," Tank said. "Where are we?"

"Turn left up here," instructed Abel. They drove about a quarter mile. "Check it out." On the right was the El Luz Loco.

"The MS-13?" said André. "That's gotta be a coincidence. We haven't seen or heard from those bastards in two years."

"Yeah, maybe," Abel said but didn't sound that certain. "Alright, let's call it. I'm wrecked. Head back to Harm's house."

By then, their adrenaline had completely cratered, and the guys were subdued for the trip home. Tank retraced their path and eventually pulled into Harm's driveway. Rabbit and Harm were standing in the driveway smoking, a shotgun drooping in Harm's hand.

The guys got out of the F-150 and walked up to Rabbit and Harm. "We chased them to the El Luz Loco," said Tank, immediately.

"They were Maras?" asked Harm, incredulously.

"We lost the guys in the area around The Loco," said André.

"We don't know," said Abel. "Just seems weird. We coulda gone anywhere in the city, and we end up there?"

"We aren't one hundred percent positive we were on the right car. We chased them in the dark for half an hour, at least," André said.

"I don't know what that means," said Harm. "But I'm pretty sure it was Guidry's men. Williams said to me this morning they were going to track me down. It feels like it was them trying to figure out what they're dealing with."

Abel said, "And if it was them, by chasing after them like that, now they're probably convinced they found us."

"I'm wiped out. I can hardly think. What are we doing here?" asked André.

"Guys, go home. I'll stick with Harm tonight. Rabbit, you need to go home to your bride. André go check on Isabelle, make sure she's OK, and Callie's in the middle of her nightshift, so she's fine. Tank, you go, too."

"I'm staying," said Tank. "Harm, get me a shottie."

FORTY-NINE

Isabelle answered her front door. "Hello, Harmon. Where y'at, cher?"

"Oh, I'm alright," said Harm.

"C'mon in! How's your mama doing after those people broke into the garage?"

"She's fine. She was more mad at me for not answering my phone than anything."

"Wasn't she scared?

"Yeah, I guess, but she was sitting on the couch with one of my shotguns, and if one of those guys came in, she woulda blasted the guy. She did make me promise to keep my phone charged and the ringer turned on, though. She'll probably bug me about that forever."

"Well, I would have been scared to death. I'm going to go check on her this week sometime. It's been a while. Anyway, I'm sorry, Thomas and André aren't here right now. I think they're doing something with Abel. Were they supposed to be here this morning?"

"No, actually, I was hoping to talk to you," said Harm.

"To me? Are you OK, cher?"

"Yeah, yeah, I'm fine. It's just I don't know who to talk to. Maybe I should talk to Callie, but I decided to talk to you first."

"What's wrong, honey?"

"I know it's none of my business, but I have bad feelings about Abel's new girlfriend, Maria."

"Tell me about that," said Isabelle.

"I think there's something up with her."

"What exactly do you mean? Give me an example."

"Well, she showed up downtown at that bar where I meet with people. I told Abel about her being at the bar, and he just laughed. But the thing is, she was hitting on me and asking questions about the past and Abel's finances and stuff."

"Do you think it's possible that she was just trying to make friends with you, and maybe you're blowing it all out of proportion?"

"That's what Abel said. And yeah, I know I sometimes don't have a clue about people, but I'm getting a bad feeling."

"Is that all? Or is there something else?" Isabelle asked with just a touch of concern.

"Didn't you see what happened at Rabbit's party?"

"I caught the tail end of it," Isabelle said without any expression.

"Yeah, I was there for the whole thing. Maria went from nice to psycho in a heartbeat. And also, you know, those people that broke into my garage took us down by the El Luz Loco. And Maria's Hispanic, too."

"Hmmm," said Isabelle.

"It sounds like you think I'm imagining it, too. Maybe I am getting all excited over nothing." Harm sighed. "I'm glad I came here rather than trying to talk to Callie. I don't want both of them pissed at me."

"I'm glad you came to me first, too," Isabelle said. "Go tend to your flock. A storm is coming. The wind is picking up, and I have work to do."

Chapter Forty-Nine

"What are you going to do?" asked Harm, but Isabelle ignored him and quietly closed the door in his face. "What am I supposed to do?" he asked the door.

CHAPTER

FIFTY

Abel was sitting in a chair down by the bayou, staring at the water and thinking. The sun was still high and hot, and the breeze was heavy with humidity. Occasionally, a mullet would launch out of the water and land with a slap, disappear, then suddenly reappear ten feet away and repeat the process. He wondered if it was being chased or whether it was just scratching an itch.

Maria had called him earlier and invited him to a dinner with her cousin and aunt that evening. She had suggested Palmettos, the same restaurant that that they had gone to on their first date. Abel thought it was funny that she didn't want to go to one of the great places down in the city and told her he'd be fine driving down, but she insisted that her cousin and aunt would love the place. Abel wasn't going to argue, as she was making good on her promise to start introducing him to her friends and family. That was all great, right? So what was he doing hanging down by the water stuck in his own head?

Maria was beautiful, intense, and insanely sexy—the perfect girlfriend—and she actually liked him. Why couldn't he get Olivia out of his head? Callie had been right; he'd been messed up since Olivia had broken up with him two years ago. He'd basically given up, and when Maria started paying attention to him, it started to feel pretty good. Then he'd seen Olivia in the grocery store, and the wound had started bleeding again. She'd shown up the other night, and now he couldn't get her out of his head. He was thinking about her constantly. But Maria was talking about taking it next level, and now he was going to start meeting her family.

He was getting in deeper with her, and it felt like he was being torn in two directions—Olivia and Owen on one side and Maria on the other, both with a strong magnetic field pulling him toward them. He knew he had to choose. If he went toward Olivia, it was a life thing. A life of family with a little boy that he'd already bonded with and a woman that felt right when he was with her. Maria, on the other hand, was like getting a drug spiked in his vein, intoxicating and frightening at the same time.

Sitting by the bayou, away from everything, he could see things clearer. The heat, the buzz of the cicadas, the smell, and the stillness. He could go down into himself and see what he really wanted—no, what he really needed. Maria was like a Fourth of July firework, bright and explosive but temporary. A bright flash that lit up your retina, and when you closed your eyes, the images danced around and then faded. Olivia was like the earth you stood on while watching the show. It held you up. You lived on it. You breathed its air. It was part of you, and you were part of it.

All he'd been really doing was treading water and avoiding ending something that he knew deep inside was wrong for him. When Olivia had come over the other night, all he had ever really wanted came true, and he should have jumped on it. It was too late to change plans for the dinner date, but he'd tell her after.

This time, Abel was late to the restaurant. He walked up to the entrance, the back of his shirt damp and stuck to him. He reached around and pulled it away, allowing a bolus of air to briefly cool him, before gravity pulled his shirt down and glued it to his back again. He wiped his hand on his pants and walked up to Maria, Carlita, and Carlita's mother who were all sitting in the white rockers lined up on Palmettos' porch.

Maria rocked forward and stood in one motion, wrapping him up in a hug. She released him and turned to the older woman. "Tía, this is my amigo, Abel." The old woman struggled out of the chair and grasped Abel's hand in both of hers. She released a torrent of Spanish which washed over him, only the kind tone sinking in.

The aunt stepped back and pushed Carlita forward, and Abel moved to hug her as Carlita reached out a hand. Carlita dropped her hand and accepted Abel's embrace stiffly.

Maria said, "Let's go in. Our reservation is ready." She reached for Abel's hand and pulled him through the door with Carlita and her mother. And just like last time, the waitstaff sat them at a comfortable table out of the main traffic flow and took their drink orders.

Over drinks, Maria kept the conversation moving, asking about Abel's day and the situation with his friends. She kept it in English, and after every few sentences, Carlita translated quietly to her mother who nodded but didn't ask any questions. Abel had been under the impression that Maria's cousin spoke little English, but from Carlita's rapid-fire translation, he realized that she was completely fluent. He didn't quite know why, but that bothered him at some level. The previous time he'd met her, he'd felt a coldness from her and had chalked that up to her inability to speak the language.

During dinner Abel tried to pull Carlita and her mother into conversation, but each attempt petered out quickly with Maria settling the talk back around Abel and their relationship. He figured that the weird dynamic was due to Maria not being close to this part of her extended family, but it was all she had to offer locally. Still, it felt awkward to Abel, and he was uncomfortable anyway because part of his head was focused on how he was going to break the news to Maria that he wanted to pursue his previous relationship with Olivia. So when dinner finally came to an end, he was relieved, even though it put him closer to the break-up conversation that was hanging over his head.

After Abel paid the bill, they all walked out to the parking lot. Maria dragged her feet a bit, and she said to Abel, "How about we go to your place? I've got some information for you that you are going to want to hear. It's about Guidry."

"Sure," said Abel. "But what about your cousin and aunt?"

"We drove separate cars. I mean, I love my aunt and cousin, but I want to spend time with you, too, tonight." She gave him a look. "Don't you want to spend time with me?"

"Yeah, definitely," said Abel, feeling a little bad.

They sped up so that they caught up with Carlita and her mother who were standing next to their car. Abel hugged them both, then Maria spoke quickly in Spanish, getting her relatives in their car and on the way home efficiently. He was bemused by the goodbye. Goodbyes for him and his friends and family usually dragged out a bit. Maria seemed anxious to get them on the road.

"That was quick work," said Abel.

"I don't want mi tía getting home after dark. She's getting on. And Carlita still doesn't completely know her way around."

"It's still early. Do you want to stop and get a drink?" asked Abel.

"No, I'll follow you to your place, and we can sit on the porch."

Abel drove out of the lot first and headed home, keeping an eye on the mirror to make sure that Maria was following. She knew where he lived, but he drove home slowly, and she followed like she was connected to him. They passed through Slidell quickly, and shortly, Abel turned into his drive and wended his way through the trees until they opened up and he pulled in to the front of his house. Maria pulled up next to him, and they both got out at the same time.

"Is Callie home tonight?" she asked.

"Nope, we have the house to ourselves."

Maria practically skipped up the stairs, and Abel rejoined her at the door and fished out his keys. "I can't believe you lock the door way out here in the woods," Maria said.

"Well, I have a few guns, so I like to button up. Out here in the sticks, it's about the only thing of value people have."

They stepped into the front room, and Maria excused herself to go to the bathroom. Abel yelled that he would be on the porch and went through the kitchen to the screened-in deck, stopping along the way to grab a couple of beers.

She came out a few minutes later, and by then Abel had settled on the couch. He handed her the bottle. "So what's up with Guidry? You said you had some info?"

"Right. The last time we talked, you said you had tried to get information on Guidry but that it didn't work out. I could hear in your voice how upset you were and worried about your friend, André. So I went back to Juan."

"I thought you said he wasn't banging anymore."

"Well, that's what he said, but I didn't totally believe that. I tracked him down and pressed him. I wasn't very nice and told him I was going to tell his mother some of the things he'd been doing."

"Wow, ratting him out to his mother. Yeah, not nice! You're evil!" Abel chuckled.

Maria punched him on the shoulder and said, "Anyway, he told me he was doing security on a transfer this Saturday."

"What does that mean?"

"Apparently, the Maras bring the money from the last shipment, and the Bastards motorcycle club brings a new load of crystal for the MS to sell."

"How does Guidry play in this?"

"He is going to be there with a couple of his men. He makes sure that things go smoothly and is like a guarantee that there isn't gonna be any heat. And I'm sure he's going to rake off his share from the payout."

"That's good," said Abel. "Where is this going down? What time?"

"On the east side of the canal, in one of those empty warehouses. I made Juan show me." Maria took her phone out of her purse and bent over it, working with both thumbs. Abel's phone pinged. "That's the GPS coordinates, the address, and a photo. Everything you need to catch Guidry in the act of a drug deal. Enough to take him down."

"I don't know how to thank you, Maria. We all owe you big time. I'm worried about you; this is dangerous shit."

"I know what I'm doing." She stood up and stepped away from the couch. "And I can think of a way for you to thank me." The sun had gone down below the trees, and the porch was in twilight. She took a step back from Abel and reached behind her neck with both hands. The last of the light barely illuminated her dress. Its large colorful flowers of the day were now shades of gray and black standing out from the white background. The dress came loose, but she caught it with one of her arms and held it up, partially covering herself.

She bent down and took Abel's hand, the dress draping loosely, and his mind emptied of all other thoughts.

Once again, Abel woke up to an empty bed. He laid there, thinking about how the night had not gone exactly the way he'd planned. He sighed and got out of bed. He noticed the pillow had streaks of blood on it, the sheets, too. He moved to the mirror over his dresser. His lower lip was slightly swollen, and there were bruises on his neck and bite marks on his chest and shoulders. He wiped at the dried blood on his shoulder and sighed again.

FIFTY-ONE

Setting aside his disappointment in himself, Abel finished doing his morning ablutions and escaped the house before Callie woke up. He figured she'd bug him about Maria versus Olivia, and he wasn't in the mood. He went straight to Tank's house and went through the back door to the kitchen. Isabelle wasn't around which was good because he didn't feel up to her insight, either. The coffee pot was full, so he helped himself and went up to Tank's bedroom.

"Wakey wakey," he called in a fake Isabelle voice outside Tank's door.

"What?" he heard Tank moan in a muffled voice, like the pillow was over his face.

"It's me. We gotta talk. I'm waking up André, too."

"I'm already awake," yelled André. "I'll be down in a minute."

Abel clomped back down the stairs and sat at the kitchen table. He sipped his coffee, prepared to wait, knowing it was gonna take Tank more than a few minutes to get his morning act together. But he was surprised when

Tank shuffled into the kitchen in a ratty plaid bathrobe hanging open with only his boxers underneath.

"What color is that robe? I'm pretty sure that's called morning baby poop."

"Haha." Tank groaned. "Do you know it's not even eight yet? Didn't you have a date with Maria last night?"

"Yeah, I did. What's your excuse?"

"Kisha and I went out, and we had 'the talk.'"

"Uh, which talk?" Abel had been subjected to many *talks* over the years and "the talk" didn't narrow it down much.

"I'm talking about the where-is-this-relationship-going talk."

"So where is the relationship going?" asked André as he came into the kitchen, fully showered and dressed.

"Jesus, you guys are as bad as she is."

"To be fair," said Abel, "you guys have been going out for two years. Even I'm getting impatient!"

"What did you tell her?" asked André.

"We agreed to take it next level," said Tank, and obviously hoping to avoid explaining what that meant, he went on the offense. "And what are you doing with respect to riding the fence with Maria and Olivia, Abel?"

"I was going to break up with Maria last night but fumbled the ball on the five-yard line because she told me some stuff, which is why I'm here. We have to defer the discussion of our love lives till later, and don't think you're getting off, André . . ."

"What did she say? More Guidry info?" asked Tank, happy to move on.

"She got more scoop from that Juan guy. There is a big money and meth transfer happening on Saturday between the Bastards and the Maras. She gave me all the details. There is this bankrupt, dilapidated warehouse down by the canal where it's all going down. We need to creep the place tonight to figure out how we're going to use it to put Guidry in a vise."

Chapter Fifty-One

"Do we need everybody?" asked André.

"Yep, I'll let Harm and Rabbit know. We'll leave from my place at eight. We can cram into my truck."

"No, it's better we have two trucks. I'll drive, too," said Tank.

The guys collected at Abel's house and did a little vehicle shuffling, finally splitting off into André riding with Tank, and Harm and Rabbit going with Abel. Rabbit insisted on driving, and Abel took shotgun so he could navigate from Maria's directions. Harm sprawled in the back seat with his eyes closed. They went over Lake Pontchartrain on the Twin Span and made their way to the canal on the edge of the Ninth.

It was dusk by the time they found the warehouse on the west side of the Inner Harbor Navigation Canal where the exchange was supposed to happen. It was part of a long strip of industrial buildings, some occupied and some empty and broken down. They cruised by slowly and made sure that the area was as quiet as Maria had described but kept going, continuing on another hundred yards and parking behind another decrepit building.

They got out and clustered together, talking strategy for a minute. Harm said, "Let me scout it out first and make sure there are no surprises. I'll text Abel if it's clear. You're all carrying, right?" They gave a chorus of yeahs.

Harm loped off toward the target warehouse, while Abel and the guys stood there silently waiting for the all clear. Abel had his phone in his hand so he could react to the text as soon as it rolled in.

He was starting to get worried, wondering whether Harm had gotten into trouble, when Tank whispered loudly, "So did you call Maria and break up?"

Rabbit immediately said, "What? That's the hottest girl you'll ever see. You can't end it. That's like a one breaking up with a ten. That just doesn't happen. Unless you're insane or something."

"Jesus, you idiots! Not now," said Abel. Then, his phone buzzed. He held it up. "OK, let's go. Don't bunch up."

When they got close to the building, Harm stepped out of the shadows. "Relax! We're good. There's nobody around."

Abel examined the warehouse. It was about a hundred feet wide by two hundred feet long with a big opening facing them. They could look straight through the building to a similar doorway on the back wall. The building had been designed to allow trucks to drive straight through it apparently. It had a lot in front of the opening, and there were other empty buildings on each side of the space.

Abel explained what Maria had told him. "These guys are gonna be here late afternoon next Saturday, so we have a week to get ready. They drive the truck with the drugs into the warehouse, and the rest of the Bastards' security roll in on their bikes. The Maras come in a couple of vehicles, and Guidry and Williams show up. Who knows, maybe they'll roll up in a cruiser."

"Do you think they go deep inside or just hang by the front door?" asked André.

"My guess is they are going in with the vehicles, and they'll stand in front of their cars and bikes in the light," said Harm.

Abel said, "I've been thinking about this a little. Harm you need to find a place out here for overwatch. You can get a good sight line with your rifle, and if shit goes south, you can start shooting. And Rabbit, think about how we get in here and outta here fast if we have to."

"I'm going inside the building to see where I can put the electronics. I've got a week to put this shit together. It's not going to be a replay of the rally. I'm going to make sure we are wired. I'm going to have redundant cameras and mic the shit out of the place. We'll stream it all off-site immediately. So if we lose the gear, we won't lose the data," said André.

Harm grabbed Rabbit and they moved off, and Tank, Abel, and André walked into the warehouse. The light was fading fast so it was a little difficult to see, but the inside of the place had some industrial machines or furnaces to either side of the passage that bisected the length of the building. There were beams crossing the space from either side going over the road about every twenty feet. A catwalk circled the perimeter of the building at the same height as the girders. About forty feet in, another catwalk was sitting on one of the beams crossing the space from right to left. Right in the center of the catwalk, directly above the passageway, was some kind of winch or crane assembly.

André was snapping photos of everything, and Abel asked him if it was going to work. "Yeah, this is perfect. I'll put in some parabolics and cameras here and there aimed at the center."

Tank said, "Put me on the catwalk right above the middle and stash Abel someplace with some gear, and we'll be all set."

Abel pointed at a big piece of industrial equipment that was sitting next to the path that ran through the building. "Check out this thing. I don't know what it did, but it's basically empty. Whatever was inside it has been ripped out, and that big duct runs up to the catwalk and then out the roof."

"It's some kind of large-scale flash dryer. That conveyor took stuff in, the heater dried it, and the stuff got dumped out the other side," said André semiconfidently. "It looks like it was decommissioned a hundred years ago."

André went around behind the machine and yelled out to Abel, "You're right. This is perfect." He came back around and said to Abel in a normal voice, "You can climb inside and film through one of the holes. It looks directly out to where the deal is probably going down. I'll set you up with the right equipment, and you'll be able to capture it in wide-screen Panavision."

"And if shit goes south, I can scamper up that vent pipe and exit on the roof," Abel said.

"Try it, dude. If that works, then you got a back door," said Tank.

Abel climbed into the machine, and André and Tank could hear him knocking around, then a banging noise started coming off the duct. The sound tracked up the duct, and then they heard a muffled, unintelligible yell.

A few minutes later, an unrecognizable man came around from the opening in the back. It was Abel, covered in soot from head to toe. Tank and André laughed. "It looks like you're riding in the bed of the truck on the way home," said Tank.

"Yeah, no shit," said Abel, laughing, too.

"Were you able to get all the way up?" asked Tank, making sure Abel wasn't going to be trapped if the plan went sideways.

"Yep, but it's slippery, and it goes up at a really steep angle. Knee pads and a rope ladder, and I'll be all set. When we come back, we can saw through the vent on the roof and stage some ladders. Good to go."

"We need to bolt some metal over that opening and the conveyor openings so if someone gets wise to you, they can't get in," added André. "I hope you're not claustrophobic, dude."

"Nope, just melanophobic and cacophobic," answered Abel, immediately." Then, he stood there with a grin on his face.

"What's that mean?" asked Tank.

"I'm afraid of ugly black things."

"Haha, fuck you!" said Tank. They all laughed.

"And it's good that you aren't a leukophobe 'cuz then you couldn't look in the mirror," tacked on André a little late.

"Joke's over, dude. Nerds!" said Tank, shaking his head. "To get real for a minute, we're gonna be spread thin given the number of bad guys that're probably going to be here. We need more men. Want me to call Didi and see if he and his ghosts can help?"

"That's a good idea. Remember, he said he wanted to help take down Guidry? Alright, let's go hook up with Harm and Rabbit and see what they found. Talk this shit over."

André had spent all week thinking about the issues at the site and getting the gear together, and by Wednesday night, he had it all ready to go. The first problem had been that there was no power at the shutdown warehouse, and he'd solved that by getting some heavy-duty auto batteries and a two-kilowatt 120 V inverter. That way he could just use standard extension cords to get power to the places he was going to install the gear.

He bought all the cameras and microphones from Amazon and had them overnighted. It was amazing what you could get nowadays. For the parabolics, he bought a couple of handhelds and cobbled together a WiFi interface for them. But then, to be sure they captured the audio, he went old school and built his own with a microphone and a big metal bowl he got from a restaurant supply store.

He painted the bowl flat black and figured that he could mount it up under the catwalk, and the dipshit gangbangers would just think it was some part of the industrial equipment left there from its previous days. He'd aim it at the spot where he figured the deal was going down, and the big bowl would gather all the sound waves and funnel them to the microphone at the focal point of the bowl.

And finally, he needed a way to talk to all the surveillance devices on site. He purchased a rugged enterprise router with an extended WiFi range, that had a 4G LTE cellular modem. At home, he tweaked his server to catch all the audio and video data that would be streaming from the warehouse. Guidry, the Maras, and the Bastards would have no idea they were gonna be the stars of their own TV show, and it was going to be recorded and saved for posterity.

Around nine o'clock, Abel came over to the Chevals' house and helped the brothers get the gear primed for a quick install at the warehouse, putting together a kit of tools, black duct tape, and about a thousand zip ties of various sizes. Rabbit was supposed to bring some tools, sheet steel, and hardware from his dad's auto shop.

Finally, Harm and Rabbit showed up, and they all headed to the warehouse to set up. When they got there, Tank and André split off to mount the cameras and microphones, and Rabbit and Abel started working on the industrial dryer, making it a perfect hide. Harm went out to stand guard, making sure they didn't get surprised by some teenagers looking for a place to make out or a security guard.

Abel and Rabbit made their way to the dryer. "Dude, I still can't believe you're gonna lock yourself in this thing," Rabbit said.

"Yeah, that's why you're helping me. I want to make sure that if it gets crazy, I can get the fuck outta Dodge."

They closed off the conveyor belt openings on the sides by bolting sheets of steel over them and then moved inside the unit and cut a hole in its front with a battery-powered angle grinder that had a cutting disk installed. This opened up a window so Abel's camera would have a good view of the festivities. For the parabolic mic that Abel was going to be aiming, Rabbit cut another opening and then bolted a piece of coarse screen over it. The sound waves could travel through it, but it would obscure the parabolic.

Abel pointed out the duct that was his escape route, and Rabbit shook his head. "Fuck me! We have to fix that thing so you can move up it fast."

They climbed out of the piece of equipment and moved over to the side of the warehouse where there was a set of stairs to the encircling catwalk. Rabbit followed Abel up, and they found the door to the roof. Rabbit busted the lock, and the door swung open to another set of stairs on the outside of the building that gave access to the flat roof above. Clambering onto the roof, they made their way to the vent box above the duct from the industrial dryer.

Rabbit whipped out his angle cutter and buzzed one side off. Abel covered the sharp edges with duct tape, then he tied a rope around the unit and dropped it down the duct. He shook it and watched it slide down and disappear into the blackness. "Alright, now it's time to practice getting up and out."

"Before you do that, I need your help carrying some sheets of metal up to where Tank is gonna be. It's mostly protected, but there are some spots where I've got to put some armor. If he has to run, he needs cover to get to the door to the roof. I don't have much steel, so we may have to scrounge some shit to stack along the catwalk to give him more protection."

Abel helped Rabbit, then made several practice runs escaping from the dryer unit. He stood at the front of the dryer, then pressed the timer on his phone, shoved it in his pocket, and climbed up the duct to the roof as fast as he could, occasionally giving himself a hand with the rope.

This time he was smart and wore a boiler suit, but still, after a few runs he was covered in grime, and every time he wiped sweat from his eyes, he left another big black streak on his face.

By the end, he was covered in gummy black dust and dead tired but had managed to get onto the roof in thirty-three seconds. That would be an eternity in a shootout, but it would have to do. He hoped it wouldn't come to that.

After somewhat reassuring himself that he had an escape, he went back to helping Rabbit do the same for Tank. By the time they were done cobbling together protection, Tank would be able to scuttle along the catwalk to the roof door and be mostly protected.

Next, they went back outside and unstrapped an extension ladder that they had tied to Abel's truck and carried it around to the far end of the warehouse. After stacking up some pallets, they were able to lean the fully extended ladder against the building's outside wall and tie it in place.

Abel ran back inside the warehouse, up the catwalk stairs, out the roof door, and up to the roof. He ran the length of the building, climbed down onto the ladder, and speed dropped, sliding down the ladder while barely hitting a wrung. He controlled himself with his gloved hands and his toes. Going down the ladder was a lot faster than climbing the duct.

He walked back to the front and met up with Harm and Rabbit. "You see anything out here?" he asked Harm.

"No, this place is dead. Probably why they picked this place. Are they almost done inside?"

Rabbit and Abel walked back inside to help Tank and André finish while Harm continued to guard the outside. André assigned them some hardware to install, and they finished up getting the gear in place inside the warehouse.

Finally, the four of them finished the job and stood standing in the middle of the building. "Now, we test it," announced André.

Rabbit groaned. "It's three in the morning!"

André said, "I have to know if there is something fucked up now so I have time to fix it."

"Wait a second," Abel said and ran out to his truck and grabbed a cooler from the back. He brought it back to the guys and handed out icy Cokes. "We'll take a rest and then check everything out."

After the break, André walked out to the shed where he had hidden the communication equipment and turned everything on. Then, they simulated what they thought was going to take place on Saturday. It took another two hours, and they had to move some cameras around, but by the end they had proved that the surveillance system worked. André was even able to check the server at his house using his phone and watch the recording.

They shut everything down, and Tank and André carried the batteries back to the truck so that they could take them home and top off the charge before they came back for the real deal. Harm and Abel made arrangements to come back several times before Saturday to make sure their stuff hadn't been interfered with.

"Let's go," Rabbit said. "Crystal's gonna kill me. I told her I was going to be back before midnight."

"Aw, she's probably asleep," said Harm. "I gotta meet with Maroni in a couple of hours. If I look like shit, he's gonna bust my chops. I'm going to go park somewhere and grab a nap."

"Yeah, this took a long time. I'm sorry. But thanks for helping me. Not just now, but the last few weeks. I don't know what I woulda done without you guys," said André emotionally.

Abel hugged him. "You don't have to say thanks. We got your back. Always."

On Saturday morning, the guys met Didi and a couple of his ghosts at the warehouse. Maria had said the deal was going down at four in the afternoon, but Abel wasn't taking any chances, and he wanted to get there and make sure their surveillance equipment was all good to go.

Rabbit had brought Tank and André's dirt bikes, KTM 300 XCs, and Abel's Yamaha on a trailer, and they needed time to get them staged in an accessible place near the warehouse where they had the ladder to the roof set up. The location had numerous battered and decaying vehicles strewn about, and it was going to be easy to hide the bikes and their escape vehicles in plain sight.

Rabbit had been the crew's transpo guy forever, and besides the bikes, he'd brought down two anonymous late-nineties Chevy Impala SS four door sedans. They were almost twenty years old, and looked it on the outside, but inside they were running with meaty 350-cubic-inch LT1 V8s.

Since Abel was going to be stuck inside the industrial dryer in the middle of the warehouse and Tank would be twenty feet overhead on the catwalk, André was going to orchestrate the scene when the deal went down. He led the guys in a run-through before lunch, putting Harm and Didi on overwatch with their rifles on the roof of adjacent buildings.

Harm had brought two Bushmaster AR15s with 4x Leupold scopes that he'd picked up from a pawn shop in Houston for cheap and that he was prepared to lose if he had to. When Didi had offered to help and insisted he could shoot, Harm went up to the Blood River to get proof.

Harm recounted with amazement that Didi had been shooting one-inch groups at a hundred yards. Didi had explained that besides all the herbs and plants he had to find, he also provided dried brains and other organs from various varmints to his voodoo and hoodoo customers. Harm hoped that under the pressure of real people shooting at him Didi would retain his composure.

Didi had brought a couple of his friends who had been the ghosts in the woods spooking Abel when they first met him near the Dollar Place up off the Blood. André used one of them hidden behind the building, covering Abel and Tank's escape route down the ladder. They'd given him an untraceable Glock, and they all hoped he didn't have to use it.

André put them all in place and called all their phones in conference mode. They walked through the deal scenario as they imagined it, and then André told them to escape. Tank and Abel ran up to the roof, across it, and down the ladder. Didi's friend, Kevon, mimed a few pretend shots in the direction of the building, and the three of them ran to the bikes and took off.

At the same time, Harm, André, and Didi went over the sides of their respective buildings. Didi had it easy with a ladder welded to the side of his building, but Harm and André had to climb down a fragile wooden extension ladder they'd found on site. Rabbit was there waiting in his Impala, and the second Harm and André piled in, he laid thirty yards of rubber as he rocketed through the canal complex.

Didi wasn't left hanging. Another of his ghosts, James, was waiting for him in the other Impala. They tore through the complex in the other direction and left through the southern exit.

After the practice run, the guys grabbed some lunch, hit the bathrooms, and rehydrated. They went back to the site and settled in for a long wait in the heat.

It was overcast, so they didn't have to contend with the blasting sun, but it was still in the low nineties and humid. It was the worst for Abel; he was essentially in an oven. He was pounding bottles of water and jammed in a little area with sharp metal edges everywhere he turned and was getting drowsy. His head nodded forward, resting against the metal side of the dryer. His phone vibrated, and he jerked upright. He answered and reset the earbud. He heard André's voice. "Someone just pulled up! Everybody get ready!" Abel's heart went into overdrive, and he could feel it thumping against his chest wall.

FIFTY-TWO

André was lying on the roof next to Harm, looking at the scene in front of the warehouse through a pair of binoculars. He could see some distance into the building through the doorway as the afternoon light reached deep into the warehouse. A Harley had just rolled up with a throaty rumble and driven straight through the open doorway, down the lane inside the building, and out the other end. It circled the warehouse and parked in front of the warehouse in the open area.

The rider leaned the motorcycle to the side and heeled the stand. He pried the helmet off, shook his lank hair out and dismounted, then hung the helmet off the handlebars. André could read his cut, which proudly displayed *The Bastards* in red block letters in an arc across his broad back. Turning around, the man eyeballed the lot and the surrounding buildings, stopping for a moment as he checked out the roof they were lying on. André's heart jolted, even though he knew they couldn't be seen.

Earlier, Rabbit had set up some steel boxes that looked like generic HVAC units, which gave them cover and allowed them to hunker down and not be seen as long as they didn't move around or do anything stupid. The building that Didi was on already had real HVAC units that served the same purpose.

The man down below did a quick walk around, looking here and there, then pulled out his phone and made a call. André watched him wait, noticing his shiny white bald spot glinting in the sun. The scout shook out a cigarette and lit it. Five minutes passed. An old-school white delivery van pulled in, and the advance man waved the vehicle into the warehouse. The van jockeyed around and backed into the space, stopping in plain view. *Good,* thought André, *that's gonna make it easy to watch what happens.*

Three more motorcycles roared into the lot. Then, a small truck with the word *Produce* on the side drove straight into the building and parked next to the white van. The driver of the produce truck opened the back doors, and two men jumped down and stood at alert holding what appeared to be AKs. The truck driver leaned against the side of the truck.

Harm whispered, "Now, all we need is Guidry!"

André was whispering into his phone, giving a one-sided status to everyone else. A car drove up. It was immediately followed by another. Guidry and Williams stepped out of the first vehicle, and two bangers rolled from the second. One of the Maras was wearing a flannel shirt with the long sleeves buttoned and the collar button fastened tight to his neck despite the heat. The other was wearing a white V-neck undershirt. The two detectives weren't in uniform but still managed to broadcast the message "I'm a cop."

The four men walked into the warehouse, the gang members moving with a rolling gait, their arms away from their bodies like they were bodybuilders with big lats, trying to dominate the space. Oddly, Guidry couldn't seem to walk in a straight line and periodically had to adjust himself back and forth like a sailboat. Once, Randy even grabbed his upper arm as if to guide him, but Guidry shook him off.

André gave the play-by-play. "Looks like they are all here. Guidry, Williams, and two MS-13 bosses. Guidry looks drunk or high—he can't walk straight."

Inside the dryer unit, Abel could see Guidry come into the warehouse. André was right. The fucker looked drunk, or sick even, slightly swaying back and forth as if he was standing in the ocean and trying to stay anchored against the waves. Randy had a concerned expression on his face, but no one was paying attention to the cops. Instead, the Maras and the Bastards were moving product.

The double doors on the back of the white van had been opened, and four of the Bastards were ferrying cardboard boxes from the van to the small panel truck. Two bangers were inside the produce truck stacking the boxes in an orderly fashion, while the Mara bosses supervised the operation.

Abel texted Tank: "Are you getting this?" He received a "y."

When the last box was loaded, the motorcycle men moved closer to Abel's hide, out of his direct line of sight. Then, one man leaned against the industrial dryer with a clunk right next to the opening where Abel had his camera. Abel could see the man's shoulder. He froze and slowed his breathing, but he couldn't stop his heart. The beating sounded loud to him, and he imagined the guy could hear it. He made like a statue, the sweat dripping into his eyes, stinging. He blinked repeatedly, but it wasn't helping, and he had to will himself not to wipe his eyes.

There hadn't been much talk while the drugs were being transferred, but when the overhead door on the produce truck clattered down, the Mara boss gave a curt order in Spanish, and the MS-13 truck driver went to the cab and dragged out a large duffle bag. It was heavy, and he pulled it along the floor until it was in front of the Bastards head honcho who was standing next to Guidry.

The man kneeled, unzipped the bag, and plunged his inked arms into the duffle like he was a surgeon going deep to remove a gallbladder. He came out with a brick of cash and handed it to Guidry.

"There's your piece," he grunted and looked at one of his men. "Count it." He turned to the Mara gang leaders. "Not that I don't trust you!" He laughed like it was a big joke. The MS-13 bosses didn't say anything; they just stood there, stone faced.

Man, I sure hope we got that on all the cameras, Abel thought, his eyes still burning. He continued to stand like a statue.

The man who had handed the detective his cut started talking. "Guidry, you said you had something you wanted to talk about?"

"Uh, yeah I did."

Abel could see Guidry's face over the camera he had pointed at the scene. It was slightly confused looking. His forehead wrinkled like he was thinking as hard as he could, then his expression morphed into a scowl. He said, "I just wanted to remind everybody that we're all in this together. We have to keep our own houses clean, or we all go down." He wheeled around, bringing up his pistol, and shot Williams in the cheek. Matter spewed out of the back of his head, painting the white van with gray chunks and crimson splatter. The Bastard who had been standing next to Williams wiped his face off with a stunned look.

As the echo died away, Guidry said, "The fucker wasn't being careful enough . . ."

"Holy shit!" said André over the comms. "I think you guys should get out of there!"

"Throw the body in the van, and dump it somewhere," Guidry ordered the men still standing there in shock. He started moving toward the exit.

Tank started moving, too, and in his haste, he popped up high enough that a piece of his shirt was momentarily visible over the side of the catwalk.

"There's somebody up there!" one of the motorcycle guys yelled, pointing at the structure above them. Suddenly, everyone had a gun out and was firing up at the catwalk. Abel could hear Harm and Didi methodically firing round after round at the men in the warehouse who were shooting up at Tank. Most of the men inside the building turned around and started firing back at Harm and Didi.

Abel didn't know what was exactly happening outside his hide but knew he didn't want to be caught in a firefight, and he dropped the gear he was holding and ran for the vent stack. He leaped into the duct and grabbed the rope and started up, making frantic scrabbling sounds like a cat caught in a chimney. The noise of the guns covered the sounds, and he made it up and out to the roof.

"Tank where are you?" he said over the comm channel.

"I'm almost to the stairs," Tank said breathlessly.

Abel ran back through the roof door and peered down. Tank was there taking the stairs to the roof two at a time. Suddenly, there was a great rending roar, then a crash could be heard above the gunfire. "There go the stairs," said Tank, as the inside stairway leading from the ground to the catwalk collapsed.

Thank you, Rabbit! thought Abel. It had been Rabbit's last-minute idea to saw through all the bolts that held the stairway up to the catwalk. Now, nobody could follow Tank up the roof stairs. Tank crested the stairs and he and Abel blasted across the flat roof toward the ladder. They reached the end of the building, and Tank clambered over the edge onto the ladder and did a speed drop, barely touching a wrung. Abel glanced over his shoulder to make sure no one had climbed onto the roof behind him, then grabbed the top of the ladder and swung around and slid down, controlling his speed by pressing his insteps against the side of the ladder frame.

Tank was standing at the bottom of the ladder in a shooting stance aimed at the open back door of the warehouse when suddenly a man burst through the opening. Before he could get a shot off, Didi's ghost Kevon popped up out of the shrubbery behind the building and shot the man. Abel grabbed Tank by the shoulder and got him moving toward the dirt bikes hidden with Kevon.

The three of them mounted the bikes and kicked them to life. They tore off cross country each spewing a rooster tail of gravel behind them. The Bastards might have been able to go after them with their motorcycles, except no fat hog was going to be able handle the path they'd taken over debris, under overhangs, and between buildings. The motorcycle gang couldn't give chase anyway because Harm and Didi had them pinned down. They couldn't get to their own Harleys.

Back on the roof, André was getting antsy. "Harm, we gotta git! They're going to break out any second, then we'll be trapped up here."

Harm paused his shooting for a second, speaking without taking his eyes off the scene below, "Roll the cars! Get Didi off the other roof. André you go, too! Get down the rope now!"

"I'm not leaving without you," André said, then urgently told James and Rabbit over the conference line that it was evac time.

"Fuck, man! Go now! I'll be right behind you," yelled Harm.

André bear crawled to the rope and dropped over the side. Ten seconds later, Harm heard the rumble of Rabbit's Impala. He scrambled to the roof edge, turning and firing bursts back at the warehouse, then slung the AR over his shoulder and fast roped down.

André was already in the car but had left the backdoor open, and Harm dived in just like the old days. Rabbit smoked his tires as he accelerated toward the warehouse complex exit, then took the ramp at speed, the bump throwing all three of them into the air. The car slammed back down, and Rabbit wrestled it back into control. He blew through Didi and James's dust cloud, then put the hammer down and caught up.

The two cars headed to the neighborhoods east of the canal zone. They turned off the main road and were out of sight in seconds. Rabbit followed Didi into a large apartment complex where they stashed the Impalas. Transferring into André's Super Crew that had been parked there since the morning, they sedately drove off, heading for the rendezvous location.

Tank, Abel, and Kevon were already there and sitting on their bikes in an unused lot at the New Orleans Lakefront Airport when André pulled in. Rabbit's trailer was there for the bikes, and it was all set to go, hitched to Abel's F-150. The men piled out of the truck, and they congregated around the three dirt bikes.

"Holy shit!" said Tank. "Can you believe Guidry shot his own man? He just turned and plunked him in the head."

"Yeah, splattered his brains all over everybody and the white van," said Harm.

"It was like a Jackson Pollock painting," added André.

"Who?" asked Rabbit.

"The American abstract artist who was famous for splashing paint all over his canvasses," said Harm.

They all looked at Harm. "What? I know some things," he said. They all laughed, releasing some of the pent-up tension.

"Guys, we better split, but I'd say we nailed that motherfucker. Hebert puts that shit in front of a jury— Guidry will be history. Hell, the prosecutor sees that video? The charges will be dropped. I'd say both André and Didi are off the hook."

For the first time in several weeks, André's expression relaxed. "Guys, I can't begin to thank you—"

"Yeah, yeah," Tank said and gave his brother a big hug. Then, everybody was hugging each other and giving high-fives.

Finally, Abel broke up the celebration and said, "Let's load up the bikes and get the fuck outta here!"

CHAPTER

FIFTY-THREE

Abel and Callie were sitting in the living room talking about the Guidry takedown. Abel had gotten home after dropping off all the bikes and unhitching the trailer at Rabbit's dad's garage. Callie had met him at the door, anxious to find out what had happened. She had been taken through everything up to the detective shooting Williams.

When she heard that, she sat back with a look of amazement on her face. "And you guys have that all on video? His face and all the stuff he said?" she asked incredulously.

"Yep, André reviewed the video on the way home. Somehow, he can magically check his personal server with his phone. He said it's perfect. The audio was crystal clear, too."

"That means he's off the hook. The DA has to drop the charges. There's no way they are going to put that in front of a jury."

"Yeah, they are going to have to open up an investigation on Guidry for corruption and murder. And they won't be able to sweep it under the rug because of the Consent Decree, either."

"I'm so relieved—" Callie was interrupted by a pounding on the front door.

Abel stood up and went to the door and looked out the sidelight. It was Rabbit. He opened the door and started to say, "Hey, it just seems like—"

Rabbit spoke over him. "Is Crystal here? I got home, and she wasn't there. Then, I checked my mom's. She's not there, either. No messages on my phone. I called her girlfriends, and she's not there. They don't know where she is. She didn't leave me any messages. There's no note."

"Whoa!" Abel said. "Slow down!" He grabbed Rabbit's arm and dragged him in the house and sat him down. But Rabbit stood back up and started pacing. "Something's wrong. I can feel it. Something's wrong."

"Is her car at home?" asked Callie.

"Uh, I didn't check the whole lot. I just checked her usual spot. It wasn't there."

"Maybe she took a walk? She's almost due, so maybe she's getting antsy," said Callie.

"Look," said Abel, "we'll all go over to your place and look around. We can call her doctor and see if she's there. We'll look for her car and maybe get one of the bikes and check the paths in the woods and see if she's out walking."

"I'll start calling people and get the guys back over to your house," said Callie.

"Let's go. We'll follow you over," said Abel.

Rabbit took off down the driveway and was in the trees before Abel even got his truck turned around. They followed after him, and as soon as they pulled out onto Fish Hatchery Road, Callie said, "Is he blowing this out of proportion? Maybe having post-traumatic stress triggered from this afternoon?"

"I don't know. I've actually never seen him in this state. Even back in the day when shit was going down, he'd be running off at the mouth, making jokes."

Chapter Fifty-Three

As they neared the garage, they could see Rabbit standing and waving at them frantically. Abel pulled up next to him and rolled down the window. "I found her car! She didn't take her car!"

"I'll go into the apartment with you," said Callie. "We can call her doctor and anybody else you can think of. Abel can drive around here and see if he can find her."

Callie got out and put her arm around Rabbit, and they started heading toward the stairs to his apartment. Abel reversed out of the lot and headed down the road. He called the rest of the guys and told them Crystal was missing and Rabbit was freaking.

Abel spent a half hour driving in ever-widening circles from the auto shop but didn't see Crystal. Then, he went back to the garage and parked his truck. There was a path through the woods near there that that he wanted to check out. He sprinted down the path, running with more and more urgency until he popped back out of the woods. He was bent at the waist, his hands at his hips, gasping for breath when his phone rang.

He straightened and fished it out of his pocket, expecting it to be Callie telling him they'd found Crystal. Instead, it was Maria. He listened for a minute. "Oh no . . ." A terrible expression came over his face, then he turned toward Rabbit's apartment and started running.

CHAPTER

FIFTY-FOUR

A bel went up the steps to Rabbit's apartment and then through the open door. Callie saw his stricken face. "What? What happened?"

Abel stood there looking at Rabbit, Callie, Harm, Tank, and André who were all staring back at him. "I got a call. It was from Maria. She said they have Crystal."

"Maria? Why is Crystal with your girlfriend?" asked Rabbit.

"Who are *they*, Abel?" asked Harm slowly, a strange blankness on his face.

Abel, sick to his stomach, said, "MS-13. Maria said she runs the clique. She wants the money we stole from them. She says we took them for over a million, and she wants it all back. And that we are going to pay for killing all their leaders."

"But she's nice. She's your girlfriend. She likes us . . ." Rabbit couldn't seem to catch up. He sat down, his eyes jittering crazily around in the sockets.

"That psycho bitch was pretending the whole time. What kind of person can do something like that? She wiggled her way in, finding out all about us, finding out how to get the best leverage," said Callie with an ugly expression on her face.

Harm said, "You should have listened to me. I told you something was wrong." He had the same calm tone, but it belied the waves of anger boiling off him.

Abel suddenly ran back out the front door and vomited over the porch railing. He was gripping the black metal so hard that his hands were white, the spasms wracking his body until all that was coming out was bile. He stood up and wiped his mouth with the hem of his T-shirt and went back inside.

"This is all my fault. I should have seen through her. I let her into our world."

"It's on all of us. We all were part of ripping off the Maras," said André.

Tank had been standing there in shock. He rubbed his face with both hands, then said, "What does she want us to do? What instructions did she give you?"

"She told me to shut the fuck up and listen. She's gonna call back tonight with the details. We have till Monday at noon to get the money together. When I told her I didn't know what she was talking about, she said that René told her all about us before he died. Said, 'How could I think that she really liked me?' What a bunch of weak, stupid pendejos we all were and that she couldn't believe we were able to kill Garcia. She hung up laughing. She fucking killed my cousin!"

"Shit!" said André. "You do realize she's been playing us since the beginning, right? She probably had Guidry attack and arrest me to keep us all distracted while she infiltrated us."

"And that telling us about the drug deal and setting up Guidry was a move by her to get us out of the way so she could snatch Crystal," added Tank.

Abel groaned and started to say something, but Harm cut him off. "This isn't about the money. This is about revenge. It's a demonstration of power. Pretty unusual for a woman to be running the MS clique. She's got to be over the top. The Crystal thing is to get us crazy and get what money she can from us. Then, she's gonna try to kill us all. She's got to show her soldiers she's ruthless, otherwise she can't hold power."

Abel went over to Rabbit and sat down next to him and put his arm around him. "Don't worry. We'll figure something out. We'll scrape together the money. It won't be a million, but it will be everything we all have. Then, we'll go get Crystal and your babies."

Harm bent down and looked into Rabbit's eyes. "Remember why you made me godfather?" Harm waited till Rabbit nodded, then squeezed his shoulder and stood up.

Tank said, "Let's move over to my house. There's more room, and we're going to need everybody. My mama will want to help."

FIFTY-FIVE

E veryone was milling around the Chevals' house: Rabbit and his mother and father, Harm and his mother, and Callie and Abel who had made a stop and shown up with three extra-large pizzas and some liters of soda. Isabelle had gotten out the old-school percolator and had brewed a giant batch of coffee, and Tank and André were walking around making sure people had what they needed.

Callie had laid the pizza out on Isabelle's big dining room table, but no one was exactly able to sit down and eat like it was a meal. Tensions were too high; although, Abel and the guys were at least walking around with a slice. Like soldiers, they knew they had to eat while they had the chance.

Rabbit was standing next to his parents and Harm's mother in the dining room, looking around with the dazed expression that had taken over his face. Abel gave the rest of the guys the eye, and they migrated to the kitchen. Isabelle had her back to them and was putting together a salad.

"Maria said she was gonna call before midnight. I'll tell her we're going to need to hear Crystal on the phone, or we aren't doing anything."

"OK, Abel, that's good," said Harm. "I got to believe they have her either in The Loco or one of their gang houses. I wonder if they are still using Garcia's house."

"Basically, we don't know where Crystal is," said Tank. "But she's probably in the Ninth somewhere. André can't you hack the phone company and figure out where her cell is?"

"I've never done it, and I don't think I could figure it out by Monday."

"OK, that's out," said Abel. "But we know she wants the money, so there's gonna be a swap of some kind on Monday. I doubt that Maria will bring Crystal to the meet."

Harm said, "We either backtrack Maria to Crystal or we snatch Maria for reverse leverage."

"It all depends on what Maria says when she calls," said André. "We gotta wait. It's killing me."

Tank, André, and Harm went back to the dining room to check on Rabbit, leaving Abel alone in the kitchen. He sat down at the kitchen table and halfheartedly tried to finish his piece of pizza. He took a bite and chewed it, then tried to swallow. It felt like he had accidently swallowed an ice cube; the pizza was barely going down and hurting the whole way. Isabelle stopped messing with the salad and came over and sat next to Abel. She put her bony hand on his and leaned in. They began talking quietly. After a while, they both stood up and Isabelle gave Abel a quick hug, and they joined everybody else in the dining room.

Then, time stood still for a while as they all tried to support Rabbit, but it was brutal. It was like watching an unlit candle in the sun gradually slumping. Around midnight, Abel's phone rang.

Abel answered, "We are all here. You're on speaker. We want to hear Crystal before we go any further."

Chapter Fifty-Five

"Of course." There was a rustling noise, then, "Speak!"

"Charlie?"

"I'm here, baby," choked out Rabbit.

"I wanna come home."

"I know," said Rabbit. "We're gonna bring you home—"

Maria interrupted. "Aw, that's sweet. Now, this is how it's going down. On Monday at three pm, I'm going to call you again. By then, you'll have had all day to get the money put together. And I know you've got it, probably in safety deposit boxes. I'll tell you where to go, and Abel, you're going to come without all your buddies. But here's the deal. Your sister is going to walk the money to me. You aren't gonna even get out of your truck. Once she hands me the money, I'll tell her where to go to get Crystal."

"Just a second, let me check with my sister." Abel put the phone on mute.

"I can do it," Callie started to say, but Abel interrupted her. "No, we have a different plan."

Abel switched the phone off mute. "Callie can't. She's got a shift at the ER. Isabelle said she would do it."

"That old Black lady, Tank's mama?" Maria snorted. "That's even better. And you better have all the money! And you better not try any of your bullshit, or you'll never see Crystal again. Alive, anyway . . ."

Maria terminated the connection, and the second the line dropped Tank said "Mama, what the—"

Isabelle glared at her son. "Don't!" Tank bit his lip and looked at André, who shrugged.

She went over to Rabbit and embraced him, and he let out a spasming sob. She stepped back and said, "We have a lot to do tomorrow. We all should get some sleep. Or try, at least."

FIFTY-SIX

From Saturday night to Monday at three o'clock seemed like an eternity had passed, but at the same time, it felt like they hadn't had enough time to prepare. Sunday was spent getting vehicles and their weapons and body armor ready. They wanted to use all anonymous cars, but the plan required a raised truck, so they had to use Harm's jacked up F-150 and slap some stolen plates on it. Monday, they emptied their safety deposit boxes.

They'd gotten all their money together, but they were south of the million. Short by a long shot. Even after the robbery from two years ago it wasn't a million, and they'd all been dipping into it to live. Now, it was in a duffle in the back seat of the truck. If you zipped the duffle open and took a quick look, it appeared to be a lot of money.

Abel's phone rang. He looked at everybody. They stared back grimly. He answered, "Where do we go?"

The phone was on speaker, and everybody clustered around. Maria said, "You've got forty-five minutes. At exactly three forty-five I'm going to be waiting on the lane between the two fields at Digby Park in the Ninth. You go in off of Virginia Street. Stay in the lot. Send the old lady to us with the money."

"OK."

"Just you and her. You bring more people? Crystal's dead. You fuck with me? She's dead. If you don't have the million? She's dead."

"Got it!" said Abel. The line dropped.

Harm climbed into the bed of his raised pickup. Abel got into the driver side, and Isabelle climbed into the back with the money bag. Abel started moving slowly. Callie got into her Toyota and followed after Abel. Rabbit was in one of the Impalas from Saturday, and Tank and André were in the other. It wasn't ideal. They should have dumped the two cars and replaced them, but Rabbit was low on inventory. The truth was, he was barely functional.

Once they got on the road, the two Impalas moved ahead of Abel. Callie did, too. Her job was to take a first pass around the park and scope out the scene and see if there were more MS-13 soldiers staged. If she saw something, she'd give Rabbit, Tank, and André the heads up and hopefully the guys could neutralize them.

They crossed Lake Pontchartrain and headed to the meet. The park was in the middle of a small residential neighborhood in the Ninth. It was not likely to have much of a police presence, if any. Abel and the other's hung back, and Callie took a slow tour around the park, driving down Pines, Hermes, Dwyer, then back up Virginia.

She gave a steady report on the conference call linking them all together. "No one standing around. North side of the park. Houses are way back on Pines. Now I'm going south on Hermes. Lots of residential houses, but everybody must be at work. Houses look dead. Some cars parked in the front yards. Can't see behind them. I'm on Dwyer heading west. Big elementary school here, but it looks like the kids have all gone home—thank God. Alright, turning back north on Virginia. I'm looking into the park entrance. I see a car parked down the dividing road. It's near the Hermes side of the park."

"Tank, you guys need to get on each end of the park on Hermes and cover that area. The Maras are either in the houses or maybe the trees on that side of the park," said Abel.

Tank started talking. "Rabbit, stage the southeast corner of the park. I'm going to drop André in the trees on the northeast. Then I'm going to sit at that end of the street and watch for shooters from the north end. Abel, give us three minutes. I'll give you the go."

Two minutes went by. Tank said, "Go, Abel. We're set."

Abel drove Harm's big black raised truck into the lot of Digby Park. It wasn't exactly a parking lot with curbs and neat lines painted on it. It was more like broken concrete with patches of gravel and grass befitting the city's investment in the Ninth Ward. Abel lined the truck up with the lane that stretched from the lot to Hermes on the east side of the park. Abel reported that he could see a car parked at the far end. He rolled to a stop.

The truck's bed cover obscured Harm but the tailgate had been left down, and the second the vehicle stopped moving Harm scooted forward and flowed over the gate onto the ground like a drop of mercury sliding off the top of a table. The previous day, Rabbit had extended the front air dam on the truck so that people in front of the truck couldn't see under it. Harm wormed his way up to the front on his belly, the AR15 in his hand, the drive train of the truck looming over him. They had made a hole large enough in the air dam to accommodate the barrel and scope so that Harm could see enough to shoot.

Harm looked through the scope and watched Maria and her sicario, Carlita, exit their car. Harm could hear Abel answer the phone above him. Then, he heard Isabelle get out of the truck. The heavy duffle bag of money hit the ground, and he could hear it being dragged. Soon he saw Isabelle walking ahead of him toward Maria and Carlita.

She'd been instructed to stand off to the side so that she wasn't in his shooting lane. Belle had picked up the duffle, but a corner was still dragging on the ground. Every now and then Isabelle gave a hitch and managed to hold it up off the ground, but then it would slip back down.

Over the conference line Abel had given the heads up that Isabelle was moving. Tank responded, "I don't see anybody." Then André said, "Nobody in the woods." And finally, Rabbit, unusually terse, said, "Southeast clear." Everybody could hear the crunch of gravel through Belle's phone as she made her way to the kidnappers.

Isabelle made it to the two women at the end of the lane and dropped the duffle onto the ground. She was slightly to the right of Maria. Carlita was standing next to Maria on Isabelle's left and had a handgun pointed down next to her side.

"I thought you were going to collapse before you got here," said Maria nastily. "That better not be a bag of rocks."

"A million dollars is heavy," said Isabelle with no inflection.

Maria bent down in front of Belle and unzipped the bag and started rooting her hands through the stacks. "Well, well, well, you came through with the money."

Harm was watching through the scope and giving the play-by-play to the rest of the crew. Suddenly, he saw Carlita raise her pistol and aim it at Isabelle. Mindless muscle memory kicked in and he made a minute adjustment and pulled the trigger.

Red gore burst from Carlita's head as the sicario collapsed like a puppet whose strings had been cut. Quickly, Belle reached into her own hair and withdrew a metal tube the length of a drinking straw. Putting it to her mouth she briskly blew through the straw toward Maria whose hands were still in the guts of the duffle bag. A cloud of powder enveloped Maria's face. Isabelle took three fast steps backward. She raised her arm into the air, and

Abel hit the gas and started forward. He reached Isabelle and jumped out of the truck and pointed his handgun at Maria. Isabelle held up her hand. "Watch!"

Maria had partially stood up after Isabelle had blown the Devil's Breath on her but froze as if her legs had stopped working. Abel watched as Maria slowly sank to the ground where she ended up sprawled over the duffle. "Is she dead?" asked Abel.

"No. When it first hits, everything shuts down. She'll be like that for a few minutes. You could put someone down for twenty-four hours or kill them if you get the dose wrong."

Harm jogged up, laughed, and said, "I can't believe you know how to turn someone into a zombie."

Isabelle turned to him, deadly serious. "She's not a zombie, yet. If I do this wrong, she will be too far gone to help us. There was a lot of other stuff in the dust besides the burandanga—a fast-acting anesthetic for one. Put her in the truck. I have to give her more stuff before she comes to if she's going to do what we want."

Abel and Harm zip-tied Maria's hands, then her feet, and wrestled her into the back seat of the truck. Harm opened up the bed cover, and then they picked up Carlita by her hands and feet and tossed her into the back of the truck. Harm spread a tarp over her and closed the bed cover and tailgate.

At the last minute, Abel went to Maria's car and grabbed her purse and the car keys still stuck in the ignition, then climbed behind the wheel of Harm's truck. Harm got in the back on one side of Maria, and Isabelle sat on the other. Abel reversed down the lane. "We're moving. We got Maria," he announced on the conference line.

"Take us somewhere quiet. I have to give her more drugs and move her into the next stage."

"Yeah, do something quick. We have to get her talking so she can call the people who have Crystal," said Abel.

"Park there!" said Harm, pointing to a house with no cars in the driveway. As Abel pulled in, Isabelle snapped on a pair of blue nitrile gloves. "Hold her head," she ordered Harm. She pulled a little salve jar out of her conjuring bag and dipped her gloved index finger into it. Isabelle faced Maria and cupped her jaw with her left hand. She put her thumb and index finger at the corners of Maria's mouth and roughly pried open her mouth. Belle jammed her finger in and wiped the goop from the jar under Maria's tongue and over her gums.

"Now what?" asked Harm.

"Now, we wait."

Maria's head jerked upright. Her eyes opened, and her neck spasmed. Her eyes rolled up, and a stream of vomit shot out. The veins on her face bulged, and she vomited again, a putrid mess of food and bile.

"Glad we drove your truck," said Abel, taking shallow breaths.

"Fuck you, dude. You're gonna help clean it."

"Shut up you two," said Isabelle angrily.

Maria sat there seemingly unaware that she had vomited all over the truck.

Isabelle pinched Maria's cheek and slapped her twice. "Maria! Maria!"

"Ahhh . . ." A groan.

"What's your name?"

"Lúcido."

"Can you say, 'This is Lúcido. I'm coming. Don't harm the girl'?"

"This is Lúcido. I'm coming. Don't harm the girl."

"Louder!"

"This is Lúcido. I'm coming. Don't harm the girl."

Harm fished out Maria's phone from her pocket. He held Maria's finger against the screen. It opened up, and he went to the phone log and saw a number that had been called repeatedly. He dialed it.

Chapter Fifty-Six

He waited till the phone was answered on the other end and put it on mute.

Isabelle slapped Maria again. "Say 'This is Lúcido. I'm coming. Don't harm the girl.'"

Harm immediately unmuted the phone and held it to Maria's face.

Maria mumbled, "This is Lúcido. I'm coming. Don't harm the girl."

Harm shook his head and muted the phone. Isabelle commanded, "Louder!"

Harm hit the unmute. Maria said clearly, "This is Lúcido. I'm coming. Don't harm the girl." Harm hung up the phone.

Maria's eyes were drifting closed. Belle pinched her cheek again. "Where is Crystal?"

"Stop."

Isabelle slapped her. "Where is Crystal?"

"Mi cuñado," she said softly.

"Who?" demanded Isabelle, leaning in.

"Diego, Diego Garcia."

"What did she say?" yelled Abel from the front seat.

"Garcia's house! Go!" yelled Harm as he let go of Maria who slowly tipped forward until her face was resting in the pool of vomit on the console.

Isabelle pulled her back, wiped the puke off her face with a gloved hand, and quickly ran her finger around the inside of her mouth to make sure her airway was open. Placing her elbow across Maria's chest, she pinned her upright.

Abel was on the conference line telling the rest of the guys to head to Garcia's. Then, he called out to his sister. "Callie, you need to go home. I don't want you in the middle of this next thing."

Of course, she pushed back, but Abel didn't want to have to worry about her. It was bad enough that Isabelle was there. Eventually, Callie veered off and headed back to Lacombe. He breathed a sigh of relief. As much as

Callie was outraged about Crystal, she was about helping human beings—that was why she worked in an ER. What was going to happen in the next few minutes wasn't about helping anybody but Rabbit and Crystal, and it wasn't going to sit well with Callie. She still believed that people were basically decent and kind, and this was going to get ugly.

By the time they got to Garcia's place on the edge of the Ninth, Maria was a little more with it. She was compliant, and Belle had been able to make her dig the key to the gang house out of her purse.

Abel took the door key from Isabelle, then took out his Glock and stood there waiting for Harm. Harm told Isabelle to stay in the truck and he got out, then leaned back in and dragged Maria out. He pulled out his knife and cut the zip ties around her ankles.

They had parked down the street from the gang house so the bangers couldn't see them and started walking to the house from the blind side. Harm put Maria in front of him and pushed her toward the house. Abel was behind him. Harm directed Tank and André to the back of the house. Rabbit came up tight behind Abel.

The three guys moved toward the house slowly. Maria could barely manage a shambling pace, and Harm was propping her up.

Before they went through the front door, Harm handed over Maria to Abel, and Abel went through the door first. Harm was on his shoulder holding the AR up to his face in house-clearing mode. The went down the hall, Harm covering the right and Rabbit taking the left. A blast came through the wall, and Harm took it on one of the plates in his vest. He fired six quick shots through the wall, then went low and went around the doorjamb. He fired two more shots into the guy who was already flat on the ground.

He straightened and joined the Maria train, and they pushed into the back room. A man started shooting wildly at them. Suddenly, the back door crashed open and the boom from Tank's shotgun crushed their ears. The Mara soldier was knocked back against the wall. He slid down, leaving a smear of blood. Abel threw Maria to the floor, then he and Harm cleared the house while Tank and André covered Rabbit and Crystal.

Rabbit cut his wife loose and started heading for the vehicles. The rest of the guys followed, eyes darting back and forth in case anybody else popped up out of the woodwork. Abel had pulled Maria up off the floor, but Harm ripped Maria out of Abel's hands and threw her back to the floor. He pointed his gun at her, but Abel stopped the muzzle from pointing at her. "No, man! Time to go."

Abel pushed him out of the back room, a pissed look on Harm's face. When they cleared the front door, Isabelle passed them, going back into the house. "Jesus!' Abel yelled and turned around and followed her back in. Abel caught up with her, kneeling over Maria. She had dipped a big gob of the stuff from the little jar and was sticking it in Maria's mouth. She held Maria's mouth closed for what seemed like an eternity but was probably only a few seconds. Maria's eyes went vacant.

He grabbed Belle by her bony arm and pulled her up. "Can we go now?"

Harm dragged Carlita's body out of the truck and carried her back into Garcia's house and dropped her next to Maria. He ran back to his truck and jumped in. Abel hit the pedal and headed back to Lacombe with the two Impalas close, leaving behind them a zombie and three dead bodies.

FIFTY-SEVEN

W hen they got back to Lacombe, Abel and Harm dropped off Isabelle and then went straight to Rabbit's apartment. The white Impala was parked in front of the auto shop's office, and Rabbit was upstairs packing some clothes for the two of them. Crystal had refused to go up to the apartment and was sitting with Rabbit's daddy in the garage. The guys went up to see how Rabbit was doing.

Abel yelled through the door, then went in, and they found him in the bedroom grabbing clothes willy-nilly and stuffing them in a suitcase.

"We're going to Crystal's parent's house in Lake Charles. She's gonna be OK! A little messed up right now, but she's down with my dad. He's watching her. She wouldn't come up here, but sure, who would after being kidnapped? Gonna stop at the doctor's and make sure she's OK, then we're getting out of town for a while. Probably have the babies up in Lake Charles. That's gonna be better, right?"

Abel thought, *He's kinda like the old Rabbit, but still messed up.* Euphoric and manic at the same time. More manic than usual, but it was better than the Rabbit from last night. Abel went over and gave him a big country hug. Rabbit embraced him and then quietly started crying. He pulled away from Abel and turned his back on them and wiped his eyes. He sniffed. "I was just so scared, ya know?" He turned back around, his eyes red and watery, a weak grin on his face. "I'm not sure I'm cut out for this anymore."

"Hey, man," said Harm, "we all have one thing on our minds. Get Crystal with her parents, and y'all take care of her. We'll make sure you guys have everything you need. You let us know as soon as she starts getting contractions, and we'll be there. Hear me?"

Harm embraced his best friend and left, leaving Abel alone with Rabbit. "Abel you gotta watch out for Harm. You know he can't take care of himself." Abel snorted. "You know what I mean. We're all he's got."

"Yeah, I know. Call us as soon as you get there. Let us know how Crystal's doing." Abel grabbed Rabbit's hand and squeezed it. "Drive safe." He left quickly, too. He was getting choked up and didn't want Rabbit to see that. He somehow felt responsible. Like it was his fault that Maria snatched Crystal.

He got to the bottom of the apartment stairs and saw that Harm was already in his truck. Abel climbed up into the passenger side. Harm wheeled out of the garage lot and glanced over at Abel. "Do you think we have to worry about the dead bodies and Maria?"

"Maria isn't gonna be able to do shit."

"I still can't figure out why you stopped me from killing that bitch."

"Isabelle told me not to. She said that Maria was going to be locked up in her own private hell for a long time, and that was worse than just dying. I mean, can you imagine? Having your mind just do whatever anybody tells you? Trapped in your body like you're a vegetable?"

"It's like that forever?"

"Well, I guess not. But she told me that it was a slow-acting poison, and she'd never be the same."

"I don't know, man." Harm sighed. "That Maria was like the evilest person I've ever met. Stone cold. Acting like she was in love with you and friends with all of us. If I ever see her again, I'm gonna kill her. No matter what Isabelle wants."

"Harm, I don't think Isabelle told us everything. She said we couldn't kill Maria because she was now connected to her."

"You believe that shit?" asked Harm.

"I think Isabelle believes it."

"Yeah, maybe . . ."

Harm dropped Abel off on his way home, and as soon as Abel went through the front door, Callie immediately started in with the questions. Abel held up his hand and breezed through the living room into the kitchen. He grabbed a beer and then took a second one for Callie.

Abel handed off the beer, then crashed on the couch. "Rabbit is taking Crystal to Lake Charles. She's pretty messed up."

"No doubt," said Callie. "That's a good idea."

Abel went on to describe extracting Crystal from the gang's house. He didn't mention the casualties but went on at length about the whole Isabelle-voodoo-zombie thing. Neither of them had ever explicitly seen Belle do anything beyond gris-gris bags, and Callie asked a thousand questions.

"I always thought it was just rituals that made everybody feel good, like the placebo effect."

"Yeah, me too," said Abel. "Even when she hexed or cursed the MS two years ago, I kinda thought that we imagined some of that stuff. But today, she wasn't hoodooing. It was scary. She was a different person—nothing like I've ever seen. She was brutal to Maria. Rough. Maria started doing the things Isabelle commanded. And the weird thing was, at a certain point, she was in charge, and we were just facilitating her."

"Did you kill Maria?"

"No. Isabelle wouldn't let us. Get this! She said she was connected to Maria, and we couldn't kill her."

"Like you weren't able to kill her?"

"No, like we weren't allowed to kill her."

"That means you aren't done with the Maras."

"I guess we are gonna have to keep our eyes open. Anyway, I'm beat. I'm going to bed."

Late the next morning, Abel went to find Tank. He parked in the Chevals' front yard and walked up the porch steps. Isabelle was rocking on the porch swing, staring at her African violets that were arrayed on a low table in front of the living room window. Abel stood there for a minute, watching Belle move close and then away. Finally, she looked up at him. Abel was shocked at how old she looked. His mind went back in time to Isabelle's kitchen after the whole conflict with the Maras two years ago.

Back then, she had look tired and had been talking about evil storms. He thought she would get over it. But she hadn't. The bright morning light cast her eye sockets in dark shadow, and he could see all the bones in her face pushing against her black, translucent skin. A vein throbbed in her temple.

He remembered the warning from Lovelie Mondesir. The trip to her apothecary seemed like it was a year ago instead of just the weeks it had really been. She had said Isabelle was going to a dark place. He hadn't taken it seriously—just old ladies creating drama in their passing lives.

Abel said, "Good morning, Belle. How are you?" She continued staring at him. Her shadowed eyes were seemingly bottomless. A ripple of goose bumps went up his arms and across his neck. He waited a moment for a response that never came, then went inside without saying anything else.

"We're in the kitchen," yelled Tank.

Abel went on back. André and Tank were sitting at the table eating biscuits with honey and drinking coffee. "Has your mama been like that since she got back?"

"Like what?" asked André.

"Like in a trance or something. She's rocking in the swing like she's the zombie."

Tank said, "She's fine. She just made us these biscuits." He changed the subject. "Ya know, I think we shoulda killed Guidry at the warehouse. Hebert basically told us to do it. It woulda been the end of the story."

André immediately disagreed. "Naw, it woulda made me look more guilty. This way I'm a victim of a corrupt cop. And anyway, I just got back from Hebert's office. I showed him all the video. He's confident I'm off the hook. Didi, too. And probably every other guy Guidry has arrested. Basically, the NOPD is skating on thin ice, what with the Consent Decree, and the Feds are still up their ass. His exact words were 'the DA is gonna shit himself when he sees Guidry pop Williams.'"

"So you think you're in the clear?" asked Abel. "I mean, how could a jury believe anything the guy says after seeing that video?"

"Yeah, Hebert said there is no way the district attorney will ever let this go to trial. But that if the DA was stupid enough to do it, he would enjoy stomping on him with both feet."

They all laughed, then André pushed away from the table. "I better go check on the Voodoo Queen." He laughed some more as he left the kitchen.

Abel looked over at Tank. "It's not a joke. You didn't see what she did to Maria."

"That bad, huh?"

"You know, I love your mama, but she's changed."

Tank sighed. "Yeah, I know. So does André." They sat there quietly for a second, and then Tank said, "She told me I couldn't be a bounty hunter anymore. She didn't ask me to stop. She told me to stop. She said it was wrong."

"I'm not feelin' it, either," said Abel. "Plus, we aren't making jack shit. All of our money, every last dollar, barely filled that duffle."

"What are we going to do?"

"I don't know. We'll think of something. But right now, I gotta roll. I've got something I need to do."

The sun was low in the trees, casting dappled light across the bayou, and the warm breeze pushed Abel's pirogue up against a snag. *Perfect,* he thought. He put his arm around Owen's shoulders and then his hands around the six-year-old's little ones. "Look! Look at your bobber. It's jittering. Now we give it a little jerk! And set the hook . . . Now, slowly reel it in."

Abel helped him land the mullet, and the both of them watched the beautiful little fish flop around on the bottom of the boat for a few seconds. "Should we take it home and fry it up?" asked Abel.

Owen looked up into Abel's eyes. "Let's put him back in the water with his mama and daddy."

Abel grabbed the slippery fish and tossed it over the side. They watched it float, unmoving for a second, then with a flash shoot away. "Now it's back with its family!" said Owen.

The boy put more bait on the hook, then held up the tip of the rod and cast the line away from the pirogue. The bobber splashed, then sat there waiting for another fish.

Abel leaned back and watched the child intently staring at the end of the fishing line, feeling a kind of completeness. He looked around the beautiful bayou, pausing a beat on Olivia. Maybe things were going to be OK.

CHAPTER

EPILOGUE

L uis had fussed over the breakfast plate he had in his hand for an hour. He had used his rudimentary kitchen to lovingly craft a meal for Lúcido of huevos rancheros, frijoles negros, and some fried plantains—her favorite.

He placed the plate in front of her on his small kitchen table, then sat across from her and leaned across the table, taking the fork off the plate. Maria was in her chair, slumped to the side, her head awkwardly resting on her shoulder with a thin ribbon of drool hanging from her chin.

"I brought you your favorite, mi amor! Here, have some frijoles, cielo." Luis took some beans with the fork, then with the other hand tried to straighten up her head. He put the food in her open mouth and closed it by pushing up on her chin with his knuckle. He took his hand away from her chin, and her mouth dropped open and the black beans fell out. One bean was still stuck to her lip, but the rest were splattered on her crisp white shirt. He heard a noise and looked over his shoulder.

A wiry man in a black T-shirt was standing in the doorway, a gun in his hand. The man's pistol was pointed at him, and Luis noticed his corded forearm and the stillness of the gun.

Harm squeezed the trigger, but Luis didn't hear the report. A black hole appeared in his forehead, just slightly above the bridge of his nose. He collapsed in his chair, then slowly slid to the floor.

In Lúcido's eyes, a vague light flared, and her head came up off her shoulder a bit. The suppressed pistol made another loud clapping sound, reverberating in the tiny room. Her head flew back and her body rebounded, flopping forward, and her face landed on the plate of eggs and beans.

Harm watched Lúcido for a moment, whispering something to himself. "Sometimes you have to be sure," he said louder, then backed out of the doorway.

Acknowledgments

I couldn't have written this book without the help of so many generous people. **Sarah Fraps** gave me the editorial clarity I needed, and **Vinnie Corbo at Volossal Publishing** brought the story to life with his cover and interior design. To my wonderful beta readers—**Margaret Dickson, Doug Wilson, Cynthia Gabriel, Sue Ellen Larkin, Kevin Wilson, and Joseph Wilson**—thank you for the time, care, and honesty you poured into reading draft after draft. And to my friends at the writers' club—**Eliah, Cody, Sherman, Emma, and Chris**—your encouragement, honest comments, and camaraderie carried me through the hard days and kept me going.

About the Author

John Wilson is a former engineer and inventor with over a hundred patents. After a career developing computer systems, a life-altering accident led him to pursue writing. He is the author of the crime novels *A Shadow of Black Water* and *The Devil's Breath*. John lives on the Gulf Coast with his wife and their exceptionally furry dog, Blaze.

Website and further developments

www.johnwilsonbooks.com

Disclaimer